Also by Carlos R Savournin

NEVES

Hidden Square

Isa & Kim —

NAME NOT ONE MAN

Thank you so much for your support —

Carlos R. Savournin

Copyright © 2014 Carlos R. Savournin.

All rights reserved. No part of this book may be reproduced, stored, or transmitted by any means—whether auditory, graphic, mechanical, or electronic—without written permission of both publisher and author, except in the case of brief excerpts used in critical articles and reviews. Unauthorized reproduction of any part of this work is illegal and is punishable by law.

ISBN: 978-1-4834-1015-9 (sc)
ISBN: 978-1-4834-1017-3 (hc)
ISBN: 978-1-4834-1016-6 (e)

Because of the dynamic nature of the Internet, any web addresses or links contained in this book may have changed since publication and may no longer be valid. The views expressed in this work are solely those of the author and do not necessarily reflect the views of the publisher, and the publisher hereby disclaims any responsibility for them.

Any people depicted in stock imagery provided by Thinkstock are models, and such images are being used for illustrative purposes only.
Certain stock imagery © Thinkstock.

Library of Congress Control Number: 2014905645

Lulu Publishing Services rev. date: 3/27/2014

Acknowledgements

A special thanks to those who made this possible:
Daniela & Doug, my editors
Maggie, thanks for the hand
Cover and Author Photography by Bernard Bohn
www.b3pics.com

For Mom, Dad & Karina

The Soul is not subject to the laws of space and time.
~ Carl Jung

CHAPTER ENO

I T WAS THEIR SECOND TRIP to the pig farm. On the first one, they advised the owners, James and Hilda Bayer, that if they did not fix their violations within a week, they would return with an official state order to close the farm. It wasn't a pleasant trip – one rarely ever was. James was rude, not allowing them inside to seek refuge from the strong Miami heat and instead slamming the door in their faces.

Despite not being invited inside, they could see the quality of life the Bayers provided, not only for themselves, but also for their livestock. James Bayer was tall and lanky, dressed in a sweat-stained under shirt and pants that hung from his waist with rope. The scent of his body odor was masked only by the wretched smell of manure pouring out of the house and hovering over the entire farmland. The swine were unhealthy, barely moving.

When they left the first time, they had no doubt the violations would not be corrected, so when they arrived a week later, they assumed they would find the farm in the same condition as before. Were they ever wrong.

At first, they thought they were seeing things, but the closer they approached, the clearer the picture became. Blood was everywhere, saturating the earth beneath the pigs that were slaughtered over the entire property. Pig carcasses and intestines were strewn over the vast field; blood marked the tractors and equipment surrounding the house. A decapitated pig's head greeted them at the steps of the house.

The scent of rot was strong enough to make them wish for the manure that burned their nostrils the week before and it was all they could do to not vomit over the front of the house.

They discussed calling the police, but were distracted when they noticed the same door James Bayer had slammed in their face was now open, exposing the house's dirty interior. From the front porch, they could see more dead swine scattered about the inside of the house, their stomachs sliced open and their intestines exposed.

At the top of the staircase, James Bayer hanged from an exposed ceiling truss at the landing of the second floor. The odd angle of his neck made it clear that the noose tied around him snapped it in two.

Both of them ran to their car, one of them on the verge of vomiting, the other holding back a need to scream for help. They called the police and described what they saw in the hopes they could flee the property and never have to face it again. But they were told to stay put until officials arrived.

Mason Bayer watched their reactions and the expressions of horror on their faces as they stood by the car, looking at the whole scene before them, completely disgusted and terrified.

And he laughed.

Darkness

Samantha Cabello promised herself she wouldn't get drunk. She wasn't a big drinker, aside from enjoying the occasional glass of wine with dinner. When her colleagues were threatening to get her "rip-roaring drunk", she told them time and again that it wouldn't happen.

As she stumbled into her house late that night, she realized that she drank much more than she thought. It was her retirement party, after all, and colleague after colleague kept bringing her a drink from the open bar. A martini here, a Scotch there, Samantha didn't disappoint as she sipped each drink, recoiling each time from the taste of the alcohol, but then politely accepting another.

She stripped off her suit jacket and threw it onto the dining room table along with her purse as she made her way to the bedroom. The clock radio beside her bed showed it was also later than she thought; almost two in the morning. Normally, she would have scoffed at others who were trying to persuade her, but tonight, she only shrugged. What does it matter? She didn't have to report in the next morning. She paid her dues; nearly thirty years with the Department of Health, and now, she was free to do what she wanted. And at just fifty-five years old, she was still young enough for freelance work.

It was worth it, she concluded, while thoughts of her friends and coworkers at the party lingered in her head. She smiled for a moment, then laid down in her bed. Her smile instantly faded as the room began to spin. She closed her eyes and put both hands on her head. *I shouldn't have drunk so much.*

She rubbed her face in a failed attempt to settle the room trying her hardest to will her body off the bed for a glass of water or a piece of bread to absorb the alcohol, but to no avail. Before long, she was on her side, hugging her pillow and breathing heavily. Her thoughts on her friends again, it wasn't long before she was on the journey to an alcohol induced slumber. One she knew she'd pay for with a headache in the morning.

It was that same headache that woke her nearly an hour later. Her heavy eyes opened and she was thankful for the darkness around her instead of the light of the beaming sun. She rolled onto her back and for merely a second, she forgot how she had gotten home. Richard. Her friend, Richard, brought her home and said he would pick her up in the morning to retrieve her car from the celebration hall.

The noise that echoed through her house suddenly was not liquor induced. It was a loud *thump* that made Samantha sit up immediately. It took a few seconds for her to gather her time and place; she hadn't realized she was sweating profusely, but that could have been caused by the fact that she was still fully dressed. The heavy breathing was strictly caused by the start of the noise that still echoed in her head, though she couldn't pinpoint where it had come from much less what caused it. It was a heavy noise, the sound of something falling.

She sat still – thinking, pondering the possibilities. Did she leave the door unlocked when she came in? Surely, she was drunk enough to do something so irresponsible. And if she did leave the door unlocked, did that mean someone had entered and worked their way through the house? A stranger had come for her, and her gut told her that the stranger's intentions were not kind. She could feel it as though the air itself carried the warning and covered her like a blanket – telling her to stay absolutely quiet amidst the darkness, and she would be safe. The intruder would eventually leave, but she knew it wouldn't be so simple. She could *feel* it.

She thought of her husband who passed three years before. He would be on his feet, calling out to whomever, whatever had come for them, and warn them to leave. She thought of her daughter who told her time and again to sell the house and move in with her. She thought of the damn darkness in her room and how it allowed her no vision – not even as she waited for her eyes to adjust. She was paralyzed; sandwiched between her fears and the shadows that once held still and were now prancing around her, moving through the dark, through her as she realized the imminent silence that had taken over the room. Not even the whirling of the ceiling fan could be heard as she tried to listen for the singing crickets that soothed her to sleep nightly. She heard nothing more than the sound of her own breath as though the intruder had murdered the entire house and its surroundings before he came for her. Shaking the terrible suspicion that she was next, she barely attempted to move off the bed, but her better judgment told her to stay right where she was, for something *within* the room itself was not right.

Her eyes searched through the abyss of black trying to hold her own breath. Stripped of one sense, her others heightened; her nose sniffing for the distinct smell of sweat that was not her own; her ears listening for the breath of the intruder in the event he was already in her room. She could feel he found his way to her private resting area and was perhaps standing in the very corner which hid beneath the shadows; the very corner beside her bed. Who knows how long the uninvited stood there, watching her as she slept, planning the manner in which she would die. She would fight her way to freedom if she had to, but the killer was hideous; an abomination to science and humans. A monster.

She beckoned to the killer; a pathetic whisper of a noise her parched throat produced. Her fear multiplied at the thought the she would receive a response. A growl, a deep rumbling voice that would shake her every bone – and it would not be an answer from the dark corner of her room, but a mere whisper in her ear to let her know that the killer was already with her on her bed. Just as the call left her dry lips, she wanted desperately to take it back, but alas, there was no answer. Still, she remained motionless on her bed until her heart rate settled, deciding that her emotions were at their peak caused by the drinking, the headache, and the sudden atmosphere in which she woke.

Slowly, she reached to her night table in search for the portable phone. Thankful she had left it on its charging station the morning before, she found it and hit the power button unsure of who she should call; the police? Tell them she thought there might be an intruder in her house though she wasn't sure? Her daughter who was travelling on business and who could do nothing about her mother's situation? Either way, it didn't matter. She hit the power button, but there was no dial tone. The phone was dead. The intruder must have cut the lines before making his way in. She had seen it done in a thousand horror movies, but didn't really think it could happen. Now, there was proof. She immediately thought of her cell phone, but she left it in the dining room, in her purse. She was left with no choice but to investigate her house and hope she found the intruder before he found her.

Slowly, she stood from the bed and took her steps to the closet door from memory, her footsteps muffled against the plush carpeting. Since her husband's death, there were two things she would check before going to sleep, a habit she could not sleep peacefully without fulfilling – 1) to ensure the doors were locked, and 2) that the closet door in her bedroom was closed. But since she was drunk, she wasn't sure she did either. She prayed that she would find her closet door closed as she approached it, convincing herself that these habits were all a prelude to the night which she now stood.

A small bit of relief fell over her when she did, indeed find the closet door closed, and without a sound, she slid it open. She reached for the baseball bat tucked in the far corner – the only weapon she allowed in her house though she was familiar with the use of an automatic gun. Her anti-gun policy seemed a bit foolish now, though. She held the chrome bat and always thought that if the situation arose where she needed to use it, she would feel protected. Nothing could harm her. Bring on your every gender-bending, shape-shifting monster, and she would face them. But her sweaty palms found no comfortable grip around the bat, and though her will told her to run to the light switch – reveal every hidden corner of the room, she decided against it. As much as the darkness was her own enemy, she could not risk the possibility that perhaps the darkness was the only reason she was still alive. As much as it hid the intruder, it hid her as well. And she knew her house much better than anyone else. She made her way toward the bedroom door to face the rest of the house – after making sure she closed the closet door, of course.

Slowly, she opened the door to her room and looked out into the hallway that provided a clear view to the large picture window leading to acres of nothing that was her backyard. As though the moon were biased, its pale light cascaded throughout some of her home in such a brilliant manner which she had never seen before. Her home was part of a secluded neighborhood which provided a clear view of the night's stars and the moon – but never so bright as she witnessed then. The darkness was so prominent, even the slightest of lights were more powerful, and for that, at least, she was thankful.

She stepped onto the tile, her feet beneath her feeling the warmth of what was normally chilled throughout the night. The air conditioning usually cooled the ceramic floor, but the stuffy atmosphere only convinced her more of someone else's presence. Her entire body was still sweating as she slowly crept through the living room. She could feel the drops of perspiration rolling down her bare back, and she knew it was not caused by the fear within her. The house itself was warmer than usual. She could feel the invaded space around her by someone following or watching her. A ghost, perhaps, that would show its pale, wicked face just as she passed it, a raven perched on her windowsill that would call out "Nevermore", or the demon she expected to find in the darkest corner of her house. But despite the aid of the moonlight, she saw no one.

The wet grip on her bat tightened as she paced her way to the dining room table where her cell phone rested in her purse. It was her final resort. She decided she couldn't look for the killer herself, fearful of what she might find; something more terrible than her overactive imagination was producing; a maniac with no control over his mind or body – someone who took pleasure in tearing his victims to shreds with his bare hands. She saw enough movies to know that only stupid people were killed in situations like the one she was in; the girl who should have run out of the house instead of checking for the killer in the basement with nothing more than a candle to light her way.

With one hand still on her bat, she blindly searched for her phone in her purse, but she couldn't find it no matter how much she rummaged. Her heart raced against her chest. Her breath fell heavier and her shoulders slumped as the last bit of energy drained through her feet. Her cell phone had been taken. She knew then that her attempt at running for the front door would be in vain. If the intruder went to such lengths as to kill the phone lines and secure her communication to the outside world by being so efficient as to taking her cell phone, then no doubt he was watching her every move now. The intruder would not allow his meal to escape, but he would play with his food until his undoubted appetite to kill would strike.

She felt her finger tight grip on sanity slowly slipping. The room stretched and the darkness enveloped her as much as her own fear did when she heard the noise again. *Thump*. She spun in the direction from which it came, and she found herself staring in the direction of her front door. She approached it slowly and found it was locked. She wasn't relieved by it because she wasn't sure if it was the killer who secured the bolt once he was in. She looked through the peephole, the small, magnifying outlet allowing a distorted, elongated glimpse of the dark, outside world. All appeared still – an eerie calm that was the prelude to the storm. Once she opened the door, there was no telling what she would find on the other side; the monster she expected, or worst, nothing at all. What if the intruder wasn't inside the house, after all. Her instincts weren't wrong about feeling threatened, but what if the killer was trying to get in? The *thump* was a knock on death's door. Suddenly, running out of the house didn't seem like a good idea after all. Once she was out, she could find the killer and struggle for her life, or she would realize her fear was nothing more than the product of her time and place. Though one would seem irrefutably worse than the other, at that precise moment, she wasn't so sure. Finding an answer to her fear was diagnosing the mysterious illness that befell her. Without an answer, she was left with her own mind to refute the questions that would not stop, not even when the sun began to rise over the eastern skies.

She opened the door and looked upon her front yard, looked at the porch set before the seemingly undisturbed parkway. With her bat in hand, she stepped onto the chilled cement taking slow steps and kept her eyes everywhere at once. The night was silent – slumber falling over the entire neighborhood as it normally does at such an hour, but it was darker. She didn't take the time to look at the brilliant stars that twinkled above her, nor did she realize that none of the neighboring homes' porch lights were burning. The darkness inside her house engulfed the entire land once she opened the door.

If there was an intruder in her home, he did not enter through any windows. The only possibility was the front door, but the more she thought of it, the more she realized that locking the door when she arrived home was not so much a task as it was a reflex. Drunk or not, she would have locked it. And perhaps the portable phone didn't charge at all on the station explaining the dead line. And perhaps she left her cell phone in her car which was still parked at the celebration hall. Perhaps.

Slowly, she returned her gaze into the dark foyer. Standing outside, she listened for any movement, but the sounds in her house were not unlike the ones she heard nightly; the house settling onto its foundation beneath it, the plates shifting in their cabinets, the sound of the battery operated clock in the foyer *tick, tick, ticking* away. But there was a difference. They were all happening at once. And amidst all of these noises, the prominent silence was still as loud as a jackhammer pounding on her brain.

...*tick, tick, tick...*

She entered the house again, cursing herself as she did so. Her eyes scanned every square inch the darkness allowed. The swaying trees caught in the moonlight were the source of dancing shadows upon the floor, cascading impossible figures that played with her mind, but she held her own. Nothing seemed out of the ordinary.

...*tick, tick, tick*...

And suddenly, there it was again, the noise that originally set Samantha Cabello on her paranoid night; the hollow *thump* that filled the house with a terrible mechanical cling nearly making her knees give out underneath her as she couldn't pin point the original source. It was all around her. And one by one, the electrical hum of the kitchen appliances were resurrected. The refrigerator sang with power, the microwave beeped, as did the portable phone in her bedroom. And just as she began to realize what was happening, the lights above her flickered then remained burning at full power. The darkness disappeared. The silence exorcised.

And the intruder, reduced to nothing more than a power outage, was gone.

She jogged back to her front door and found all the houses on her street, as well as her own, lit with their porch lights. She took a calming breath, let her shoulders relax, and she closed the door, locked it, and shook her head.

There was no intruder. No killer. No monster in her closet. But she was indeed a victim – a victim of her own imagination, a victim of the dependency on appliances to aid her sleep, a victim of that which is the most terrible to face and can vary from person to person; the fear within.

She walked back into the dining room and placed that bat against the table where she found her cell phone. In the darkness, she rummaged through her purse trying to find it, but it was never in her purse to begin with. It was resting beside her purse. She picked it up, cursing herself for being such a brainless coward, then made her way back to her bedroom where she closed the door and locked it.

And Samantha Cabello was able to sleep again – without the worries she woke with. The various noises echoing in her house soothed her to the land of slumber where she found her own comfort.

And somewhere, in the back of her mind, she couldn't wait to call her daughter in the morning to tell her about what a horrible, and somewhat humorous night, she had experienced.

And those same sounds that soothed her to sleep; the sound of the whirling fan above her, the sound of the AC, were the sounds that prevented her from hearing the closet door slowly opening.

Saturday: January 7<u>th</u>

When Todd Grazer woke up, the first thing that came to his mind was that he hadn't had a nightmare in over a year though the remnants of the one he just had were still fresh in his mind. Horrid images of the young man's insides exploding outward, the smell of the gunpowder that lingered in the air; it was all as though it just happened right in front of him. But it was a dream, one he conquered before, and one he'll conquer again. He controlled his heavy breathing and wiped the sweat from his brow as though erasing proof of the nightmare would expunge the dream itself.

The second thing he thought of was the eight o'clock meeting his lieutenant scheduled. He wasn't worried about it; probably a standard meeting to discuss the results of the John Doe case that he and his partner, Hector Corona, closed the day before. He was, however, concerned about being late. Before he went to bed the night before, he made sure the night clock beside the bed was armed for a five AM wake up call, and as he slowly turned to face it, the digital display showed it was only 3:37. He took a deep breath, and looked to his right, toward the empty side of his bed.

He and his wife, Mary, hadn't shared their bed in over two weeks. He knew why, and he vowed to talk to her about it, resolve this issue. But he was out of the house before she was up, and usually came home after she had gone to bed in their guestroom. Just the night before, he went to the room to speak to her, resolve the issue and found her in a deep slumber.

She looked more beautiful at 43 than she did when they first met over twenty years before. A strand of her red, curled hair had escaped the tight bun she prepared for her sleep and laid against the flawless skin of her high cheek bone. He moved it behind her ear carefully and watched as she slightly flinched at the disruption of her space. He wanted to wake her with a kiss, join her on the small bed and press his body against hers, lose himself in the passion of the late night.

He knew she was tired from dealing with their two teenagers who were on winter vacation and free to run their mother crazy all day. He decided it was best to let her sleep.

His train of thought was lost when he heard the noise.

His back stiff, he immediately focused on his bedroom door. Twenty years of police work taught him where his attention needed to be when something wasn't quite right. The sound was distinct; someone taking slow, methodical steps up the stairs to the second floor of the house – the floor where his bedroom, and the bedroom of his two teenage children, resided. The steps were muffled by the carpeting, but whoever was making their way up was wearing heavy shoes, and no amount of light footing would prevent the noise.

Slowly, he stood from his bed. His issued handgun was kept in a locked drawer beside his bed, and his personal gun was in a lockbox under his bed, but he didn't move for either. Instead, he slowly made his way to his bedroom door, and pressed his ear against it, listening as the steps moved closer and closer to his room. He held his breath as he listened, careful not to make any noise as he reached for the doorknob – waiting for the moment when the footsteps were at his door and spring upon the heavy shoe wearer before they made it any further. The element of surprise. It worked every time.

He threw the door open and his son gasped, taking a few steps back in surprise.

"Dad," he said between breaths. "You scared the crap out of me!"

Luis was fifteen years old and working on his malicious teenage ways. Todd looked him up and down, studying his jeans, t-shirt, and the black work boots his son was wearing.

"Coming in, I take it?" Todd asked, crossing his arms over his large chest.

Luis hesitated. He stuttered for a moment and Todd could tell the boy's mind was searching desperately for an answer. Especially after he said, "Do you have any idea what time it is?"

"Dad, I –"

"Lucky for you I have a meeting in the morning so I am not going to deal with you right now. We'll talk about this tomorrow. And if I catch you doing this again, that'll be the end of your vacation. Do you understand me?"

Luis looked at the floor. "Yes, sir."

"Go to bed."

"Yes, sir." Luis slowly turned and began making his way toward his room.

"And Luis," Todd said in a high whisper. "If you're gonna be coming in so late, have the decency to wear lighter shoes so you don't wake anyone up."

Luis nodded slowly and continued toward his room.

Todd shut the door and shook his head, a small smile settling upon his face. Once making his way back into the bed, he took a deep breath and looked at the clock again. 3:41 AM.

*

Detective Hector Corona was running late. He ran into the Miami-Dade Police Headquarters and took the stairs to the second floor, two steps at a time, careful not to spill the coffee in his foam cup. Swiping his ID badge to gain access to the Homicide division, he ran through the door and almost knocked an officer off her feet. She was carrying a folder that flew out of her hand, papers falling to the floor and his coffee spilling over them.

"Shit – I'm so sorry," he told her, and as she looked upon the veteran Detective, he was on his knees picking up her files and doing the best he could to get coffee off of them using his loosened tie. "You'd think I'd learn that door opens inward and someone could be behind it."

"Running late as usual, I take it?" Officer Tina Hood asked, smiling at the scrambling man on the floor before her.

Corona smiled back handing her the coffee stained papers. "I got most of it off."

"It's okay. They're just copies. I still have the originals. You got lucky this time."

He smiled at her, looking upon her flawless pale skin and light blond hair pulled back into a tight bun. "I won't consider myself lucky until you have that drink with me. That offer does have an expiration date, you know."

"But my ability to say 'no' does not, thankfully," she said playfully.

"Coffee then."

"I've had enough coffee for today," she said, holding up the stained papers. "Have a great day, Detective Corona."

She walked toward the way from which she came, presumably to make a fresh set of copies as Corona watched her backside until she was gone. He shook his head and began to walk in the direction of his desk where he found his partner, Detective Todd Grazer, leaning, with arms crossed and a disapproving shake of the head.

"Way to make a grand entrance," Grazer said.

"Got her attention, didn't it?"

"She's young. You're old. It's not gonna happen."

"Get your ass off my desk, will you?" Corona said, taking his seat and immediately looking through his drawers.

"You're late."

Corona gasped. "No wonder they made you detective!"

Grazer took the seat opposite Corona. He inspected the loosened tie and ruffled shirt that looked very similar to the one he was wearing the day before. "Rough night?"

"Yeah, I was up all night helping my daughter build a dresser for her room," Corona said, still looking through his drawer. "I barely had time to take a shower this morning, I woke up so late. Where the hell is my hand sanitizer?"

"You're out?" Grazer asked with a smile. "Impossible!"

"Not funny, asshole. I took the stairs and you know how many germs are on that handrail? It's disgusting. Give it back, will you?"

Grazer shook his head again and reached into the inside pocket of his blazer. He tossed the small bottle toward the Corona which he opened and used immediately. "Lieutenant hasn't called us in yet, so you didn't miss anything."

"Did he say what it was about?"

Grazer shook his head. "All I know is that we were supposed to be here at eight. Do us all a favor and go freshen up before he gets here. You look like hell." Grazer slapped Corona's shoulder as he walked off toward his desk a few feet away. But before Corona could move, the phone on his desk rang. He looked at the caller ID – it was an interoffice call, and the ID showed Jack Roth; their lieutenant. Corona's shoulders slumped as he reached for the receiver. "You ready for us, sir?" he asked. Grazer turned to his partner in time to hear him say, "We'll be right in." Corona stood from his desk, tightened his tie, ironed his shirt with his hands and nodded to his partner. They had been summoned.

Lieutenant Jack Roth stood from his chair in his grand office when the two men entered. His desk, nearly as big as the man that used it, was covered in paperwork and case files, and it was this reason the two detectives assumed they were being called in. Their last case was closed, but plenty of paperwork is involved with a John Doe that no one wanted to claim.

"Gentlemen," Lt. Roth said, his voice booming in the office. "Good morning. Please, have a seat."

Both men did as they were told and took seats opposite the lieutenant's desk.

"I've called you both in this morning because I have a task I would like to assign to you both," Roth continued, handing them both file folders. "There's a transfer from Pinkney County up north who is joining our team. He's supposed to be a hot-shot up and coming officer, and I'd like for you two to show him the ropes when he gets here."

"Pinkney County?" Corona asked. "Never heard of it."

"It's a small town up north," Grazer answered. "Kind of like a Mayberry in the middle of nowhere. I didn't even think they had a police force, to be honest."

Corona sighed and rolled his head back clearly showing his disapproval. "Lieutenant, with all due respect −"

Roth held up his finger. "I know, I know. It's a bullshit assignment, but let me explain why I want you two to do this. You're the only detectives out there that insist on working as a team. All the others prefer to work alone. Your success rates are better than anyone else's and I think we need more of that here. You'll let him ride with you for a week. That's it. Once that's done, we'll partner him up with Officer Hood."

"Lucky bastard," Corona said, almost to himself.

"If this guy's so good, why is Pinkney transferring him?" Grazer asked flipping through the file Roth handed him. It contained everything about the new officer they needed to get to know him without actually meeting him.

Roth shrugged. "Because Pinkney's boring, I guess."

Grazer nodded after a moment. "It would be our pleasure, sir."

Roth nodded and smiled. "Good! And Corona, please be sure to be nice to the guy. I think you scarred the last officer you showed around. He's become just as cynical as you. Speaking of which, he and forensics are at a crime scene this morning. I'd like you two to go over and see what you can find."

"You let Officer Leddy go to a crime scene on his own?" Corona asked. "That prick probably has his fingerprints all over the place by now."

"Well, I would have sent you, but you were running late," Roth said. "Again."

Corona swallowed hard and glanced at his partner who was fighting a smile.

"Thanks again, gentlemen. Get in touch with Officer Leddy when you can and keep me posted on what's going on."

"Will do," Corona said and both men began to walk out of the office.

"Detective Grazer," Roth called.

They turned back to face the lieutenant.

"Can I speak to you a moment, please."

Grazer turned back to Corona and gave him a tight nod. Corona left the office and closed the door behind him while Grazer resumed his seat before the desk.

Roth folded his hands over each other on the desk. "How are you doing, Todd?"

Grazer tried to hide the surprised look on his face. It was rare that anyone called him Todd in the building let alone Lieutenant Roth. The question that prefaced the name weighed heavy on him because he didn't expect it, and because as soon as Roth asked it, the nightmare came screaming back. Todd closed his eyes for a second, fighting the image of the dead man from seeping into his brain. "I'm fine," he said, finally. "Thank you."

Roth nodded, and Grazer felt relieved. He bought it.

"I want to commend you on your last case," Roth said.

"Thank you, sir," Todd said, "but in truth, it was closed only because there are no leads. That John Doe is still lying in a coma in a hospital where he'll probably die."

Roth was already nodding. "I understand, but the way you exhausted all avenues looking for a clue has led us to close this case knowing, one-hundred percent, that there are no other options. That's why I commend you. In fact, I think it's time you received recognition for all the work you've done for us for the past twenty years."

Detective Grazer nodded. "I appreciate that, sir, but Hector – Detective Corona is as much to recognize as I am."

Roth nodded, "And I will thank him in due time as well. But, I wanted to let you know first that there's been talk from upstairs about making you sergeant soon. Both of you eventually, but you have seniority because of your tenure."

"I'm flattered, sir. Thank you."

"Do you know what they call you upstairs?" Roth asked.

Grazer shook his head and ran his hand through his salt and pepper hair. "I do, but…I don't like it."

"Grazer the Great."

"I've heard it before."

"You are the detective with the most solved cases in this building. You should be honored by your accomplishments, not ashamed of them."

Grazer shook his head again. "Don't misunderstand me. I am very proud of what we've done. But I've done that only because I have a great team behind me; Detective Corona, Officer Hood, Officer Leddy. I don't work alone."

Roth nodded and pointed his finger at the detective. "That's what makes you successful. This department can use more people like you."

"Thank you, sir."

"This stays between you and I. Tell your wife, your kids, but don't say anything to anyone until I get the chance to speak to them myself."

Grazer nodded knowing that it would be difficult to keep the news from Corona. Aside from the fact that Corona's first question would be about what the lieutenant had to say, Grazer and Corona hardly kept anything from each other. But, he told Roth "Yes, sir," anyway.

He left Roth's office and met with Corona at his desk. He was on the phone, writing an address down on a piece of paper quickly. "Okay," he said into the receiver. "We'll be there in about twenty." He slammed the receiver down and stood from his desk in a hurry.

"What's going on?" Grazer asked him.

"That was Officer Leddy. That scene he's at? Says it's really bad. Wanted to know if we had breakfast this morning."

Grazer frowned. "Why?"

"Because he threw his up after arriving at the scene."

"I'll drive," Grazer said, already making his way toward the department's exit.

Corona followed closely behind; "What'd Roth tell you?" he asked.

"Not now," Grazer returned, and just as quickly as Corona had entered the building minutes earlier, they both were gone.

*

While neither enjoyed the fact that a crime had taken place, both men looked forward to arriving at the scene of a crime for the first time for very different reasons. Todd Grazer found the search exciting. Observing the situation, looking at the evidence, getting information from the forensics team and putting all the pieces together in his head like a puzzle in the hopes of solving whatever case was before them. But the arrival was exciting in its own right as there was nothing more pure than evidence when it's first discovered. Meanwhile, Hector Corona was a pro at talking to witnesses, questioning suspects, taking notes and identifying the lies. It was said Corona could make someone confess to anything; whether they did it or not. They worked as a team for over fifteen years, and since day one, their strengths complimented each other and ensured one would not step on the other's toes.

Both of them got out of the car; Grazer adjusting his tie before draping himself in a tan trench coat. Corona, snapped on his wind breaker, looked at his partner, let out a chuckle and shook his head. "Really," Corona said. "You wouldn't be any more of a stereotype if I called you Dick Tracy."

Grazer waved him off quickly observed the scenario around them. The upscale South Miami neighborhood of Coral Gables was usually quiet, but by the time they arrived, there were news crews amidst police cars, an ambulance and several other marked vehicles.

"Seems the action's in full swing," Grazer said. He looked over at Corona who was snapping on latex gloves. "Why do you do that while questioning people?"

Corona frowned at his partner as though his glove wearing was something new. "How many hands do you shake in a day?"

Grazer frowned. "A few."

"And do you know where those hands have been? Do you know how many germs are transmitted on a simple handshake?"

Grazer shook his head and was already walking toward the house that had been lined with yellow police tape. "You're sick, man."

Corona held up his gloved hands. "Nope. That's what these prevent."

They pushed through a few spectators and ignored several news reporters shouting questions at them as they walked underneath the police tape being guarded by several officers. The large front yard to the house was a little less busy, but almost immediately, both men saw Officer Scott Leddy, dressed in the county's brown and khaki uniform, trying hard to calm a woman who was being treated by a paramedic and crying hysterically. Officer Leddy noticed them, said something to the paramedic then jogged over to the detectives, his forehead and shirt both drenched in sweat despite the chilled winter morning.

"Good Lord, man. You need a towel?" Corona asked.

"Thank God you guys are here," he said to them, taking Grazer's hand to shake.

"What's happening?" Grazer asked.

Leddy offered his hand to Corona who shook his head. "No, thanks."

"The woman over there," Leddy proceeded, pointing to the hysterical lady. "She came to check on her mother and found her dead in the bedroom. And it's bad."

"How bad?" Corona asked.

"Better you see it yourself. Forensics is in there now doing their thing, so I asked everyone else to leave."

"Did anybody touch anything?" Grazer asked.

Leddy shook his head. "She said she ran out of the house the moment she saw it and hasn't gone back since. I walked in just as forensics arrived. No one came or went in between."

"So, we're not going to find your prints all over the place?" Corona asked. "Like we did in the Johnson murder?"

Leddy sneered at the detective. "Not unless you planted them."

Corona and Leddy engaged in a quick staring competition, until, "Children, please," Grazer said. "This is a crime scene. Let's try to be professional."

"He started it," Corona said.

"What about the victim?" Grazer asked. "What do you know?"

"Her name was Samantha Cabello," Leddy said from memory. "Age fifty-five. She just retired from the Department of Health, but no one's heard from her since the night of her retirement party. Her daughter flew in from a business trip because she was worried about her and, well, that's when she found her." Leddy looked back at the woman, still hysterical. "I can't imagine having to walk into what she did."

"Why don't you go find out what the daughter knows, then go do your thing and question the neighbors," Grazer said to Corona. "Leddy, you come with me and see what we can find inside."

Leddy hesitated. "If it's all the same to you, I'd like to maybe go with Corona."

Both men frowned. "Really?" Corona asked.

"Make fun of me if you will, but I don't need to go back in there. Seeing that bedroom once is enough. It's burned in my memory."

Grazer nodded and looked to his partner waiting for his approval.

Corona sighed and shook his head. "Fine," he said to Leddy. "But you say nothing to them. I'll do the questioning. And don't touch anything."

"I'll go talk to forensics and see what I can find," Grazer told him. "Keep me posted."

Both men nodded to each other and as Grazer began to approach the house, Corona and Leddy made their way back toward the paramedic and the victim's daughter.

When Grazer entered the house, the forensics team didn't even acknowledge him. They went about their business, dusting for prints, taking pictures, inspecting and turning over every single item in the search for something that would tell them who committed the crime and how it all transpired. Grazer was always amazed at their work and how they could recreate an entire crime scene by finding something as insignificant as a cigarette butt.

He looked around the living and dining rooms and from the looks of things, he would never have been able to tell that a crime had been committed. Everything seemed clean and normal enough. He was about to call the closest technician to ask him which way the bedroom was, but the flash of light coming from the hall told him where he needed to go.

As he reentered the living room toward the hallway, another flash of light filled the room. Seconds later, a man emerged from the bedroom with a large camera in his hand. He looked pale and sickly. He and Grazer exchanged glances.

"Prepare yourself before you go in there," he told Grazer. "In all my years, I've never seen anything like it." He excused himself and Grazer watched him hurry out of the house, his mouth covered and his back hunched over.

Grazer reached into the pocket of his blazer and extracted a pair of latex gloves. He snapped them on, took a deep breath, and began his descent into the hallway toward the victim's bedroom.

The first thing he noticed was the amount of blood. It was everywhere. On the ceiling, on the walls, covering every bit of furniture, the bed and floor. Samantha Cabello once had blood pumping through her veins, but every ounce of it was now spilled before him. He looked upon the bed and found the mass that, a few days earlier, was the body of the victim. It was nothing more than a mushy mess, and though he couldn't tell for sure, the mess that was hanging off the bed and puddled on the floor were her entrails. It explained the overwhelming smell of feces in the room.

"Jesus," he whispered to the air, and then a reflexive gag settled at the back of his throat when he realized he could make out her face on the bed – her eyes and mouth open as though she were still screaming in pain. Most of her teeth were missing now, and her eyes were red with blood. As though she exploded from the inside out, it was impossible to think that a human could do this to another.

He had seen enough. He closed his eyes for a second and as his brain registered the last image he saw, he stopped. Could he be mistaken? He looked again, and there it was. Almost camouflaged in the rest of the blood on the wall above the victim's bed, the blood pattern changed. It wasn't a splatter like the rest of the room had. There were strokes and lines forming three letters that, though not distinct, were visible enough to anyone who looked closely.

Grazer's eyes narrowed at the letters and without realizing, he read them out loud.

"E-N-O" he said.

Probable Cause

It wasn't unusual for Kelly to not speak to her mom for a couple days, but that was always it; just a couple days. The two would always check in with each other – especially since her father passed away. The night of her mother's retirement party, Kelly was in Manhattan on business, and she felt horrible about missing the event. She called her mother that night, left her a message, and figured she'd talk to her in the morning. But several days and countless voicemails later, Samantha never returned Kelly's calls, and that's when she began to worry. She took the first flight she could, drove straight to her mother's house, and found the horrid scene. She told Officer Leddy and Corona the same story over and over again before she was taken away on a gurney and pumped full of sedatives.

Grazer read the reports countless times while sitting at his desk back at Homicide, and unfortunately, it was the only evidence they had; Kelly's testimony. Forensics would take a few days to analyze the blood for any narcotics or something telling that the killer might have used to sedate Ms. Cabello. There were absolutely no fingerprints in the house aside from her own, no sign of forced entry, nothing indicating there was even someone else there. The only thing Grazer had to go on was the fact that the last time anyone heard from Ms. Cabello was at her own retirement party. Detective Corona was already on the phone with several of her associates who attended the party to ask who she left with, was she drunk, were there drugs involved, etc.

Then there were the letters. *ENO.* Grazer sat back on his chair, examining the picture taken at the scene. Leddy was right when he said the image was seared in his memory because Grazer experienced the same. Still, he studied the picture in case he might have missed something caused by the shock of seeing the room for the first time. *ENO.* He rubbed his temples and closed his eyes, his brain working tirelessly trying to figure out what the letters could mean – if anything at all.

He tossed the picture aside and it landed beside a frame containing a different picture entirely; a picture of his family. His wife, Mary and his two teenage children, Cynthia and Luis, were smiling gleefully back at him unaware of the horrid things he had seen earlier that morning. And so long as he could help it, they wouldn't know. Todd and Mary Grazer were married for just over twenty years, and in all that time, he would keep his work to himself – especially when it came to cases like the one on his desk.

"Really?" Corona said, suddenly in front of Grazer's desk. "We got a killer to find and you're daydreaming?"

Grazer nodded slowly, pointing at the picture of his family. "It's terrible to think there are people like the one who killed Samantha Cabello out there while we have kids, you know?"

Corona took a deep breath and sat on the chair opposite his partner's desk. "You can't think like that or you'll never work in law enforcement. You know that."

"How do you do it, Hector? Being a single father, your daughter's out there while you're dealing with maniacs like this," he said, showing him the picture of the blood drawn letters.

Corona smiled, "That's why she's always at your house." There was a moment of silence. "How are things at home?"

Grazer shook his head. "We're on night 17 of sleeping on separate beds. We talk when we need to. That's about it."

"Are you ever going to talk about the issue?"

"This is the type of conversation to have over a few drinks. Not here," Grazer said. "What do you think E-N-O means?"

"I don't know," Corona said, taking the picture and looking at it. "Initials, maybe? I haven't looked it up yet, but maybe it's Latin for something. Maybe it's a message from the killer."

"And how it is possible for someone to do what they did without leaving something behind?" Grazer asked, taking the picture back. "All that blood in the room, you'd figure there would be a foot print, a finger print. Something. It's like this guy vanished."

"We still haven't ruled out the possibility that maybe Ms. Cabello did this to herself."

"Impossible."

"Not any more impossible than someone doing this and not leaving any kind of trace. She was cut across the gut – that's the only injury that caused her death that we know of. That takes time to bleed out."

Grazer was already shaking his head. "She wasn't just cut across her stomach. She was disemboweled."

"I don't know," Corona said. "I'm as lost as you are with this one. And the few people I got a hold of who were with her at the party know nothing. They were about as useless as a nun's vagina."

Grazer cracked a smile then stood from his desk. "Let's get some lunch. I need to get out of here for a while; think this through."

"I'll go tell Leddy to make the rest of the calls. There are a couple names I didn't get to."

*

At almost thirty years old, Officer Scott Leddy was still rather disappointed in his career in law enforcement. As a child, living in a bad neighborhood in Miami, his mother wouldn't allow him outside to play, so his only source of entertainment was the small black and white television he would share with his two older brothers. They would watch action movies mostly, and when he went into the academy, his dreams of high speed car chases and Hollywood type shootouts lingered in his head. But years later, he found that life as an officer was much more subdued than the movies he watched as a child with countless hours driving in a patrol car, responding to calls made up of drunken brawls, pulling over the occasional pot-smoking speeder, or going on a wild goose chase by way of Corona's instructions. And he hadn't ever fired his gun outside of the shooting range.

What he hated more than anything else though, was the paperwork. The amount of paperwork that came with every action he took was astounding, but it was also a part of his evaluation, so shortcuts were not tolerated. Sitting at the desk he shared with Officer Tina Hood, he was working on documenting accounts surrounding the response to the call he received from Samantha Cabello's daughter when Detective Corona suddenly appeared before him.

"Teddy," Corona called, startling the officer.

"I'm sorry?" he responded.

"Your name. Teddy."

The officer rolled his eyes. "It's Leddy. You know that."

Corona shrugged. "Whatever. I need you to make some calls for me."

"Why? Your hands broken?"

Corona's eyes widened and his brows furrowed. "Very nice, officer! I'm impressed."

Leddy smiled – one of the very few times he did with Corona around.

"I need you to find out if anyone else at Ms. Cabello's party saw anything. The few people I've spoken to know nothing and Detective Grazer and I have other business to attend to. Lunch, mainly."

And Leddy's smile was gone. His shoulders slumped.

"And you call me if you find anything out," Corona said. "The file's on my desk."

"Sure. Fine. Whatever."

"I knew I could count on you. And hey, isn't this Hood's desk?"

"It's my desk, too."

"Huh. I wouldn't have thought you two would have been paired up. Go figure."

"Why?" Leddy frowned. "Because she's a female and I'm not? Because she's in better shape than I am? Or is it because I'm black and she's not? Which is it?"

Corona had both hands up in surrender. "Actually, I was gonna say because she's less experienced than you and she might slow you down a bit. That, and she's much better looking than you are. Settle down there, cowboy."

Leddy looked down and shook his head. Ready to apologize and explain he was just fed up with the clerical aspect of his job, he looked back to Corona, but the detective was already gone. Leddy took a deep breath, shook off his aggravation and went off to look for the numbers on Corona's desk.

*

Despite their increasing weight, tussles with high cholesterol and increased blood pressure, the one diner the two detectives would go to discuss a case was called the Latin Corner, and it was famous for their fried plantains, Cuban sandwiches and deep fried chicken bites that may or may not have been made of real chicken. Both men walked in, greeted their regular waitress and sat at their usual table where they awaited their complimentary basket of Cuban bread slathered with butter.

The diner was only half full as the lunch hour in Miami was still about an hour away. This was a strategic move on their behalf as it would allow them to speak freely regarding whatever case they worked on, and it almost always ensured their favorite table, set in the corner of the diner where the sun cascaded its brilliant rays upon, was available. It was also a place where Detective Grazer and Detective Corona were just Todd and Hector, respectively. There were no badges, no other officials, just both of them and the delicious, greasy food.

Their bread arrived and their glasses of water were filled. Both bid the waitress *gracias* and Todd ravaged the basket of bread as Hector rubbed his hands with sanitizer before helping himself.

"Mary would kill me if she knew I was here," Todd said.

"Statements like that make me glad I'm single," Hector responded, taking a bite of the bread. "Never want to marry again."

"Mary looks great, but let's face it, I'm not in the shape I was ten years ago."

Hector nearly choked on his bread laughing. "Ten years? Try twenty, Mr. I-Lost-Interest-in-the-Gym-Right-After-College."

"You're one to talk."

"I'm not the one complaining."

The waitress bounced back to the two men, smile on her face, pen and pad in her hand. *"Estan listos?"* Are you ready?

"*Si*," Hector said, his half smile gleaming and his eyes twinkling at the young woman. "*Chicharones de pollo, maduros, y un sandwich Cubano con papas fritas, por favor.*"

Todd shook his head slowly at his friend. It didn't matter what woman was around, Hector would turn on the charm and make her feel like she was the only woman that mattered.

"Nada mas?" Nothing more?

"Nada mas. Gracias, mi amor," Hector said with a wink.

The waitress smiled and bounced away to place their order.

Hector reached into the inside pocket of his blazer and extracted a sealed package containing a plastic fork, spoon, knife and napkin and pushed the ones on the table aside. He opened the package, gently set down the napkin and placed the plastic utensils on top of it. Satisfied, he looked at his friend who was smiling in return.

Todd had learned years ago to stop harassing his friend's habits, even when Hector would ask him to pour the ketchup or mustard from the bottles on the table for him.

"So, any theories?" Todd asked.

"About what?"

"The Cabello case. You said you think she did that to herself."

Hector shook his head. "It was just an idea."

"I'm just completely baffled by it. None of her neighbors saw anything suspicious, she didn't seem to have any enemies…"

"That we know of. Let's see what Leddy comes up with. And besides, the blood results aren't back yet. Maybe all of it wasn't hers."

Todd slapped his thighs. "That's the problem; waiting means this guy will have the chance to do it again."

"*If* he's gonna do it again. We don't know that yet."

Todd took a deep breath. "Honestly, at this point, I hate to say it, but if he does, that might actually lead us somewhere. A one off doesn't make sense. Two murders, maybe we see a pattern."

Hector nodded. "Maybe."

A moment of silence fell between them suddenly, and for a split second, Todd considered telling Hector that he had another nightmare – just like the others that he had before – in the hopes that Hector told him it was nothing. As though hearing it would make it true, Todd wanted Hector to shrug it off even though he wasn't sure of it himself. He took a breath, phrasing the words in his mind when -

The cell phone in Hector's pocket erupted and both he and Todd exchanged glances. It never failed; once food was ordered, they'd be called out to a crime scene or forced out of the restaurant in an emergency. Hector reached for it, looked at the display and sighed. "It's the station."

"Of course it is," Todd replied.

Hector was already on the phone, and by the way he stood up, Todd could tell the call was urgent. While Hector ran for the front door of the restaurant, barking something about bad reception, Todd was calling the waitress over to cancel the meal in broken Spanish.

The sun was in full force when Todd walked outside to meet Hector. The chilled wind wasn't enough to keep the sweat from forming the moment air conditioning was no longer available. Though it was winter, it was still Miami. Todd lit a cigarette and walked to the east of the small parking lot where his partner was just hanging up the phone.

"What's going on?"

"That was Leddy. He's got something big."

Grazer's eyes widened. "They found him?"

"Not exactly. But he was on the phone with some people who were with Ms. Cabello at the party and they saw her leaving with a man named Richard DeCocq. It's pronounced *DeCook* but spelled more like *DeCock*. He should be arrested just for that. He's a Dick, either way. Richard. Get it?"

Grazer motioned his hand in a quick, circular motion. "And the point is..."

"Turns out these two go back. Way back. They worked together at the DOH, he retired a couple years ago as well. They had some kind of affair, but it got ugly because she was married. Anyway, supposedly, he drove her home that night."

"And did they try to contact him?"

Corona nodded slowly. "Yes. So have several other people. No one's been able to get in touch with him, either. They figured the two went somewhere for the week."

"The son of a bitch took off," Grazer said. "Address?"

"Got it already. Leddy and Hood are on their way."

"I'll drive," Todd said, flicking his cigarette to the floor, and both men jogged to their black sedan.

*

Leddy anxiously bounced his leg while Hood weaved the marked cruiser in and out of traffic. He looked at his watch; it had been nearly five minutes since he spoke to Corona, and based on the Detectives' location, they would probably arrive at the scene before he and Hood did. But this was his lead.

"Maybe we should take Bird Road," Leddy told Hood.

She rolled her eyes. "Relax. I know my way."

Leddy was about to remind her that 88th Street, the road they were on, was gridlocked at this time of day, but she would only snap at him. He wanted to drive to their suspect's residence, but Hood already had the keys and arguing with her would only waste time.

He looked at his watch again. Six minutes.

Though the siren blared, drivers in Miami seemed to be oblivious. Some moved out of their way, most didn't. If he had the time, Leddy would ticket them all. He took a deep breath, tried to calm himself and give way to the fact that perhaps it was better the Detectives get there before he did. He closed his eyes, took a deep breath, but within seconds, his leg began bouncing again.

Hood looked at him for a second. "Relax," she said. "We'll get there."

He nodded, returning a forced smile.

Hood and Leddy were assigned as partners immediately after his run with the Detectives – nearly two years before. They could read each other's signals and body language. Leddy knew when Hood was nervous and Hood knew when Leddy was anxious. And although he wouldn't admit it to her, a break like the one Leddy found was just what he needed to prove to the Detectives that he was indeed a good cop.

The two-way radio on the cruiser's console suddenly came to life. Detective Grazer's voice filled the car, and all hopes of reaching the site first drained from Leddy's gut.

"What's your location?" Grazer asked.

Leddy reached for the receiver before Hood had the chance. "Making our way toward US1 and 88th Street," he said. "ETA five minutes – traffic depending."

"Good," Grazer responded. "It's gridlock on Bird. You'll probably get there before we do."

Hood smiled at Leddy in that *Told you so* way he was familiar with. Leddy smiled in return. This time, it was genuine.

"Be careful when you get there," Grazer said. "If this guy is who we're looking for, he may be dangerous."

"Yes, sir!" Leddy responded with enthusiasm. He put the receiver back in its place as Corona's filtered voice warned something about not leaving fingerprints on anything. He rubbed his hands together, turned to his partner and said, "All right, let's do this!"

Hood laughed at his boyish excitement and sped through the city streets until finally, they pulled into the neighborhood where their suspect resided.

It was a middle class neighborhood with homes lining on each side of the streets. Their trifling front yards were barely visible as they made way for the driveways which were mostly empty except for –

"That one," Leddy said, pointing to the right.

About a hundred yards ahead of them, an old white Cadillac was parked on the driveway of a house identical to the rest. Hood led the cruiser, sirens off, to a crawling stop before the house, and both officers were out of their cars in seconds. Hands on their weapons, both of them approached the house slowly, Leddy in the lead.

As he approached the car, he placed his palm flat on the hood. The car was cool, indicating it had not been used recently. He looked back to Hood and shook his head. He continued toward the front door as Hood made her way to the closest window and peered in.

"Anything?" Leddy asked her, almost in a whisper.

"Nothing," she responded.

Leddy nodded and swallowed hard as he fisted his hand preparing to knock on the door. This was his chance – question the suspect, and if everything was in his favor, make the arrest that closed this case.

"Wait," Hood said, still looking through the window. "I think... Come here."

Leddy frowned. "What is it?"

"Come look," she demanded, and Leddy did as he was told. Hood made way for Leddy to look through the window. "What does that look like? On the floor just beyond the doorway there."

At first, Leddy couldn't even make out a doorway. He could see an old couch in the small darkened living room through a small opening in the heavy curtains. His eyes scanned the wall beyond the couch until it parted. He looked to the floor.

It was hard to see at first, but a second later, he recognized it. A hand was on the floor, turned upward, fingers curled at rest.

"Oh shit," he said quickly.

"That's what I thought," Hood returned.

He looked again — it was difficult to tell if the hand was severed or if the rest of the body it was attached to was hidden behind the wall. Either way, Leddy had his way in.

He took hold of his gun — a 9mm Glock — and approached the door.

"What are you doing?" Hood called out. "Shouldn't we wait for…"

"No," Leddy returned. "We have probable cause."

"We should call it in," Hood argued as Leddy reached for the door.

"You call it in if you want. Grazer and Corona will be here soon," he stopped when he unwillingly opened the door by simply touching it.

They exchanged glances, and a second later, Leddy put both hands on his gun, pointed it straight down, and he entered the house.

Hood took a deep breath and shook her head. She drew her gun and followed.

The humid smell was the first scent that hit them as they slowly entered the living room. It was small and filled with clutter to make it appear even tighter. There were no lights turned on, there seemed to be no signs of life, but Hood called out either way: "Miami-Dade Police. We're armed. If anyone is here, come out with your hands up!"

Both of them kept their eyes on the hand on the floor in the next room. It didn't move.

The humid smell suddenly gave way to a rancid scent that made both of their faces cringe. Hood let out a cough. "What the hell is that smell?" she asked. Leddy didn't answer because he couldn't identify it. It was rot and sulfur combined, the smell of spoiled milk and feces all combined in one horrid odor. The more they approached the opening of the room, the stronger the stench became.

"Leddy," Hood said in an attempt to get him to stop, but he continued.

He approached the opening, an arm attached to the hand revealed. It wasn't severed. In fact, the body it belonged to was all there, but barely intact.

Except for a few places, there was no skin on the body. Its red and white tissue was glistening back at Leddy and rendered the body asexual. Its face was propped up against the corner, a mess of bone and tissue. He didn't want to look at it anymore, but he couldn't tear his eyes off the fact that the skull had one eye missing. The other hand, stripped of its casing, was holding on to, what Leddy assumed, was a telephone covered in slime. This person was alive while whatever happened to them took place.

"What is it?" Hood asked. He was going to warn her not to enter, but it was too late. She covered her mouth and her throat made a noise indicating she was going to become sick.

There was blood. Everywhere. And a mass of slime and cream colored mucus was piled in the furthest corner of the room. A few flies circled the mess.

"What is that?" Hood asked through her covered mouth.

Leddy fought the gag back. "Skin," he answered.

Hood spun quickly and though Leddy didn't watch her, he knew she ran out of the house.

His eyes remained on the room and his knees grew frail. A dining table was in the center of what was once a quaint dining room. Another pile of mess was set atop it - the victim's intestines - were left displayed as though whoever, whatever did this wanted it to be seen first.

Leddy looked beyond the table, on the sliding glass door that led to the small backyard. His back stiffened and his knees almost buckled. The letters O-W-T were scrawled on the glass, in blood.

Nausea and dizziness took hold of him and Leddy turned feeling light headed. He was going to faint, and he didn't want to do it in the victim's mess. He hurried to the doorway and took a breath of the humid Miami air in the hopes of ridding the stench burned in his nose. It didn't work. He dropped himself onto the door's step, taking a seat and breathing heavily. He looked at his partner who was vomiting beside the patrol car and he fought the urge to do the same. The darkness was starting to circle his head and he was fighting it off. He didn't want to faint. Not when Grazer and Corona were on their way.

Almost instantly, their black sedan pulled onto the curb. Both men jumped out of the car and looked at the two officers – one sick, the other pale as a ghost. Corona ran to Hood's aid while Leddy watched Grazer approach him.

"What's going on?" Grazer asked.

It was then that Leddy realized he was hyperventilating. He tried to tell the detective not to enter. He tried to warn him about what was inside, but all he could muster was, "Another".

Grazer frowned. "Another?"

Leddy nodded.

"Another what?"

Leddy closed his eyes trying his hardest to compose himself. "Another victim," he said between breaths. "Like Cabello."

NAME NOT...

As lieutenant of the Miami-Dade Police Department's Homicide Unit, it was Jack Roth's job to lead his team in the performance of law enforcement services. Throughout the years, he had built a team that he was comfortable with; a team that did not need his constant supervision. His sergeants were top-notch and his detectives were stellar. Grazer and Corona were amongst his favorites as he felt he molded them into the men they were today. Even his newest recruits like Leddy and Hood were shaping up to be prodigious which is specifically why he asked Grazer and Corona to include them on anything the detectives were working on. There was no doubt throughout the department and all the way up to the Chief of Police, Jack Roth loved his job. There were certain aspects however, that he despised; the clerical work, the budgeting, and the massive amount of paperwork involved when a case landed on his desk or when it was closed.

"If I wanted to sit behind a desk, I would have been an accountant," he had said many times before – but never to anyone who could hear him.

It's exactly why he was all too excited when he got the call from Grazer. Cool and collected, Grazer told him of the crime scene they had stumbled upon, though Roth knew him long enough to tell there was a hint of alarm in his voice. He could already picture Corona bathing in hand sanitizer somewhere in the background. Within seconds, Roth grabbed his blazer and the keys to his sedan and was headed to the scene.

The sun was beginning its descent over the western skies, cascading an orange glow over the city. Traffic on the streets was beginning to die down as most citizens had already arrived home from their nine-to-fives and while they were spending time with their family, Roth sped through the streets, his brain making the shift from desk worker to investigator. The usual questions he asked once he arrived on scene were on his tongue and the notepad in his brain was ready to absorb the information.

Roth pulled up to the scene as closely as he could without hitting or running over any of the dozens of spectators before parking his car on the curb and outfitting his jacket. As though he were a celebrity allowed into an exclusive club, the few officers standing beyond the yellow caution tape lifted the proverbial velvet rope and allowed him to step onto the scene. His eyes scanned the area, taking everything in at once but observing all the details; forensics were already on scene, from where he stood, he could see the inside of the house bustling with activity, a few uniformed officers were talking to neighbors, and beside one of the patrol sedans, Roth could see a puddle of sick someone left behind. His money was on Leddy.

Just before he made his way into the house, Corona stepped out, his hands protected by latex gloves that were covered in blood. He snapped one off, his right hand, and tossed it to the floor, careful not to get any blood on his exposed skin. Reaching into his pocket he replaced the glove with a clean one then removed the stained one on his left hand. After both hands were protected again, he picked up the soiled gloves and properly disposed of them. All the while, his face displayed disgust.

"Talk to me, Corona," Roth said to him after the ritual was complete. "What do we have?"

Corona shook his head. "Pardon the expression, Lieutenant, but we don't have shit."

Roth frowned.

"No finger prints, no sign of forced entry, none of the neighbors saw or heard anything. We came here on a lead related to the Cabello murder only to find another body."

"Same M.O." Roth said as both men stepped away from the house to let more of the forensics team in.

"In every way except the cause of death. This man was skinned. Well, we think it's a man, Richard DeCocq."

"You think?"

"There was probably some kind of chemical used to skin the victim. There was no sign of a…" Corona hesitated and swallowed hard. "Um, there were no genitals."

"Jesus," Roth whispered, almost to himself. "Poor bastard."

"Forensics is analyzing a sample of the tissue to see what they can find, any trace of chemicals and to ensure that this was, in fact, Richard DeCocq."

Roth nodded. He was about to ask for the whereabouts of Grazer when, as if on cue, he stepped out of the house and approached the two men quickly. Grazer's gloves were also stained with blood. Corona eyed his partner's hands and took a step back.

"Estimated time of death is about seventy two hours," Grazer said without greeting Roth. "We need to confirm because if any chemicals were used on the victim they might have altered the rigor mortis. However, by the temperature of the corpse and the dried blood in the room, specifically on the writing on the glass doors, it's estimated at seventy two hours."

Roth held a hand up at Grazer. "I'm sorry. The writing on the glass doors?"

"Yes, sir." Grazer said.

"O-W-T," Corona jumped in.

"Like the E-N-O in the Cabello case." Roth concluded.

Both detectives nodded.

"Any clue as to what it means?" Roth asked.

"Initials, words, or part of a word," Grazer said, stripping off his gloves. Corona took another step away. "We're working on it."

"I think they're being numbered," Leddy said, suddenly appearing from behind them.

All of them turned to face him, and the speed at which they did visibly startled the young officer. His face tightened and he stepped back.

"Say again," Corona ordered.

Leddy took a deep breath. "They're being numbered. E-N-O and O-W-T. One and two. They're written backwards."

Lieutenant Roth, Detective Grazer and Detective Corona all looked at each other for a brief moment then looked back to Leddy – each of them wondering why they hadn't realized it sooner, and impressed with the young man for doing it before them.

"Good job, Leddy," Roth said. "Why don't you and Hood see if you can figure out if there's any relevance to the backwards writing and the manner in which they were murdered?"

Leddy nodded and nervously smiled. "Will do, sir. Thank you." He disappeared.

"Son of a bitch is numbering his victims," Corona said, letting his mind absorb the fact.

"We need to find out who is doing this, gentlemen," Roth said, "before a third victim. The last thing we need is a serial killer on our hands."

"There's one more thing about the time of death," Grazer said. "If we're accurate and this man was killed less than three days ago, then that puts the time of death very close to Cabello. Whoever did this killed Cabello, came clear across town and killed DeCocq all without a trace, and within minutes of each other. We might be dealing with more than one killer here."

Roth shook his head. "This just keeps getting better."

*

At the end of the night, Roth watched the crowd disperse at the hands of his two best detectives aided by some of the uniformed officers. When they were done, he thanked them for a job well done, and told them to wrap up their teams and call it a night.

"I can handle the rest from here," he told them. "You've had a long day. We'll regroup in the morning."

Grazer and Corona looked at each other and nodded.

"Call us if anything comes up," Corona ordered and Roth agreed.

They called Leddy and Hood to share the good news, and without hesitation, the two young officers jumped into their sedan and sped away as Roth disappeared into the house to gather information from the forensics team.

Grazer drove through the city streets, Corona secured in the passenger side, back to their station to retrieve their own vehicles. "Two murders in one day," Grazer said. "Can't think of the last time we had a day this hectic."

"In one night," Corona said.

"Say again."

"If the time of death was correct, both murders happened in one night. Not in one day."

Grazer nodded. Both men rode in silence, the information fresh in their heads and trying to make sense of it all. Two murders, both of them numbered in backward English. One was mutilated, the other skinned. Both were obviously linked, and it was only a matter of time before they found out how. And if it was done in one night, within minutes of each other, then there had to be two killers.

"What are you thinking?" Grazer asked Corona, finally breaking the silence.

Hector looked at his friend and frowned. "The last time someone asked me that in that tone, she was naked in my bed."

Todd rolled his eyes. "About the case, asshole."

"Too much and nothing at all." He closed his eyes and rested his head on the window of the passenger door. "Roth was right. It's been a long day, and I can't get my head around everything. I'm tired, and quite honestly, the shit we saw today kind of jarred me. Add that to the fact that we still haven't eaten and I'm fucking starving."

Todd laughed. "I hear ya. Why don't you go pick up your daughter and come to the house for dinner? We'll order something."

Hector frowned. "You sure it's safe? I don't want to get in the middle of anything."

Grazer laughed. "If anything, you'll help ease the tension."

"Well, call her and make sure. I don't want to impose, especially if she's tired."

"She'll welcome the adult conversation, and the kids will keep each other busy. Believe me, she won't mind. It's the reason for all our troubles. I'm not around and she hates me for it."

"She doesn't hate you."

"You should see us when we're on our own."

"Do you think there were two?"

"Two what?"

"Killers. One murder clear across town from the other."

"It makes sense," Todd answered. "But there were striking similarities; no finger prints, no fibers, nothing to indicate anyone was there at all. For one person to pull that off is nearly impossible, let alone two."

"My thoughts exactly. But how do we pursue this investigation with the idea that there's just one killer?"

"And give Roth a heart attack?" Todd asked, laughing. "No way. We continue as though there are two until we find out otherwise. We'll wait for forensics to do their thing and see what they come back with."

"And if they come back with nothing?" Hector asked.

After a moment's thought, Todd answered, "Well, then we hang up our badges because in all my years, they've never come back with nothing."

*

It was almost ten when the last of the team left the crime scene. Roth thanked each and every one for their help and cooperation on their way out. He yawned and rubbed his glazed eyes. It had been a long day for everyone involved, and Roth thought of nothing but resting his head on his pillow and drifting to sleep, even after seeing the things he saw at the crime scene.

The body had to be taken out in pieces. The body's muscle, void of any skin, tore apart when moved and the liquid and slime it left behind was horrid. The memory of the victim's innards spilled across the floor was enough to turn anyone's stomach, but Roth worked under such circumstances for many years. To say he was used to seeing the kind of mess left behind would be a lie, but he learned, very early, that he could not allow such scenes to bother him too much otherwise his run as lieutenant would be short.

He shook the images from his head and yawned again. Making his way to his car, he thought of stopping somewhere for food when the mobile phone in his pocket came to life with a high pitched ring. For a split second, he grew excited hoping whoever was calling had some kind of answer to the case, but when he didn't recognize the number on the phone's display, the anticipation faded. He answered the call.

"Roth here."

He listened intently to the panicked voice on the other line.

"When did this happen?" he asked. He glanced at his watch then slapped his thigh. "Okay. I'll be right there."

He switched the phone off then cursed into the air. "Son of a bitch!" Putting the phone back in his pocket, the thought of eating and sleeping disappeared. It was a long day for Lieutenant Roth, and it was going to be an even longer night.

...One Man

Roth was kind enough to let them have the rest of the evening off, and though Todd appreciated it at first, he would much rather had stayed working the case. It's all he did that evening, anyway. Mary was happy to see him and Hector, accompanied by his daughter, arrive at their house, and despite Todd's insistence of ordering food out, she immediately went to the kitchen and began preparing a hearty meal for the two detectives. The three adults ate together while their children spent their time in the pool house in the backyard, and never once was the case brought up. It was however the only thing on Todd's mind.

The elusiveness of the killer, or killers, baffled him. It would be a while before forensics returned with their findings, if any since it appeared they had nothing to go by; no hair, skin, DNA at all left at either scene. Impossible, he thought to himself, but the evidence, or lack thereof, spoke for itself.

His train of thought was broken only when either his wife or Hector said something directly to him. He would respond then return to his thoughts. He glanced at Hector several time throughout their dinner and wondered if he was as wrapped up in the case as he was. Hector laughed and took part in the conversation flowing around the table, his eyes focused on whoever spoke or on the plate of food before him. Never once did he falter, not even when Mary turned her attention to her distracted husband.

"Where'd you go, Todd?" Mary asked.

Todd's concentration broke, the question resonating in his head though he actually didn't hear it. He shook his head, placing his fork on the almost full plate, then wiped his mouth with a cloth napkin. "You don't want to know," he responded.

"I wouldn't have asked if I didn't" she said. "It's gotta be a big case because I haven't seen you this distracted in a long time."

"You know Todd," Hector said, pushing his empty plate aside. "Always working."

Todd smiled, sheepishly. "Sorry. I'm just lost in thought. I didn't mean to be rude." He smiled at Mary. "I'm here. Promise."

Mary shook her head. "He never tells me about your cases," she told Hector. "Only once they're closed, and sometimes even then, it's like pulling teeth. That John Doe case you just closed? I wouldn't have known about it if it wasn't for you."

Hector laughed.

"I do it because you and the kids don't need to worry about me or the filth that's out there in our streets."

"He's right," Hector added. "This particular case that fell on our laps is pretty terrible. You don't need the gory details."

"When we close the case," Todd said, "I'll tell you everything."

Defeated, Mary shook her head and turned her attention to Hector, placing a hand on his. "I'm glad he at least has you," she said. "If he won't talk to me, I hope he leans on you."

Hector's pulse raced suddenly. He quickly slipped his hand off the table, away from Mary's, a neat line of sweat forming above his brow.

"We got company," Todd said, suddenly.

Three teenagers approached the sliding glass door beyond the dining room that lead to the expansive back yard. Joanna Corona, Hector's daughter, was the eldest at eighteen. She was followed closely by Todd and Mary's children, Cynthia, and the youngest of them all, Luis.

The three teenagers entered the house, all of them in mid conversation and laughter, but they stopped cold and stared at the three adults who were already looking at them.

"Well, those are some guilty faces, if I've ever seen them," Hector said. "I assume you three are up to no good?"

"Those two are," Joanna responded, referring to the Grazer teens. "I'm an angel, as usual."

"She may have her mom's looks, but she's got your sarcasm," Mary said to Hector.

He nodded with a smile. "That's my girl. But wrap it up soon because we're leaving. I have an early start tomorrow."

"That's what we were coming in for," Cynthia spoke up suddenly, looking to her mom. "Do you think it's okay if Jo spends the night?"

"If it's okay with her father, I don't see why not," Mary responded.

"You don't have your hands full with two teenagers already?" Hector asked. "You want one more running amuck in the house?"

"Jo's great," she said. "Really, I don't mind."

Hector shrugged and looked to Todd. "We'll probably have a busy day tomorrow, so I don't see why not."

Both Cynthia and Joanna bounced with glee as Luis' shoulders slumped. "Any chance I can crash at Nick's for tonight then?" He asked. "It's bad enough with just one sister in the house, let alone two."

"You, young man, should be thinking about the conversation we had at about three this morning," Todd said, waving his finger at his son. "I haven't forgotten about that. I hope you didn't, either."

Luis hung his head. "No, sir."

"Good. Now it's late. Everyone to their rooms. You'll have all day tomorrow to... to do whatever it is you all do these days."

The two girls wandered happily out of the dining room, both of them gossiping and laughing all the way up the stairs as Luis dragged behind them.

"Good night, dad! You're the best!" Hector called out to his daughter.

"Love you!" she yelled from the second floor as her father shook his head.

"Poor Luis," Mary said, stifling a smile. "Did you see his face?"

"He's had his fill of fun," Todd said, then turned to Hector. "Caught the punk sneaking back into the house at three this morning reeking of cigarettes."

"Ouch."

"Jo can stay here whenever you need her to," Mary said. "She really isn't a problem, and she'll keep the kids busy and out of my hair."

"I appreciate that, considering she won't be visiting her mother in California this summer because she said she wanted to spend it with her friends."

"That's sweet. They're good kids," Mary said, "and you know, my sister in New York said she wanted to bring her daughter down to visit. I know the kids would love to see her. It's been like two years now."

After insisting he help with the dishes, Mary kissed Hector on the cheek and ordered him to go home for a restful night's sleep. Hector blushed, careful not to hold her embrace for too long. Afterwards, Todd walked his friend out of the house and waited until they were outside to light a cigarette.

"You know what I was thinking," Todd said, blowing a cloud of grey smoke into the air. "While we were at lunch discussing the Cabello case, I said had this guy killed again, it might help our case. Well, he did, and it didn't."

"Are you saying you want there to be another victim?" Hector asked.

"God, no. And if victim number three does show up with the same time of death as the other two, then I'll throw my hands up in surrender."

"And we'll have a serial killer on our hands. This case will be bigger than either one of us even realized."

Todd thought about it then shook his head. "Serial killers typically have a sort of 'down-time', if you will. They kill, return to their normal lives, then kill again later on. They usually do it out of anger or just for kicks, not like this."

"Did you not see the victims? One body was disemboweled and the other was skinned beyond recognition. There was definite anger in those killings."

"Whoever did this took time to plan his entry so that he would be completely undetected. He probably knew his victims well enough so that they willingly allowed him into their homes. This guy is more of a spree-killer; two people, different locations, same night - hell, virtually at the same time."

"That's *if* we're dealing with one person."

"Yeah. Right."

"Well, we don't know enough to start profiling anyone yet. Let's find the connection between the two victims and regroup."

Todd took another puff and nodded.

"Get some rest tonight, will you?" Hector said. "And talk to your wife."

Todd nodded, and watched Hector as he pulled out of the driveway and left the neighborhood. Rest. He did need it, but with the case banging at the forefront of all his thoughts, rest was far from an accomplishment.

*

When Roth walked into the hospital, his eyes burned with the bright lights after coming in from the darkness as he scanned the vast waiting area. As the automatic doors slid to a close behind him, he avoided the patients waiting to be attended to and made his way to the nurse's station in the center of the room.

"I'm here to see Eugene Morrison," he said to the nurse behind the desk who was busy looking at files.

"Dr. Morrison is with a patient at the moment," she said without looking at him. "How can I help you?"

Roth reached into his jacket and flashed his badge. "You can help me by getting Dr. Morrison out here so that I may speak to him about the patient under his care that went missing."

The nurse glared at the badge and made eye contact with the lieutenant for the first time. She nodded slowly then picked up the phone and punched in a few numbers. It wasn't long before Dr. Eugene Morrison, a large, burly black man, came from behind two swinging doors marked *ER, Authorized Personnel Only*. He was dressed in scrubs and a lab coat draped over his large shoulders. Though they had never met, Morrison approached Roth quickly and extended his large hand.

"Lieutenant Roth, thank you so much for coming. Can we speak in my office, please?"

"Right here is fine," Roth said, looking at his watch. It was quickly approaching 11:00 PM.

Morrison nodded, but Roth could tell it was against his will. "One of my nurses went into the patient's room to perform routine checks on him, and that's when she saw he was missing."

"Is this nurse still here, can I speak to her?"

Morrison nodded then pointed to the nurse behind the station. "Nurse Johnston, this is Lieutenant Roth of the Miami-Dade Police Department."

"Ms. Johnson, is there anything you can tell me about the missing patient that struck you as strange?"

"You mean beside the fact that he got up and walked outta here without anyone noticing after spending almost a year in a coma?" she asked, every word dripping with sarcasm.

Both Roth and Morrison glared at her.

"Nothing before that," she continued, handing Roth a folder. "Here's his file. It's got all his vitals while he was here, heartbeat, brain function, blood pressure. Nothing out of the ordinary, nor any indication that he woke up or anything."

Roth flipped through the paperwork but didn't quite know what he was reading. There were graphs with colored lines forming mountain peaks and intersecting with each other, a chart with all kinds of numbers, even something that looked like a sonogram. He nodded, taking Nurse Johnston at her word. "Any witnesses say they saw him leave?"

Both Morrison and Johnston shook their heads.

"What about security cameras?"

Morrison nodded. "We have security looking at the tapes right now. So far, nothing."

"In the morning, I will send two officers to collect whatever tapes you have," Roth said. "In the meantime, I'll put out an APB and contact local patrol." He put a couple of his cards on the nurse's station. "Call me if you think or hear of anything else."

Without wishing them a pleasant evening or thanking them for their cooperation, Roth spun on his heel and began making his way out of the hospital, his mobile already on his ear.

"I need to put out an APB," he demanded. "Male, Caucasian, forty five to fifty five years of age, graying hair, grey beard, possibly shaved and possibly wearing a hospital gown or scrubs." He waited a couple seconds. "Name? No name, unfortunately," he said into the phone. He received the confirmation he needed then snapped the phone closed. Taking a deep breath, he looked at his watch once more and wondered if it was too late to call Grazer and Corona that their John Doe had gone missing from the hospital, and the case was about to be reopened.

*

At sixty-six years old, Mark Shaw was in the best shape of his life. His first doctor's appointment after retiring scared him into shape, so to speak. His cholesterol was high, his blood pressure was off the charts, and he was about eighty pounds overweight. Sitting at a desk for an entire career span would do that to anyone. His doctor wanted to put him on all sorts of medication for every ailment, but Mark objected. He made a deal with his doctor; give him one year to lower his blood pressure, his cholesterol and weight on his own. If he didn't succeed, he'd take the meds. His doctor agreed, and the very next day, Mark signed up for his very first gym membership – even paid for a personal trainer.

Three years later, Mark was still losing the weight and his blood pressure was back to the ideal 120/80. Unfortunately, diet and exercise were not enough to lower his cholesterol, so he had to take medication every day. One pill was better than three or four, he thought. Though he still went to the gym, he didn't frequent it six days a week like before – especially not during the summer. Aside the fact that a gym in Miami during the summer months was overcrowded with model types showing off their glistening, toned bodies in fashion show mode, Mark preferred the nightly runs on his own to clear his mind and plan his next day.

His wife, Melinda, was proud of him, to say the least. Though she didn't particularly enjoy sweating, or raising her heart rate, she supported her husband without question. Which is why when he suggested going to a ski resort in Oregon, she hesitated only for a minute. She watched him fall when he tried rollerblading on the streets of Miami Beach, she cringed when he twisted his ankle during his first tennis match, and barely laughed out loud when he suggested they take dancing lessons (though she enjoyed this activity the most, he only went to two classes). She didn't think that skiing would be the safest activity since neither of them had ever even seen a pair of skis, let alone tried them on, but she thought the get-away would be nice; the two of them in a log cabin, in the mountains, a blanket of snow surrounding them. It was the perfect escape from Miami and the countless grandkids they watched while their children went to work.

For weeks, Mark had been buying all sorts of gear and equipment to take on their trip; thermal underwear, heavy coats, thick tube socks, ski pants and jackets, protective goggles, and all other sorts of paraphernalia that would make their luggage weigh more than both of them combined. Melinda was overwhelmed at the amount of items sprawled out on the bed and wondered how much of it she could "forget" to pack without Mark noticing. At almost ten that evening, she insisted he go on his nightly jog so that she could work at getting their luggage prepared without his supervision. The moment he left, she closed herself in their spare bedroom, laid all of their travel items out, and didn't know where to begin. Once she got started however, there was no stopping her. She managed to pack most of the items, except for a few articles of clothing such as matching black jumpsuits and black ski masks that she found ridiculous, though Mark was excited about. She left them locked in her closet, hoping he wouldn't notice they were missing.

When she was finished, Melinda opened the door to the guest bedroom and froze. The hallway between her and the other rooms had gone dark, and it did so the moment she opened the door. The light in the hall had been switched off just as she entered, and it took a moment for her eyes to adjust to the darkness that had enveloped her suddenly.

"Mark," she called out instinctively, and was surprised by the authority in her voice despite the sudden jolt of her nerves. "Is that you?"

Her eyes scanned the darkness, especially the end of the hall that gave way to the remainder of the house. As though the power had been cut, the rest of the house appeared just as dark as the hall – even darker, in fact.

"Mark, this isn't funny," she called out to the air, taking a step toward the hall's entrance, toward the switch. "If you keep this up, I swear I will cancel tomorrow's trip," she warned, the authority leaving her voice. Her anxiety gripped her throat and the words that came out of her mouth were just as shaky as she was.

She took another step toward the light switch, and that's when she saw the silhouette standing at the end of the hall. Amidst the darkness, she could see the figure of a man standing absolutely still, watching her. "Mark..." she said, almost in a whisper, her eyes tearing up in fear.

The silhouette let out a loud breath, its shoulders barely moving up and down as though it were quietly laughing at her. Whatever it was standing before could smell her fear and found it amusing.

She could sense his intent simply on the fact that her fear was making him laugh. She was frozen as she watched his arm rise to the wall beside him, toward the switch. He flipped it on, and when she saw the man wearing the black jumpsuit and ski mask, Melinda's fear turned to pure anger.

"You're an asshole!" she said between her teeth. "You could have given me a heart attack!"

Mark stripped off the mask, his flushed face gleaming with a sheepish smile. "Oh, come on. You knew it was me. *Mark...*" he said, mimicking her fearful voice.

"That's not funny. Go on your ski trip alone." Melinda flipped him her middle finger and disappeared into their bedroom.

He chased after her, laughing like a child. "That's what you get for not packing these awesome jumpsuits!" he said to the door after she slammed it in his face. "I saw you forget to grab them from the closet!"

"Because they're hideous!" she yelled back.

"Well, would it help if I told you yours came with that necklace you wanted?"

Melinda's response came in the form of opening the bedroom door slowly. "What's that?" she asked, a smile growing on her face.

"It's in the pocket of your jumpsuit. I was going to give it to you when we were in Oregon, but what the hell. Go get it. You can wear it on our flight out tomorrow."

"Really?" she smiled.

Mark smiled. "Really."

Melinda bounced back into the room like an excited schoolgirl and Mark watched her search for the necklace. His smile surpassed hers when she found it and jumped into his arms, kissing him.

With all the commotion, neither one of them noticed the bearded man peering into their bedroom window, watching them.

Sunday, January 8th

As usual, Corona was the last one in. The briefing was supposed to begin at 7 AM sharp, and when he entered, the faces on those waiting for him showed neither displeasure nor surprise. He looked at his watch. It was half past seven.

The room was void of any windows save for the small glass partition on the door. It was large enough for a few desks and a dozen or so chairs, but no more. Its walls were grey, the fifty inch monitor and the whiteboard that covered the east wall were the only sources of color, though what they displayed did not illuminate the room. Pictures of their current case were taped to the white board; the same images of Cabello and DeCocq that danced in Corona's head the entire night were now displayed before him in analytical fashion.

Grazer was standing before the whiteboard, studying the pictures as though they would reveal something they missed while at the scene. Roth sat behind one of the desks reviewing whatever paperwork had been turned in from the case; forensic reports, witness accounts, or physical and trace evidence. Truth was, there were little of any, and the few thin folders before Roth was not enough to reveal what he was revising.

"Now this is a party," Corona said, finally.

Roth broke from the paperwork. "How nice of you to join us, Corona," he said. "Please have a seat so we can begin."

Corona looked around the room and observed the few other people who had spun on their seats to see him. A few he knew from the forensics team, he saw Leddy, naturally, sitting in the front row beside Hood, and beside them was an officer Corona frowned at. His brown hair was closely trimmed, military style, and his build showed he was probably in the service, though his face, young and seemingly naïve to a wrinkle, was hidden behind permanent stubble. He was in the khaki and brown uniform of the Miami-Dade Police Department, though Corona didn't recall seeing him before.

"Who's the newbie?" Corona asked, looking to Grazer.

The newbie stood from his chair and was about to introduce himself when Roth interrupted.

"Introductions were made when we began," Roth said to Corona. "Since you were late, you can wait until we're done. Now please, let's continue."

The newbie retook his seat as Corona, maintaining eye contact, made his way toward his partner at the front of the room. Though he wasn't looking at him, Corona could tell Leddy was avoiding meeting eyes at all costs, but the newbie never broke Corona's glare. His intimidating welcome did not seem to be working.

"As I was saying," Grazer continued, "We were able to establish that the two victims knew each other and had an affair when they worked together at the Department of Health. DeCocq was a person of interest until we arrived at his place of residence and found his body in worst condition than Cabello's."

"It appears as though the killer, or killers, worked very quickly as forensics have confirmed the time of death to be within an hour apart," Corona jumped right in.

"We're still waiting on reports from the medical examiner to determine if there was a chemical used to skin DeCocq," Grazer continued. "And, as you know, evidence in this case is very scarce. Aside from the bodies of the victims, there were no finger prints, no signs of forced entry, nothing to indicate that anyone was even inside the house aside from the victims themselves, though we have concluded that they did not do this to themselves."

"And how is that?" the newbie asked.

Corona frowned at him again as though he had no right to speak up.

Grazer nodded in Leddy's direction. "Officer Leddy," he called. "Will you please fill us in on your findings?"

Leddy stood up, clearing his throat as Corona frowned again. Avoiding eye contact with Corona, Leddy slowly made his way to the front of the room and picked up a small remote from Roth's desk. He aimed the remote at the monitor and it came to life with an image of a blood-stained wall. Though the blood covered nearly every bit of the space, the letters *E-N-O* were clearly defined.

"The-um, this picture was taken from the-ah-Cabello residence," Leddy said, the remote in his hand shaking almost as much as he was. He pushed a button and the picture changed to another wall and more blood. *O-W-T.* "And-uh, this picture was taken at the DeCocq residence." Leddy looked at the room, to Hood specifically who smiled and gave him a slight, encouraging nod. He took a deep breath, and the remote shook even less. "It appears as though this is a signature left behind by the assailant at both scenes."

"It doesn't appear," Corona said. "It *is* a signature."

Leddy swallowed hard, the remote shaking again.

Grazer elbowed Corona into silence. Corona smiled at his partner. He couldn't resist.

Leddy pushed on the remote again and the two pictures appeared on the screen side by side. "At first, um, it was thought that, uh, they were initials or part of, like, a larger word," he said, looking at Hood again. "However," he pushed the remote once more, and both pictures turned over so that they can be viewed through a mirror-image. Suddenly, the words *ENO* and *OWT* now read *ONƎ* and *TWO*. "It was-ah- determined that the victims are being numbered in backward English."

"Thank you Officer Leddy," Grazer said.

Leddy nodded, put the remote back on Roth's desk and almost ran back to his seat where Hood immediately patted him on the back – job well done.

"Do you have any theories on motive?" Newbie asked the two detectives.

Corona leaned in toward Grazer and whispered, "Who the hell is this guy?" so that no one else can hear.

"We're working on it," Grazer answered. "Leddy and Hood here are currently working on finding anything related to the two victims we can go on."

Hood immediately stood to her feet. "So far, it's been ascertained that both worked on several cases together while at the DOH. We're starting there."

Newbie nodded, but didn't appear to be pleased by her answer.

"Anything else, detectives?" Roth asked. "Anything aside from what we can all read on the reports?"

Corona shook his head while Grazer looked at his shoes for a moment and cleared his throat. Corona immediately eyed his partner. In the fifteen years they worked side by side, Corona could read his partner better than his wife could. He saw the look on Grazer's face and immediately, Corona's expression went cold. *Don't do it* he thought.

Grazer glanced at Corona for a second then took a deep breath. *I have to.*

"Evidence, or lack thereof," Grazer started, "suggests that these murders were done by one person."

Corona closed his eyes, dropped his head and rubbed his temples as the rest of the room shifted uncomfortably around him. Some whispers erupted as Roth folded his arms across his chest and sat back on his chair absorbing the information. "You do realize that both of these victims lived more than thirty miles from each other, yet they were killed less than an hour apart." he said to Grazer.

"Here we go," Corona said, almost to himself.

Grazer nodded. "Aside from the time of death, everything else suggests that there is only one killer. The simple fact that there was nothing left at either crime scene, not one print, it seems very unlikely that two or more people could have gotten away with that." He made his way to the monitor where the two bloody numbers were still showing. "I'm no handwriting expert, but take a look at the two words here. Both appear to have the same structure, both obviously done with enough time, and neither done with a bare hand because there were no finger prints on here, either. Whoever is doing this is numbering his victims for a reason."

"Do you agree with this theory, Corona?" Roth asked.

Corona took a deep breath. "It was something we discussed."

"But do you agree with it? Should we treat this investigation as though there is one killer?"

Corona looked at Grazer, then to Roth. "Yes," he said. "I believe this was done by one killer."

"As do I," Newbie said. "I agree with both Detective Grazer and Corona."

"Seriously, who is this guy?" Corona asked Roth.

"Okay, since we're thinking one killer," Roth said, "any suspects?"

"Our only suspect showed up dead," Grazer said. "I was going to get in touch with the local news crews and have Leddy and Hood review any footage they have of the crowd."

Roth nodded in approval.

"And as Hood said earlier, she and Leddy are working on making more of a connection between the two victims," Corona added.

"I may have something," Newbie said, raising his hand. "May I?"

"May you what?" Corona asked. "Introduce yourself? For crissakes, please do so."

Newbie stood from his chair, taking hold of a manila folder and a notepad he had on the floor beside him. He made his way to the front of the room, approaching Corona. Extending his hand, he waited for Corona to shake it. With a firm grasp, he looked at Corona and said, "My name is Officer William Kux. I transferred to Miami-Dade from Pinkney and Roth assigned me to you and Detective Grazer because you're supposed to be the best. Now, if I may, I have information on your case that I think might help. May I proceed?"

Corona glared into the young man's ice blue eyes. Their frowns were identical, but slowly, Corona's grasp firmed up and he smiled. "Welcome aboard, Officer Kux. Please let us know what you have."

He stepped aside and let Kux have the floor. Turning to Grazer, Corona whispered, "this guy's awesome."

Grazer shook his head.

"Lieutenant Roth provided me with the case files late last night, and I did my own research," Kux said, then looked to Hood and Leddy, "certainly don't mean to step on anyone's toes. However, though Cabello and DeCocq worked several cases together, as Hood said, there was one that was very high profile."

"How so?" Roth asked.

"Media attention," Kux responded. "News coverage went national."

"The Bayer farm," Hood said, nodding. "Leddy and I read about it."

"That's correct," Kux said. "The Department of Health closed down a family pig farm in Homestead nearly twenty years ago after an outbreak of salmonella. The owner of the farm, one James Bayer," he continued, looking at the notes scribbled on his notepad, "allegedly killed his wife before hanging himself. Corona and DeCocq were the ones who found their bodies."

"How is that related to this case, exactly?" Grazer asked.

"The Bayers had a son that went missing. There was a statewide manhunt for the boy, approximately ten years old at the time, but he was never found."

"And you think he's the one that killed Cabello and DeCocq?"

Kux shrugged. "It's possible. Both victims were on the board that closed down that farm. If this boy is still alive, he's almost thirty now, and he blames them for losing his family. Seems logical enough."

Roth nodded. "How many people were on this board?"

Kux looked at his notes, flipped a page, then flipped it back. "Seven. There were seven people."

"Get me their names," Grazer said, approaching Kux. "We'll need to question every one of them."

"Their names are right here," Kux said, handing Grazer his notepad who immediately began reviewing it.

"We'll get in touch with the ones we can," Corona told Grazer. "The ones we can't, we'll go check out immediately. If there's another victim out there we'll need to find them ASAP."

"Not so fast," Roth said. "I need to speak with both of you. Privately."

Both Corona and Grazer exchanged glances. *What now?*

"The rest of you can be excused," Roth said. "Leddy, Hood, hang tight until you receive further instructions."

Both officers nodded then left the room.

"Kux, good work. I'll have the detectives here instruct you on your next move."

Officer Kux nodded then began making his way out of the room.

"Hey, Kux, wait a second," Grazer called. "What's his name?"

Kux frowned. "I'm sorry?"

"The boy who went missing from the farm. What's his name?"

"Oh. It's Mason," Kux answered. "His name is Mason Bayer."

*

Melinda sat up on her bed quickly, gasping as though she just woke up from a nightmare, when in fact she was having the best sleep she'd had in a while. It was almost one in the morning when she and her husband finally turned off the lights in their room and laid beside each other, both excited about the coming day's trip to the Oregon ski resort. However excited Mark was though, his heavy breathing filled the room within minutes, and while he was off in the land of dreams, she kept checking the alarm clock on her side of the bed. The minutes turned to hours, and Melinda thought she would not sleep well at all, worried they would wake up late for their 7 AM flight. By 2:30, only two hours of sleep seemed feasible, and when one of their three alarms erupted, ensuring they wouldn't oversleep, she would be tired, no doubt, but the excitement of the trip would get her out of bed without hesitation. She would sleep on the plane, she decided.

But when she sat up on the bed, she knew very well that she had slept more than two hours. She looked at the alarm clock, it was almost 7:30. Neither her alarm, Mark's alarm, nor her mobile phone set to 4:30 went off as they should. The room was still dark as the sun, ascending in the eastern skies, was blocked by the black-out curtains she swore she left open the night before.

"Shit," she said to the air, throwing the sheets off of her. Their flight had left without them. "Mark, we missed our flight," she said, but he didn't respond. He was still sleeping.

With thoughts of how much it would cost to get replacement tickets, Melinda swung her feet off the bed and onto the cold floor. When she stood, she realized the floor wasn't cold at all, rather, it was wet. Nearly slipping, she muttered, "What the…" and slowly made her way toward the light switch near the bedroom door. She flipped it on, first looking at her feet, then immediately to her bed.

Blood. It was everywhere; all over the floor, all over her bed, all over her husband who still lied where he fell asleep, his stomach torn open and a pile of a gelatin like substance on the floor beside him.

Her first reaction was to scream, but she couldn't. Frozen, terrified and confused by what she was looking at, her throat locked up and her knees almost gave out when she looked above her husband, above the headboard of the bed, and onto the wall beyond it. She didn't know what it meant, but she knew it was Mark's blood that she was looking at; the word read *EERHT*, and after she processed it, after her brain finally registered what was happening, her body went cold.

The scream she finally let out was loud enough to wake her neighbors, however it did not last more than a second or two when the scene before her turned to darkness and she fell to the floor, faint.

*

"Where did you find that guy, Kux," Corona asked after Roth shut the door to his office.

Roth requested they speak in private, and the trek back to his office was a quick one.

"I didn't," Roth answered, taking a seat behind his desk. "He found us."

"Why do you think he wanted to come here?" Grazer asked. "He's in for quite the culture shock. And Corona, tone down the tough love, will you? Leddy can barely look at you. Don't mess this guy up, too."

"He's got my respect," Corona said. "Can't wait to work with him some more."

"That's why I called you in," Roth said. "Unfortunately, I'm splitting you two up."

"What?" Grazer asked.

Corona followed quickly with, "Why?"

"I don't have a choice," Roth explained. "Something's come up, and believe me, I prefer leaving you two on this case, really. But I received a call last night that led me to the hospital where your John Doe was in a coma."

Both men nodded, waiting for Roth to get to his point.

"He's gone. He went missing, and no one knows where the hell he is."

"How is that possible?" Grazer asked, his shoulders slumping. "The guy was in a coma. We closed the case because the doctor told us it would be unlikely for him to come to."

"I know," Roth said, "but it happened. I need you to find him and put this case to bed once and for all before word gets out."

"I can't believe this," Corona said. "Of all times for this to happen."

"Never a good time for this to happen," Roth said. "That's why, the sooner you get this done, the sooner I can put you back on the Cabello, DeCocq murders."

"You want me to find John Doe?" Corona asked.

Roth nodded. "Use Leddy and Hood. Detective Grazer, continue the investigation on this Bayer thing with Officer Kux."

Both men nodded, somber looks on their faces.

"I'm not happy about this, either," Roth said. "But fortunately we have the manpower to get this resolved. Corona, I need you on the murders, so get this done fast. Grazer, keep me abreast of anything you find out. And in the meantime, keep the Bayer name under wraps. If Kux was right, that it was all over the news nationwide, then that kind of attention will hit again. We don't want that until we have something concrete. Understood?"

"Yes, sir," Grazer answered.

"You're both excused. Good work out there. Keep it up."

Without another word, both detectives stood and left the office, leaving Roth on his own. Once they closed the door behind them, Roth took a deep breath and looked up at the ceiling. Clasping his hands behind his head, his thoughts began to race at a hundred miles an hour. When he heard the victim's names, he had a suspicion. When he saw the blood soaked walls and the words they contained, he feared it was true. Now, his newest recruit confirmed it.

His name is Mason Bayer, Kux told them.

Roth picked up the phone and dialed a few numbers. *Mason Bayer*, he thought as he waited for a response. It was a name he had not heard in nearly twenty years, and for twenty years, it was a name he prayed he never heard again.

John Doe

"Who the hell does that guy think he is?" Leddy whispered to Hood. They stood clear of earshot from Roth's door where Grazer and Corona had been summoned. Officer Scott Leddy was looking in the direction of the newbie; William Kux, who was making his rounds throughout Homicide, introducing himself with a vivid smile and firm handshake. "I agree with both Detective Grazer and Corona," he said, mimicking Kux's contribution. "Kiss-ass."

Hood frowned at her partner. "Like you were any different when you first started," she said, then looked back to Kux. "Besides, he's not *that* bad. He did bring up the Bayer case that..."

"That probably has nothing to do with this case," Leddy fumed. "It's a shot in the dark."

"And it's our only lead," Hood reminded him. "Stop being so jealous. It's not very becoming of you." Hood returned her gaze to Kux and watched him introduce himself. She smiled slightly – and Leddy saw it.

"Oh for crissakes," he said, almost to himself.

Hood snapped from her daze. "What?"

The door to Roth's office opened and both Grazer and Corona exited. Both seemed in a hurry, and without a word to each other, they parted ways; Grazer toward Kux and Corona toward Leddy and Hood.

"You two," Corona barked. "You're with me."

Leddy and Hood frowned at each other. "What's going on?" Leddy asked Corona.

"I'll explain on the way. Let's go."

Hood immediately followed the detective and Leddy looked back in Kux's direction. Grazer was already whisking him away, off to a more important assignment, no doubt. He shook his head and followed Hood.

It wasn't until they piled into Corona's car, Hood in the passenger side, Leddy behind her, did Corona finally tell them what Leddy suspected; they had been split up. For the time being, Grazer would continue to work the murders with Kux, and the three of them were off to investigate another priority.

Leddy shook his head at the news.

"What's the other priority?" Hood asked as Corona drove onto the main road.

"A missing person's case."

"You gotta be kidding me!" Leddy said. "We're homicide! Why would we be looking for a missing person?"

"Because this particular missing person confessed to two murders then went into a coma for no damn reason before we could get info out of him."

Leddy frowned. "Wait, that sounds like…"

"Yeah," Corona said. "Our John Doe woke up and apparently walked out of the hospital without anyone noticing."

Hood frowned and strained her neck to look back at Leddy. "I thought you said he wasn't going to wake up."

"That's what the doctor said."

"He was wrong," Corona said.

"We put out all sorts of information on this guy," Leddy said. "No one claimed to know him, he had no visitors, and no one from Missing Persons had anyone that looked like him. It's like he never existed. Where would he have gone?"

"That's what we're going to find out," Corona said. "First thing we're going to do is review the hospital's security tapes for the last few days; see if anyone suspicious entered or left the place…"

"Least of all, our John Doe," Hood added.

"That's right."

"So, let me get this straight," Leddy said, "while Grazer and this new guy are doing real police work, we're stuck on security detail? This is bullshit."

"This *is* real police work, Leddy," Corona said. "It's not all cops and robbers one hundred percent of the time, and the quicker you realize that, the better. Understood?"

Leddy didn't answer. He sat back in his seat and shook his head, silently staring out the window until they arrived at the hospital.

*

Officer William Kux was sitting at Corona's desk reviewing a list of names; the names of those who served on the board that closed the Bayer Farm nearly eighteen years before. Some were circled, others were crossed off. The two names at the top of the list were marked *deceased* – Samantha Cabello and Richard DeCocq. After making his last phone call, he gathered his paper work, stood from Corona's desk and after making sure everything was how it was before he sat there, including the coffee mug that read *Fuck Off, I'm Doing Police Work*. He walked to Grazer and put the list before him.

"I was able to make contact with three of them, we know Cabello and DeCocq are accounted for, and these two," he said, pointing at the list, "I can't locate."

Grazer picked up the list, sat back in his chair and reviewed the list, "Mark Shaw and Tomas Brewer."

Kux nodded.

"Find relatives, their residential address…"

"I already did, sir," Kux said.

Grazer looked at the young officer, his brows arched.

"Tomas Brewer has been on some sort of self-sabbatical, according to his ex-wife. She hasn't heard from him in the better part of a year or so. Really bitter about it, too."

"What about Mark Shaw?"

"I'm told by their neighbor that the Shaws are currently on a flight to Oregon. They should be landing within an hour or so."

Grazer nodded, looking at the list, then back to the young man before him as though his brain was working on what the next steps should be. Kux awaited his orders, his hands behind his back, standing at attention. In the background, phones were ringing, papers were being shuffled and the men and women of Miami Dade Homicide were bouncing around with pending investigations, but none of that existed to Kux. He kept his eyes locked onto Grazer and silently waited.

"Good work, kid," Grazer said. "Did you confirm that they made their flight?"

Kux frowned and took a breath in hesitation. "Uh, no, sir. They're due to land in an hour, so..."

Grazer shook his head and waved his hand. "Don't call me 'sir', I'm not your boss."

Kux nodded.

"Call the airline and confirm the Shaws made their flight," Grazer said, handing the list back to the officer. "Let's eliminate the possibility that they're victims and we don't already know it. Get the others in here for questioning. If they refuse, we'll go to them."

"You think one of them is the killer?"

"Until we find him or her, everyone's a suspect, Kux."

Kux accepted the list and turned toward Corona's desk. He hadn't made it three steps before Grazer called him back. Kux spun on his heals to face the detective.

"What can you tell me about Mason Bayer?" Grazer asked.

Kux shrugged. "Not much, I'm afraid. I don't know that anyone can. He's been missing-"

"Yeah, I know, for the better part of eighteen years. It's just that..." Grazer trailed off, standing from his desk, and rubbing his temples. "I've been sitting here looking for anything that has to do with the Bayers, and it stops right where you told us; search for the boy was called off, case closed. There's nothing else. That's it."

"But the search went on for a while, sir. It's not like it was dropped after a day."

Grazer shook his head. "That's not what I mean. And don't call me 'sir'."

"Then what do you mean?"

"You said yourself that this was a very high profile case; national media coverage, newspapers ate this case up; I've read dozens of articles about the events surrounding the case since the Bayer name was brought up. But then suddenly, nothing. Like it never happened."

Kux frowned. "You think someone buried it?"

Grazer smiled and shook his head. "This isn't an episodic television drama, Kux. I just find it curious. And I can't help but connect this to our John Doe."

"I'm sorry?"

"Think about it. No one claims John Doe, missing persons didn't have anything on him. Suddenly he wakes up and walks out of the hospital and now we have two people dead."

"You think John Doe is Mason Bayer?" Kux asked.

"Kid goes missing for nearly twenty years. No one knew him. No one knows Doe. It's possible, isn't it?"

Kux nodded, slowly stepping toward the detective while formulating his next words within his head. "Possible, yes. But not likely." Grazer frowned and Kux felt his heart drop to his feet. "The... ah – um..." He cleared his throat and collected his thoughts. "The Bayer boy was ten years old when he went missing. That would make him about thirty years old. The APB Roth put out on John Doe describes him as a Caucasian male age forty five to fifty five. That eliminates him. Furthermore, Doe has been in a coma for too long and his body is more than likely too weak to carry out the elaborate murders performed on Cabello and DeCocq. That also makes him a very unlikely suspect. Also, I've been formulating a profile on the murderer, and John Doe does not..."

"Okay, okay, I got it," Grazer said. "It's not John Doe. It was just a thought."

Kux swallowed hard. "Sorry, sir."

Grazer shook his head. "Don't be. This is what we do; bounce these kinds of facts off each other so we're not chasing empty leads."

"Yes, sir. I'll call the airline now and let you know what they tell me."

Grazer nodded. "Good work, Kux."

The officer nodded and quickly turned toward Leddy's desk making sure he left on a high note, though he wasn't sure correcting a seasoned detective was such a high note at all.

Grazer sat at his desk and cleared his computer screen of the Bayer case files. He watched as Kux sat at Leddy's desk and picked up the phone and dial numbers. He envied Kux's eagerness, his keen sense and bright ambition. Grazer saw a lot of himself in Kux because he, too, was once a rookie who was trying to prove his way through the department, stumbling and making mistakes, but proving himself in the end. There were moments where bright ideas and tidy thinking solved cases, but Todd Grazer also knew that there were also moments when blind luck had a hand. He could count on one hand the moments it happened, but when it did, it seemed magical. When cases came to a dead end, when all options were exhausted, and the investigation had stopped, a break would occur that seemed to manifest out of thin air.

It was too early in the current case so Todd wasn't hoping for such a stroke of luck. Reports from the medical examiner had not come in yet, and there were still others that needed to be spoken to; the Shaws included, not to mention the connection between the two victims. But all those pieces of the puzzle were time consuming. Todd wanted a break now, an answer from the heavens that would set him on the right path. He wanted luck.

Suddenly, the phone on his desk rang.

*

When there was a knock on Ruth Brewer's door, the last person she expected to see was her ex-husband, Tomas. It wasn't moments before that she received a call from someone asking for him, and suddenly, there he was.

Nearly a year before, when their divorce was finalized, he disappeared with all their money, and she assumed he went to "find himself", something he constantly mentioned wanting to do during their twenty-two years of marriage. Australia, Mexico, Wine Country, any of the other places he'd mentioned time and again were all possibilities, but there was no way to track him down. He simply left her with their teenage daughter, Katherine, to fend for themselves while he was off exploring whatever it was he needed to explore.

So when she opened the door and saw Tomas standing on the porch, she was surprised her feelings of anger were instantly replaced by fear. Standing before her was not the clean-cut, well-manicured man she married (or divorced); rather, a bearded vagabond with hair nearly as long a curly as hers. The stench off his body indicated he hadn't showered in, what smelled like, the year he was missing, and the well pressed suit he was wearing the last time she saw him was replaced by a tattered shirt and jeans marked with dried mud. But the emptiness in his grey eyes is what struck her the most. Tomas was standing before her physically, but she wasn't even sure that he knew it.

"Tomas?" she said to him, stepping out of the house and into the crisp Miami morning. "Are you okay?"

She reached out toward him, but he slowly turned away from her and toward the swinging bench suspended from the porch's ceiling. He took a seat, and without a word, began to methodically swing back and forth, his mind somewhere Ruth could not see.

She quickly closed the door to her house so that their daughter would not see what her father had become. Taking the few steps toward the bench, Ruth saw Tomas' bare feet were covered with dried grime and dirt up to the ankle. His hands, each resting on his knees, were just as dirty. She thought about calling the police or an ambulance, but the need to know what happened to him was much greater.

"Tomas, are you okay?" she asked again. "Do you need help?"

Still, he did not answer. He did not even make a movement to indicate that he knew someone was speaking to him. He stared out into the vast area that made up the house's front yard which was as beautifully manicured as the rest of the neighborhood.

"Are you okay?" Ruth asked again, slowly approaching him, placing a hand on his frail shoulder.

He flinched, shaking his head.

"What is it?" Ruth asked him. "What happened? Do you need me to call someone?"

He shook his head again, mumbling incoherently.

"I can't hear you, Tomas. What's happened?"

He spoke louder, but still not loud enough. All Ruth understood was "I...it". He began repeating the words over and over, each time louder and louder, until finally, Ruth understood him. "I did it," he said.

Ruth stepped back away from him, her hand slipping off his shoulder. "What did you do, Tomas?"

He slowly turned to face her, his empty eyes making her flesh erupt with goosebumps.

"I killed them," he said. "I killed them all." His head rolled forward, his back losing support, and within seconds, Tomas Brewer was on the floor of the patio, his body limp and his eyes closed.

CHAPTER OWT

⸻◦◦◦⸻

THE SUMMER SUN AND HUMIDITY was not helping with the smell.

Detective Phil Chiovitti and the young officer sitting on the passenger seat could smell the rot a few miles out, growing stronger the closer they got. By the time they arrived, both of them had their mouths and noses covered. The farm grounds was swarming with officers and investigators, all of them wearing particle masks. Det. Chiovitti and the young officer were each handed one upon their arrival, and though the mask helped, it didn't completely disguise the scent.

"What do we have here?" Chiovitti asked one of the officers that were already on the scene. Both men approached the house set upon the farmland as they spoke.

"Two dead, James and Hilda Bayer," the officer said from memory. "We're figuring James Bayer killed his wife, slaughtered the pigs, and hanged himself when he was done."

"Where is he now?" Chiovitti asked.

"Right this way, sir," the officer responded, pointing toward the house's open door. "Per your instructions, we left him right where he was."

Chiovitti entered the house, the mentored officer directly behind him. Both looked up at the dead James Bayer hanging from the second floor.

"Tell me what you see," Chiovitti told his protégé.

The young officer was barely in his twenties. Fresh out of the academy, this was only his second trip out to an actual crime scene and Chiovitti picked him out of the freshest batch of recruits because of his visible eagerness to learn.

He took a deep breath and looked at the body from the first floor, and moments later, began ascending the stairs for a closer look.

"I don't think he killed the pigs outside," he told Chiovitti.

"Why do you say that?"

"The pigs outside were disemboweled. There's blood everywhere, in and surrounding the house, even on most of the equipment outside. Bayer here doesn't have a drop of blood on him. Someone else did."

Chiovitti nodded. "Then who did?"

The officer took in his surroundings. He studied the body, then moved on to review the second floor. Several officers were in the master bedroom where Hilda Bayer had been strangled on her bed, then moved to the room next door, a smaller room.

A twin sized, unkempt bed was set in the center of a small room. The floor was dark wood, just like the room where Hilda Bayer had been strangled. There were no windows, and the small closet at the south of the room was open revealing shirts and other clothing that were small enough to fit a child. The room he was looking at was a child's room. The room was painted a pale blue, and decorated with illegible writing. Random letters were written in red paint, scattered about haphazardly.

"They have a son," the young officer told Chiovitti who was standing at the doorway of the room. "Has he been accounted for?"

Chiovitti nodded again. "Very good. He has not been accounted for yet, but we are already on it. His name is Mason Bayer, which we know because of an engraved frame found in the dining room.

We estimate his age to be eight to ten years old. Do you think he's responsible for these pigs?"

The officer nodded. "It's possible. He saw his dad kill his mom, flipped a switch, killed the pigs and ran off."

"Precisely," Chiovitti said with a smile. "Now let's see if we can find this boy before he leaves us all without bacon."

Both men laughed and worked their way back downstairs to the rest of the crowd.

Carlos R. Savournin

Separated

EERHT. It is written in blood on the wall of the Shaw's bedroom, just above their bed and above the mangled bloody mess that was once a man. *EERHT.* Written with such precision, the hard angle of most of the letters not seeping into the rest, the curves of the "R" almost artistic. Like a template was used to paint the word, blood was dripping from beginning and end points of each letter as though strategically placed. *EERHT.* In its own way, it was beautifully done.

Officer Billy Kux could not pull his eyes from the killer's artwork since he walked into the room. He knew what to expect based on the case files and his own research into the previous victims. When Detective Grazer received the call from dispatch claiming a frantic woman's husband was murdered and there was blood writing on the wall, Kux knew to expect the number – even pictured it in his mind. But now, actually standing in the room, it was like nothing he imagined.

There was blood everywhere – not just on the wall. It was all over the bed, the floor, some even on the ceiling. The victim was just as red as the word written above him. His body, void of any skin, lay in a slimy mess on his bed, its midsection torn open. From where Kux stood, he could not see the other side of the bed, but knew very well that the victim's intestines were piled there in another sloppy mound. The disgusted look on the others' faces told him so – the forensics team taking pictures and making gestures toward the area all displayed a sickly look of repulsion. Kux wanted to see the pile himself, but he couldn't bring himself to take a step away from where he stood.

Being from Pinkney County, a small town with a population of less than 6,000, Kux was not used to this kind of crime scene. His patrolling was made up mostly of teenagers trying to buy a six pack of beer from the local gas station or assisting the town's sole lawyer sort the facts of an old woman's claim that her neighbor was spying on her. Murder, disembowelment, cryptic messages left from a killer were never a part of his routine despite how much he'd read about the tasks of larger police forces and found himself yearning for the excitement. So when the opportunity to work for Miami Dade arose, he jumped at the chance, only to find himself standing before the horrific scene just days later.

He fought the urge to gag once he allowed the rest of his senses take in the room. The rancid smell of melted flesh raped his nostrils and settled in the back of his throat, his eyes watering almost immediately. The sounds of footsteps tracking through blood with a sickly squish turned his stomach, and the soft mutter of the forensics team was not enough to smother the sounds of the victim's wife sobbing outside while more officers tried to get her to explain what she knew. It all became almost too much to absorb, and an unexpected feeling washed over the young officer at last; he wished he'd never left Pinkney.

The flash of the high powered camera snapped him out of his daze, and almost immediately, he locked eyes with his mentor; Detective Todd Grazer was standing a few feet away from him, at the east corner of the sizable bedroom. Grazer nodded tightly in his direction.

"You doing okay over there, officer?" he asked. "Looking kind of pale."

Kux nodded slowly.

"It's not like Pinkney County, is it?" Grazer asked, looking back to the body on the bed. "Welcome to Miami."

Kux swallowed hard. "Didn't picture it like this," he responded.

"You never do," Grazer answered, his eyes scanning the room. "And you never get used to it, either."

"Is it like the others? The murder, I mean?"

Again, Grazer nodded. "We're taught that no two murder scenes are exactly the same, and in my years, I've known that to be the truth. But this is different."

"Different how?"

"Different in that it's exactly the same. No point of entry, no signs of a struggle, no trace of anyone being in the room except for the victim. And in this case, his wife." He took a deep breath. "Now, tell me what you see."

Kux cleared his throat, observing the scene before him. "Cabello and DeCocq were alone. Our victim here was killed right beside his wife while they slept." Kux shook his head. "Do you think she could have done this?"

Grazer shrugged, making his way toward the redwood dresser on the opposite side of the room. It was adorned with perfumes, several picture frames and other miscellaneous items all sprinkled with blood. He picked up one of the frames with a gloved hand and studied the picture of the elderly couple; both in their mid to late fifties, but both in considerably good shape. Kux watched Grazer as he gazed at the picture, the cogs of his mind turning. "It's doubtful," he finally said. "She must weigh a hundred pounds, soaking wet. He's closer to a buck eighty, maybe more. He could have easily overpowered her."

"Not in the dead of sleep," Kux retaliated. "She could have given him a dose of something to knock him out and waited."

Grazer nodded, returning the frame to the dresser. "It's possible. But that would mean she was responsible for the other two victims as well."

"Maybe she read the details of the other two in the paper or saw it on the news..."

"We haven't released details to the public," Grazer shot back.

Kux shoulders slumped. He knew the odds of the woman being the killer were unlikely no matter how much he tried to pursue the notion.

"I think we've gotten what we need from here," Grazer said. "We'll have to wait for forensics to get back to us. As of right now, we're exactly where we were before victim number three here."

"Where's that?" Kux asked.

Grazer was already half way out of the bedroom, snapping off his latex gloves when he responded; "Looking for a fucking ghost."

Both men walked out of the house side by side, but it was Officer Kux who stopped at the front porch and took in the scene. It was unlike anything he'd ever seen in Pinkney; late morning sky filled with flashing lights from the half dozen patrol cars blocking the scene beyond the yellow police tape, the crowd of spectators that had formed on the streets surrounding the property, and three news vans parked just beyond them. His gaze settled on the newly widowed Melinda Shaw, sitting in the back of an ambulance, still hysterically crying while several officers tried to ask her questions. Grazer was already questioning them on what they were able to find out, but they shook their head. She was obviously too distraught to talk. She'd have to be sedated, Kux thought. Maybe then she can tell them something. But judging from the scene she woke up to, it would be a miracle if she didn't just plummet to insanity, never to recover.

"Still think she could have done this?" the detective asked once Kux joined him. Before Kux could answer though, Grazer was on the move, ducking underneath the yellow tape, storming passed the patrol cars and the crowd of spectators. He could see the detective was frustrated. And Kux decided it was best to not follow.

*

John Doe had confessed to two murders just before slipping into a coma. He walked into the Miami Dade Police Department Headquarters and asked for Detectives Todd Grazer and Hector Corona by name claiming he had important information to a case they were working on. He was escorted to an interrogation room where the two detectives were waiting for him and within seconds, the old man confessed to two murders then collapsed into a coma. That was nearly a year ago.

After his wife, Ruth, called for help, Tomas Brewer was whisked away to the hospital. She informed his caretakers of what he told her; that he had killed them all, though she didn't know who *they* were. As if on cue, Detective Corona and Officers Hood and Leddy entered the hospital amidst the commotion, fully expecting a full day of viewing security tapes in the hopes of finding the missing man.

After Doctor Morrison filled them in on the events that transpired, Corona was stunned to hear of the similarities to John Doe's confession. He watched as Ruth Brewer sat in the lobby, her face buried in her hands, and Corona instructed Leddy and Hood to review the security tapes while he spoke to Ms. Brewer. They did as they were told, Leddy mumbling something about not being fair.

Corona approached the woman and introduced himself. She looked up at him, her eyes bloodshot and stained with tears. After wiping her cheeks and nose, she nodded at him, Corona praying she wouldn't extend her hand to avoid the awkward moment he didn't accept it; not after she wiped her nose. Luckily, she didn't.

"May I take this seat?" Corona asked her, pointing to the empty chair beside her.

She nodded.

He took his place beside her, adjusted himself then cleared his throat. "Ruth...may I call you Ruth?"

She nodded again.

"Thank you. Ruth, what can you tell me about your husband's whereabouts in the past week?"

She wiped her nose again, tears streaming from her eyes. Corona reached into the inside of his jacket, pulled out a white handkerchief and handed it to her. She accepted it, thanked him then wiped her nose.

She may have been the same age as Tomas Brewer, but didn't look a day over forty years old. Though her face was marked with streaks of makeup that had smeared with her tears, Corona could see she was a woman who normally cared about her looks. She probably woke up, and before she left the bedroom, her face was already dolled up, her hair styled, and her perfume that smelled like vanilla and spice was applied.

"I don't know," she said, between sniffles. "I haven't seen him since the divorce. He disappeared, and this is the first time I've seen him since."

Corona sat back. She wasn't lying, he could tell by the way she looked at him as she spoke.

"You say he told you he killed them all? Do you know who *they* are?"

She shook her head.

"And he didn't mention anything else?"

Again, she shook her head, then wiped her nose with the handkerchief.

"I know you may not remember, but I need you to think back about this," he said. "Do you ever remember your husband mentioning the names Samantha Cabello or Richard DeCocq?"

Ruth glared at him. "What does that have to do with anything?"

"Please, Ruth. It's important."

She took a deep breath and looked at the floor. After a moment, she shook her head. "No. I don't remember if he has."

Corona nodded and handed her a business card. "I'll let you be, but if you can think of anything you think you should tell me, please call me."

She accepted the card and nodded. Corona thanked her and was getting ready to stand when she asked, "These people; Cabello and DeCocq. Is that who he killed?"

Corona gnawed his jaw. Answering either "yes" or "no" could prove problematic depending on the outcome of his investigation. So, the only response he could muster was, "you'll be the first to know once we find out."

It provided no comfort for her. She continued to cry as Corona left her behind to join Hood and Leddy.

*

"You're not going to believe this," Leddy told Corona the moment he entered the security room.

It was a large room filled with monitors all displaying black and white images of all different angles of the hospital. Corona looked at the monitors, then back to Leddy and Hood who were seated just before them. "What am I looking at?"

"This one," Hood said, pointing to the largest monitor in the center. "This is surveillance video of the night John Doe walked out. And that's just what he did. He simply...walked out."

Corona frowned and stood behind them, looking at the frozen image on the screen. Leddy pushed a button, and the monitor came to life and a grainy picture split into four quadrants filled the small screen.

"This is the ward he was being held in," Hood said, pointing to the feed on the upper right hand corner of the screen.

It was of a hallway, several closed doors lining each of the walls. "That's his room there," she said, pointing to the middle door on the left. The door opens slowly and large man dressed in scrubs exited the room, followed closely by a thin, bearded man, also dressed in scrubs – John Doe.

Corona frowned as both Leddy and Hood turned to face him for his reaction.

"Whoa, wait a minute," Corona said. "Did that guy give him scrubs?"

"Keep watching," Hood said. "It gets better."

The feed on the upper left hand side of the screen showed a hallway filled with doctors and nurses crossing each other, each acknowledging the other. Doe slowly walked down the center of the hall, no one even noting his presence.

"What the fuck!" Corona yelled at the screen. "Does no one notice him?"

The final feed was of the hospital's lobby, several patients waiting to be attended on. Dr. Morrison and Nurse Johnston were standing at the center station, revising a chart of sorts.

John Doe entered the feed, slowly passing the station. Morrison and Johnston looked his way for a moment, then turned back to their report.

John Doe stood before the doors as they slid open, revealing the outside world. Before he left however, he looked up to the security camera.

Corona's back stiffened as though John Doe was looking directly at him. After almost a year of seeing the man in a coma, it was chilling to see his features come to life in the grainy picture; sunken temples around his head, eyes large enough to bulge out of their sockets, his narrow nose prominent amidst his caved in cheeks. His wiry hair was jet black and just as unkempt as the dirty beard that was long enough to cover his neck. Then, revealing his crooked teeth.

The feed suddenly turned to static, and John Doe was gone.

"What…the fuck…was that about?" Corona asked, his eyes wide.

"Told you you wouldn't believe it," Leddy said. "He just disappeared."

*

The house had been given the all-clear. After a zone search, all the evidence had been collected, bagged and tagged, and the team reported the house was completely empty. The suspect was at large, but they would find him.

Grazer entered the house once more, this time alone. He was known for reviewing crime scenes once it was empty, and most times would come up with nothing more than his expert team had already determined, but on some occasions, he would find something that was missed; a single strand of hair, a fiber from the suspect's shirt, a drop of blood that was camouflaged against the marble counter top. *There goes Grazer the Great*, his team would say, then place bets as to whether he would uncover something they missed.

The house was silent and dark. Most of the investigation had been done by aid of flashlight since someone (presumably the murderer) cut all source of power to the house. Grazer held his flashlight in one hand, its brilliant light shining down the long, desolate hallway that led to several rooms he had already memorized – bedrooms, bathrooms, a home office. He guided the light to every corner, against every inch of wall and floor, watching specks of dust dance in its ray and studying every crevice.

A sudden flash of light lit the house for a split second, and a few moments later, thunder rolled in the skies above the house. It was then that Grazer realized that he wasn't alone in the house at all – the lightning revealing two men standing in the doorway to one of the rooms, one of them a young officer, the other holding him at gunpoint. Their killer had been hiding, and now, he had a hostage.

All Grazer could do was blink forcefully to clear the stinging sweat from his eyes as he quickly drew his gun and aimed it and the flashlight at the murderer; a tall, thin man with dirty hair and even dirtier clothes.

The rookie's hands were handcuffed behind him, and the perp used the rookie's gun to control him. Grazer recognized the standard issue pistol immediately. His heart pounding against his temples, Grazer locked eyes with the rookie, trying to convince him that it was going to be okay with a simple glare, but the fear in the young man's eyes made it clear that he did not get the message.

"Take your shot!" the perp yelled. "Shoot me and this pig gets it before I hit the ground!"

Grazer's sweaty palm gripped the gun tighter. "There's no way out of this," he told the killer, trying his best to remain composed.

"Come on!" the perp yelled. "Do it! You fucking pig!"

The explosion that followed was deafening. Grazer wanted to yell out, but his throat would not produce a sound as the explosion echoed in his head like a jackhammer – as though God himself was knocking on his brain with all his might. *Knock! Knock! Knock!*

He bolted up in his seat, his breath short and his heart still beating in his temples. The *knock* on his brain was nothing more than a knock on the window to the driver's side door, and it jolted him from his dream. It took a moment, but Grazer found his place in the driver's seat of his sedan, and the knock on his window was from Officer Billy Kux.

The dream still in his head, Grazer lowered the window and allowed the cool air to seep in. He took a deep breath of the freshness then glanced at the officer. "What is it, Kux?"

"You okay, sir?" Billy asked with a frown.

"Fine," Grazer returned. "I haven't been sleeping much, lately. Must have dozed off."

Kux nodded, his face showing much more than concern. "Corona has been trying to get in touch with you, sir. Said it's important."

Grazer reached for his mobile phone and saw its display had four missed calls; one from his wife and three from his partner.

"He wants to meet back at the office," Kux continued.

Grazer nodded. "Let's go then," he said, starting the car. The fifteen minute drive back to the building was silent making it seem much longer, the dream still lingering in his head.

The first thing Grazer noticed when he walked into the briefing room was the look on Corona's face. His brows were furrowed and his lips were pressed tightly together. He wasn't his normal chipper, flirtatious, germ-phobic self. Corona looked downright worried. He was standing at the podium at the front of the room, Roth standing beside him, his arms crossed over his chest and gnawing his jaw. Both Leddy and Hood were seated before them, both at attention until Grazer and Kux walked in. Suddenly, everyone's attention was on them.

"What's going on?" Grazer asked as Kux made his way to sit beside Officer Tina Hood.

Leddy rolled his eyes.

"Forensics finally came back," Roth said. "You're going to want to take a seat for this."

Carlos R. Savournin

Reproach

CASE#: 10-28-KAS-1028 DECEDENT (L,F,M): Cabello, Samantha R						
CORONER OF **MIAMI DADE COUNTY**						
DECEDENT (L,F,M): Cabello, Samantha R		**DOB:** 7/7		**AGE:** 55	**RACE:** Hispanic	**SEX:** F
ADDRESS: 12846 Anastasia Blvd		**STATUS:** S			**OCCUPATION:** Retired	
CITY: Coral Gables		**STATE:** FL	**ZIP:** 33177	**SSN:** 0000	**EMP:** Retired	
	Location		County		Type of Premises	
DEATH	Occurred in Home		Dade		Residence	
VIEW OF BODY BY CORONER	Miami Dade Police Dept		Dade		Medical Facility	
	Last Seen Alive			**Injury/Illness**	**Death**	
Date	1/3				1/3	
Time	2 AM				Appx 4 AM	
Death reported by Daughter: Kelly Ortiz							

NARRATIVE SUMMARY OF CIRCUMSTANCES SURROUNDING DEATH:

Victim was attacked in home. Neck was cut with clean blade, severing jugular.
Body drained of blood.
Stomach sliced open to disembowel victim.
No evidence of drugs found outside trace of alcohol.
No chemical was used to skin victim.
Water was found in hollowed out hair follicles (no inner root or connective tissue) indicating boiling water was used.

CASE#: 10-28-KAS-1029	DECEDENT (L,F,M): DeCocq, Richard D						
CORONER OF MIAMI DADE COUNTY							
DECEDENT (L,F,M): Decocq, Richard D		**DOB:** 5/28		**AGE:** 55	**RACE:** White		**SEX:** M
ADDRESS: 3376 N 152 Ave			**STATUS:** S		**OCCUPATION:** Retired		
CITY: Miami		**STATE:** FL	**ZIP:** 33181		**SSN:** 0000	**EMP:** Retired	
		Location		County			Type of Premises
DEATH		Occurred in Home		Dade			Residence
VIEW OF BODY BY CORONER		Miami Dade Police Dept		Dade			Medical Facility
	Last Seen Alive			Injury/Illness		Death		
Date	1/3					1/3		
Time	2 AM					Appx 4 AM		
Death reported by Daughter: Officer S. Leddy, MDPD								
NARRATIVE SUMMARY OF CIRCUMSTANCES SURROUNDING DEATH:								
Victim was attacked in home. Neck was cut with clean blade, severing jugular. Body drained of blood. Stomach sliced open to disembowel victim. No evidence of drugs found outside trace of alcohol. No chemical was used to skin victim. Water was found in hollowed out hair follicles (no inner root or connective tissue) indicating boiling water was used.								

Grazer looked between the two reports silently as the others watched, waiting for him to come to the same conclusion they did: "The only difference between the two is the name," he said, finally.

"Precisely," Hood said.

"Now there's no doubt we're dealing with just one person," Leddy added.

Grazer pushed the reports aside and sat back on his chair, rubbing his temples. Another dead end. "How?" he asked as Kux took the reports to look them over. "How does he do this? How does he kill these people, moments apart, and doesn't leave a damn fingerprint, nothing."

"Maybe we're looking for someone who cuts off their prints," Leddy said, "dissolves their prints in acid, or something."

"Right, but that doesn't explain the lack of everything else," Corona said. "No fibers, no hair, nothing else left behind. Unless this guy cocooned himself before entering these peoples' houses…"

"It's like he's a ghost," Hood said.

Grazer glanced at her having thought the same thing at the Shaw murder.

"Wait a minute," Kux said, suddenly. He was still looking at the reports. "These say there were no chemicals used to skin the victims."

"Boiling water was used," Roth said with a nod. "What about it?"

"Pigs."

Everyone else glanced at each other, unsure of where Kux was going.

"It's how pigs are skinned," he said, popping up from his chair. "Pigs are first cut across the neck then hung upside down to be drained of blood. Next, boiling water is poured over them to remove hair and skin. Then, they're disemboweled."

"Exactly like our victims," Corona said, snatching the reports to review them again.

"Precisely," Kux answered, winking at Hood.

Hood blushed.

Leddy rolled his eyes.

"And who do we know was raised on a pig farm?" Kux asked.

"The Bayer boy," Grazer said. "Mason."

"Correct."

"Okay," Grazer said, clapping his hands once. "It's official. We're looking for the Bayer boy. What now? He's been missing for eighteen years."

"Everybody hold on," Roth said suddenly, pushing himself off the desk. "There is a man in the hospital who confessed to the murders. Are we just dropping that?"

"He didn't confess to these murders," Corona said. "He confessed to *a* murder. Who he confessed to killing is still not clear. I don't think he murdered Cabello or…"

"He knew them, they knew him," Roth said. "That explains why there was no sign of forced entry."

"But not everything else," Grazer said.

"Besides, the guy's the eldest of the group," Corona added. "He's thinner than the folder containing his file. He didn't do this."

Roth took a deep breath, rubbing his temples. "Okay, so where would you start on this Bayer boy? How would you find him if he's been missing for twenty years?"

"We start with his family line," Grazer suggested. "See if there's a next of kin; someone he's related to in the area."

"Odds are he's got his eye on four other people," Kux said. "There were seven people who closed his farm. Three of them down, four to go."

"Maybe we need them in protective custody."

"Let's make sure we know what we're doing before we blow our budget on protecting four people who may or may not need it," Roth told Corona. "Let's start by bringing them in one by one. See what they know or don't know. It's possible one of them is doing this and making it look like Mason Bayer."

"I'm on it," Corona said.

"In the meantime, this stays under wraps. The Bayer name made national headlines last time, and we don't want this getting out. If it makes it look like we never found the boy and now he's killing people, it looks bad for Miami Dade."

"Alright," Grazer said. "There's a lot to do. Let's get on it, people."

The room suddenly came to life – everyone on their feet, shuffling to make their way out of the room. Grazer gathered the coroner's reports, and before he took a step away from his chair, Roth called to him. "Close the door," he ordered.

Grazer did as he was told. He turned to his lieutenant and took a deep breath.

"Relax," Roth said, "This will only take a second."

Grazer nodded.

"You doing okay, Grazer? You're looking a little peaked today."

Though he tried to stifle it, Grazer laughed a bit. "With all due respect, it's been a long couple of days. I just came from another murder scene. Three murders in two days will do a number on anyone."

Roth nodded. "I'm sure," he said. "But falling asleep at a crime scene is not like you."

Grazer's blood pressure dropped to his feet and he immediately thought of Kux. The conniving rookie must have called the lieutenant before he woke him, and within seconds, anger began to take over the feeling of betrayal. He took another deep breath and cleared his throat. "I haven't been sleeping that well lately. That's all."

"Are you having the nightmare again?"

Grazer was already shaking his head. "I just haven't been sleeping much. Don't read into it. It is what it is."

He turned to leave when Roth said, "I need you one-hundred percent on this, Grazer. If you're having troubles, you can talk to…"

"I've had enough therapy for two life times, Roth," Grazer said, spinning on his heel. "I'm good."

Roth's hands were up in surrender. "Just trying to help."

"Thank you, but I'm good."

"One more thing before you go."

"What?"

"This Mason Bayer thing," Roth said. "I wouldn't put money on the fact that it's him."

Grazer frowned. "I beg your pardon."

"Kux himself said that he was missing for eighteen years. I find it very unlikely that, in this day in age, he would have been able to stay under the radar for that long without someone noticing. Go about your investigation, but don't put all your eggs in that basket."

"As the lead detective in this case sir, I'll look into whatever lead we have and right now, it's the only one we've got."

"Start with the rest of the group from the DOH."

Grazer took an aggressive step toward his lieutenant. "Are you telling me to ignore a possible suspect?"

"No, I'm telling you to focus on the rest of the DOH group first. Then, if you don't find anything, move on."

Grazer nodded, then without another word, left the briefing room after throwing the door open.

"What do you think happened there?" Leddy asked Corona as they watched Grazer storm by his desk.

"Mind your business," Corona responded, then jogged to catch up to his partner.

"Hey!" Corona called after him. "Where you off to, speed-demon?"

Grazer turned to face his partner, his face flushed and his jaw clenched.

"What happened in there?"

Grazer shook his head, glanced back at the briefing room where Roth standing in the doorway, then looked at his partner. "Get me everything you can find on the Bayer boy," he said.

*

The Cell Block was appropriately named because it was the bar most of Miami Dade's law enforcement team would visit at the end of a long day. Lucky for them, it was open from noon to midnight every day, so the only ones out of luck were usually those who worked the over-night shift. Though the place was usually filled with officers, detectives, sergeants and lieutenants, titles and last names were left at the door. Everyone, including the staff, was known on a first name basis, and it didn't take too long before the bartender or wait staff had your drink ready as you walked into the place.

It was nearly eight o'clock in the evening when Kux walked in for the first time. He stood at the doorway looking for the one who invited him, all the while taking the opportunity to observe the scene like any good detective in training would.

Smoke danced in the air around him as it was one of the few bars in Miami where smoking was still allowed. It seemed as though the only light source in the place was coming from the several neon beer signs scattered about the vast area and the jukebox in the far corner which played classic rock only loud enough for the patrons to hear it outside their conversations.

He found Leddy and Hood seated at a bar table and worked his way through the crowd of faces he recognized from the building. One of them shouted "Hey Billy!" as he approached.

Leddy and Hood, or Scott and Tina respectively, were in mid-conversation – and mid-drink – when Billy reached the table. Both were surprised to see him, but their reactions were very different; Tina smiled, let out an excited "Hey you!" and moved in for an awkward hug, while Scott simply gave him a quick nod then continued sipping his whiskey.

"This is a surprise!" Tina said, putting her hand on Kux's shoulder. "What are you doing here?"

Kux smiled in return and gave her a once over; dressed in jeans and a tight fitting tee, he would not have recognized her had she not been beside Scott, especially since her blond hair, which was normally in a tight bun, was now draped over her slender shoulders.

"Shouldn't you be researching the pig boy?" Scott asked. "Seems like you have the answers to everything lately, thought that by now you would have found him."

Tina shook her head. "Don't mind him," she said to Billy. "He's upset that you cracked this case before he did, so to speak."

"I don't mean to step on anyone's toes, Leddy," Billy said. "Especially not yours. Either way, I'm here to see Corona. Have you guys seen him?"

"We came in with him," Tina said, "but he's never at a table for more than a minute before he's off flirting with whoever gives him the attention." She signaled to a table behind Billy, one filled with middle aged, dolled up women. In the midst of all their giggles and amusement was Corona, swinging his drink in the air as he told a story that had them all quite entertained. "He always finds them," Tina said. "Women come into this bar looking for the hot cop dressed in uniform, but somehow, Detective Hector Corona captures their attention and makes them fall in love with him for the few hours he's here. It's quite a gift." She looked to Scott. "You can learn a thing or two from him."

Leddy retaliated, but Billy simply thanked them and made his way toward Corona, leaving the other two to continue bickering. Corona was happy to see him, but Billy couldn't tell if it was genuine or because there were drinks involved.

"Ladies," Corona told the crooning women, all looking at the young meat that had made its way to their table. "This has been fun, but my friend and I have business to take care of." He bid them each farewell, calling each of them by name and promised to see them soon. His attention on Kux now, Hector led the young man toward the bar's exit.

"Can I get a drink first?" Billy asked. "Not yet," Corona said. "You'll need one more after what I'm about to tell you."

The Miami winters were mild during the sun's hours, but once it set, the darkness allowed for the temperature to drop. Though the winters in Pinkney were more intense, Kux felt the thin air penetrate his jeans and windbreaker, allowing a small chill to erupt through his body. "What's going on?" he asked Corona, wondering what was so important or secret that he preferred to speak outside the bar.

"You're new to the station," Corona began. "And we appreciate everything you've brought to the table, we really do."

Billy nodded.

"But there's something that you have to learn if you're going to continue working at this station – especially if you want to continue working with us."

Kux was already frowning, playing the day's events in his head. To his recollection, he did nothing that warranted a scolding which, as of yet, Corona had not unleashed. However, the tone in his voice was more than just an indication.

"We're a team," Corona said. "More so than just a team, when we're in that building, or working on a case together, we spend more time together than we do with our family which, in its own fucked up way, makes us family."

"I understand."

"I don't think you do. Someone who understands wouldn't have ratted Grazer out for taking a nap in his car."

Kux shook his head. "I didn't rat…"

"I'm not here to argue about it. The fact is, it happened, and that's not how we deal with things around here, do you understand?"

"Sir, Roth called looking for him. What was I supposed to say?"

"That he wasn't available. That he was taking a shit. That he was doing something other than sleeping in his car for crissakes."

Kux looked to his shoes in defeat.

"Look, as I said, you've brought a lot to the table, but don't let it get to your head. We work together or this case falls apart. Are we clear?"

"Yes, sir," Kux said. "I'll apologize to Grazer first thing."

"Don't you dare. He'd kill me if he knew I spoke to you about it."

Kux shook his head. "Then why did you?"

"Because it's what partners do," Grazer responded. "The sooner you realize that, the better you'll be."

Billy took a deep breath and watched it leave his mouth in a mist in the cold air. He nodded, gnawing his jaw.

"Now go back inside and mingle with your team," Corona said. "Have a couple drinks with Scott and Tina. Forget about this conversation and this case just for tonight. You've had a long day, and it's still your first day. We'll regroup tomorrow."

"I was actually thinking about going back to the station and looking up more info on Mason…"

"Go inside and have fun. That's a direct order. Forget it for now."

Kux nodded. "Yes, sir."

Without another word, Corona turned to his sedan and drove off. The conversation still in his head, Kux realized the detective was right about many things, especially about the fact that he wanted a drink now more than when he was inside the bar.

Order

His home office was his escape. Once Todd entered the room and closed the door, it was a clear notice to his wife and children that he was not to be disturbed. A hardwood desk was set in the center of the room, and along the east wall as a brown leather couch. At any given time, he'd be seated at either, pondering his thoughts about cases or reports, usually accompanied by a drink from the small bar behind the desk; whiskey – neat.

He chose to sit at the desk to review the dozens of bloody pictures from the crime scenes. He studied each picture, one by one, with the help of the small desk lamp. There was a stronger light fixture on the ceiling above him, but the faint light of the desk lamp helped him concentrate. As did the small radio set atop the bar playing classical music so low, one could barely hear it unless they knew it was playing.

Three victims so far; Cabello, DeCocq and Shaw. Amongst the pictures were countless files and notes that he had made to keep his thoughts in order but the more he studied them, the grander the mystery became. So many deaths, so little answers. And if they were on the right course with the Bayer boy, then there were at least four more people that were in danger of becoming numbered backward in their own blood.

Before the end of the day, he and Corona reached out to three of the four would-be victims / suspects and scheduled them all to be at the station in the morning. The forth, Tomas Brewer, was safely kept under watch at the hospital. Roth had given the order to forget Mason Bayer until the others were cleared, but everything on the desk before him pointed to the missing boy. He told himself time and again that none of it made any sense - that was the only thing he knew for certain about the case.

It wasn't long before he moved to the couch, laid down and stared at the ceiling. He rubbed his temples, the thoughts of the case dancing in his head. Whether the remaining members of the group that closed the Bayer farm would turn out to be suspects was yet to be seen - and he'd find out come sun up, but Grazer closed his eyes, taking a deep breath, wanting an answer now. If for any other reason than to save another possible victim.

He played the scenario over in his head; seven members of the Department of Health closed down the Bayer farm. Mason Bayer went missing. Eighteen years later, three of the seven members have been murdered in less than a week...

Grazer sat upright suddenly, his heart skipping a beat at the thought that took over. He was surprised he didn't think of it before, and considering Roth's orders, he'd have to keep it quiet if he was to pursue it. And he was going to.

Without another second passing, Grazer stormed out of his office, slammed the door behind him, and told his wife that he'd be back in a couple hours.

If Mason Bayer was, in fact, responsible for the murders of the members of the DOH, and he still was not accounted for, odds were he was hiding in the most obvious of places - yet a place no one yet thought to look.

*

Hector Corona gave his daughter a longer hug than usual when he got home. The need to hug her took over him the moment he saw her in the dining room, eating the dinner she made for herself; lots of greens. "Hey daddy," she said to him. "You're home earlier than I thought."

"That's right," he said, "to make sure you're not sneaking any boys in here."

She stood to give him the usual hug they shared when they saw each other; a light embrace, a rub on the back at best, but he took her in close and squeezed with both arms. And he held her near for a while, making her frown.

"Are you okay?" she asked.

He released her from the hug but still held her by her arms, looking into the blue eyes she received from her mother; the woman who abandoned both of them forcing the young woman before him to miss her childhood and become an adult faster than she could process what was happening.

"Everything is fine," he told her. "Have I told you how proud I am of you lately?"

Joanna rolled her eyes. "Yes, dad. Can I finish eating before my food gets cold?"

"Cold?" he asked, releasing her from his grip completely. "Looks like you're eating a freaking salad."

"You should have some. It's good for you."

He walked away, shaking his head. "I had a burger at The Cell Block," he called back, a smile on his face from the interaction with his daughter. It was then that he realized where the sudden urge to hold on to his daughter had come from.

The gruesome murders flashed in his head like a slide show of blood and intestines. Only a monster would be capable of such atrocities, and that monster was still out there, lurking and waiting for the opportunity to strike at its next victim. To know such fiends walked the same streets as his daughter made Corona uneasy.

Suddenly, he wanted to rush back into the dining room and beg his daughter to stay indoors until the killer was caught, but then shook his head at the thought.

"Hey Jo," Hector called from the hallway, the thoughts rushing through his head. "Anything strange happen today?"

"Like what?" she replied.

Hector smiled. "Nothing. Never mind." No use in getting her worked up. He began making his way toward his bedroom, the case and the worries slowly replaced by thoughts of showering and relaxing.

Then the phone in his pocket erupted to life.

*

The three officers had moved on from The Cell Block and were back at Tina Hood's immaculate apartment. Small as it was, it was kept very clean and neat. She had promised to make them a dinner they wouldn't forget, but upon arriving at her townhouse, she quickly ordered a couple pizzas and assured the men they were free to help themselves to the beer in the fridge.

After a bit of coaxing (and a few drinks) Billy told the other two about what Corona had told him outside the bar. He was embarrassed by it, but Tina assured him he shouldn't be.

"You got the 'We're a family' speech," she said. "We all get it."

They were seated around her spotless living room, a spacious area with a sofa, love seat and recliner; however, the three sat on the floor around the coffee table adorned with empty beer bottles and several note pads. Tina's dog, Sandy, a yappy little mutt with short sandy hair (hence the name), bounced between the three of them hoping for a pat on the head or some kind of attention.

"Grazer and Corona are like brothers," Leddy said with a nod. "Never a good idea to pit them against each other."

"I didn't!" Kux said after a swig of beer.

"Doesn't matter. Take Tina over here. She's Roth's niece – literally family."

"I am not," Tina countered. "You know that."

Kux looked at both of them feeling as though they shared an inside joke he was not privy to.

Tina rolled her eyes at Scott then turned to Billy. "I made the fatal mistake of calling Roth 'Uncle Jack' once at the station and this one here has never let me live it down."

"Why'd you call him Uncle Jack?" Billy asked.

Tina and Scott exchanged glances, the look on her face telling Scott she would make him pay for bringing the whole thing up. Billy picked it up immediately. "You don't have to tell me…"

"My parents abandoned me as a child," Tina said. "I was in and out of foster homes when I was a kid, and when Roth was a young officer, he used to volunteer at one of the centers I was in between homes. We've been in touch ever since. He's the reason I became an officer."

"So, he's Uncle Jack," Billy said with a nod. "Makes sense."

"But I assure you he gives me no special treatment."

"Let's talk about the case," Scott said. "There's gotta be an order. I refuse to think that Cabello, DeCocq and – uh…"

"Shaw," Tina said.

"Right, Shaw. There must be a reason they were murdered in that order."

"Enlighten us, oh wise one," Billy said. "What would that reason be?"

"I don't know why yet," Scott said. "But I guarantee there's a reason."

"Well, thanks for your shrewd observation, Officer Leddy," Hood said. "You'll be sure to make detective real soon."

"No, wait a minute, I think he might be on to something," Billy said.

"Thank you, Billy," Leddy said, lifting his bottle to him, then taking a sip.

Sandy barked - a shriek of a noise.

"So what would the order be, then?" Tina asked.

"Alphabetical!" Leddy yelled. "Cabello – C, DeCocq – D, Shaw…"

Kux was already shaking his head. "Greer, O'Neill, Rodic and Brewer," he said from memory. "The others have names that don't follow alphabetically. Good guess, though."

Sandy barked again.

"See?" Kux said, petting the small dog's back. "Sandy agrees."

Tina rolled her eyes and stood from the table. "Excuse me, I'm going to the rest room then grabbing another beer. Does anyone want one?"

"Me!" Scott called.

"Pass," Billy followed. "I don't want to be hung over tomorrow."

"Wuss," she called as she made her way toward the hallway, Sandy close on her heel.

She shut the door to the bathroom once she was inside, the voices of her guests now just muffled noises. She looked at her reflection in the mirror, her eyes turning blood shot as the moisture came forth.

Trying to hide her emotions as much as she could in front of the men was more difficult than she thought. She took a deep breath, trying to compose herself, and wiped her eyes with the soft tissue from the dispenser on the sink.

"It's okay," she told herself in a whisper.

Speaking of the past was never easy, much less her past.

She opened the medicine cabinet and amongst the half dozen prescription bottles, Tina picked the one marked Pamotine Antidepressants. She bounced two into her palm, tossed them in her mouth and chewed them down as she left the bathroom to rejoin her guests.

Kux watched her cross the room from the hall to the kitchen, casually admiring her backside, careful not to stare or gawk. But the look on Scott's face made it clear that he wasn't casual enough. Leddy's disapproving eyes stared Kux down making him feel as though he were a child and he was caught with his hand in the woman-jar. "So, you came up with the idea," Kux said. "Any theories?"

"On the order?" Scott asked. He shrugged for a moment. "Maybe the order in which they signed the affidavit closing the farm."

Billy took a sip of his beer then nodded. "That's actually a very good theory, Leddy."

"Are you surprised?"

"Not at all."

Tina Hood walked out of the kitchen and slowly made her way back toward the two men seated on the floor around her coffee table. She stood before them silently, her blue eyes glossed over, her lips pale and partially open. She was breathing heavily through her mouth. Both men noticed her, but only Billy Kux frowned.

"Where's the beer?" Scott asked.

She didn't answer.

Billy stood from the floor and rushed before her. "Tina," he said. "Are you okay?"

Tina didn't respond. She didn't even look in his direction when he placed a hand on her shoulder. She stared at the table before her, but Billy could see she wasn't focused on anything at all.

"Someone's had too much," Leddy said then laughed to himself.

"Tina," Billy said again, gently shaking her. "Hey, did something happen?"

Slowly, Tina turned her gaze to Kux. A single tear dropped from her right eye, and Billy couldn't tell if it was because she was emotional or because her eyes were begging for moisture. She hadn't blinked once since she walked back into the living room.

"What is it?" Billy asked, almost in a whisper.

"I did it," she said.

Leddy was on his feet and beside Kux. "What did you do?" he asked. "What happened?"

"I killed them," she said. And the last words she said before she fell to the floor unconscious was, "I killed them all."

SIMULTANEOUS DEEDS

He drove for miles, heading west on 88th Street. The roads weren't completely free of other cars that night, but the further west he traveled, the less traffic appeared.

He turned south once he reached Krome Avenue, a street dubbed The Avenue of Death. It was a desolate, two-lane road tucked far enough away from society that people often forgot it even existed. There were no street lamps, and the forest of trees surrounding the road prevented even the moon's light to penetrate come nighttime. Drivers often sped through the road since even the officials stayed clear of the area, and when automobile collisions occurred on Krome, they were usually fatal.

Grazer continued driving further and further away from the city lights, heading south for miles.

"What the hell am I doing?" Grazer asked the air, half expecting an answer. But he didn't receive a response from not even his consciousness, aside from the fact that the case was weighing heavy on his mind.

He turned right, onto a side road off Krome he never knew existed, but according to the map by his side, it was the right way to go. Suddenly, the road became unstable.

Ditches and hills the size of speed bumps made the ride turbulent, dust and grime kicking up behind his car.

The sound of the black sedan's tires crunching rocks beneath him filled the cabin. He glanced out the windows to his left and right as his speed dipped below twenty miles per hour.

"There it is," he said.

A wooden fence ran alongside the road, barricading some sort of field behind it. It seemed to stretch for acres, the darkness of night preventing him from seeing further than a few feet.

He traveled alongside the fence for nearly two miles, until finally the wooden fence gave way to two aluminum panel gate doors. They were shut, but not locked.

Todd stepped out of his car, for the first time in nearly an hour. He took a deep breath of the thin night's air then exhaled, watching his breath dance around him until it dissipated. He looked into the darkness around him, then back to the gate doors.

He pushed both doors open one at a time with more ease than he anticipated. After locking them down, he got back into his car and drove past them onto a makeshift driveway.

The moment the headlights of his black sedan illuminated the structure, Grazer regretted his decision. No one knew where he was, if he had to call for back up, it would take at least an hour for anyone to find him, and his spur of the moment idea could very well cost him his life – if he found what he was looking for, if he found Mason Bayer.

Against his better judgment, Grazer turned off the engine of his car, but left the lights on to illuminate the grand building before him. The windows of the second floor were boarded with plywood, as were a few of the windows on the first floor. The unkempt grass surrounding the house stretched upwards toward the stairs that led to the porch. It was obviously abandoned and had been so for years, left untouched and forgotten about completely.

He glanced to the right of the building and found a pigpen just yards away. It was empty.

"So this is where it all began," he said, almost to himself, hoping that it would be the place where it all would end. He reached into the glove compartment of his car and took hold of his handgun. He checked the magazine – it was filled – and he holstered it to his side once he stepped out of the car and into the cold air again. After retrieving a flashlight from the trunk of his car (one of the benefits of working for the police force), Grazer lit a cigarette. He listened to the sound of its burn as he puffed it slowly taking a deep breath to inhale the sweet poisons. Grazer's head fell back as he closed his eyes. He puckered his lips and exhaled, watching the gray smoke dance around him until it vanished. His shoulders relaxed, slumped in fact, as though the tension was lifted. Mary, his wife, had been on him to quit smoking, and he promised himself that if he survived the night, he would.

After only a few puffs, Grazer flicked his cigarette aside, turned on his flashlight and made his way into the Bayer farm.

*

Corona didn't want to leave his daughter alone for the night, so when he received a text message from Roth called him back into the office, he asked Mary Grazer if she could take his daughter in for the evening. It was common practice; so of course, she said she was happy to have her.

The first thing he noticed when he arrived was that Todd's car was not in the driveway. Once Mary opened the door, Hector, once again, thanked her for taking Jo in for the night then asked, "Where's your husband?"

"I was hoping you could tell me," Mary said. "He stormed out of here about an hour ago. Didn't say where he was going."

Hector frowned. "Do you know if Roth called him in, too?"

"I don't think so. He was in his office here, and then flew outta here like a bat out of hell."

"Huh," Hector let out. "Interesting. Okay, well, if I hear from him, I will let you know." He turned toward his car. "Thanks again for watching Jo."

"She'll keep the kids busy, so I should be thanking you."

He reached his car and opened the door. Before he got in, Mary called out to him. He looked back toward the house where Mary was standing at the doorway. The light from the porch illuminated her brilliant red hair and cascaded shadows across her flawless face. The white t shirt she was wearing was almost translucent in the soft light, he could make out the outline of her light colored bra. He tried not to stare at her for too long, but he couldn't help it.

"What is it?" he asked, not moving from his car.

Mary looked back at the house, presumably to ensure the kids weren't around. Whether or not they were, she decided to close the door behind her and take a slight jog toward Hector's car. He took a step back once she reached him.

"Is he okay? Todd?"

Hector shrugged, trying his hardest to act unfazed by the question, but feeling relief at the sound of her husband's name. "Of course he is," he said. "Why do you ask?"

She hesitated and looked around as though she were about to reveal a secret and wanted to be sure no one was around to hear it. "After he left," she said softly, "I went into his office to see what the rush was about. I saw some pictures on his desk."

"What kind of pictures?"

"I'm assuming they're of your case. Lots of blood. Some letters written in blood. I don't know what I saw to tell you the truth."

Hector took a deep breath and shook his head. "Mary, that's why you shouldn't know about what we're working on. There's no need for you to see that shit."

"I know, but I'm worried about him, Hector. Something like this could trigger the nightmares again."

"If he was having nightmares, he would have told me," Hector assured her, placing a hand gently on her slender shoulder. "He wouldn't hide anything like that from me. We're partners. Best friends."

She took hold of his hand and grasped it firmly. "Promise me you'll tell me if he tells you he is. He'll tell you before he tells me."

Hector looked at his large hand in her slim ones. He swallowed hard. "I promise."

She hugged him, took him in quickly and held him close. Her arms around his back squeezing firmly, Hector closed his eyes and returned the embrace half-heartedly. "Thank you," she said, her cheek brushing up against his. The contact made his hair stand on end, and as much as he wanted to continue the embrace, he pulled away.

"I'll call you as soon as I hear from him. He's probably at the station with Roth which is why I was called in."

Mary nodded, and then smiled.

Without another word, Hector got into his car, started it, and turned the heater onto full blast.

He watched as Mary made her way back toward the house, her backside watching him as much as he was studying it. She turned back to the car once she was at the door, waved good bye then entered the house.

Hector smiled at her wave, but the smile was gone once she was out of sight. He put the car into reverse as he took a deep breath then exhaled the word *Fuck*. In seconds, he was off the Grazer property, but Todd Grazer's property still lingered in his head.

*

Though Kux did most of the lifting, Leddy helped carry Hood onto the couch.

"Tina," Kux said, gently patting her pale cheek. "Tina, come on, wake up."

Sandy was on all fours, her small tail tucked under her hind legs, barking at Kux.

"Should we call an ambulance?" Scott asked, standing behind Billy who was kneeling beside the couch.

"I'll call the ambulance," Kux said. "Go to her bathroom and see if you can find some alcohol or something."

Sandy continued shrieking.

"And for fuck's sake, shut that damn dog up!"

Scott nodded and ran into the hall, leaving Billy tending to Tina. "Come on," he said to her, reaching for the mobile in his pocket. "Wake up."

Before he could dial for an ambulance, Tina moved. Her head moved to one side quickly as she let out a small breath of hesitation. He watched her hands clench into fists and her eyes squeeze tight, her body reacting to something she was seeing beyond her eyelids as though she were having a vivid nightmare.

"Tina," Billy said softly. "Tina, can you hear me?"

Her eyes opened.

Billy slowly stood from the floor as Scott entered the room behind him, a bottle of rubbing alcohol in his hand.

"What's going on?" Scott asked.

Billy shook his head. "I don't know."

Tina slowly stood from the couch to face the two men.

Sandy's bark morphed into a growl, and she was growling at Tina.

"Tina, take it easy," Billy said softly, the words trailing out of his mouth despite what he was witnessing. "You need help."

Tina Hood was standing before them; staring at them both though they were several feet apart. Her skin had gone pale, almost translucent. Billy could make out the network of blue veins on her cheeks and forehead. Her eyes were solid black as though her pupils had dilated enough to cover the entire surface. They were wide open, her eyebrows arched and her forehead creased beyond any form of normalcy. A small trail of blood began to fall from the duct of her left eye and down her swollen cheek.

"Tina," Scott whispered.

She showed her teeth through clenched jaws, blood flowing from her mouth the moment she parted her lips. Her teeth were all stained crimson.

"She's having some sort of seizure," Billy said.

Her head suddenly jerked in his direction as though she coherently understood what he said. He took a step back at the quick action, his heart jumping a beat.

"I killed them," she growled through her clenched teeth. "And you too."

"Billy," Leddy called. "What's happening to her?"

Her attention was suddenly on Leddy. "You fucking pig," she said, blood splattering from her mouth.

"Tina, sit down," Kux said, slowly taking a step toward her.

She looked to him again, the snarl in her lip slowly descending. The tension in her body was gone suddenly, and she closed her eyes.

Billy and Scott exchanged glances.

Sandy had run somewhere to hide.

Her knees grew weak, visibly beginning to give way underneath her, and both men rushed toward her as she collapsed. Billy caught her before she fell to the ground and guided her back toward the couch.

"Call an ambulance!" he yelled to Leddy who was right beside him. Within seconds, Leddy was on the phone.

Billy took hold of Tina's face, feeling her skin burning and the cold sweat forming from every pore. "Tina," he called to her. "Stay with me."

Her body began to convulse, first with her hands, then arms, then her entire body was writhing with spasms. Billy tried to hold her head in place, but the seizure was too powerful. He was losing his grip.

Leddy was yelling instructions on the phone, giving a play by play of the events happening before him.

The spasms began to subside, her body slowly falling to rest. Her breath was shallow and quick, and her skin slowly began to fill with color.

"That's good," Billy said to her, still gently holding her head. "Come back to us."

She slowly began to open her eyes, and to Billy's relief, they were the hazel color he had come to enjoy. She slowly turned her head to face Billy.

"Hey you," he said softly, with a smile. "You gave us quite a scare."

"What happened?" she whispered.

"You had an episode. You're okay now. Scott called the ambulance and they should be here soon."

She closed her eyes again, her face losing strength. "I'm so tired."

"I know, but stay awake with me until the ambulance arrives," Billy told her. "Stay awake."

Her head rolled to the side, falling limp. Her arm dropped to the side of the couch and her lips parted, blood drooling from her mouth in a sickly stream.

"Tina, wake up!" Billy yelled, patting her face a bit firmer than before.

Leddy rushed to his side, opening the bottle of rubbing alcohol.

The blood she vomited in a violent stream hit them both suddenly. Billy and Scott jumped back, Billy falling over the coffee table, as Tina's steady stream of vomit surprised them. She was still on her back, still unconscious, but the growl that accompanied the sick was very much awake.

It ended almost as quickly as it started. Billy made his way to his feet, wiping as much of the blood off of him as he could. He looked to Leddy who was equally soaked.

Both looked to Tina Hood, still on the couch, still on her back. Her chin and torso were covered in vomit and blood, and her body lied still.

"Tina," Billy whispered.

She did not move. He could see that her stomach was not rising and falling with breaths.

"Billy," Scott said. "I think she's…"

"I know," Billy said.

Both men, stunned and unsure of what to do next, stared at the body on the couch and waited for the ambulance.

Descent

Hector Corona was downright pissed. Not an hour before, he received a text message from Roth. *Meet me at office. Important.* He left his daughter at the Grazer house, and rushed back to the Miami Dade Police Department Headquarters. He took the elevator to the seventh floor; Homicide, and when the doors slid open, he saw no one. Not even Roth.

The expansive floor was empty save for the scattered desks and file cabinets. The lights were off – no one as working the graveyard shift when Monday morning was just a few hours away. He flipped the switch, and the florescent glow of the halogen lamps above filled the room instantly.

"You've got to be kidding me," he said, looking around the empty room, passed the briefing room and toward Roth's office.

From where he stood, he could see it was empty, the door closed and the darkness pouring from the small window was enough indication.

"Roth," he called into the room. "Are you in here?"

Of course, there was no response.

He quickly withdrew the mobile phone from his jacket and checked the text log. 9:34PM. He looked at his watch; 10:27.

Corona hit the send button on his phone to dial Roth's mobile. Several rings later, Roth's voicemail filled his ear and fueled his anger even more. He thought of leaving a message; a nasty rant to sting the lieutenant about taking time away from his daughter, but thought the better. Instead, Corona hung up his phone and holstered it in his pocket.

"Fuck it," Corona said to the air. "I'm going home."

He was ready to leave, turned toward the light switch to diffuse the halogens, but stopped just as his peripheral took in something that wasn't quite right on the desk furthest from his view; his desk. A box sat atop the surface; a box he hadn't left there when he and the rest went to The Cell Block a few hours before. He frowned, looked around the space again as though Roth would suddenly appear hidden in a place he hadn't seen before then slowly made his way through the expansive space toward his desk.

It was from evidence storage – Corona could identify the markings on the box almost instantly. *Was this what Roth wanted to meet about?*

Grazer told him earlier to get him everything he could on the Bayer case from nearly two decades ago. Corona figured it would be a daunting task; trying to recover any evidence from the case for several reasons; primarily because the evidence box was nearly twenty years old, but secondarily, because Roth instructed Grazer to forget about it. Not directly, but by telling him to forget the Bayer boy for the time being meant drop the theory. Leave it alone. Move on. So naturally, the box Corona mysteriously found on his desk was a surprise; but what was more striking was the label; *Case # 11-02-5047. Bayer Farm.*

Once again, Hector looked over his shoulder. He was still alone – as far as he could tell. The thought of opening the box and studying its contents immediately consumed him, he wanted nothing more than to study the case files, reexamine the old evidence and solve the case on his own as though the box not only contained the whereabouts of their prime suspect; Mason Bayer, but the answers to all of life's mysteries. So, to fulfill his need, he slowly lifted the lid and peered in.

The smell of the storage room was the first thing that hit him. The box had not been opened in eighteen years, and the scent that poured out of it was clear indication that it was hidden in the sterilized, cold rooms of storage. It was the same scent he found in hospitals and airplanes – the kind that made his nostrils instantly feel like the arid sands of a desert – and he loved it because it was *clean*.

From what he could make out, the box contained several items in plastic bags tagged with a faded *EVIDENCE* stamp. Most of the tags on the items had been frayed and were, more than likely, very difficult to read. He also saw an accordion file than, no doubt, contained all the details to the previous case in countless pages of paperwork filled out by whoever was the team of detectives, officers, and the fine men and woman who served Miami Dade before he did. He couldn't wait to get his hands on it, tear it open and start piecing the puzzle together, but more than that, he couldn't wait to show the box to his partner; Todd Grazer.

Before his anticipation got the best of him, Corona picked the box up off the desk, carefully carried it with both hands and headed toward the elevator at the far end of the office. He switched the light off with his elbow, and with a smile on his face, he left the station with all the answers in his hands.

And it was that same elation that prevented him from noticing that someone in that very office was watching him the entire time.

*

Despite the thin, cool air just outside the tattered structure's walls, the inside was moist and humid. The moment Grazer walked in, he regretted having worn his trench coat. He didn't want to turn back to his car, though. If he did, he wasn't sure he'd walk back in. His decision to come alone as a stupid one – he knew it. But the moment he saw the state of the farm, he found it very doubtful anyone could live there; psychotic-backward-numbering-killer or not.

He opened the door; its hinges desperately crying for oil, filling the air with a horrid noise that sounded more like the wail of a cat in heat and being raped by a cactus. Grazer froze; the beam of the flashlight illuminating the darkened entrance, the moan of the door announcing his arrival. He waited for a few moments, until the noise of the door was nothing more than an echo in his head – waited for any sign that someone or something inside the house now knew he was there.

There was nothing.

Grazer stepped inside, slowly closing the door behind him to avoid awakening its hinges, and that's when the stench of humidity hit him. It appeared as though the structure, completely made of wood, had not been tended to since the events that occurred nearly twenty years before. Abandoned and desecrated, the Bayer farm was in no condition for even Grazer to be in for a quick search. Still, he moved forward into the small rectangular room, the beam of his flashlight illuminating the small room almost entirely. To his right, there was a staircase leading upward to the second floor. He glanced upward, but the darkness emitting from the second floor prevented him from making out anything that might have been there for him to discover.

He entered the room to his left, and found it to be just like the one before; small and rectangular. However, unlike the other room, this one had a door at the back which Grazer quickly discovered led outside. He wasn't going to take the chance of opening the door and having the house fill with its sounds, but the door was equipped with a small window which allowed him a view of his surroundings.

A wooden boundary fence circled the field; it was part of the same fence he followed just off the main road. The field was an ocean of overgrown grass and weeds stretching over ten acres of land. Behind the house, there was an opening; the fence broke apart, giving way to a concrete path that led to a barn just meters from where he stood.

It was tall; nearly twice the size of the house and nestled completely in darkness. From his standpoint, he couldn't see its condition, and he had no intention of investigating the barn without the aid of a team. He was already in over his head and there was a difference between being efficient and being foolish.

He turned back, inspected the rest of the room from where he stood, observing every corner, taking in the textures of the wooden walls and floors, and he wasn't sure if his mind was playing tricks on him or not, but Grazer swore the room itself was actually moving.

It didn't take long for him to realize that the room wasn't moving, of course. The moon was the only source of light in the desolate area, and outside of the city lights its brilliance was matched only by the scatter of stars that surrounded it. The resonant air just outside was enough to rustle through the branches, moving them slightly and cascading shadows through the small window on the door and into the room – even with the high powered flashlight in Grazer's steady hand.

He left the room and made the short walk back toward the entrance. He glanced at the stairs again, contemplating whether he should take the journey upward, but he shook his head. He'd done enough. He should be at home, in the comfort of his own walls instead of the abandoned house he now stood. But the need to know more was much stronger than rational, so he pushed forward. Instead of taking the stairs upward though, he studied the wall opposite the entrance, the corner where the wall met the floor of which he stood.

The wood beneath his feet creaked as he made his way toward the wall. As if from memory, he placed a hand on the center of the wall and gave it a slight push. The wall gave, moving inward with the momentum of his arm, launching dust particles all around him and into the ray of his flashlight. It was possible that the makeshift door could have opened more, but the dragging sound it made, though not as loud as the front door, was enough to warn anyone who might have been in the house of his presence. He pushed it open enough to squeeze his large frame through; then, studied the new space he was now in.

It was a small area that served as the landing to a set of stairs that, unlike the one he saw before, led downward. A basement, perhaps. Or a cellar where a serial killer had temporarily made his home – the prodigal son who had returned to exact revenge on the seven people who had destroyed his kith and kin by closing the family business. The monster he had become could very well be just beyond the staircase that was before Grazer, and so the question instantly became: *Take these steps or not?*

"Miami-Dade Police," Grazer called, extracting his firearm from its holster with his right hand, aiming it down the staircase, his left hand crossed on top holding the flashlight. "Come out slowly, your hands where I can see them." For good measure, he added, "We have the place surrounded, so there's nowhere to run." After a few seconds and no response, Grazer swallowed hard and took a step downward.

His footing was slow, taking each step one by one, waiting for both feet to meet on a single step before moving to the next. The sweat that formed above his brow leaked into his eye, and all he could do was blink the sting away so as to keep the aim of both the flashlight and the gun in front of him. The further he descended, the heavier the air became. Beneath his coat, Grazer could feel his dress shirt stuck to his back; his sweat acting like glue and the humid air surrounding him instantly weighing heavy on his shoulders.

The staircase wasn't more than twenty steps, but it seemed much longer. It landed in a room much larger than the ones above as though the three rooms on the first floor were combined into one massive space. The moment his flashlight illuminated what the basement contained, Grazer knew being there alone was a mistake – probably the biggest one he had ever made.

Before he could make the slightest attempt to leave however, a noise filled the room that Detective Todd Grazer felt in his bones. It echoed throughout the house, travelled down the staircase he just descended and penetrated his ears like an unwelcomed spirit possessing the body of an innocent child. The noise created a chill in the back of his waist that travelled up his spine, gripped the back of his neck, took over his scalp and resonated on his tongue. He could taste the gripping fear. For more than few seconds, he was frozen, his brain registering what he was hearing. It was the sound of hinges crying for oil. The horrid sound of a cat wailing.

Someone else had entered the house.

REVELATIONS

Normally, no one was allowed beyond the double doors where patients were being attended to while on the verge of death, but Kux and Leddy were quick to flash their badges, and access was granted. Only to an extent, however.

When the ambulance arrived, one of the techs detected a faint pulse on Tina's neck. She was whisked away, oxygen being forced into her system, out of her partners' sights.

"Can one of you tell me what happened?" one of the rescue techs asked them. But neither Billy Kux or Scott Leddy could. They looked at each other, most of their shirts stills drenched with the blood she vomited, the scene playing out in each of their heads, and no, they could not tell the tech what happened. They had no idea.

They followed the ambulance to the hospital and ran in past the nurses' station and toward the ER. The commotion died down eventually and both men were asked to wait in the doctor's lounge – an area usually reserved for only staff, but Dr. Eugene Morrison allowed the stay. He even gave them access to the shower stall and a clean set of scrubs for each.

It was close to midnight when the door to the lounge opened, and Kux looked up from his soda to see Leddy enter the room carrying a plastic bag that contained the blood soiled clothing. Kux, already cleaned and donning the dark blue scrubs, nodded toward the east corner of the room, toward a large trash bin he had tossed his own clothes into.

"I knew I shouldn't have worn my favorite shirt tonight," Leddy said, throwing the bag away. "Any word yet?"

Kux directed his attention back to the can of soda before him and shook his head.

Leddy took a seat beside him. The room was dimly lit – two halogen bulbs set on either end of the room buzzed with efforts to fill the room. To the east, beside the trash can, a large refrigerator was set beside a brilliant white counter that was home to a sink and microwave. It was that same refrigerator that Kux found the soda, told Leddy about it, and Leddy declined. The other side of the room was taken up mostly by a large green couch that, though it appeared older than Leddy himself, still looked comfortable enough to sleep on.

Kux rubbed his eyes, blinked hard, took the final sip of his soda, and tossed the can into the trash bin from here he sat.

"Nice shot," Leddy said.

"What happened in that apartment, Leddy?" Kux asked,

And there it was. On the way to the hospital, while showering, even as he sat beside Kux, Leddy had been asking himself that same question. Knowing that it would have to be talked about, the images still so horrifically fresh in his mind, he didn't know if he should bring it up or allow Kux to. Though he was relieved Kux did, he was not too eager to talk about it.

"Honestly, I don't know."

"Drugs, maybe? Do you think Tina might have taken something then mixed it with alcohol causing that violent reaction?"

Leddy was shaking his head before Kux even finished his question. "No, I know Hood. She's clean. She doesn't do drugs."

"How well do we really know anyone?"

"I've known her a lot longer than you," Leddy snapped back. "You just got here. I know she doesn't do drugs."

Kux nodded, picking up on the defensive tone coming from the officer and deciding not to pursue it further. "Well, then why don't you tell me what you think happened in that apartment?"

Leddy looked to his hands which were folded over each other on the table. Taking a deep breath, he stood suddenly, and then made his way toward the refrigerator. "On second thought, I think I will have a soda," he said. "You want another?"

"Not unless you can find some whiskey to pour into it."

Leddy opened the refrigerator and took his time selecting his soft drink from the variety. He chose the caffeine free kind, opened it immediately then took a long swig.

Kux watched the officer intently. The moment he turned the table on Leddy, he avoided the question and looked as though he would run out of the room if he could. "You doing okay there, man?" Kux asked.

Leddy nodded slowly, still facing the refrigerator. "Great. My partner threatens to kill us then vomits blood all over us. I'm doing awesome."

It was then that Kux noticed that Leddy was trembling. He wouldn't have seen it Leddy not been holding a can in his hand, but the moment he picked up on it, he couldn't see anything else. Leddy was a nervous wreck. "Why don't you take a seat," he told Leddy. "Come talk to me about Tina."

Leddy shook his head. "It's all I've been wanting to talk about, but you know what? I don't want to any more. I don't know what happened to her, and at this point I think it's best we just wait for the doctor to tell us."

"But you must have some idea or some thoughts about what happened. I'm just trying to figure it out."

"You said it yourself, Kux. She had some kind of seizure. That's probably it."

"No," Kux said. "I've never heard of a seizure where someone does that. She called us 'fucking pigs'. She said she was going to kill us – *then* she went into a seizure."

Leddy didn't respond.

"I wonder if maybe she has some sort of schizophrenia in her family, or something," Kux said, almost to himself.

"She's not crazy," Leddy whispered.

"What was that?"

"I said, she's not fucking crazy!"

Kux was taken aback at the anger in Leddy's voice. Leddy had turned to him, took a quick step toward the table and almost yelled his response as though Kux had said something that fueled the volcano of anger in the pit of Leddy's stomach.

"Relax," Kux said, his hands up in surrender. "I'm just thinking out loud."

"Well, keep it to yourself!"

Kux nodded, and Leddy turned back toward the garbage bin and fired the half full can of soda toward it.

He missed.

Kux watched the can fall to the floor, the soda spilling outward much slower than he anticipated. He glanced at Leddy who seemed unfazed by the rolling can.

"It just seemed to come out of nowhere," Kux said. "She went into the kitchen just fine, came out a second later saying she killed them all. Who was she talking about?"

Leddy's head rolled backward. Finally, he slapped his thighs and spun toward Kux. "You want to know what I think happened?" he asked between grit teeth.

"Yes, please."

"I think that, whatever it is that happened to Tomas Brewer, is happening to her."

"Tomas Brewer?"

"Yes. Tomas Brewer said those same exact words before he was admitted here. That he killed them all. I think that whatever it is we're investigating, what we've gotten too far into is doing this to them, and it's going to happen to us."

"Whoa, hold up," Kux said, frowning. "What are you talking about? What did we get too far into?"

Leddy's back stiffened. "Forget it."

Kux stood from the table. "No. I want to know. What are you talking about?"

Leddy swallowed hard, locked eyes with Kux, then nodded. "Honestly? You want to know what I think?"

"Yes."

"I think Tomas Brewer and Tina Hood were possessed."

*

Hector called Todd's cell phone for the seventh time, and for the seventh time in a row, Todd's voicemail greeting answered. "Where the fuck are you? Call me back. Fast." Hector tossed his mobile aside and his focus went back to the box before him.

He was seated at the head of the dining room table, the same spot his daughter was seated when he arrived home earlier. The evidence box was just before him, still sealed, taunting him. He had promised himself that he wouldn't open it again without Todd, but he couldn't be found, not even Mary knew where he was (she still hadn't heard from him by the time Hector returned to pick his daughter up). With no mention of the evidence box, he instructed Mary to have Todd call him should he show up.

A little less than an hour had passed since. Still, no Todd.

The thought did cross his mind that maybe something had happened to him, but he knew Todd could take care of himself. Mary, on the other hand, was very worried – especially after seeing the pictures Todd had left behind. Hector continued to assure her that he was fine – that if, God forbid, something had happened to him, he would have known by then.

His mobile came to life suddenly, echoing throughout the dining room and into his very bones. *Finally!* he thought as he reached for it, expecting to see the name Det. Todd Grazer's on the unit's display. Instead, word *Unavailable* flashed at him.

"Who the fuck..." He checked his watch. A little over midnight.

He was close to hitting the Ignore button but a second thought prevented him from doing so. What if Todd was in some kind of trouble? Finally, on the fifth and last ring before the call was sent to voicemail, Hector answered it.

"Corona," he barked into the phone.

At first, there was nothing but silence. No filtered voice that responded, no background noise to indicate the caller's whereabouts, not even the crackle of a dead-zone call. "Hello," Corona said into the phone, then checked its display to ensure the call was connected. It was. "Who is this?" he demanded, and it was then that he could hear the breathing. It was barely audible, but Corona heard it as though the breath was on his ear, warming his skin and making the hair on his neck stand. "Who is this?" he asked again.

The call went dead.

Hector frowned, looking at the display on his phone as though it would suddenly tell him who the mystery caller was. He placed the phone down and stood from the dining room table, his eyes scanning the large area around him; the separate openings to both the kitchen and the living room. Both were darkened, the lights retired for the evening. The call, though quick, was enough to put his senses on alert, and he couldn't shake the feeling that he was being watched despite the fact that all windows were curtained, and all the doors were locked – at least he hoped they were.

The fact that his house phone began ringing just then nearly made him jump out of his skin. He rushed to the kitchen, grabbed the portable receiver and clicked it on.

"Who the hell is this?" he said into it.

"Good, you're up," Todd's filtered voice said. "You busy?"

Hector shook his head, and pinched the bridge of his nose. "Todd. Where the hell have you been, man? I've been calling you nonstop."

"My phone's on the fritz," he said. "I'm at a payphone down the street from your house. Can I swing by? It's important."

*

"You went where?!" Hector asked loudly, but not loud enough to wake up his daughter who was asleep a few rooms away.

"I know, I know," Todd said. "But I thought of it, and I had to."

Both men stood in the foyer, Todd making in clear his visit wasn't going to be long.

"And did you find anything?"

Todd shook his head. "The place is in shambles. But someone found me."

Hector's eyes widened.

"I heard someone enter the house after me and I snuck out before they found me."

"Mason Bayer?"

"It's possible," Todd said. "My phone stopped working so I couldn't call for help, so I just left. We need to get a team out there first thing in the morning, but Roth won't go for it. He'd have my badge if he knew where I was tonight."

"I'm not so sure," Hector said. "My night was pretty eventful as well."

When Hector walked toward the dining room, Todd wasn't sure if he should follow. When he arrived, he was excited to tell his partner about the farm, but now, the tables were reversed. Once Hector walked back into the room, holding the box marked *EVIDENCE*, Todd's jaw dropped. "You found it?"

Hector shook his head. "Got a message from Roth. Told me to meet him at the station, and when I get there, this was waiting on my desk, Roth nowhere to be found."

Todd frowned. "But that doesn't make any sense. He told me to stay away from…"

"I know. But here it is," Hector told him with a crooked smile. "Haven't gone through it yet."

Todd nodded. The excitement that began growing in the pit of his stomach was almost too strong to ignore, but it was late, and he already had an exciting night. "We'll start going through it soon. Roth told me to concentrate on the remaining board members that are still alive, and I'll do that first thing tomorrow morning. Soon as we're done with that, we'll start going through the box, maybe scope out the farm some more."

Hector nodded. Agreed.

"We're going to get this son of a bitch, Hector" he said, a smile spreading across his large face.

"We always do."

The two men shook hands and before Todd bid him a good evening, he said, "Let me ask you a question; what do you think of this new kid, Kux?"

Hector arched his brow. "He's good. Eager. I like that. Smart."

Todd nodded. "I think he needs some work, but Leddy and Hood can learn a lot from him. Have you heard from them tonight?"

"I left them at the bar," Hector said. "They're probably having one hell of a night."

Possession

Billy Kux rubbed his eyes for, what felt like, the hundredth time in less than ten minutes. They were dry and were beginning to sting despite the fact that each yawn made him teary. He looked at his watch – it was near one in the morning.

If I get home now, I can still get at least four hours of sleep, he thought to himself.

He glanced at Leddy, lying on the couch of the doctor's lounge. He wasn't sleeping, his eyes locked onto the ceiling as though it were displaying the answers they were desperately awaiting. As much as Kux wanted to leave, he felt it was his duty to keep Leddy company – at least until they received an update on Tina.

They hadn't spoken in nearly an hour, not since Leddy mentioned the word that echoed in Kux's head. *Possession*. Sure, it made sense in its own twisted way; Tina spoke in a voice that was not hers, acted out violently, and short of levitating off the floor, she certainly did seem very different than she did in the short amount of time he knew her. But really? Possession? That only happened in the movies. He didn't know which was worse; the fact that Leddy mentioned it, or the possibility that Leddy actually *believed* it. The only thing Billy Kux knew for sure was that 1) he was dead tired, and 2) he wanted to go back to Pinkney.

"Can I ask a favor?" Leddy asked suddenly.

Kux wanted to tell him "No. Let's just sit here in silence like we have been," but he settled for, "Sure."

"Can you just forget what I said before? You know, about Tina being…"

"Already done," Kux lied.

There was another moment of silence, and Kux's mind was anything but. He knew he would hate himself for continuing but the words seemed to have come out of his mouth as if involuntarily. "Do you believe in that stuff?" he asked Leddy.

Scott did not move. His eyes were still locked on the ceiling, his hands clasped over his stomach, and his feet crossed at the ankles. He said nothing for a few seconds, and Billy thought, hoped, he wouldn't answer at all.

"My dad died when I was very young," Leddy said. "I only remember his face because my mother had a picture of him that she carried around in her purse. As a kid, I used to take the picture when my mom wasn't looking, take it to my room and talk to the picture. I knew my dad was gone, in heaven, my mom used to say. But I just knew that he could hear me wherever he was.

"One day, my mom was cooking for me and my brothers, who are older than I am. They were off doing their thing, so sure enough, I go to her purse, grab the picture, and ran off to my room to tell my dad about this new toy I saw on TV that I really wanted. It was this little toy gun from a cartoon I used to watch, but I remember seeing it and knowing mom wouldn't be able to afford it. I never asked her for it, never told my brothers about it because they would just make fun of me. But my dad? I could tell him about anything. So I told him about the cartoon gun.

"I was in my room, telling him about it, and all of a sudden, I spill water all over the place; all over the nightstand, the floor, and all over the picture. Ruined the thing in an instant. It almost dissolved right before my very eyes, and I was destroyed. It was the only thing I had of my father, the only picture of him I'd ever have, and aside from that, I was so afraid my mom was going to kick my ass."

Kux listened to Leddy tell his story, even watched as his eyes watered at the memory of destroying the picture, but he couldn't help think; *what the hell does this have to do with anything?*

"Years passed, two or three, maybe. And my mom started dating this guy, Craig Something-or-other. Tall, lanky dude. I mean tall, like seven feet or something. And he always wore white and smelled like cigars. Anyway, he scared the crap out of me. Every time he would come over, before he got to the house we lived in, I could feel the air around me becoming colder and thicker. Sure enough, minutes later, he would knock on the door. One day, he showed up at the house and I didn't feel scared. He had this brown paper bag with him that he carried under his arm for the longest time, and I sat across from him wondering what the hell was in that bag, and why, from one day to the next, I wasn't afraid of him. I was a kid; figured I was just used to him being around.

"I don't remember why, but mom left the room and suddenly it was just him and I sitting in the living room. He looked at me and said something like, 'I know you want to know what's in this bag'. And I did. I couldn't see it, I had no idea what it was, but I just knew I wanted it. So, he handed it to me. Guess what it was."

"The gun," Billy said.

"The gun. I was stunned. I stared at it for what felt like an hour, shocked. I never told anyone that I wanted it. Only the picture of my dad, and by the way, at this time, I don't know if mom even realized that his picture was missing. Anyway, when I finally looked up to Craig, to thank him, he was staring at me with these piercing green eyes. I'd never noticed them before. They always seemed black as night to me. And mom always told me that of my two brothers and I, my eyes were the ones that reminded her most of my dad's. They're green, just like Craig's were that day.

"I couldn't speak. I didn't know whether to scream or hug him. Then he looked at me and said, I'll never forget this, he said, 'Just because the picture is gone doesn't mean you can't talk to me anymore. I miss you.' And that's all I remember. I don't know what happened after, nor do I remember what happened to that toy gun – never saw it again. Almost like it was a dream, but it wasn't."

Leddy sat up suddenly, but never once did he look in Kux's direction. He kept his head low, his shoulders slumped and his back free of support. He played with his hands as he spoke, and Kux realized that it was very possible Leddy was telling this story out loud for the first time. He listened as Leddy continued.

"About a week later, he was at the house, and the fear was back. I remember thinking I had to look in his eyes to see if they were still as green as mine, as they were the day he gave me the toy, but for the life of me, I could not bring myself to look at his face. I was scared of him again, and I remember going to bed that night, scared out of my mind that he would spend the night with my mom and come into my room in the middle of the night and kill me or something. I eventually fell asleep, only to wake up at some point throughout the night because I heard these noises coming from somewhere in the house. They were like grunting noises, animal like. I was too young to think my mom and Craig were having sex, so that thought never entered my mind. I tried to wake up my brothers – we shared a room at the time – but neither of them would wake up. It was like…like only I was meant to wake up. Only I was meant to hear those noises.

"So, I did what any scared kid would do. I went to my mom's room looking for protection. Little did I know that's where the noises were coming from. Her door was closed, so I opened it slowly," Leddy said, his hand turning an imaginary door knob. "I looked inside, and there he was, sitting at the edge of my mother's bed, looking directly at me as though he knew I was coming. There are a few things I remember about what happened next – I remember his eyes. They weren't green. They weren't black. It was like they weren't there, just these gaping holes that were staring back at me with more intensity than if he had eyes. I remember immediately trying to scream, but the fear within me was so grand that I couldn't. It literally robbed me of my voice. It's hard to explain, but he mocked me because of it. I heard him laughing though his mouth never moved. And I remember my mom, sitting up behind him, completely still and in some kind of trance. She couldn't stop him from scaring me, she couldn't run to my rescue though I knew in my bones that she wanted to. It was like he had some kind of power over us that kept us frozen.

"Then he opened his mouth. Like he was yawning, you know? Wider than that. And without moving his lips, he started with the grunting noises, like a mad dog that just saw a cat. It was a deep rumble that resonated in his chest, God knows I'll never forget that noise. And just after it was gone, his mouth still open and not moving, I heard him say 'Leave us, you piece of shit. I'm not done raping your mother's soul.' And again, that's all I remember."

Billy watched Scott rub his arms as he told the story, but it wasn't because Scott was cold. Billy could see his skin erupting with goose-bumps.

"All I know is that the next morning, my mom wasn't herself. She was depressed and no matter how much I asked what was wrong, she wouldn't say. I never saw him again. He was out of our lives, and though he was only around for a month or so, his face is burned in my brain. I can pick him out in a crowd if I needed to. Hell, I walk down the street and sometimes think I see him still, looking just as intimidating and scary as he did before. But I never saw him again.

"Years later, when I was eighteen, my mother was in the hospital, dying. My brothers and I were all there, we knew she didn't have long. She told everyone to leave the room, and as we were walking out, she called me back. It was just her and I. She took hold of my hand softly, God rest her beautiful soul, she barely hand the strength to grip my hand. And she told me, 'I'm sorry I let him around you. I'm sorry he touched you.'

"Though I knew who she was referring to, I also knew that he never *touched* me. Not in a sexual way. And it took a while for me to realize that she meant he *reached* me. I saw that he had many things inside him that would manifest whenever he needed them to; my dad to bring me close, a demon to tear me down. Then she opened her mouth, like in a yawn, and I heard something that I can't describe, but it was beautiful. Like a release of years of being tortured; like her soul was finally released from the grip of Craig."

Kux witnessed a tear fall from Leddy's face and onto the floor.

"So," Leddy continued. "You ask if I really believe in that stuff? If I think possession is real?" He let out a small, forced laugh. "I do. But I guess I wouldn't either, unless I had witnessed it firsthand."

"If she was possessed," Kux asked. "Why? Why her?"

Leddy shrugged. "She's the perfect candidate, really. Rough past. She battles depression. Leaves her open to other things."

The door to the room opened suddenly and both men quickly turned their attention to the man who entered; Doctor Morrison.

Leddy and Kux exchanged glances before standing.

"How is she?" Kux asked.

"What happened to her?" Leddy followed.

Morrison shook his head. "She's fine. Weak but fine."

"What caused the episode?"

"Your guess is as good as mine," Morrison answered. "We've run all kinds of tests, and we cannot find anything wrong with her."

Again, Kux and Leddy exchanged glances.

"She's going to need her rest tonight, so if you'd like you can come back in the morning. If anything changes, I will let you know."

He left the room, leaving the two officers on their own again.

"Well there you have it," Billy said. "She's fine."

Scott nodded. "For now," he said. "But if I'm right, then we are in way over our heads."

Billy swallowed hard, watching Scott reaching for his keys then heading toward the door. "How will we know?"

Scott looked to his feet, took a deep breath then said, "When we realize there's no way to save her."

CHAPTER EERHT

───◆◇◆───

"**W**HAT IF THE BOY'S RESPONSIBLE for his parents' deaths?" the young officer asked.

Chiovitti's eyebrows shot upward in surprise. "How so?"

They walked out of the house where the activity was still in full swing. Amidst the crowd of officers, squad cars and a cleanup crew removing the dead swine, news cameras and spectators were starting to form on the outskirts of the farmland.

"Well, we're assuming he slaughtered all these pigs which means he is capable of it. What if the boy was the one who strangled his mother and hanged his father before going on a pig-killing-spree?"

Chiovitti considered it for a moment, and then shook his head. "How would he get his father to hang himself? The kid probably weighs 50 pounds soaking wet. No, don't lose focus here. This kid may be fucked in the head, but he's not a killer."

Thunder rolled above and both men looked upward toward the dark grey clouds that were rolling in. Chiovitti shook his head at the sky. "Typical Miami. Let's search the grounds for this kid quickly," he said. "Storm's coming, and I don't want to get my shoes wet."

The young officer watched as Chiovitti started calling in a few of the officers to help him search the property for the boy. *The kid may be fucked in the head, but he's not a killer,* Chiovitti had told him. The young officer shook his head at the sentence. "Not yet," he said, almost to himself. "Not yet."

Monday, January 9th

Like a child on Christmas morning, Grazer jumped out of bed before the sun was up, thoughts of the Bayer evidence box prancing in his head. Despite only getting four hours of sleep, he was showered, dressed and out the door before six that morning. On the way to the station, he thought of calling Hector to ensure he was up, but no matter how much his partner would insist he was on his way, Todd knew he would be late – as usual. Instead, he settled his thoughts on how to review the contents of the box and the case files without making it obvious to Lieutenant Roth. Hector thought Roth left it for them to find, but no one was sure, so to be safe, it would have to be reviewed discreetly.

In the meantime, Grazer would spend the day doing diligent police work; rounding up the rest of the board members that were still alive and question them about anything they may or may not know regarding the other deaths, and more than likely illuminate them as suspects. In his gut, Grazer knew they weren't guilty of killing their coworkers. Whoever was doing this was younger than they were, more skilled, someone the likes of which they'd never encountered – someone like Mason Bayer.

His stomach turned with excitement, the box back on his mind. Upon entering the parking lot of the Miami Dade Police Headquarters though, his excitement dwindled as Hector's car was not amongst the others. And it diminished completely when he entered the Homicide Division and was immediately called into Roth's office. This time, Roth left the door to his office open.

"Have you heard from Kux or Leddy this morning?" Roth asked after taking a seat at his desk.

Grazer frowned and looked at his watch. It was just before 6:30AM. "No, sir," he said. "Why? Has there been another murder?"

Roth shook his head. He filled Grazer in on the events that occurred the night before; Tina Hood's *incident*, as Roth referred to it.

"Both Leddy and Kux were with her when it happened," he said. "She's in the hospital now, and they're still trying to determine what caused it."

"I appreciate the update," Grazer said after a moment's silence. "Will Kux and Leddy be in today? I need the manpower on this."

Roth was already nodding. "They will be. Just be sure they are allowed their time to rest if needed. They had a long night."

Grazer was already on his feet and, once again, thanked Roth for the info. One foot was out of the office door when Grazer stopped himself. He knew he should have just kept walking; the conversation should have ended where it was. But he couldn't help himself.

"Roth," he said, "I know you told me to leave the Bayer boy out of the investigation for now." Grazer could feel Roth's stare burn his back at the mention of the name Bayer. He turned to face the lieutenant. "And I know I shouldn't have, but in my anger, I disobeyed your order and went to request the evidence box. Only it had already been checked out. Do you know who might have done that?"

Lying was something Grazer learned how to do in his years of law enforcement. Learning the science behind how polygraph machines worked, Grazer learned how to cheat one. Endless lies coming from suspects' lips, Grazer learned how to spot one. Body language, eye contact, pauses in sentences were all a part of lying as much as they were a part of hiding a lie. When Grazer lied to Roth about trying to check the box out of evidence, he told the lieutenant casually just as he would if he was telling the truth.

And just as Grazer had learned to tell a lie during his years in law enforcement, he knew that almost everyone he worked with had as well. So, when Roth answered, "No, I don't," he didn't know whether Roth was telling the truth or not. "I can appreciate your passion for this case, Grazer," Roth continued, "but the next time you disobey a direct order, you will be reprimanded. Understand?"

Grazer nodded and left the office.

*

Patricia Greer was the only one out of the seven board members that continued to work. The others had retired from the DOH with hefty pensions and lived their golden years travelling or falling into comas after confessing to murders they didn't commit, and though Patricia Greer had indeed retired two years before, she worked as a volunteer at a local university's library. For a year and a half, she helped students find the specific books they needed for courses, and aided in the organization of said books upon their return.

Kux, especially, thought she looked the librarian type. Her tall and thin frame was draped in a light blue dress that was outdated, her silver, curly hair was kept short, and her wire rimmed glasses sat on the bridge of her reedy nose. She spoke softly, and slowly, her voice soothing enough to make Kux even sleepier than he already was.

He was seated next to Grazer in the small interrogation room, Ms. Greer across from both of them separated by the small table. The room was made for questioning, but set up so whoever was being questioned was not intimidated. There was a couch along one wall, and a large plant covered the other. There were no two-way mirrors, though a small hidden camera was affixed to the ceiling to record the entire room. The walls were decorated with scenic shots of Miami Beach – the kind of pictures found in cheap motels and the countless tourist traps around the city.

"Do you work full time in the library, Ms. Greer?" Grazer asked. Though Kux was invited to join the questioning, Grazer made it clear that he was to do nothing more than listen – and learn.

"Since I volunteer," she said, "I go in when I'm need. Sometimes two to three days a week, sometimes more, sometimes less."

Grazer nodded. "Well, we appreciate you taking time out of your schedule to come speak to us today. I'm going to ask you some questions and it's up to you whether or not you want to answer them. Please be aware you are not a suspect in anything, but we are looking for some information that might help us in the murders of your coworkers."

"I'll do anything I can to help," Patricia said.

Grazer nodded.

Kux yawned.

Patricia was very quick to answer all the questions Grazer had for her:

How well do you know the victims? *We worked together for a while, but I retired before them. Hadn't heard from them since.*

Do you know of anyone who might want to hurt them? *Not that I can think of.*

I really hate to ask, but for the record, I have to; can you tell me your whereabouts on the night of Saturday, January 7th and early morning of Sunday, January 8th? *My ex-husband and I went to have dinner with my son and his wife at their house. Afterwards, I went home and went to sleep.* She even offered to give her son's contact number, and though Grazer accepted the offer, he knew it would be useless.

Within half an hour, the interview was over, and it ended with a pleasant handshake and another yawn from Kux. "If you think of anything that might be important, please do not hesitate to contact me," Grazer said, handing the woman his business card. She accepted it with a warm smile.

Kux stood to his feet the moment Patricia left the room. "You didn't ask her about the Bayer case," he said.

Grazer shook his head. "She probably wouldn't tell us anything more than we already know. And besides, the less she knows the better. We need to confirm that it is Bayer before we do anything else."

"And how are we going to do that?"

Grazer honestly had no idea. "Let's hope Corona and Leddy are having better luck with their questioning."

*

Leddy couldn't care less about Michael O'Neill or Mercedes Rodic – the two interviews scheduled for the afternoon. While Kux and Grazer worked from the station, he and Corona hit the road to meet up with the last two names on the list and clear them as suspects. Leddy, however, knew it would be a waste of time. Michael O'Neill nor Mercedes Rodic were killers. The thing that took hold of Tina the night before, however...

He wanted to go back to the hospital and spend time with her, to ask if she felt okay or if she remembered anything; basically all the questions he couldn't ask her the night before. But duty called, and on the other hand, once O'Neill, Rodic, and whoever it was Kux and Grazer were interviewing (he forgot the woman's name) were cleared, the sooner they can concentrate on what was actually happening.

Before they left the hospital, Kux asked Leddy to keep the possession thing under wraps. "All anybody knows is that she had some kind of episode," Kux told him, and though he agreed, Leddy wanted nothing more than to reveal the truth.

"Hey Teddy," Corona suddenly said. "What really happened to Hood last night?"

Leddy snapped from his daze, Corona's question coming as if on cue. He sat up on the passenger seat of the sedan and glanced at Corona with a frown. "What do you mean?"

Corona shrugged. "You tell me. She's perfectly healthy, and all of a sudden she has this violent episode that lands her in the hospital? I mean, you guys were there. What do you think happened?"

Leddy took a deep breath. This was his chance.

"I'll tell you what I think happened," Corona continued. "I think Kux tried to drug her. Slip her a roofie or something. What do you think?"

Leddy frowned and looked at his superior, unsure if he was being serious or not. And time has proven that if he was unsure, odds were Corona wasn't.

"Oh come on," Corona said. "Tell me you haven't noticed the way Kux looked at her. He wanted to tap it, she wouldn't let him, and so he tried to slip her a drug. What do you think, Teddy?"

"I think it's a mystery how you became a detective," Leddy said, looking out the window.

Corona laughed. "Okay, you're tired. I get it. But tell me it didn't cross your mind."

Indeed, it had not. And now, more than ever, Leddy wanted to tell Corona what he really thought – if only for the shock value. He kept his mouth shut, though. Even during the interviews with O'Neill and Rodic that eventually crossed them off the suspect list. He kept his mouth shut.

But his mind was never off what spoke through Tina and what it said; "I killed them," she growled through her clenched teeth. "And you too."

The Bayer Case

Case Number: 11-02-5047
Incident: Bayer Farm Investigation
Reporting Officer: Det. ███████   Date: July 07, ███

At 0710 hours on July 1, ███, we received a call from the Bayer Farm in Homestead regarding the mutilation of pigs, and a possible murder / suicide. First on scene was, Officer ███████, and upon arriving, we found twenty to thirty pigs all slaughtered amongst the field; blood soaking the earth, the farming vehicles and most of the ranch.

We both interviewed witnesses ███████ and ███████ who were there to issue a close order from the DOH. They told us they had come a week before and spoke to James Bayer, the farm's owner.

Upon entering the premises, I saw more blood on the floor and the walls (pictures included) as well as another pig slaughtered on the dining room table. James Bayer was hanging from the second floor landing, and his wife, Hilda Bayer, was found in the master bedroom strangled in her bed sheets.

██
██
██
██
██
████████████████

"Everything else is blacked out," Todd said tossing the folder containing the report aside. "Five more pages of nothing but black lines. What the fuck!"

Hector picked up the report with gloved hands and flipped through it.

"Why? Who is trying to cover something like this up?"

Hector shook his head reading the first page. "Well, we know who went to the farm from the DOH, Cabello and DeCocq. Every other name is blacked out. And why black out the years? We saw that in the newspaper clippings. It doesn't make any sense."

Todd stood from the table abruptly. They were at Hector's dining room table, his daughter, once again, at the Grazer's. They decided to review the contents of the box there for several reasons, but mostly so that Todd's kids wouldn't be exposed to any horrific items they might find stored as evidence.

"Where you going?" Hector asked.

"Outside. I need a cigarette."

"Sit down. Light one in here. The report mentions pictures."

Todd shook his head. "Yeah, they've probably been blacked over, too." He lit a cigarette as Hector reached for the box and slid it between them. Aside from the folder containing the report, there box didn't contain much more; a cement mold of a footprint, and empty wooden picture frame, and a small box containing vials of what looked like dirt or mud – all bagged and tagged as *EVIDENCE*. The final item was another box, larger than the ones containing the dirt samples, but small enough to hold in one hand.

Hector held up to show Todd. "The pictures, maybe?"

"We can hope," Todd answered, smoke dancing around him.

Hector carefully opened the box as though it contained the ashes of James Bayer and would blow away with the slightest gust of wind. He flipped the top over and, holding the box in his right hand, he looked at the contents, looked to his partner and smiled.

Todd felt the drop of excitement soar throughout his body. Finally, something they might be able to go on.

A stack of color pictures, all 4x6, were neatly wrapped in a plastic bag, all snug so they wouldn't bend or rip. Hector delicately flipped the box so the stack would fall out into his left hand, and the weight of the set surprised him.

"There must be a hundred pictures in there," Todd said, standing to his feet and staring at the stack with hungry eyes.

Hector nodded. "We'll split them up, see what we can find. Hopefully a picture of the Mason or something."

Todd reached for the stack, but Hector recoiled, holding the pictures further away. "First things first," he said to Todd, then waived his gloved hand at his partner. "Rubber up before you touch these."

*

The pictures told the story of the Bayer case better than any case file could. Both Hector and Todd sat side by side reviewing the photos, reading them like a book, telling each other the stories the pictures formed, the puzzle pieces falling together.

The sky above the farm grounds were grey with looming clouds from a coming storm. The farm was in better condition than when Todd saw it – almost looked new, and if it wasn't for the pig carcasses that were scattered about, mostly in the pigpen just east of the farm house, Todd could picture it as a quaint place to work. Blood saturated the earth, intestines and other unidentifiable pig guts were strewn about, and several mounds of what looked like skin were piled together resembling the last three cases the detectives visited.

A close up of the steps leading to the front door of the farm house revealed dozens of flies that were glued to each landing by aid of the drying blood. There was a footprint on the step; breaking the blood pattern and revealing the same footprint that was cemented and found in the evidence box.

It was a man's print – wide and long, size 10 or 11, Todd quickly estimated, his detective training kicking into gear.

The first room in the house was set up as the living quarters; couch, loveseat, recliner; the makings of a perfect family home. Everything in the room seemed normal, but upon closer inspection, the dark panel floor wasn't dark wood at all. It was blood stained. As was some of the ceiling. Someone or something had exploded in the room – the blood spatter having no identifiable tracings and could not tell the story of what happened in the room. It was as though a hose had been turned on in the living room, only instead of water spewing out of the nozzle, it was blood.

"Whatever happened in here," Hector said, "it was bad."

Once in the dining room, the personalized touch like the family pictures in the china cabinet or the large plant placed in the southwest corner of the room were overshadowed by the slaughtered pig on the dining table. It was on its back, its underside sliced from groin to gullet. The way its purple tongue lolled out of the corer of its stout mouth was just as sickening as the intestines, blood and mucus that had spilled out of the gaping hole and onto the floor beside the table. A serrated steak knife was beside the carcass, bound to the table by way of drying blood – the swine's murder weapon, no doubt.

The stairway that led to the second floor was door-narrow, no room for two people to ascend side by side. It made the hanging body at the top of the staircase all the more prominent. James Bayer was a tall man, his shoulders almost touching each wall on either side of him. The other side of the noose around his neck was tied to an exposed ceiling truss above him, and his face was transmogrified into a lifeless guise. It was hard to tell if his eyes were open, but it was certainly clear that his mouth was. Like the pig in the dining room, his tongue slouched out of his mouth, black by lack of circulation. The chair that was on its side beneath him made it obvious that Mr. Bayer hanged himself, as did the feces that fell out of his pants leg, staining his bare feet, and landing onto the floor beside the chair.

It seemed that whoever had slaughtered the pigs ran out of energy by the time they reached the second floor. The hallway was pristine, and so was the sizeable master bedroom. The hardwood dresser that matched the floor was clean, the flash of the camera reflecting off its glossy finish, the photographer staying clear of his or her own reflection on the massive mirror hanging on the wall above it. The king sized bed was housed in the center of the room, its white sheets bringing clarity to the otherwise murky atmosphere brought on by all the dark wood surrounding it. Even the bed frame, exaggerated by large bed posts on all four corners, were made of the same wood as though the Bayers had torn down an entire forest just to build the second story of their quaint farmhouse. Amidst the white sheets was the body of a naked, pale woman – Hilda Bayer.

Her black hair cascaded against the large pillows like spider webs, her eyes wide open, hauntingly bulging out of their own sockets and blood shot to the extreme where her eye color could not be identified. Her nostrils were flared and her mouth was open as though frozen in mid scream. Though fear may have contributed to her death, what ultimately killed her was the brilliant white sheet that was tied around her neck – leaving her naked body exposed, her breast falling lifeless beside her, and the white sheets between her legs stained yellow with urine. There was definite fear in her dead face though, but Todd knew it wasn't from fear of dying – it was the dread of whoever did put her to rest.

Todd swallowed hard, hesitant to move on to the next set of pictures. He lit another cigarette, took a long drag, then exhaled and watched the smoke dance around him. "I need a drink," he said, almost to himself, rubbing his temples.

"Bourbon okay?" Hector asked, already on his feet and making his way toward the kitchen.

"Bourbon's perfect," Todd replied, staring at the picture of Hilda Bayer's lifeless body.

The cigarette between the fingers of his right hand, he scattered the pictures before him, looking at each one and all of them at the same time. A part of him couldn't believe that he stood in that same farmhouse less than twenty four hours before, and a larger part of him wanted to go back, to see the room where Hilda Bayer had died, to study the truss that James Bayer hanged himself on. It seemed surreal.

As Hector walked out of the dining room, Todd moved on to the next picture.

It took less than a few seconds for Todd to register what he was seeing, though to him, it seemed like an eternity.

A twin sized, unkempt bed was set in the center of a small room. The floor was dark wood, just like the room where Hilda Bayer had been strangled, but the walls in this room were painted a pale blue. There were no windows, and the small closet at the south of the room was open revealing shirts and other clothing that were small enough to fit a child. The room he was looking at was a child's room, and it was apparent that whatever child this room belonged to had been there for a long time.

A baby's crib was set against the east wall, beside the twin bed. Toys and dolls made of hay, straw and wood were strewn about, and there was one that Todd could not stop fixating on.

It was set atop the center of the twin bed, its eyes, made of old rusted buttons, staring back at the camera as though it knew its picture was being taken. Its long black hair was strewn against the dirty sheets, like spider webs. Like Hilda Bayer's own hair. The dress it wore was white with a yellowish hue, age and the dilapidated room it lived in leaving its mark. The smile on her face was stitched in black, the left spreading across the length of her face, and the right side curling upward as though she were sneering directly at Todd. A sinister look that made her lifeless body all the more intimidating. The same black stitch could be seen around the sides of her face, down her uneven arms and at the soles of her bare feet. The doll was homemade, that much was obvious. What curled his stomach was what the doll was made of; her skin glistened in the flash of the camera. Leather-like in its appearance, it didn't take Todd long to realize that the skin on the doll was the same as the mounds of skin in the pig pen. This doll was made of pig skin.

The doll, the crib, the state of the dirty room wasn't what Todd was concentrating on. It was what was on the pale blue walls around the bed. Random, angry, threatening words were written all over the walls. Whoever massacred the pig on the first floor used this room as the finale. All the words were written in blood, trails dripping from the curve of each letter. And it wasn't until Todd saw *gip nicuf* that he realized all the words were written backward.

Hector walked back into the dining room with two glasses of brown alcohol.

Todd's eyes on the same 4x6 image stood slowly, his forehead creased and his hand slightly shaking.

"What is it?" Hector asked.

Todd swallowed hard. "Everything we need to prove that Mason Bayer is who we're looking for," he said.

Tuesday, January 10th

A sudden flash of light lit the farm house for a split second, and a few moments later, thunder rolled in the skies above the house. It was then that Grazer realized that he wasn't alone in the farm house at all – the lightning revealing two men standing in the doorway to one of the rooms, one of them a young officer, the other holding him at gunpoint. Their killer had been hiding, and now, he had a hostage.

All Grazer could do was blink forcefully to clear the stinging sweat from his eyes as he quickly drew his gun and aimed it and the flashlight at the murderer; a tall, large man draped entirely in black, including a ski mask that covered his face.

The rookie's hands were handcuffed behind him, and the perp used the rookie's gun to control him. Grazer recognized the standard issue pistol immediately. His heart pounding against his temple, Grazer locked eyes with the rookie, trying to convince him that it was going to be okay with a simple glare, but the fear in the young man's eyes made it clear that he did not get the message.

"Take your shot!" the perp yelled. "Shoot me and this pig gets it before I hit the ground!" His voice echoed in Grazer's head and rattled his bones. It was a deep grumble, one that is produced by a snarling animal, not a human.

Grazer's sweaty palm gripped the gun tighter. "There's no way out of this," he tried to tell the killer, but the words were caught in his throat.

"Come on!" the perp yelled. "Do it! You fucking pig!"

The explosion that followed was deafening. Without Grazer even noticing, he pulled the trigger. He heard the body fall to the ground but he couldn't see which one it was since he shot with closed eyes.

Sweat poured from his brow when he sat up on his bed and found himself in his darkened room instead of the farmhouse. His heart raced against his chest as he tried to catch his breath, and his dry mouth made it almost impossible to swallow. *Another fucking nightmare*, he told himself in a failed attempt to calm his nerves.

"You can't keep doing this to yourself," Mary said to him. She was standing at the doorway to the bedroom, watching him.

Todd swung his legs around the edge of the bed and rubbed his face. "I'm fine." He glanced at the alarm clock beside the bed. 4:37 A.M.

"Bullshit," Mary said. "You're having nightmares again. This needs to stop. I heard you from the other room. The last time this happened..."

"I know, Mary, believe me, you don't have to remind me." He walked to the bathroom on the east side of the room and flipped on the light switch. Though the light burned his eyes, he welcomed it. The dark of the early morning mixed with the remnants of the nightmare was a cocktail he no longer wanted.

He splashed cold water on his face from the sink with Mary standing behind him.

"I know you're not going to stop what you're doing," she said.

"That's right," he said. "I have a responsibility."

She watched him as he dried his face with a washcloth. "Then promise me you'll talk to someone about it."

He laughed. "A lot of good it did last time."

"I saw the pictures in your office, Todd," Mary said finally. "I don't want the details, but I saw what you're investigating, and that's enough to put anyone over the edge. It's no wonder you're having the nightmares again."

Todd hung his head then slowly shook it. "That's why I don't want you to know what I'm working on, Mary."

"I know, but I was worried," she said, stepping into the bathroom and taking a gentle hold of his face. She pushed it upward so that their eyes met. "Please, promise me you'll talk to someone. Do it for me. For Cynthia and Luis. Please. Do it for yourself."

A moment of silence fell upon them and Todd took a deep breath. Finally, he nodded.

She kissed his stubbled cheek and gave him a tight hug. He reciprocated.

*

The sun had barely begun ascending over the eastern skies, and it was colder than usual. The fog hovering over the parking lot was barely noticeable, had it not been for the lamp posts, Leddy wouldn't have seen it at all. When he exited his car, he saw his breath dance around him, and he shivered, second guessing the Miami Dade Police Department issued windbreaker he was wearing. Should have gone for something a bit more substantial.

He checked his watch; 5:47 A.M., far too early for visiting hours, but it was the only chance he would have to visit Tina. Since her *episode*, his nights were sleepless and his mind was restless at the thought of being around something more sinister than they could imagine.

He walked into the hospital and made his way toward the elevator, looking over his shoulder to ensure no nurse or doctor would ask him where he was going. His hand in his pocket, he had his badge ready to flash in the event he was told he could not visit anyone. But the elevator arrived without incident, and he quickly entered.

The ride to the seventh floor was a long one – his heart pounding against his chest and his hands becoming moist. Suddenly unsure of what he was doing, Leddy closed his eyes and took a deep breath. He knew that, if his suspicions were true, he could do nothing to save Tina, but he had to have confirmation outside of the events that had taken place. He *needed* to know that he was right.

The elevator doors menacingly slid open allowing Leddy view of the desolate hallway that housed rooms where in the sick, dying and possessed were lying. He stepped onto the tile floor, the soul of his shoe squealing against the surface and making the only noise heard in the hall. He eyed the door to the Tina's room, several paces away from the elevator, and took each step slowly not looking away. Once he reached it, his clammy hand gripped the door lever and he prayed against hope that it was locked. It wasn't.

His mind, proving ever the enemy, had made the situation much worse than it actually was. Upon seeing his friend on the hospital bed, he felt somewhat relieved; her pale face resting, her blond hair tied in a bun above her head, and her slender arms resting at her sides outside the white sheet that covered the rest of her body. An IV bag rested above her, dripping nourishment into her right hand. She was not the evil, transmogrified monster spitting vile insults and poisonous deformations like he was expecting. She was simply Tina Hood, and she was sleeping.

He didn't enter the room. Deciding to let her rest, he began closing the door, but stopped when the faint voice that filled the air called out to him.

"Scott," she said, almost in a whisper.

He smiled in her direction. "Sorry. I didn't mean to wake you."

She shook her head slowly. "It's okay. Come in."

He did as he was told and shut the door behind him. He sat at the foot of her bed, and took hold of her cold, pale hand. "How are you feeling?"

"Like I was hit by a truck," she said. "My whole body hurts."

"Has anyone here told you what caused it?"

She shook her head slowly and took a deep breath. "They don't know what happened. I don't know, either."

"What do you mean?"

"I don't remember any of it. How did I end up here?"

Leddy frowned. "What do you remember?"

"You and Billy at my place. Then me waking up here. That's it. What happened?"

Leddy thought carefully about his response; revealing what she did would undoubtedly upset her. So he left it at a simple; "You had an episode. A seizure or something."

Tina nodded slowly. "You're lying."

Leddy smiled, stood from the bed and kissed her forehead. "Get some rest. I'll find out how much longer they're going to keep you here if they can't find anything wrong with you. You'll feel much better once you get home."

"Can you do me a favor?" she asked softly.

"Of course."

"Sandy. Can you make sure she's okay?"

Scott smiled. "Of course."

"I don't feel like myself," she said as he walked toward the door.

His stomach turned. He closed his eyes for a moment, gnawed his jaw then turned to face her. "How do you mean?"

Tina took a deep breath. "All day yesterday, I keep having these thoughts, like memories or something. And they're horrible. Disgusting. They're sad. Full of hate. It's like I'm trying to remember something I locked away in my brain somewhere and these images are flashing at me suddenly. And I can't control it. It's happening even now."

"What are they?"

She didn't answer right away, and Leddy wasn't sure if it was because she didn't know, or didn't want to.

"Death," she said finally. "Evil."

*

"Fuck!" was the first word out of Hector's mouth when he woke up to sunlight. He had over slept, once again.

He jumped off the bed and performed what was becoming a morning ritual; running into the shower, shaving in the shower to save time, and dress for the day all within fifteen minutes. Storming out of his bedroom, he called out to his daughter who was usually in the kitchen with two slices of toast and a to-go coffee cup filled with the fresh brew. He'd thank her profusely, kiss her on the forehead and wish her a great day as he ran out the door and hauled to the station. But this morning, she wasn't in the kitchen.

Hector frowned, "Joanna," he called out again, wondering if she was still sleeping. He checked his watch; 7:37 A.M. It was strange that she slept past seven on most mornings.

His decision to check on her was certainly not to wake her, but to simply make sure she was okay. If she wanted to sleep in, she had every right to do so. The love of his life, his daughter worked hard at both school and home, and there were days Hector felt for her; the fact that her mother wasn't around, that she was forced into adulthood because he worked long hours. But she never complained. And her friends were a great support system.

He opened the door to her room slowly and peered in. It was dark in the room, the black-out curtains doing their job of keeping the sun from seeping in. He could hear the heavy breath of someone sound asleep, but once his eyes adjusted to the darkness of the room, he could make out the silhouette of his daughter sitting up on her bed.

A small chill ran up his spine as he called out to her, opening the door and flipping on the switch. Immediately, he wished he hadn't.

Joanna was staring back at him with large black eyes, her face cut in several places on her forehead as though shards of shattered glass broke her skin. Her cheeks were bruised and a thin trail of blood trickled from her smiling mouth.

"Joanna," he gasped, stepping into the room and almost not realizing the drop in temperature the moment he did. Though he was looking at her, he knew, could *feel* that what he was looking at was not his daughter at all. It was her face, her body he could see, but both completely different. She was swollen, her skin was as grey as her eyes, and the smile upon her lips was crooked – sinister.

"Joanna is dead," she said, but it wasn't her voice coming from her grit teeth. It was a deep voice, beast like in its growl.

Hector was robbed of his words, especially when he realized the blood above her bed. On the wall above the headboard, in blood, was the word *ENO*.

Joanna, or the thing she had become, tilted its head toward Hector. "I killed this pig," it said.

The words echoed in his head as he tried to scream, but he couldn't. Sitting up on his bed, Hector's body erupted in goose bumps, the image of his daughter becoming something she wasn't, taking hold of his head. But he was in his room, sitting up on his bed, breathing heavily, the scream of horror still lingering in his throat.

If it was a dream, he did not remember waking up.

He looked at the clock beside his bed; 7:37 A.M.

After jumping off his bed, he made his way to the bedroom door and opened it slightly for a view of the hallway. Joanna's bedroom door was open, the sun seeping out of her room. He walked to the kitchen and found her spreading butter on his toast, the coffee brewer hard at work.

"Joanna," he called to her, his heart still racing.

She spun to him, the smile on her face turning into a frown. "You okay, dad?"

His shoulders slumped at the sound of her voice, at the sight of her flawless face and green eyes.

"You look like you've seen a ghost," she said.

"I'm okay," he said, swallowing hard.

"Well, you better get a move on. You're late."

He nodded. "Yeah." He rushed in her direction and hugged her – tightly. He kissed her cheek then held her by the shoulders so that they were face to face. "I love you, you know that, right?" he asked.

"Alright, weirdo, you're freaking me out," she said, the frown holding.

"Good enough," he said. After kissing her cheek again, he headed back toward his room proceed with his morning routine. Still uneasy about what he had dreamed, the image of his broken daughter still in his mind, he took a deep breath.

His only response to it all was, "Fuck."

Mason Bayer

Roth looked at the picture then looked at Grazer and Corona standing on the other side of his desk – both of them cross armed and neither braking their stone cold stare. He looked to the picture, then back to the detectives. Did it once more before finally asking, "Where did you get this?"

"Doesn't matter where we found it," Grazer said. "The only thing that matters here is the fact that it proves Mason Bayer is the man we're looking for."

Roth studied the picture some more.

"You do realize what this is going to cause, don't you?" Roth asked. "What's going to happen to the department?"

Grazer and Corona exchanged frowned glances then looked back to their lieutenant.

"How so?" Corona asked.

Roth shook his head. "This case was closed almost twenty years ago, and now it's coming back to bite us in the ass. Once the mayor and the chief get wind of this, they're going to reopen all the case files and see where we went wrong. This is not good news for us."

"With all due respect sir, this is great news," Grazer said. "It's the largest break we've had in this case."

"One that you obtained by some means I don't even want to hear about," Roth said. "And this stays between us. Where are we on the remaining DOH members?"

"They've all been cleared," Corona answered.

"I'm officially requesting round the clock protection for the remaining four," Grazer followed. "There's no telling when or where Bayer will strike next."

Roth closed his eyes and pinched the bridge of his nose. "So much for keeping this under wraps."

"We can use Leddy and Kux for that. All we need is two more bodies to cover the others."

"With Hood in the hospital, we're already shorthanded, and you're asking for round the clock protection?"

"We'll use Vice," Corona said. "It won't touch our budget."

Roth tossed the picture onto his desk. "Do what you need to do," he said. "But keep it as quiet as possible. The last thing we need is to have people think all of this could have been avoided because we didn't do our jobs twenty years ago."

Both men gave Roth a tight nod. Grazer picked up the picture and both men left the room leaving the lieutenant on his own.

When the dynamic duo walked into his office moments before, closing the door behind them and tossing the picture on his desk, his stomach sank. Fortunately Roth was good at hiding his facial expressions when unpleasant surprises slapped him, so he simply shook his head before asking the men "What is this?" Though he knew very well what it was. He knew where the picture was taken. He knew that the moment he dreaded for longer than he could remember was finally surfacing.

The picture had come from the evidence box for the Bayer case – a box that he held in the basement of his home for over ten years. After the Cabello and DeCocq murders, he handed that box to someone who he trusted, and he was wrong.

His blood pressure rose, and it was difficult to hide the heat on his face when the detectives stood before him. But now that they were gone, Roth grit his teeth in anger. He had been betrayed.

He snatched up the phone, punched a few numbers, and waited. "It's me," he said into the receiver. "We have a problem."

*

Mason Bayer has died more than once. He was too young to understand his first death; the same night his parents died, the same night his many pets died – all at his hand. He liked the blood. He liked the noise the swine made, the squeal of agony that screamed out of the same throat he was slicing open. He enjoyed the feel of the intestines falling onto his hands when he sliced their stomach, the feeling of the blood sticking to his skin when it began to dry. He liked it so much, he could feel his groin tightening, his pelvis overcome with a feeling he didn't quite understand, but he knew it felt good.

He had the same feeling when he overcame his mother's strength. Standing over her bed and watching her sleep, he looked upon the black rosary tangled around her right hand. A nightly prayer became routine for Hilda Bayer, and on this particular night, she fell asleep mid entreaty. He touched the crucifix before he moved his fingers toward his mother's soft face, waking her. The look on her face like something he never experienced, but her dark eyes were similar to those of the swine he slaughtered moments before; filled with horror. Her face revealed the speechless thoughts that entered her head at the sight of her young son standing before her, dirtied with blood and intestines. Before she could call to her husband, Mason's hands were on her throat, squeezing with a force that even surprised him. His mom thrashed about the bed, the sheets flying off her nude body and giving Mason the tool he needed to keep her still. As though his hands were being controlled by an outside force, Mason took the sheet and tied it effortlessly around her neck, tightening the knot. He watched his mother's eyes as they began to bulge, their veins turning blood red, until finally, she stopped the fight. Coughing up blood, her head went limp – turning awkwardly to its side as her arms fell lifeless, one off the edge of the bed, the other to her side. Her eyes; however, remained staring at her son. Motionless though they were, he stared back to them, and he smiled.

That was the night that Mason Bayer died the first time, and a different Mason was born; one who sought the feel of the intestines on his hands, drying blood on his skin. As he left his dead mother's body behind him, his search for his father was a short one. His father stood at the doorway of the room, and Mason knew that he had witnessed what he had done. The look on his father's face was sufficient proof. Mason smiled an innocent grin in his father's direction.

Twenty years later, he stood in the same room, in the same spot where he innocently smiled at his father – a smile painted in gore. He looked around the room, seeing it with eyes that found it just the same as it was the night his mother died. The wood screaming for relief beneath his feet with every step was as new to him as the day the house was built. The place he stood was his home, and it had been for longer than even he could remember. And he vowed, long ago, the day that someone showed up at the door with an order condemning the property, that he would make those who trespass regret their decision.

He took the short walk to the first floor, studying the walls, looking over every square inch of the property ignoring the imperfections, smelling the air around him as though searching for a hidden trespasser. The walls, watermarked and splintering, were perfect to him. Satisfied, he moved on to the center wall and slid his hand across the coarse surface. He pushed the hidden door open slowly, as though mimicking the actions of the trespasser that was in his house a few days before. Just like the trespasser who was draped in a trench coat, he placed a hand on the center of the wall and gave it a slight push. The wall gave, moving inward with the momentum of his arm, the dragging sound filling the room, and notifying Mason that someone was in his house.

He pushed it open enough to squeeze his large frame through and stepped onto the platform at the top of the stairs that led downward. Mason stared at the dark opening that was where he had made his home for nearly twenty years. He remembered hiding in the darkened area – in a specific spot no one would ever think to look (and no one did) while dozens of men and women invaded his home above. Some were there to study the dead animals, others were there looking for him. He could hear the frantic, muffled footsteps, the voices of those who had taken over his home, and he would exact revenge on them as well, if only he knew who they were.

"Miami-Dade Police!" Mason called mockingly. The man had said those words as he took his first step down the stairs, followed by "Come out slowly, your hands where I can see them." Mason's ridicule echoed in the area around him, his voice carrying far enough for anyone in the house to hear, if only there was anyone else there.

Something the detective saw in the basement frightened him, Mason knew that by the way he turned and ran out of the house. There was nothing out of the ordinary – at least to Mason's perspective. Rusted farming tools; hack-saws, picks, a hatchet and various others were hanging from chains lining the ceiling as they had been for the past twenty years. Murder weapons the detective probably thought. Mason smiled at the idea.

He walked toward the east end of the room, passed the work table placed in the center and pushed open another wall concealed amongst the others. It was a room Mason's father built – no larger than the size of a closet.

"Fucking pig," Mason said as he reached into the room and extracted the black ski mask he took from the pig he last murdered – the one called Shaw. He slid it over his and fitted it around his face, the fabric fitting snugly. He took a deep breath, smelling the remnants of Shaw's scent on the mask itself, then exhaled through his mouth, his shoulders slumping and his back losing support.

It was the same thing he did just before he heard the door to the basement open, just before he heard the warning; *We have the place surrounded, so there's nowhere to run!* He stepped backward into the closet upon hearing the man's voice and slowly closed the door, concealing himself in the darkness and camouflaging the door amidst the walls of the room. He watched through a small hole in the wall as the detective descended the steps slowly, his flashlight illuminating parts of the room. He continued watching as the detective saw the tools, heard the front door caught in the wind, and run back up the stairs and out of his home. He continued to watch as the detective drove frantically through the dark streets of Krome Avenue, stopped to use a payphone, then to a house in a suburban neighborhood. Never once did the detective know he was being followed, even when he arrived at his own home. Mason watched the detective as he kissed his wife, and checked on his kids; one boy and one girl – both teenagers.

Mason stepped into the closet and closed himself in. The room was empty, save for the pile of bones in one corner, and large blade hanging on the right wall. The handle was made of wood, something Mason himself made years before when his father taught him woodwork and it was the first and only knife Mason used to slaughter pigs then and now. He sat on the floor, brought his knees to his chest, and he closed his eyes.

His thoughts were on the man who broke into his house. For that, he would pay. Mason would break into his house when he was done with his current roster of swine. He would play with his wife and children the way he played with his pets before slaughtering them.

For now though, he would simply wait.

Visitors

Todd kept his promise to Mary, and for the next six months, he visited with Dr. Jennifer Leppe once a week, preferably in the morning before starting his day.

Dr. Leppe started her career as a criminal psychologist where a large part of her job was to study why people commit crimes; why criminals do what they do. In many instances, she interviewed criminals, from thieves to murderers, from arsonists to child molesters, to try and ascertain what part of the mind is satisfied by what they do – what triggers it, and why. It was a fascinating career that ended when she was attacked by a rapist of women.

It was supposed to be a routine interview that was going to be reported to the parole board to determine whether the criminal was going to be able to function if placed back into society, and when she declined his release, he jumped the table and attempted to strangle her for several seconds before he was finally tazed and whisked away by several officers. After that day, she held her job with the Miami Dade Police Department, but as a staff psychiatrist available to all personnel.

When Grazer began having the nightmares nearly two years before, he reluctantly began regular sessions with her, and he was surprised to find that she was able to help. Relaxation exercises, relying on his support system, and most of all being open and honest about the incident eventually exorcised the nightmares from his head. And when they began resurfacing nearly six months ago, he sought her help once more.

It was Wednesday, June 3rd, and by eight that morning, his final session was already under way. After the usual exchanges, the mandatory questions and answers began:

Jennifer: *How are you feeling?*

Todd: *I'm fine.* Same answer every session. Most of the time, he wasn't lying.

Jennifer: *No more nightmares, then?*

Todd: *None.* He was lying, but the nightmares had become less reoccurring. The last one he had was several weeks before, and that was an achievement.

Jennifer: *Anxiety attacks?*

Todd: *Not since the last one.* More than seven weeks before.

Jennifer sat back and looked at her patient. Her office wasn't large, enough room for a small desk, a filing cabinet and two chairs. She at the opposite side of the desk so that she and Todd were sitting face to face, her notepad set atop her slender, crossed legs. It was the same every session, even when he began visiting her years before.

After the usual exchanges, she sat back on her chair and looked at Todd over her wire rimmed glasses. "Do you realize that you've given me the same exact answers every visit?" she asked. "It's like you're reading a script."

"It's only because you ask me the same questions," he answered with a smile. "Really, though. I'm doing very well. Much better than I was before I started coming in."

She continued looking at him as though sizing him up, seeing if he broke down and told her he was lying. But he didn't. Satisfied, she nodded. "Well, this is our final session, per your request. Because you came to me voluntarily, I don't have to report anything to your superiors unless you want me to."

Todd shook his head. "No need."

Again, she nodded.

"But could you do me a favor and tell my wife? She doesn't believe me even more so than you."

Dr. Leppe let out a small laugh. "How does that make you feel?" she asked.

"I thought we were done with the session."

She looked at her watch. "We still have fifteen minutes or so."

Todd stood from his chair. "Unfortunately, I don't. Work beckons."

"Are you still frustrated over the Bayer case?" she asked.

"You don't give up, do you?"

"That's not an answer," she said.

Todd took a deep breath then exhaled slowly. He took his seat. "Nothing's happened in the past six months. Of course it's frustrating."

"And that's what caused your anxiety attack a month and a half ago."

He nodded. "That's right. I still feel anxious about it, of course. This guy just keeps vanishing. He did it eighteen years before, and he's doing it now. I have Roth on my ass looking for answers, I have a team looking to me for something to work on, and it's frustrating as all hell. And I hate to say it, but..." he hesitated, glancing at Dr. Leppe for a second then looking to his feet. "I almost wish he would murder someone else so we can pick up the trail again."

"That's understandable," Leppe said.

"It's a shitty thing to wish for."

"And it's completely normal. You shouldn't beat yourself up over it. Now, if you have thoughts about doing it yourself, then we have an issue."

Todd smiled. "No worries there."

"Good," she said. "I know you're on pins and needles to get outta here, so I won't keep you much longer."

"Thank you," Todd said as they both stood.

They shook hands.

"You know I'm here if you need me. If anything comes up, or if you have another nightmare. I'm here."

Todd thanked her once more then left her office after ensuring none of his colleagues were lingering in the hallway. The last thing he needed or wanted was for word to get out that Grazer the Great was seeing a psychiatrist again – not that anyone would know considering her office was in a different building. Still, he looked down either side of the hallway, closed the door behind him, and made a quick dash toward the elevator. His escape was good.

*

When there was no answer, Scott Leddy decided to let himself in. He had knocked, waited, knocked again, but no one came to the door. He tried the knob on the off chance the door was unlocked, and was not entirely surprised to find that it was. He wasn't surprised to find the living room in the condition it was in, either.

Several empty beer bottles were on the coffee table, and a bottle of vodka was beside them, turned on its side. It wouldn't have been empty if the remainder of it hadn't fallen onto the carpet, but it was hard to tell how much of it was left over.

The apartment smelled of cigarette smoke and urine, though he could see neither. Perhaps it was due to the fact that the blinds were sealed shut and the only light source was coming from the open door, or maybe it was because Scott didn't want to find the puddle. Though the potent smell was enough to make his eyes water, he continued his way in.

He placed the vase of flowers that he carried with him on the coffee table, knocking over some of the beer bottles and made enough noise to wake the dead, but he froze, looked to Tina who was sleeping on the couch, and she didn't flinch. Counting the bottles, it was no wonder she was sleeping better than the dead.

Sandy rushed out of the kitchen and barked only once to greet Scott with a furious tail and exasperated tongue. She leaped in his direction, and he pet her, rubbed her belly when she rolled onto her back and told her to remain quiet. Surprisingly, the dog did.

He walked to the only window in the living room and opened the blinds, allowing the sunlight to explode its way in, and Tina stirred to life with a hiss, a moan, and jumbled words that made no sense to him.

"Rise and shine, beautiful," he said to her. She barely had her eyes open, but he could tell she had rolled them at the sight of him. "Party too hard last night?"

"What do you want, Leddy?" she asked, smacking her dry lips.

Sandy jumped onto the couch to greet her master, but Tina shoved her to the floor, annoyed.

"I came by to say hello, and I find you like this?" he scolded. "What are you doing to yourself, Tina?"

Scott could tell it was painful to do so, but Tina sat up, struggling to do so. She was fully clothed, but appeared as though she hadn't showered in days. He wasn't sure, but the jeans and light brown t-shirt she was wearing appeared to be the same she wore a week before, only the t-shirt was white before. She put her head on her hands and moaned again.

"This isn't healthy, Tina," Scott said. "I'm worried about you."

"Don't be. It's not like I do this every night. I was depressed last night, is all."

"You've been depressed for the past six months. You need help. Are you still taking your medication?"

"I got help, and you see what good that did me," she snapped back. So quickly in fact, Leddy took a step back. "They took my badge. Called me unfit to carry a weapon, and I lost my job. That bitch of a doctor did me no good and you want me to go back to her?"

"There are more doctors than Jennifer Leppe," he said. "I'm just saying that this isn't you. You're better than this."

"You don't know me," she said. "Don't act like you do, and don't fucking psycho analyze me. I'm not in the mood."

Leddy threw his hands up in surrender. "Whoa, take it easy there. I just came by to see if you wanted to grab a bite to eat or something, get you out of this apartment for a bit."

She shook her head. "I'm sorry. I'm not myself. I need water."

Leddy nodded, told her to stay put and made his way to the kitchen. It was in no better condition than the living room; more empty bottles spilled out of the trash, take out boxes half filled with food covered the counter top, as did the trail of ants. Dirty dishes were piled in the sink, and the moment he reached for a glass that looked clean, a roach startled his hand away.

He also saw that Tina wasn't the only one in need of water. Sandy's water dish was bone dry, and her food dish was empty. She sat beside them, looking to Scott with desperate eyes and a wagging tail.

He shook his head and filled the bowl with water. Sandy drank almost all of it in a hurry.

He bit his tongue to not comment on the filth, but before he even could, he heard the distinct sound that made his stomach turn.

It was coming from the hallway, from the bathroom, and it was the sound of Tina vomiting. The gurgling strain from the pit of her stomach and the splash of her sick violently hitting the toilet revolted him, mostly because it reminded him of the episode that was the onset of her downfall.

"You fucking pig," she said, blood splattering from her mouth.

Scott closed his eyes as the memory flashed in his head so vividly as though he were seeing it before him.

Her body began to convulse, first with her hands, then arms, then her entire body was writhing with spasms. Billy tried to hold her head in place, but the seizure was too powerful. He was losing his grip.

Leddy looked to the couch, to the place where it all happened, to the place where Tina was lying just moments before. Though the air in the room suddenly went thin, cold, Scott felt a tremendous weight in his chest.

The blood she vomited in a violent stream hit them both suddenly. Billy and Scott jumped back, Billy falling over the coffee table, as Tina's steady stream of vomit surprised them. She was still on her back, still unconscious, but the growl that accompanied the sick was very much awake.

And it was the same growl coming from the bathroom as Tina vomited the previous night's party.

Finally, there was silence. Tina was done with the purge. The sound of the toilet flushing filled the hall, and though that should have relieved Scott, it didn't. Especially when the front door opened and Tina stepped into the apartment still looking disheveled and hung over as he had seen her moments before.

He frowned at her, his heart racing suddenly. "What were you doing just now?" he asked.

"I stepped outside for a cigarette. I don't smoke in my apartment, but it smells like I did... Do you smell that? I don't remember smoking in here."

Leddy's frown held. He looked into the hallway. "Is there anyone else here?"

Tina shook her head. "No. Why?"

He looked into the hall again, and ordered Tina to "Stay put."

Keeping his eyes locked onto the bathroom door, which was closed, Scott entered the hallway and took one slow step after the other. He glanced back at Tina once who was watching him from the living room, but only because he felt he was being followed closely – the hair on his neck standing at attention and the chills soaring through his body not resting. With a clammy hand, he pushed the door open toward a dark room, and he flipped on the light switch.

He didn't know whether he hoped to find someone in the room or not. If he had, it would explain what he heard. But the room was empty. Even the shower curtain was already pulled back so there was no need to investigate further. Save for Tina and himself, there was no one else around.

He quickly walked back into the living room.

"What is it?" Tina asked.

"Nothing," he said quickly. "Just, do me a favor. Get some help. I'll call you later."

Without another word, Scott fled the apartment, jumped into his car, and left the parking lot, leaving a very confused Tina in the apartment on her own. When he first told her to get help, he meant psychiatric or inspirational help, something that would end the depression she was suffering. But when he told her the same thing while leaving, he meant a totally different kind of help all together.

For months, with every passing day, he believed his possession theory about Tina was more and more foolish. That morning, he was never so certain that he was absolutely right.

Idle Hands

It was business as usual at the Homicide Division that Monday morning; Grazer walked into the office, randomly greeting people and politely answering those who asked if he'd had a good weekend. He reached his desk and found the thick folder filled with reports and the work he'd put in on the Bayer case sitting where he left it the Friday before. It had not grown in thickness for about half a year, and the sight of it every morning made him resentful.

He rolled up his sleeves, loosened his tie, and was about to take a seat to review the contents of the folder once again when Office Kux, dressed in the standard issue brown and khaki uniform, suddenly appeared before him.

"Good morning, sir," he said.

"Officer Kux," Grazer acknowledged. "How are you this fine summer morning?"

"Truthfully? Summers here suck! In Pinkney it was hot, but dammit, the humidity makes it feel fifty degrees hotter."

"And the polyester doesn't help," Grazer said, nodding at the uniform.

"No kidding. I hate to ask, but nothing new, huh?"

Grazer shook his head. "You'll know when I know."

Kux nodded. "I'm going to ride with vice today. Let me know if anything comes up."

Grazer nodded as Kux walked away, happy that it meant he would have one less to answer or worry about.

The phone on his desk rang, and he recognized the extension immediately. He picked up the receiver and said, "Good morning, Roth."

"Good morning. My office, please."

He hung up, took a deep breath and made the short walk to the lieutenant's office where he was surprised to see Corona.

"This is one for the books," Corona said. "I beat you into the office."

Grazer smiled, and nodded to his lieutenant who was dressed in a suit, a rare occurrence, for Roth was a fan of polo shirts – Miami Dade issue, of course.

"Aren't you spiffed up today, sir," Grazer said, taking a seat next to his partner.

"It's easier to be a mercenary when you're wearing a tie," he said.

Grazer laughed. "How so?"

Roth eyed both men then took a deep breath. "I've been instructed to take you two off the Bayer case."

"What?" they both yelled, almost in unison.

"It's gone cold. Nothing for the past six months, and there's been no leads other than those we acquired. So, until we find more, we're moving on. The Bayer case is closed. As is the John Doe."

"With all due respect," Grazer said. He was on his feet, but he didn't realize it. "We can't close the case! He's still out there."

"And he has been quiet for six months. He could have left the country, he could be dead for all we know. The fact is its gone cold. I've been instructed to close the case, and that's what I'm doing."

"By whom?" Corona asked.

"By the mayor himself."

"This is such bullshit!"

"Be that as it may, it looks bad having this case open for so long with nothing going on. It affects his numbers, our turn-around, tourism…"

"Unbelievable! You'd rather have us not look for a killer than hurt tourism? You were right about the mercenary part."

"I'm also taking security detail off the four remaining DOH board members."

Grazer slapped his thighs. "For all you know, that's the reason they're still alive. You take them off, and you're practically handing Mason the rest of his victims."

Roth sat back in his chair. "My hands are tied. There are plenty of other cases that can use your expertise, both of you. Right now, this one is on the back burner."

Grazer leaned across the desk and got close enough so that his and Roth's noses were mere inches apart. "One more of those board members dies because we pulled their security detail, let it be on your head, you son of a bitch."

Corona stood up behind Grazer. He was ready to pull his partner away in the event he jumped the desk.

"And you can tell that slime ball mayor of ours that the blood will be on both your hands just as much as they will be on Mason Bayer's."

He stood upright and adjusted his shirt. Corona placed a hand on his shoulder.

"You're a murderer just like he is," were the last words Grazer said to Roth just before throwing the office door open and storming out.

*

They reacted just the way he knew they would. Once the two detectives left the office, Roth picked up the phone and with a few words, relieved the four officers on security detail for the DOH members. He stood from his desk, adjusted his tie, and stripped the sports coat off the back of his chair and draped it over his arm. He had an appointment to keep, and he had to leave soon if he wanted to make it on time.

He locked his office on his way out, and without making eye contact with Grazer, Corona, or anyone else on the floor, he made his way toward the elevator and pressed the button to the parking garage.

It was a three story structure, and on most days, it was partially empty due to the fact that most cars were out on patrol. Summer was the height of the crime season in Miami; kids were out of school and their idle hands were the devil's workshop, tourists with no street smarts walked the city with cash in their wallets, street drug sales were at their peak, and even though summer had yet to officially begin, the patrol cars were out in heavy force. The garage seemed desolate; only several cars, some patrol vehicles, some unmarked, were parked in their reserved spaces.

Coat in one hand, keys in the other, Jack Roth made his way to his black sedan, the heel of his shoes echoing throughout the bleak garage. They echoed almost loud enough to cover the whispering call he heard so faintly, he thought maybe he didn't hear it at all.

He stopped, the entire garage falling to silence. He looked behind him, to his left, to his right. He saw no one.

Continuing the walk to his car, Roth didn't so much shrug off the noise he thought heard. Perhaps it was remnants of the whisper he heard almost every night as he tried to fall asleep – at the moment where he was not quite asleep yet, but no longer awake, the whisper would come to him, jolting him out of any repose and startling him enough to cause an uneasy rest of the night. His subconscious, he thought. But never once did he hear it in the light of day. Never once did it call to him outside his bedroom. Until now.

Piggy, piggy…

The long, drawn out whisper was loud and clear this time, and close enough that he thought he could feel the hot breath on the back of his neck as he unlocked the door to his car.

He spun on his heel and again scanned the garage. If someone else was there with him, they were hidden from his view. No one was in sight.

"Who's there?" he called out, his deep, bellowing voice echoing throughout the garage.

Draping his coat over the hood of his car, Roth took hold of his revolver holstered on his waist, but he didn't draw it. He took slow paces toward the southwest of the garage, the darkest corner of the floor. If anyone was stupid enough to harass him in the MDPD Parking Garage, Roth figured they'd be hiding there since the rest of the floor was lit by the sun.

"If someone's there, I'd advise you show yourself!" he called, the authority in his voice masking all uneasiness.

*Piggy, piggy….*It called him again.

Roth drew his weapon, but didn't aim it. He continued walking slowly toward the darkened corner. The silhouette began to appear to him the more he approached.

"Who's there?" he called again, this time his voice cracking.

The silhouette didn't move, but there was no mistaking someone was standing there, watching Roth. Only, the frame seemed to be that of a small child, frail and demure.

Roth frowned. "Are you lost?" he asked squinting his eyes for a better look. He stood less than five feet from the child, but he still could not see more than a silhouette.

A squad car from the upper level of the garage turned the corner onto the driveway that parted Roth from the child. Its headlights illuminated the corner for a split second, but it was long enough for Roth to register what stood before him.

The small child, dressed in black, was facing the wall, his back toward Roth. The boy's head hung low, a gaping hole at the top of his head and a puddle of blood resting at his feet.

Roth gasped, his revolver falling to the floor.

The squad car passed in between them, Roth frozen in place and not acknowledging whoever was in the car that saluted him. And once the car was gone, so was the boy. Almost as though he latched onto the squad car as it passed, the boy simply vanished.

The image fresh in Roth's head, he rubbed his eyes. "What the fuck was that…" he asked the air. He didn't receive a response, nor did he need to. He knew exactly what it was. He knew what he saw – he just hadn't seen it in years.

He picked up his gun and holstered it with a clammy hand, swallowed hard, then looked back into the corner of the parking garage before making the quick walk back to his car.

"This can't be happening…It's in my head." He repeated it to himself many times, but he wasn't convinced.

As he drove out of the garage, he didn't look into the corner. He barely had the courage to look into the rearview mirror in case he saw the boy in his back seat. The fact was, he knew that silhouette was still with him. It had been with him for many years, in the back of his mind, in the darkest of his memories. Suppressing it never worked. Never once though did he think it would materialize before him.

As the he drove into the sunlight of Miami, he prayed it would never materialize again.

Awakening

When Mercedes Rodic received the call that she was no longer going to be protected by the services of the Miami Dade Police department, she was relieved. For six months, she couldn't go to the grocery store without having a cop more than three feet behind her. She was annoyed with their presence within a week, let alone for months on end. There were times when she was thankful they were there, like when she came home from the community center late at night and seeing the squad car parked on the curb of her neighborhood, but for the most part, it was a nuisance.

Being alone for the first time in six months however brought on something she didn't expect. She missed having the company. Though she never really socialized with any of the officers (they rotated weekly it seemed), she tried to be humble to them – sometimes taking them coffee and homemade cookies before she would retire for the night. She missed having someone to take care of, though it was their job to take care of her. Under the circumstances, a serial killer could be targeting her, she was thankful for their protection as much as their company.

Alone, once again, in her home, Mercedes was close to retiring for the evening. Dressed in her thin robe, she glanced out the window in her living room; the setting sun hidden by dark clouds and a roll of thunder echoing from several miles away. There was a storm brewing, which on a Miami summer evening was no surprise.

By the time she ensured her doors and windows were locked, the rain had begun. The sound of the drops on the windows were soothing, but knowing there was no squad car outside watching her house, she couldn't help but think the sound would mask anyone tapping on the glass, searching for a way in.

She set the alarm beside her front door, and thought twice about turning the lights off in the living room. Deciding to leave them on, she headed toward her bedroom. A hot shower and a good book would rid the paranoia in her system, she decided. Despite everything, she was looking forward to calling it an early night (it was barely 7).

Lightning crashed outside her window, and the lights in her bedroom flickered in a blink. Mercedes froze, her heart beat accelerating a bit, as she prayed the electricity would hold – and it did. The lights continued to burn at full power. The storm outside was building strength. The perfect setting for a horror movie, she thought.

Once in the master bathroom, she turned the knob to start the shower, allowing the water time to heat before she stepped in and began her pre-shower ritual. Living alone for the better part of twenty years, Mercedes would still close the door to her bedroom while she showered. She also turned on the television for background noise, though the thunder rolling above was louder. Still, she turned it on, tuned the television to the news channel, and made her way back into the steaming bathroom.

The lights flickered once more accompanied by the booming clouds. She paid it no mind, concentrating on the soothing shower that she was stepping into. Allowing her sixty-two year old body to be absorbed by the hot, calming water, she closed her eyes.

*

When Jack Roth walked into her office hours before, he updated her on the status of the Bayer case, told her it was officially closed, and that he would like the evidence box returned, the same box he had accused of her of handing over to the two detectives months before. Dr. Jennifer Leppe swore she didn't, ensuring him it was locked away in her home, in a safe, and that it hadn't been touched since he asked her to review it.

"I did what you asked," she told him. "I looked through the records to help profile Mason Bayer, even though I don't do that anymore. Now you're accusing me of handing over the evidence?

That's illegal!" She was offended, of course. And he apologized, and she prayed he knew she wasn't lying.

Sitting in her home office, Jennifer wondered how she would be able to get the box back from the detectives. She couldn't outright tell them what she suspected, but being seasoned detectives, she hoped they would find out on their own. Either they hadn't, or the doctor's suspicions were wrong.

The night she sent Corona the text message from Roth's phone was a tricky one. It was a spur of the moment event. She invited Roth to a business dinner where they could discuss her findings on Mason Bayer outside the office. What she told him was true – that if Bayer was indeed responsible for the murders of Cabello and DeCocq, that they were dealing with a psychotic hell bent on revenge. Numbering the victims? A form of compulsiveness – letting himself know that the job was done. The fact that the writing is backward? Probably nothing more than dyslexia. What it boiled down to was that, be it Mason Bayer or not, whoever was committing the murders was a very sick and twisted individual.

"Once he's caught," she had told him, "I know some colleagues who would be very interested in analyzing him."

The evidence box was in the trunk of Jennifer's car, and she had every intention of returning it to Roth after their dinner, but after he excused himself, said he was going to the restroom, and left the table, a new idea quickly entered Jennifer's head inspired by the mobile phone Roth left behind on the table.

Without thinking, she grabbed it and immediately searched through his contacts. Corona was amongst the first alphabetically. She hit the key for text messages, quickly typed *Meet me at office. Important.*, sent it, and then deleted the message from the phone's log. She nervously set the phone back on the table, where the lieutenant had left it, and waited for him to return.

Luckily, he didn't ask for the evidence box to be returned, and she had her suspicion as to why; he didn't want it in the hands of the detectives. But they needed it if they were to discover the truth of Mason Bayer. After paying for their dinner, she quickly wished Roth a good evening, then hauled to the station where she placed the box on Corona's desk and waited to ensure he, and only he, received it.

The plan worked without a hitch.

She decided to ask Grazer for one more session; a recap of sorts. There, she would ask for the evidence box, and tell him what she suspected. The only problem with the plan was convincing Grazer to see her one more time.

*

Grazer's cell phone rang, and for the second time in less than an hour, he ignored the call from Dr. Leppe. Slipping his phone back into his pocket, he turned his attention back to the glass of beer before him.

It was Corona's idea to take Kux and Leddy out for a couple drinks to thank them for their work on the Bayer case. Despite it being closed unsolved, he assured them they did a great job.

The Cell Block wasn't busy, Monday nights normally weren't. Several patrons occupied the pub tables, but nearly all the booths lining the walls were empty. At the center of the bar was where most of the activity was taking place – where Grazer, Corona, and the two young officers were seated.

"It's not over yet," Kux said. "I mean, he'll kill again. Right?"

Corona smiled. "You're starting to sound like someone I know," he said, patting Grazer on the shoulder.

"Don't get me wrong," Grazer said. "I don't want people to die. I just want to catch this son of a bitch already."

"What about you, Teddy," Corona asked in Scott's direction. "What do you make of it all?"

For most of the evening, most of the day in fact, Leddy remained quiet. His thoughts elsewhere. "I don't know," he said. "I think we leave it alone so long as there's nothing going on."

"Spoken like a true officer."

Leddy forced a smile.

"Well, both of you did a great job," Corona said, lifting his glass. "Here's to a great team. On to other cases, then."

The four men toasted each other then sipped from their glasses, except Leddy. He set his glass down on the table and slumped his shoulders.

"Hey, it's bad drinking etiquette to not take a swig after a toast," Corona said. "What's wrong with you?"

"Ah, cut him a break," Kux said. "He's thinking about Tina, I'm sure. I don't think he likes me as his partner too much."

Corona laughed. "Yeah, I wouldn't, either. You're not as pretty."

Again, Leddy forced a smile as the other two continued their witty banter and howled with laughter. But Grazer kept his eyes on the young officer. "Hey, Leddy, I'm going outside for a smoke. Care to join me?"

"I don't smoke," he said.

"You're not drinking the beer I bought you, either. So, humor me and step outside."

The night was humid. The storm had passed leaving behind a blanket of thick, moist, sweat inducing air. The moment they walked into it, both men regretted leaving the comfort of the air conditioner inside.

Grazer lit a cigarette as Leddy rested his back against the building's wall and crossed his arms.

"You tell me it's personal and I won't pry," Grazer said. "But what's wrong with you?"

Leddy shook his head. "Just thinking, is all."

"All day? What could possibly be that hard to think about?"

Leddy took a deep breath, unsure of how to answer. His mind was indeed on Tina, but not on her, per say. It was more so on what she had become.

"This whole Mason Bayer thing," he said. "Do you think maybe we're not really approaching it the right way?"

Grazer frowned. "What do you mean?"

His cell phone erupted again. Without taking it out of his pocket, he shut the ringer off.

Leddy took advantage of the interruption. "Nothing," he said. "Forget I mentioned it."

"Hey, if you know something that could reopen this case, you need to tell me now," Grazer demanded.

Leddy hesitated. "I... I think that what we're dealing with is bigger than–"

Grazer's cell phone rang again. "Goddammit!" he yelled into the air, reaching into his pocket.

Leddy's cell phone began ringing a moment later.

Both men exchanged glances, extracting their phones.

The door to the bar opened, Billy Kux running out followed closely by Corona who was on his phone.

Billy's cell began to ring.

"What's going on?" Leddy asked.

"We have to go," Billy said.

Corona ended the call he was on. "The Bayer case is about to be reopened, gentlemen," he said. "There's been another murder."

CHAPTER RUOF

There were four teams for the search; two teams were to search the outside grounds since the area was so vast, the third team was searching the barn on the northwest side of the land, and the fourth and final team was to search the house again.

Chiovitti and his student were the fourth group, and the search was over as quickly as it started. The house had already been cleared earlier, and the search was more of a recap than an actual hunt.

"He has to be close," Chiovitti said. "There's nothing around this area for miles."

"But it's been nearly a week since the Bayers have been dead, so he could be anywhere by now."

Both men were in the dining area, reviewing everything from floor panels to wall pressure. Anything was possible in a home built by a reclusive man and his family.

"We're wasting our time here," Chiovitti said. "He's not in here. I'm going to check on the other groups."

The young officer nodded. "I'll stay here and finish the search once more."

"Suit yourself," Chiovitti said, then left the house.

Alone, the young officer continued his inspection. The dining room was clear, nothing or no one was hiding in there.

He stepped into the middle room and stood in the center of it, beyond the dirty blood stained couch and splintered table, the room was empty. He crossed the room toward the staircase, but stopped when the center wood plank creaked beneath his feet.

He frowned, looked at the board and pressed on it again. It shifted loosely.

He tried to lift it from its space with his bare hands, but it wouldn't budge. The board ran the entire length of the area, and he followed it to the back of the room. Resting his hand on the textured wall, he pressed on the wood beam again, and his entire body shifted, but not because the wooden panel gave way. The wall he was resting against did.

It dragged inward with his weight, launching dust particles all over him.

He found an entrance none of the others did, and his first thought was calling Chiovitti to show him. His second thought was how much of a hero he'd be if he found the boy on his own.

Deciding on the latter, he entered the darkened area, turned on his flashlight and closed the wall behind him to search for Mason Bayer on his own.

Resurrection

Blood. Intestines. A carcass with no skin. It was a carbon copy of the three previous crime scenes, except for one thing.

"Where's the number?" Kux asked.

Grazer scanned the bathroom. The body was still in the tub and when they arrived, the water still running. Most of the blood had been washed away and drained. The white tiles of the shower wall were now stained pink with what remained of the blood and water. "Maybe it was written on the shower wall," Grazer suggested.

Kux shook his head. "No doubt this was the work of Bayer," he said. He was about to list the similarities to the other three murders and the complete absence of evidence, but realized there was no need. Grazer knew it as much as he did. "If there's one thing we know about him it's that he wants us to know that his victims were his. I don't think he would have written his mark in a place where he knew it would be washed off."

After a moment, Grazer nodded. "You've learned a lot these past six months, kid."

Kux almost blushed.

"Let's go see if Hector and Scott found anything," Grazer said.

Kux gave a tight nod, trying to ignore the fact that Grazer had used their first names – a rare occurrence.

The bathroom was small, so outside of the tub, sink, toilet and the small magazine rack beside it, there wasn't much to investigate. They made their notes, then headed toward the bathroom door to allow the forensics team to enter to take pictures, look for prints that weren't there, and run their course of action which would inevitably end up with absolutely nothing more than they already had. *Hector and Scott* had interviewed the victim's (identified as Mercedes Rodic) neighbor who had called the police after hearing screams coming from the inside of the house. Perhaps they stumbled upon some information that would lead them closer to the killer. Perhaps, but doubtful.

Both men were nearly out of the bathroom when they heard the slight *wheezing* – almost a whisper of sorts. Actually, it was Grazer who heard it more so than Kux. He stopped at the doorway, calling Kux back.

"What is it?" Kux asked.

Grazer brought his finger to his lips; *hush*, then pointed to his ear; *listen*.

A moment of silence passed, and Kux frowned, shaking his head; *I don't hear anything*.

And just when it appeared as though Grazer had heard the noise in his own head, it happened again – this time, loud enough for both men to hear. They both frowned, looked at each other, then slowly turned toward the bathtub, to where the open shower curtain revealed the body of victim number *RUOF*.

The hair on the nape of Kux's neck stood on end realizing suddenly why it was possible there was no blood written graffiti numbering Rodic. It was his first thought when he saw the skinned fingers on her right hand twitch right after the hissing voice coming from her parted, broken lips. *She's fucking alive,* he thought to himself, not realizing he said it out loud. "She's alive!" he screamed to the air, at the same time as Grazer yelled for medical help. The house was filled with forensics techs and officers, but neither knew whether any medical help had arrived yet.

"Someone get in here now!" Grazer yelled. "She's alive!"

Billy dropped to his knees beside the tub, ignoring the searing pain as his knees took at the fall. With a gloved hand, he moved a strand of hair from the victim's face to get a better look at her eyes – they were closed. "Ms. Rodic, can you hear me?"

Ignoring the cursing and yelling coming from Grazer and echoing in the bathroom, Billy looked to the victim's right hand. It twitched again. Slowly, he reached for it, ensuring his bare arm did not brush against the mucus and guts that had seeped from the tear at the bottom of her gut. A reflexive gag settled in the back of his throat upon being so close to the mess, and smelling it – the heavy scent of rot and feces made his eyes water. He lightly touched her hand, unsure if doing so would cause her pain – more pain than the gaping hole in her stomach. Perhaps she was in too much shock to feel pain.

She lightly squeezed his hand – so lightly he almost didn't feel it, but he could see her hand respond to the touch of his. She wheezed again.

"Grazer! Get someone in here, fast!" he called over his shoulder. "I don't know how much longer she has left!"

"Talk to her!" Grazer yelled. "See if she gives you anything!"

Billy looked to the mess around her midsection and shook his head. He doubted she could say a word let alone form a sentence, but he followed his orders. "Who did this to you?" he asked the mutilation in the tub, holding her hand. "Can you tell me who did this to you?"

The noise that came out of her mouth was much more than a *wheeze* this time. More like a weak grunt. Kux's heart skipped a beat at the thought that she just might say something after all.

"Ms. Rodic," he said, adjusting his kneeling position to allow a closer ear to her mouth. "Mercedes. We're here to help. Please, tell me who did this to you."

The soft click that left her mouth was either her choking back her own blood, or the beginning of a word that started with a *C*. She continued to make the sound, trying to swallow, but unable to.

"Stay with me," he told her. "Who is it? Do you have his name?"

Her mouth parted. "*G...g...rrr...lll.*" The noises were gurgling with blood, but he knew she was trying to tell him something – she was responding to him.

"Move aside!" someone yelled from behind him, probably a paramedic, but Billy ignored the voice.

"Who?" he asked her. "Tell me again."

"*G...*"

"Officer, let us attend to the victim!" someone said, tugging at his shirt, Billy swiped backward, nudging them away.

"*G...ir...*"

He leaned in closer.

"...*lll*..."

The grip on his hand loosened as all sounds around him became as muffled as her response. His eyebrows furrowed, he looked at the victim in the tub as her head lost the little support it had and swayed forward on the tub floor. Though she had appeared dead when they first found her, Billy knew she was dead now, her last word burning his brain.

He asked for the name of the man who did this to her – and her response came in the form of a stifled, barely audible announcement, though he heard her quite clearly.

G.....irrr....lll.... he thought. *Girl.*

He rocked back onto the floor of the bathroom as the two paramedics behind him sprung into action. Grazer rushed to his side and was speaking to him, but Officer Billy Kux didn't, couldn't hear a word from the detective's mouth. His mind was on the response.

Could it be possible a woman was committing the murders?

"Hey," Grazer said, patting the officer on the cheek.

Billy blinked hard, his focus adjusting to Grazer who was almost kneeling before him.

"What happened? Did she say anything?"

Billy simply shook his head.

"You okay?"

He nodded. "She's gone," he said. "She was holding my hand when she died. I felt her die."

Grazer blinked hard then slowly nodded. "Can you stand?"

Billy looked around him, realizing he was still on the floor, the paramedics and the body less than a foot behind him. He nodded then pushed himself upward. Grazer helping him, both men stood up, and looked back to the tub. Kux could not stomach the sight any longer.

"I need to get out of this room," he said. He looked at his hands – both covered in white latex stained crimson red with blood. His right forearm was also marked with blood, as well a wet substance that looked something like phlegm; something that came from her intestines.

He rushed to the sink, feeling the vomit surface in his throat. Choking it down, he turned on the faucet to the hottest setting and scrubbed the slime off his arm. He stripped the bloodied gloves off his hands and threw them into the sink and used a decorative soap bar placed on a pink dish to wash his hands and rid them of the fluids that once belonged to Mercedes Rodic.

He knew very well that he was contaminating a crime scene, but he didn't care. The word *Girl* fresh in his mind, the blood on his hands, he felt the weight of the experience on his shoulders and back. He needed to get out of the bathroom before he gave into the reality of it all and passed out.

He splashed water on his face, careful not to bend too far into the sink. Then he looked into the mirror, and he froze.

He could see in the mirror's reflection that Grazer had seen it, too. The look on his face told him so.

The steam released from the hot water Kux used to cleanse his hands had settled on most of the mirror. Within the steam, there were curves and lines that formed letters – and the letters formed a word.

Billy's knees almost gave as he read the word and processed it.
RUOF it read.

*

Leddy watched the action from the master bedroom, a few feet away from the entrance to the victim's bathroom. He and Corona were just outside the house, questioning the victim's neighbor when they suddenly heard both Grazer and Kux screaming for help. He even thought one of them screamed "She's alive!"

He saw it all go down; Billy leaning toward the victim while holding her hand, the paramedics trying to get him to move, even the moment when she finally passed away. He watched as a very pale and shaken up Kux stood from the bathroom floor, then rush toward the sink where he dramatically washed the blood off his skin, the word *RUOF* almost magically appearing in the mirror above the sink.

Having seen it all play out, when he finally locked eyes with Billy, he knew the look Billy gave him was one of which he had only seen once, six months before; the night he told Billy the story of his mother's boyfriend. The same night Billy asked if he really did believe in possession.

Leddy didn't know what, if anything, the victim said to him, and he knew that Billy wouldn't have been shaken up by the number *RUOF* appearing before him. Something else had rattled him to the bone.

And the only thing Leddy could think of was Tina.

ENO More

While the crime scene was being evaluated, investigated and examined, Kux sat outside the house and watched the activity from a far. Still visibly shaken, he couldn't bring himself to enter the house again, opting instead to stay seated on the hood of a squad car and breathing in the chilled Miami night's air.

He looked up to the full moon and glowing brightly amidst the darkest of skies. There were no stars visible, and he realized then that, just when he was getting used to Miami after six months, he missed Pinkney more than ever. Come nightfall in the quaint little town, stars lit up the skies brilliantly, constellations visible and it wasn't rare to catch several shooting stars every night. But, in an overcrowded city like Miami, the stars were blanketed by the countless streetlights and florescent powered buildings.

Closing his eyes, Kux took a deep breath, the humid air slightly stinging the back of his throat. Images of what occurred inside the house flashed in his mind like a quick moving slide show; the victim holding his hand, his collapse to the floor, the word *RUOF* mysteriously appearing before him. He opened his eyes quickly as though waking from a nightmare in an attempt to rid his mind of the images, and though it worked, it allowed for something worse than the images; time for his thoughts.

When they first entered the crime scene, the first thing he noticed was that the number was missing all together. Though it was a major source of confusion at first, it almost made perfect sense now; there was no number because the victim was not yet. Kux spoke to her, and she spoke back. Only after the victim's weak grip on his hand went completely limp did the number appear. As though Mason knew exactly the series of events that would transpire, that Kux would frantically wash his hands of the blood using hot water from the sink, thereby allowing steam to reveal the word he left behind.

His back straightened. He turned his neck to face the small crowd of spectators watching the crime scene, all of them desperate to see the body being wheeled out on the gurney. The crowd was smaller than some of the other crime scenes as it was a smaller neighborhood. Ten, maybe twelve men and women, some even dressed in bathrobes and slippers, stood beyond the police border and watched all the excitement. He scanned the faces of each, wondering if any could be Mason Bayer himself. If he setup his kill to have a surprise ending, then surely he would be around to watch it happen. The idea that the mysterious, elusive killer was still somewhere around gave him the chills, erupting from the small of his back and settling around his neck. He slid off the hood of the car and turned to face the crowd several yards away.

None of them were killers, of that much he was convinced in a matter of seconds. The neighborhood consisted primarily senior citizens, much like the victim herself was. Despite the amount of silver hairs and wrinkled skin amongst the group, they all whispered to each other at some point or another, inevitably gathering gossip to solve the mysteries themselves since Miami Dade Police were not forthcoming with any of their questions. Though Kux knew he wasn't amongst the spectators, he didn't know if Mason was hiding in plain sight or not.

He scanned the rest of the area around him, around the house, deciding whether there was ample room for someone, anyone to hide somewhere, anywhere around. The neighborhood was bare of large trees, and several corner street lamps provided enough illumination to reveal any darkened corners. If Mason was hiding somewhere nearby, he would have to be completely out of sight.

He, Kux thought. *He.*

Shaking his head, Kux thought of the last thing the victim said. *Girl*. Was it possible that a *woman* was committing the murders? All evidence (or lack thereof) indicated that they were looking for a man – namely, Mason Bayer himself. What if they were wrong? What if

Mason had a female relative that was committing the murders? He shook his head again. The notion was ludicrous. For all Kux knew, the *girl* uttered by the victim could have been nothing more than the sound she made while gargling the blood in her throat. Girl? Ridiculous.

It was when he saw Grazer exit the home was Kux finally able to manage his thoughts – especially when he realized Grazer was making a straight line toward him. The look on Grazer's face was determined; his brows low, his eyes narrowed and his lips pressed. "You doing okay?" Grazer asked, the tone in his voice not showing any real concern.

"I'm fine," Kux lied.

Grazer nodded. "You can go home and get your shit together if you need to."

Kux shook his head. "No need," he said, knowing that being in his small studio apartment alone would only fuel his thoughts.

"Good. Then I need you to do me a favor. Roth is on his way here. Apparently he thinks we're too slack to take care of this ourselves. If you don't want to go back in there, I understand. Stay out here and come get me when he arrives. Can you do that?"

Kux nodded, a frown appearing. He wanted to ask why, but thought the better of it.

"I want to tell that asshole that this is his fault," Grazer said, as though reading Kux's mind. "He takes detail off of our victim here and she's murdered less than twelve hours later. Son of a bitch has as much blood on his hands as Mason does." Grazer spun on his heel and headed back toward the house, muttering angrily as he walked.

Kux took a deep breath and turned to look at the street to keep watch for the sedan Roth drove. It wasn't long before he arrived followed quickly by a loud exchange of words between the dynamic duo Grazer and Corona against the lieutenant. As accusations flew back and forth, victim number *RUOF*'s body was wheeled out behind them.

Against his will, Kux stared at the body bag on the gurney, unable to peel his eyes away from it. Hours before, he held hands with the victim inside the bag, and the thought alone was enough to make his stomach turn, even before he thought of everything that transpired after.

It was because he was fixated on the body bag that Kux did not immediately notice the man standing directly beside him, staring at him with wide, black eyes. Kux took a step back in surprise, his heart skipping a beat at how close the man was to him.

His face was void of any expression, and his eyes were set completely on Kux – not moving. Not blinking.

Kux looked the man up and down – mid to late fifties, dressed in sweat pants and a worn out t shirt. He recognized him as one of the spectators he saw amidst the group.

"Sir," Kux said through dry lips. "You need to step back behind the yellow-"

"I did it," the man said slowly. His voice was deep, spoken through a parched throat.

Kux frowned, taking another step back and placing his hand on the weapon holstered to his waist.

The bickering between the Grazer, Corona and Roth ceased and their attention suddenly shifted to the man. They heard him.

"I beg your pardon," Kux demanded, his voice shaking.

"I killed them," the man said through clenched teeth. "I killed them all." His lip curled upward and he his eyes narrowed, still locked on Kux.

He lunged at the officer quickly. In a matter of seconds, Officer Billy Kux was on his back, the crazed man pinning him to the wet grass. Kux fought to push him off, but the man proved too strong. He gripped Kux's neck and began to squeeze, and the last thing Kux heard before giving into the darkness was a gun shot.

Thursday, June 4th

"His name is Roberto Ortega," Corona said.

The man's face flickered on screen and Kux's heart began to race. It was a driver's license shot, more than likely, not capturing a good image of his mug, but Kux could easily identify him as the man that attacked him the night before.

The briefing room contained the usual suspects; Leddy and Kux sat at the desks located in the center of the room, and empty desk between them that would have been Tina's had she been there. She had been gone for six months, but neither Kux nor Leddy could bring themselves to sit at her desk – for several reasons. Corona and Grazer were at the front of the room, holding files in their hands and reading from them to fill the rest in on what they may or may not already know. The routine briefings were cumbersome, but they were mostly for Roth, who was also at the front of the room, absorbing all the information.

Grazer went first, with the help of some of the forensics team to review the crime scene found at the Rodic residence. Same MO, same lack of evidence, same everything. Almost everyone in the room could sing along with the speech given by the photographer, evidence technician, medical examiner, etc. The only new nugget - what was already discovered at the scene.

"The victims are still alive at the time the suspect skins and disembowels them."

Leddy watched as Kux closed his eyes and shuddered at the thought.

Normally, being the lead detective on the case, Grazer would take over and fill the room in on any remaining facts, but it was Corona who stood before the room after forensics left. It was then that the picture of Roberto Ortega flickered onto the screen behind him, and he introduced the perp to the rest of the room.

"He lives in the same neighborhood as Rodic, and though he claimed responsibility for the murder and/or *murders*, we've ruled him out as a suspect."

"Already?" Leddy asked. "How?"

"He works at the hospital that he's currently in," Corona answered. "And we've been able to verify that he was on shift during the murders of Cabello and DeCocq, and he was home with his family during Rodic's."

Leddy and Kux exchanged glances.

"And, there's more," Corona said. "Mr. Ortega doesn't speak a word of English. That's not so shocking here in Miami, but…"

"But he spoke very clearly to me," Kux jumped in, a frown on his face and confusion in his eyes. "In English."

"That's correct. I spoke to him this morning, though," Corona said, and it was suddenly clear why he was leading the briefing and not Grazer; Hector Corona was the only Hispanic on the team. "He has no recollection of talking to you, or attacking you. Nor does he remember being shot in the leg," he said, looking to Grazer, "or getting to the hospital."

The room went silent while Corona waited for the information to absorb, and for someone, *anyone*, to comment on the information he just revealed.

Nothing.

"He has a daughter," Corona continued, looking at his file. "Angela Ortega, age 17. Leddy, Kux, I want you to talk to her today."

"Why us?" Leddy asked.

"You two are the youngest here. We don't want to scare her. He's been ruled out as a suspect, but maybe she knows why he did what he did last night. See what you can find."

Both men nodded.

Corona turned his attention to Roth. "Grazer and I are going to revisit the three crime scenes. We'd like to see if we have missed something unique in each."

Grazer cleared his throat – the first sound he made the entire meeting. "We'd also like a team to help us search the Bayer farm, sir."

Roth's face remained neutral, but he crossed his arms over his massive chest.

"We believe that if Mason Bayer is hiding anywhere, it would be there."

Roth neither nodded, nor shook his head. Instead, he took a deep breath, rubbed his temples then pushed himself off the desk he was leaning against.

"We cleared the farm several months ago," Roth said. And he was telling the truth. During the downtime, three months into Mason Bayer's vacation, Grazer was finally able to convince Roth to get a team together to search the farm and its grounds. After a full day's effort, they came up with nothing.

"I understand," Grazer said. "But he's killed again, and he may be back in the farm now."

Roth gnawed his jaw. "Leddy, Kux," he said without looking at them. "You have your orders. Please excuse the detectives and me while we speak in private."

Both men nodded and left the room without hesitation. Once the door closed behind them, Grazer and Corona turned their attention to Roth. Their faces indicated the knowledge that when Roth asked to be left in private, bad news usually followed – and Grazer knew exactly what it was.

"You shot a man last night," Roth said to him.

Grazer was already shaking his head. "It grazed his leg. Couple of stitches, and the man will be out of the hospital by tonight."

"That's not the point. You fired a weapon at an unarmed man-"

"He was attacking Kux," Corona interjected.

"I don't care if he was attacking your mother!" Roth shouted. "There's procedure to follow; protocol. There were over twenty police officers there and we could have easily pulled him off of Kux." Roth held up both hands, closed his eyes and took a deep breath in order to compose himself. He shook his head. "The point is, you do not fire your weapon unless it is an absolute last resort." He turned to Grazer. "Especially you."

"What's that supposed to mean?"

"You know *exactly* what it means, detective."

Grazer snarled his lip and shook his head.

"The last time you fired your weapon, it ended in a casualty, and I don't have to remind you what you went through because of it, do I?"

Grazer looked to his feet. "No, sir."

"Look, I'm willing to overlook the fact that you all had a couple beers in you when you showed up to the crime scene."

"But-"

"I'm also willing to overlook the hostile environment that I walked into when I first arrived. But what I cannot overlook is the fact that you fired your weapon, and I have my orders, just as you have yours."

"Which are?"

Roth took another deep breath. "You're officially relieved of duty until I get a full psyche eval."

Grazer laughed, but it wasn't a lark filled with joy. "You're kidding, right?"

Roth shook his head. "Afraid not. You haven't fired your weapon in over a year and a half, and you spiraled the last time you did. I can't afford that happening again. Not while you're on a high profile case, like this one."

"In my defense, I didn't kill anyone," Grazer said. "You know this is not the same thing."

"Are you still having nightmares?" Roth asked.

Grazer hesitated. "You asked me that before."

"And I think you were lying when you answered me before, so I am asking you again; are you having the nightmares?"

Grazer slapped his thighs then shook his head. "I'm fine. Honestly." He turned to Corona. "Will you please tell him I'm fine?"

Corona furrowed his brow, but never once looked to his partner. "Todd...I - I think Roth may be right."

The look that suddenly befell Grazer's face one of shock, surprise, and mostly, sorrow. His jaw hung open and his eyebrows arched.

Wide eyed, he took a step away from his partner, unable to produce any sound outside of "Wha..."

"I've spoken to Mary. She says two out of three nights, you wake up in a cold sweat, gasping for air. She's concerned about you. We all are."

"You...you spoke to my wife about this? How about asking me first?"

"Because you wouldn't have told me if I had."

Defeated, Grazer looked to Roth, then back to Corona, then back to Roth. "Fine," he said. He removed the badge and weapon holstered to his waist and placed them on the desk that would be Tina's. He nodded to Roth. "You at least had the nerve to tell me to my face."

Corona looked up at him the moment Todd's glare fell onto him. His eyes were bloodshot and moist. "At least he didn't fuck me over to get lead detective on this case."

"That's not what this is about," Hector told him, but it was too late.

Todd Grazer left the briefing room, and without a word to anyone else, he left Miami Dade Police Headquarters for good.

*

"You don't think it's strange that this is the third or fourth person to take credit for these murders?" Leddy asked.

"To be fair, they don't take credit for Mason Bayer's murders. They just take credit for murders in general," Kux answered. "*I killed them all.* There's no telling who 'them all' is."

Leddy, who was driving, took his eyes off the road long enough to shoot Kux a disapproving glance.

Traffic was light heading west, and the morning sun was covered in thick, grey clouds. Though the storm had yet begun, it was brewing.

"What happened to you last night?" Leddy asked, "at the Rodic house?"

Kux shook his head and looked out the passenger window. "It was a lot to take in, is all. Shook me up quite a bit."

"Did she say something to you?"

Kux inhaled slowly. He was at an advantage in that no one but he heard what Mercedes Rodic's dying word was. Expecting that many people would ask what she had said (and they already had), he formulated an answer that remained the same. "She just gurgled a lot. She was choking on her own blood. She said nothing of importance." Yet, that gurgling, bubbling sound she made rang clear and coherent in his head; *girl*. "How's Tina? Have you seen her recently?"

Leddy nodded, and the hesitation to answer matched Kux's moments before. "She's been better. I think she needs someone to talk to – professionally, I mean."

"Exorcise her demons?"

Leddy's heart raced at the sound of Kux's question. He wasn't sure it was laced with sarcasm. He simply nodded, and both men remained silent for the remainder of the short trip to their destination.

As Corona mentioned during the briefing, the Ortega residence was in the same neighborhood as Rodic's. Same street, in fact. Most of the houses seemed deserted as the residence had made their way to whatever jobs they held – except for the one that had the yellow police tape barricading it from the street. It was still very much a crime scene, and neither of them mustered the courage to look at it as they drove by.

The Ortega residence was several houses away from Rodic's and when the small house was in sight of the two officers, so was the young girl sitting on the sidewalk just outside of it.

"Is that her?" Kux asked, reminding himself of the name Corona had told them; "Is that Angela Ortega?"

"I don't know," Leddy answered, pulling to the curb directly beside her. They both watched as the girl stood to her feet and nodded in their direction.

"Did she know we were coming?" Kux asked.

Leddy shook his head. "I have no idea. But, can you do me a favor?"

"What is it?"

"If she confesses to *killing them all* too, can you promise me we go straight to Roth and tell him we quit?"

Kux laughed, but not because he found Leddy's request amusing. He was of the same mind.

Gifts

Tina woke sitting upright. Her back was stiff, her hands crossed on her lap, and her legs were locked straight on the bed. Her initial reaction to waking up in such a state was confusion, but it wasn't long before the fear set in.

The curtains she used to keep the room dark during the hours of the rising sun were open, the brightness enough to have woken her hours before despite the grey clouds. She looked to her nightstand, cluttered with empty water bottles (and a few beer bottles) and found the digital display on the clock radio flashing *3:47*.

Her intention was to jump off the bed in a hurry, her heart racing to make sense of the way she woke, but her body would not allow it. Swinging her legs around the edge of the bed shot electrifying pain from her waist all the way up to the back of her neck. Slowly pushing herself up, her arms screamed with soreness and once she stood, her knees almost buckled under the ache of her thighs. Her mind was running a hundred miles an hour, thinking of what she had done the night before to cause her entire body to suffer the agony it was in, but the last thing she remembered was falling asleep on the couch, fully dressed in her jeans and t shirt, in front of late night infomercials on her TV – the same way she had fallen asleep the past week or so.

"Sandy," she called out, her voice raspy and her throat hardly powerful enough to produce the sound. She stumbled to the dog's bed, and found it empty.

Stepping over the random articles of clothing strewn about the floor, she made her way toward the bedroom's door, which was open. Strange, considering she always shut and locked the door when she slept in her room. She stopped in the middle of her room and closed her eyes. *What the fuck happened last night?* she thought to herself, rubbing her temples to 1) aid the headache that suddenly befell her, and 2) help concentrate on any memory of the night before.

She drank. A lot. It had become common practice the last few weeks. There were mornings she woke up hung over, but the more she drank, the fewer and more far between the hangovers became. And there were moments that were blacked out – but she would at least remember certain aspects of the night before. Never did she feel like she did that morning, nor forget the entire night. In all meaning, she felt like she was hit by a truck.

"Sandy," she called again.

Dragging her feet, Tina made her way out of the room and into the hallway. The humidity in the hall did nothing for her nauseous stomach. Her hands and feet were clammy, her upper lip was beaded with sweat though her entire body felt cold despite the humid air around her. After the short walk through the hall, she realized why her entire apartment was humid; the front door was open.

The Miami summer morning was floating through her apartment like a ghost.

Her first thought was on Sandy – she was gone. And though the primary thought on her mind was on her companion, many others flipped in and out of her head; *How long was the door open? Who opened it? Was someone inside the apartment?*

"Sandy," she called again, this time, her voice gaining a bit more strength.

She took a hurried step to the door, glancing at her feet, and it brought her to an immediate stop. They were dirty – very dirty. Dried mud had crusted around the souls of her feet along with, what looked like, specs of grass. As though one had to do with the other, she looked at her hands next. Dirty as well. The mud painted on her hands were of a different kind, though. Almost red.

Being a law enforcement officer, Tina knew that what was on her hands was not mud. She just didn't want to admit it.

"What the fuck did I do?" she asked the humid ghost around her in a quivering whisper.

Her hands trembled and her eyes watered as the fear of not knowing who or what she had harmed seized her entire body. Was it possible that during her drunken slumber, she walked through the night and hurt someone – or worse? More so than the possibility of venturing out and doing something bad, something evil, what scared her was not remembering anything.

"Sandy," she called again, her trembling lip and shallow breath making it almost impossible to speak. "Please. Where are you, baby girl?"

Standing alone at the end of the hall, Tina hugged her torso, unsure of what she should do outside of call for help. Any kind of help. Her fragile state was enough to push her over the edge, and her finger tight grip on sanity was slipping fast.

Almost too scared to even move, she forced herself to take a trembling step out of the hall way. Swallowing hard, she scanned the rest of the apartment, and when her eyes fell upon the small dining table, that finger tight grip on sanity slipped away completely.

The large plant placed in the southwest corner of the room was overshadowed by the slaughtered dog on the dining table. It was on its back, its underside sliced from groin to gullet. The way its purple tongue lolled out of the corner of its stout mouth was just as sickening as the intestines, blood and mucus that had spilled out of the gaping hole and onto the floor beside the table. A serrated steak knife was beside the carcass, bound to the table by way of drying blood – the dog's murder weapon, no doubt.

Tina tried to scream, but there was no sound, and she didn't notice. As her eyes settled upon her dead dog's mutilated body, she went numb and began involuntarily convulsing. She slapped herself once, clawed at the table where Sandy's corpse laid, even threw herself to the floor as she continued her silent scream and cries for help.

And just before she blacked out again, Tina stood from the floor, looked at the dog again, and laughed.

*

Angela Ortega was smarter than either Kux or Leddy anticipated. The moment they introduced themselves, she instructed them to get back into the car and ask that they drive around.

"I beg your pardon?" Kux asked.

"You're here to ask me about my dad, right?" she asked.

"That is correct."

"Well, I'm 17 years old. You can't ask me any questions without one of my parents present. Well, dad's in the hospital, thanks to you guys, and my mom is so angry about what happened that there's no way she'd let me talk to you. So, we can get into your car and you can ask me all the questions you want, or I can go back inside the house and you can go on your way. Your call."

Kux and Leddy exchanged glances, and before they had a chance to respond, she was already in the back seat of the sedan.

"So, where are we going," Leddy asked, back in the driver's seat. "A friend's house? The mall?"

"The mall?" Angela asked, almost laughing. "No, the type of girls that hang out at the mall are not the type of girls that hang out with me. As far as friends go, I don't have any."

Kux, in the passenger side, turn halfway to face the young girl in the middle of the back seat. "You have no friends? Why's that?"

Angela shrugged. "They think I'm weird."

"Weird how?"

"I'm hungry. How about we get something to eat? You guys treat."

Kux and Leddy exchanged glances again, both somewhat amused by their passenger.

"Fine," Leddy said. "But we pick the place."

The place was a Hispanic food chain that served traditional Cuban cuisine. Breakfast was a crowd favorite, and they were relieved to find the restaurant was somewhat empty that Tuesday. They were seated at a booth, Leddy and Kux shoulder to shoulder on one side, Angela at the order. Both men simply ordered Cuban toast and Cuban coffee, but Angela ordered the special; scrambled eggs with ham, fries, Cuban toast, freshly squeezed orange juice and a side of two ham *croquetas* and a guava filled pastry.

They were stunned with the amount of food she ordered, but once it arrived, she ate it slowly and delicately. The two officers watched her for a while as she savored each bite.

"So, tell me Angela," Kux said. "Why did your father say he killed those people?"

She took a bite of the toast then shook her head. "He didn't say that."

"He said it to me," Kux said. "Loud and clear."

She was still shaking her head. "No. Dad doesn't speak English. The words came out of his mouth, but it wasn't him speaking."

Both men frowned, but it was Leddy's adrenaline that soared. "What do you mean?" he asked.

"Someone spoke *through* my dad. I wasn't there to hear what he said, but if you knew my dad, or if you spoke to him now, you'd hear that it probably wasn't even his voice."

Leddy swallowed hard. "Are you saying he was…possessed?"

Angela coughed. She covered her mouth with a napkin, nearly choking – though it sounded as though she was laughing. After composing herself, she took a large sip of the orange juice then cleared her throat. "You almost made me spit out my food, that was so funny! Was he possessed? What do you think this is, some kind of Linda Blair, pea-soup spewing movie?" She looked to Kux and pointed at Leddy. "Is this guy serious?"

Kux stifled his smile. "What do you mean that someone was talking *through* him?"

Angela pushed her plate aside, almost empty. "Look, my family on my dad's side comes from a long line of…people with gifts, if you will. For example, my grandfather was psychic. Kinda famous for it back in the day. My dad, he's different. He can be a sort of conduit."

"Conduit?" Kux asked.

"He can talk to the dead, and conversely, the dead can talk through him."

A moment of silence fell over the table as Leddy and Kux absorbed the information Angela so matter-of-factly told them.

"What about you?" Kux asked her.

"Me? What about me?"

"Do you have any of these...*gifts*?"

Angela finished the orange juice. "For starters I can tell you're a nonbeliever."

"So, you're psychic too?"

"I can tell by the look on your face." She turned to Leddy. "You on the other hand, Mr. Let's-Call-An-Exorcist. You believe me, don't you?"

He cleared his throat and shifted in his seat uncomfortably. "It's Officer Leddy."

"Oh, okay." Her attention was back on Kux. "Look, the truth is, my dad didn't kill anyone. But something in that area, a spirit of some kind, is claiming responsibility for it. Talk to my dad. He'll tell you."

"I gotta say," Kux said, "I have been working here in Miami for almost six months, and I don't think I will ever hear an alibi quite like this one ever again."

"For those who believe," she said, looking at Leddy, "no explanation is necessary." She turned her attention to Kux. "For those who do not, no explanation will suffice."

The officers exchanged glances; Leddy smirking.

"Have more people claimed responsibility for the murders?" Angela asked.

Neither of them answered. Both their faces went pale.

"Thought so."

"So what are we dealing with here?"

She shook her head. "I couldn't tell you."

"What can you tell us, then?" Leddy asked.

"I can tell you that I appreciated breakfast. And that I should get home before mom freaks."

She jumped off the booth and wiped her hands on her jeans as she made her way out of the restaurant, leaving the two officers behind.

While Leddy paid, Kux followed Angela outside. The rain had begun, so they stood underneath the restaurant's small overhang.

"I'll tell you what I do know," she said, looking over her shoulder as though she wanted no one else to hear. "Teddy in there is jaded. He believes too much."

"His name is Leddy."

"That's not what his friends call him."

Kux frowned.

"It doesn't matter. What does matter is that my dad did not commit any murders, and I think you believe me."

"It doesn't matter what I believe..."

"And by the time this is over, you will believe more. I can't tell you who or what is doing this, but I can tell you that it's not going to end well."

"But..."

"Don't interrupt me. I need to finish before your partner joins us. Unfortunately, it's all going to be on you. If you don't stop him now, it will haunt you the rest of your days. Don't let the kids get involved."

"What kids?"

Angela shook her head and shrugged. "That's all I see."

Leddy stepped out and faced both of them. He studied the blank look on Kux's face, then looked to Angela. "Did I interrupt something?"

Kux shook his head.

Leddy turned to Angela. "Let's get you home."

"Actually, I'll walk. I like the rain."

"Are you sure?" Leddy asked.

"Let her," Kux said. "We have to get back to the station, anyway."

Leddy nodded, and both men turned to the sedan parked just before them.

"Kux," Angela called.

He spun to face her.

"I'll see you again."

Without another word, Kux jumped into the passenger side of the car and out of the rain. He watched as Angela stepped from beneath the canopy and began walking home.

As they pulled out of the parking lot, Angela's warning on Kux's mind, her words rang in his ears. *I'll see you again*. She said. Was that a fact? Was it a premonition?

All Kux could think was; *Not if I can help it*.

Encounters

Todd hadn't gone home, according to his wife, Mary. When Hector called at nearly five in the afternoon, he was careful not to tell Mary anything about the day's events, and from the sound in her voice, it did not appear as though she knew. In fact, before they hung up, Mary told Hector that she hadn't heard from Todd all day. Hector thanked her, hung up, then called Todd's mobile for the tenth time that hour. And for the tenth time, it went to voicemail. There was only one place left to look, and if history served, he knew exactly where Todd would be.

There was one other time when Todd didn't show up at home after the traumatic incident that caused his reoccurring nightmares. Hector found him drowning his sorrows in whiskey and cigarettes at The Cell Block, and when he opened the door to the small tavern, he found Todd sitting on the same stool along the bar that he found him in years before. His back slouched, void of all support, both hands around a half empty tumbler filled with brown liquid, and his eyes fixated on the mahogany slab before him. History has an ugly habit of repeating itself, Hector thought.

He walked in, dusted the rain water off himself, and took a deep breath. He didn't expect the encounter to go well – not after the way he backed Jack Roth up instead of his partner. He slowly approached Todd, and halfway to the bar, Todd looked up and noticed him. As though he didn't know the man however, he returned his gaze to the glass before him without a single word or emotion across his face.

Hector sat on the stool beside Todd and ordered the same as what his partner was drinking.

"I know you probably want to punch me," Hector said, his head down. "But I want you to know what I did was for your own good."

Todd responded by taking the rest of his drink in one gulp. He stood from the stool, staggered to his feet while reaching into his pocket and tossing a couple bills onto the bar. Without even looking in Hector's direction, Todd began to walk toward the bar's exit.

"Can we please talk about this?" Hector asked, loud enough for the few other patrons to hear.

Todd forcefully pushed the venue door open and left.

It was raining much harder now than it was when he arrived, but Hector still ran out toward the parking lot after Todd who was drunkenly trying to unlock his car door.

"You shouldn't be driving," Hector said. "You're drunk."

"And you're an asshole!" Todd said quickly. Despite the slight slur in his words, he spun to face Hector so quickly that it startled him.

"Listen, I'm looking out for you, is all," Hector said.

"Oh, well thank you very much for your supervision, Hector. But I don't need you to look out for me. Not like that."

"I know you're having the nightmares again. I know that this case is starting to mess…"

"You don't know shit! You think you know what I'm going through? So you agree with Roth to kick me off the case, for what? So you can help me? Or is it so you can get all the credit once *I* catch the fucker?" Todd leaned in closer, nearly tripping over his own feet. "Because I will catch him. Before you and your little team of back stabbing cunts." He shoved Hector's shoulder with his index finger. "Do you hear me, asshole?"

Hector put both hands up, partially in surrender, and partially to protect himself. "That's not what this is about, and you know it."

"Of course it is! You've always been jealous of me!"

Hector tried his best to understand that Todd was both angry and drunk, but his anger was starting to peak. "What the fuck are you talking about?"

"You always want lead detective in any case we work on!"

"I'm happy to let you lead because I don't need the title."

"You always take credit for the work that *I* do!"

"Bullshit."

Todd took a step back and smiled viciously. "You've always wanted my wife."

The volcano that erupted in the pit of his stomach was hard to hide. Hector bit his bottom lip, and all he could muster was, "What?"

Todd waved his finger. "Don't act like you don't know what I'm talking about. I see the way you look at her when you think I'm not looking."

"Okay, that's enough."

"Your wife left you and so you start eyeing mine? You were my best friend, Hector. *My partner*! And now it's clear you set me up to get me out of the way so you can finally have everything that I worked to build."

"Todd, stop it."

But Todd didn't stop. He quickly approached Hector, their noses inches away. Hector turned his face slightly, the smell of alcohol on Todd's breath making his eyes burn.

"You can fuck me over all you want," Todd said through his teeth, "but you will never, never, fuck my wife. Do you hear me?"

The punch Hector launched at Todd's face wasn't the strongest he could gather, but he took into account that Todd was drunk, and the blow landed right against his cheek. It was undoubtedly more the alcohol that caused Todd to stumble backward and collapse onto the gravel. He wasn't unconscious, but the fall made him even more inebriated than the alcohol.

Hector shook his hand in the rain, cursing the air. Looking at Todd sprawled out and moaning on the floor before him, he said "You brought this on yourself, Todd."

During the fall, Todd's keys fell beside him and Hector picked them up. Wiping the rain from his face, he put the keys in his pocket, and extracted his cell phone. He looked at Todd once more, struggling to even sit up, and he called Mary.

*

Dr. Leppe jogged into the parking lot, a briefcase slung over one shoulder, her purse slung over the other, and holding a manila folder over her head to prevent the rain from dampening her long, auburn hair. It was failing miserably. She rushed through the parking lot in high heels, and keys in hand, remotely unlocked her car so that she can reach cover quickly. The car didn't respond, but she paid it no mind because she threw the door open anyway. Tossing her bags inside, she jumped in, slammed the door shut and let out a sigh of relief. She wiped the rain away from her forehead then adjusted the rearview mirror to check her usually flawless makeup.

Her entire body reacted to the silhouette she found staring back at her through the reflection of the mirror, and though she didn't think to just open the door and jump out of the car to safety, she did let out a frightened yell. After the initial shock, she recognized the face in the reflection, but it would be a long time before her heart settled.

"Jesus, Jack, You scared the shit out of me!" she said between breaths. "What the hell are you doing in my car?"

Roth shrugged. "It was raining. I didn't want to get wet."

"So you break into my car?"

Roth calmly shook his head. "Where's the evidence box, Jennifer?"

She turned halfway to face him. "I told you, locked away in my house. Why?"

"I want it back."

"And you'll get it back."

Roth nodded. He looked around the car, he looked out the windows, but never once did he look directly at Jennifer. "Grazer's off the case," he said, finally.

"You finally managed to do it?" she asked. "How?"

"I used his previous incident as an excuse. He fired his weapon yesterday, and I told him he needs a psyche eval before he gets his badge back. He may reach out to you."

Jennifer's heart had nearly settled, but hearing Roth's news, it jolted with anticipation. If Grazer did reach out to her, she could ask him for the evidence box and tell Grazer what she knew.

"If he does," Roth continued, "you let me know."

"He's been coming to me for the past six months," she said.

Roth frowned. He glanced at her, but only for a second. "Has he told you anything pertinent to the case?"

She smiled slightly. "Doctor-patient-confidentiality."

"I think we're past the point of procedure and morals here, aren't we, doctor?"

"What do you want, Jack? Did you break into my car just to tell me that you finally succeeded in getting Grazer off the case?" Jennifer asked. "You don't think a phone call would have sufficed?"

Roth took a deep breath. He closed his eyes and let it out slowly. Jennifer watched as his hands gripped his knees, his fingers turning white. There was something he wanted to say, that much she could tell. The trick was getting him to say it. "Grazer," she said. "Did you relieve him because he was getting close?"

"I knew it would come back to haunt me," he said after a brief moment of silence. "I should have just told them the truth."

"What is the truth?" she asked, her entire body filing with anticipation at finally getting it out of him. But he didn't respond. "It's not too late, Jack," she said. "I can help you."

Roth laughed. "Of course it is." He looked down at his hands. "I'm on his list, you know."

Jennifer didn't respond. She didn't want to gear him off track by asking a question or making a statement that would derail his train of thought.

"I don't know why he hasn't come after me yet, but he will. That much I know. I need to find him before he gets to me. And I need to do it alone." He suddenly threw the car door open and made a quick move to bounce out of the car.

"Jack, wait!" Jennifer called. "Why do you think you're on his list? Tell me!"

He leaned back into the car, rain falling onto his back. "I saw him."

Jennifer frowned. "You saw Mason Bayer?"

He shook his head. "I saw the boy. That's how I know he's coming for me." He slammed the door and within seconds, he disappeared into the storm.

Suddenly, her hair, makeup or clothes were of no concern. Jennifer jumped out of the car and into the rain, trying her damnedest to find Jack Roth. He was gone – probably in his own car and on the road already.

I saw the boy. His voice rang in her head. Suddenly, the evidence box, handing it over to the detectives, none of it seemed important.

She jumped back into her car, frantically looked for her cell phone in her briefcase, and once she found it, she called Grazer praying he wouldn't ignore her.

If Grazer was relieved of duty, it only meant one thing; he was getting close, and Jack Roth was willing to do anything to hide the truth, even if it meant getting himself killed – or killing someone else in the process.

Lingering Spirits

Grazer's heart pounded against his temples and sweat was stinging his eyes. He locked eyes with the rookie, trying to convince him that it was going to be okay with a simple glare, but the fear in the young man's eyes made it clear that he did not get the message.

"Take your shot!" the perp yelled. "Shoot me and this pig gets it before I hit the ground!"

Grazer's sweaty palm gripped the gun tighter. "There's no way out of this," he told the killer, trying his best to remain composed.

"Come on!" the perp yelled. "Do it! You fucking pig!"

There was no back up coming, that much he knew. The building had already been cleared, and the few remaining officers outside had no idea what was happening. The realization that they were completely alone made Grazer more nervous than the perp holding gun at the rookie.

"The place is surrounded," Grazer said. "Drop the gun! You're done!"

The killer laughed and said something Grazer didn't hear. He was busy looking into the eyes of the scared rookie; his eyes begging to be saved, and Grazer was his only chance.

Please the rookie said, but without making a sound. Grazer read his lips followed directly by, *Help me.*

Grazer pursed his lips, clenched his teeth and wrapped his index finger around the trigger.

"Do it!" the killer yelled.

He took a deep breath and made a conscious effort to control his adrenaline. His heart was pounding relentlessly making his hand slightly quiver.

"Come on, asshole! Shoot!"

Ignoring the perp's taunt, he closed his right eye, aiming the pistol at the killer's forehead. "Last chance," he said. "Let the officer go."

"Nope," the killer said.

The explosion that followed was deafening. Grazer wanted to yell out, but his throat would not produce a sound as the explosion echoed in his head like a jackhammer – as though God himself was knocking on his brain with all his might. He watched as the side of the rookie's head exploded outward, his body immediately falling limp and out of the killer's grip. The killer laughed, the smoking barrel of the gun now pointed at Grazer. "That's your fault," he said. "You waited too long. Now, you die."

The second explosion didn't seem as loud, and it was more than likely due to the shock that immediately took over Grazer's body, seizing his ears, his sight, even his ability to think. The only thing it didn't seize was his aim. Pulling the trigger resulted in a gaping hole between the killer's eyes, and he fell to the floor beside the young rookie. Both dead.

As if on cue, Todd woke up from the dream, but he didn't sit up, gasping the way he had every night the dream surfaced. Perhaps it was due to the fact that he actually finished the dream this time around, or maybe it was because of the alcohol lingering in his system. His body, however; that was a different story. His heart was still racing, the sweat that poured off his face was evidence of stress, and his mind reeled with images, not of the dream, but of when it actually happened.

The rookie's name was Lanza. That's all Grazer ever really knew before he was shot. He came to know him as Daniel Lanza just after, and when he told his parents of their son's death, he referred to him simply as Daniel. Grazer was hailed a hero by his peers for killing the murderer, wanted for the rape and murder of a tourist, but Grazer couldn't get the killer's words out of his mind; *That was your fault* the killer told him as Lanza's body fell to the floor. The image stained his memory, and no matter how much Grazer tried to convince himself that there was nothing he did wrong, he could not believe it. If he had the chance to do it again, he would save the rookie.

He closed his eyes tightly and sat up on his bed slowly. His head was pounding and his mouth was dry – a result of the drink. But the soreness on his left cheek came as a mystery to him for a second or two.

He suddenly remembered his argument with Hector, then remembered winding up on the floor. The pain in his cheek told him what he needed to know; Hector punched him. *Probably deserved it*, he thought to himself.

That was all he remembered. He didn't know how he got home, or how he wound up in his bedroom, in his own bed where he woke up. He looked around the room and Mary was not with him. He wondered how much she knew, and if she was sleeping in another room in anger.

He looked at the alarm clock beside his bed; *7:37 P.M.* It was still early.

Todd laid back down and closed his eyes again. He wanted to put the day behind him. He took a deep breath, and before long, he began to fall asleep again, praying he wouldn't dream the rest of the night.

*

Before Leddy opened the door to her apartment, he took a deep breath. Angela made fun of him when he suggested possession as the reason several people, including Tina, had taken claim of the murders, but he knew that it was a real possibility. He also knew Tina was in a fragile state, depressed and vulnerable, and that is the perfect elixir for spiritual interference. It was that reason he was hesitant to open the door.

He was a believer because he had witnessed it himself. There was no doubt in his belief in the supernatural and the fact that *they* can interfere with our lives without knowing it. If he placed his keys on the dining table when he got home from work and found them on the floor the next day, he was convinced it was the work of a poltergeist. And to him, just as Tina's depression opened the door to another realm, so did the simple belief in that realm.

Visiting Tina put him in as much danger of interaction as Tina was. His several visits and witnessing her episode was proof enough that *something* was tormenting her – and if he continued interfering, that something could latch on to him. As he gripped the door knob with a sweaty palm, he promised himself that this would be his last visit before finding her some kind of help, be it a witch doctor, a priest, even shock therapy. What did Angela Ortega know?

He opened the door into total darkness. Without stepping inside the apartment, he reached in, caressing the inside walls for the light switch.

He could hear breathing somewhere inside, the heavy breath of someone very close, watching him.

"Tina," he called out, still searching for the switch.

No one answered.

The thought of flipping on the lights and finding Tina, crouched on the floor, staring back at him through the face of the demon that had been distressing her made his skin erupt in goose bumps.

"Tina," he called out again.

Still, no answer.

He found the switch and flipped it upward. The lights came to life, killing Leddy's overactive imagination, and the breathing he thought he heard.

Leddy's mouth hung open in disbelief as he slowly took a step inside the apartment. His eyes scanned the entire area, his brain registering what he was seeing, but his mind refusing to believe it.

The place was clean. Spotless, in fact. The couch was no longer stained in sweat. The empty bottles and random articles of dirty clothing that were strewn about the last time he was there were all picked up and disposed of. The dining table was clear of the thick layer of dust and grime that had accumulated over the past couple months, even the strong smell of urine was replaced by a fresh, lavender scent. The kitchen was also cleaned. Dishes were washed and put away, the floor glimmering with reflection from the lights above. Scott stood in the center of the room, dumbfounded, and somewhat relieved.

Did Tina manage to wrestle her demons on her own?

"Tina," he said to the air, followed closely by, "Sandy."

Neither responded.

Name Not One Man

He was about to make his way into the hall, toward the bedroom to see if Tina was asleep, perhaps. On his way, he saw the note out of the corner of his eye. It was on the kitchen table, a piece of paper folded in half, his name scribbled on the outside. Slowly, he picked it up, and opened it.

Scott,
  I left the door unolcked knowing you would visit me, and for that, I thnak you. You've always looked out for me, and I can't tell you how much I apprceiate that.
  You were right, though. I do need help. After waking this monring with yet another hang over, I thuogth of doing something for myself – somtehing right. I claened myself (and the apartment) up, and I'm laeving town for a while. As you know, I don't really have a somwehere to go, but I will be okay. Don't freak out. I'll be in touch.
  Thank you so much for being a real frined and for looking out for me. Sorry I was scary! I scared myeslf, though. That's why I'm doing this. I'll be in touch.
                                                                  Tina.

He folded the note and put it into his pocket. Smiling, he looked around the room. "Good for you, Tina," he said to the air.

When he reached the door, he took one last look into the apartment, and for a moment, he forgot about the spirits that lingered. Maybe he forgot about them because they were gone. The air felt *clean*. He turned off the light, closed the door, and for the last time, left Tina's apartment wishing her all the best the world had to offer.

Moments earlier, he was going to check for her in her bedroom, and only the letter stopped him. Had he made his way, he would have found her, or remnants of her at least. She was crouched on her bed, her hands folded over her mouth to stifle the snarling giggles that erupted from her gullet, pieces of Sandy scattered about before her.

Inner Demons

Don't let the kids get involved Angela told him.
What the fuck does that mean?

Billy Kux was in his bed, but sleep was the furthest thing from him. Lying on his back, one hand on his forehead, the other on his stomach, Billy stared at the ceiling, but at no spot in particular.

The rain outside was normally soothing to him, one of the things he found he liked about Miami were the afternoon, nightly showers. Calming as they normally were, it did nothing to quiet his mind. His thoughts were not so much on what the case had revolved around, rather, what the young, alleged psychic had told him.

The thoughts came to him directly after showering and slipping into the comfort of his bed in the small room. He closed his eyes, expecting to drift into the land of slumber, but his mind had its own plans.

Don't let the kids get involved.

The sentence repeated over and over in his mind like a broke record, and no matter how much he tried to put it back on track, he couldn't. She told him she couldn't talk to Leddy because Leddy believed *too much* and that would be a distraction. Truth was, Kux wasn't a believer, not six months before. But after working the Bayer case, seeing what he's seen, he couldn't help but think *something* was at work; the mysterious murders, Tina's episode and subsequent spiral into depression, not to mention the cryptic words of the young psychic.

Unfortunately, it's all going to be on you, she had told him. *If you don't stop it now, it will haunt you the rest of your days.*

While Grazer and Corona were the veteran detectives on the case, how was it possible that it was up to him, a rookie cop, to "stop" it?

Billy sat up and swung his legs over the edge of the bed. His back, losing all support, arched as he rubbed his face with both hands as though it would clear his mind with the thoughts running rampant. It didn't.

Don't let the kids get involved.

There were no kids, not that Billy could think of. Did one of the future victims have children? There were three left; Michael O'Niell, Patricia Greer, and Tomas Brewer (aka victims *EVIF, XIS* and *NEVES*, in no particular order, should Mason succeed). From memory, Billy could think of only one who had a teenage daughter – Katie, or something. She was Brewer's. Would Mason Bayer go after Brewer's daughter if they didn't catch him in time? *Kids. She said kids.* There was more than one.

He stood from the bed, frustrated at his own thoughts. Crossing the small room toward the dresser, Billy cursed the air, knowing full well the night would be spent sleepless thanks to the inner demons that were his own thoughts. He picked up the digital wrist watch from the dresser, directly beside the holstered pistol, and looked at the time: 11:47 PM.

He thought of calling Leddy, tell him what Angela said without his presence but two things stopped him; 1) the time, 2) he didn't need Leddy to add more to his already conflicting thoughts. Possession and the supernatural only added another layer to his restless mind.

Is what happened to Tina somehow related? he thought, against his will.

Billy closed his eyes, disappointed in himself, then let his stream of consciousness take over as he threw himself back onto the bed.

The image of Tina's episode invaded his head like the demon that possessed her. Her grit teeth, the snarl in her lips, the blood that spewed from her mouth. Even the voice that spoke to them beyond the clenched jaw was beastly, *I killed them*, it said. *And you too.*

Tina was not the only one to claim responsibility for the murders, and though neither Brewer, Tina nor Roberto Ortega made it clear *which* murders they were referring to, the team all knew exactly which they were.

What was causing them to confess to the murders? Brewer and Tina were directly connected to Mason Bayer is some way – Brewer was on the board at the DOH, Tina was on the team investigating the murders. Did that mean the rest of the investigating team would be *touched* by the madness that they were? And what about Ortega? Was he somehow linked to Bayer as well?

Kux took a deep breath, trying to organize his thoughts, feeling as though there was something he was missing that would connect all the dotted lines, one detail he was missing that would help make sense of everything he was thinking. But there was nothing. The fact was, none of it made any sense – Mason Bayer was killing people, three others claimed responsibility if only for a brief moment, and the cryptic warnings of a psychic girl who, in their brief conversation, said enough to convince him that she was the real deal. Logically, there was no explanation for it all, leaving Billy to one conclusion; *There's more to this than we think.*

The fact was Mason Bayer would probably go down as one of the most mysterious killers that ever existed. In each and every one of the four murder scenes, there was no trace of anyone outside of the person who was actually murdered. Even in the Shaw murder, as his wife slept directly beside him, she heard nothing. No finger prints, no forced entry, nothing. It quickly eliminated the possibility of two murders, despite the fact that Cabello and DeCocq were both killed on the same night, one clear across town from the other. Victims *ENO* and *OWT* were amongst the most mysterious of the *ROUF* so far, but also the most revealing. It was one man.

Name not one man, Billy thought, a slight smile forming on his lips. The most famous of palindromes, read the same way forward as it was backward. Quite suiting for the killer who numbered his victims in backward English, and because more than one had taken responsibility for his murders.

Despite his clever thought, a small chill ran through his entire body.

Deciding that if he was, indeed, going to get some sleep, it would need to happen with the aid of something that would ease his mind. He left his room and walked into the darkened hallway of his small apartment. His bare feet on the cold tile floor, Billy cursed Angela, Leddy, Tina, and Mason for causing the sleepless night, and for the feeling of dread he felt the moment he stepped into the hall.

The light switch was at the other end of the hallway, and though it was less than five feet away, the darkened space made him uneasy. He felt a thousand eyes upon him, eyes of the ghosts that possessed his thoughts.

He made his way toward the switch and flipped it upward, the lights flickering to life and exorcising any ghosts from the hall. But as he stepped into the living room, a troubling thought entered his mind, revealing that not every demon had left his mind.

The word *NEVES* took up most of the living room wall. Blood dripped from the turn and edge of every letter, falling onto the body that was lying on the couch beneath it.

Billy closed his eyes and took a deep breath. It was his imagination. It wasn't real.

He flipped the switch to the living room, and nothing out of the ordinary appeared before him.

He shook his head, then continued to the kitchen, making sure to turn the lights on before entering. He made his way to the freezer and opened it up, standing before the cold air for a moment. His skin erupted in goose bumps as he allowed the frozen air to envelope him and relieve the heat on his skin from the rising blood pressure.

Behind the frozen steaks and ice bucket, Billy found the cure to his rampant thoughts and impending insomnia. The bottle of vodka was as cold as the air in the freezer, and as he held it to his forehead for a moment before serving a healthy amount into a tumbler glass. In three large swigs, glass was emptied, and he carried the second glassful to his room, leaving the lights on as he left each room.

"Fuck you," he told the air, but saying it to Angela, Mason, et al. He would sleep tonight – even if it killed him.

After the second glass was emptied, his mind was fogged, and much calmer. It was just about one in the morning when Billy fell into a dreamless, thoughtless sleep; a sleep so deep he didn't hear his mobile phone come to life at four in the morning.

He wouldn't be reprimanded for missing Corona's phone call. He was, after all, a rookie and it was not mandatory that he be called in. However, Billy was on the team investigating the Bayer murders, and he would have liked to know that victim number *EVIF* had just been found.

CHAPTER EVIF

He made his way down the staircase toward the basement taking slow methodical steps. He wanted to call the boy out by name, instead optioning to listen for any signs that he was in the room. The beam of light aided his way to the ground floor, and once he arrived, he studied the rest of the room.

A table was in the center of the room, streaks of dried blood staining it. The tools above; hacksaws, knives and hatchets, shined in the ray of his flashlight.

The slaughter room, he thought.

The young officer walked around the table, sweeping the light to the left and right, and finding nothing more than what was visible to him.

His shoulders slumped. His day as a hero would have to wait.

"Where'd you go, Mason Bayer?" he asked the air, and made his way toward the staircase.

The dragging noise he heard was the same as when he moved the wall to expose the staircase leading to the basement, but it was coming from the basement itself.

He spun on his heel to see the wall on the eastern side of the room moving outward. His heart skipped a beat as he moved to the other side of the table, his hand on his gun, and aimed the beam toward the wall.

The wall stopped moving. No one stepped out from the other side.

"Mason," he called out softly. "Is that you?"

The young officer smiled when the little boy stepped out from behind the wall. His hair, a tangled mess, covered most of his forehead. His wrinkled clothes were stained with dirt...or blood. His face was as thin as the rest of his body, his sunken cheeks yellowed with malnutrition.

The young officer stepped toward him quickly, and the boy took a step back, his black eyes widening as he stepped back behind the wall.

"Oh, hey, don't be scared, buddy," he said to the boy. "I'm here to help you."

The boy peeked out and stared at the officer.

"Are you Mason?" he asked the boy. "Mason Bayer?"

The boy looked the officer up and down, then nodded slowly.

Friday, June 5th

Luis was driving, Jo in the passenger side. Grazer smiled, seeing his son and Corona's daughter so close. They seemed happy; happy enough to maybe suggest something romantic was happening. The way she looked at him, the way he laughed with her. It was heartwarming.

Until he reached over, grabbed the back of her head and slammed it downward into the dashboard. Jo screamed in pain as he did it again. Blood covered her face, the skin on her forehead breaking. And Luis did it again.

The car swerved, leaving skid marks on the gravel, and sped recklessly down the darkened street until it finally crashed into a lamp post, the metal twisting around it with a horrific explosion.

The last time Todd looked at the clock, it was 7:37 PM. The time had not changed though he felt he slept at least a couple hours. He sat up on the bed slowly, rubbing his eyes as visions of the newest nightmare cursed his mind, and looked at the clock again. It was then that he realized the time read 7:37 AM.

Todd Grazer looked around the room, bewildered that he slept more than twelve hours. Odds are he would have continued his slumber had it not been for the horrid vision his brain fed him.

There was noise seeping into the bedroom.

His head fogged, Todd struggled to make sense of the noise, hearing several voices at once, some of them incoherent. He looked around the room; Mary still not beside him, and though he wasn't sure whether or not she slept beside him at all, he could hear her now, somewhere in the house. By the sound of it, somewhere downstairs; the living room or kitchen.

It was then that he remembered Mary's sister Mayra and her daughter Rebecca were visiting for the summer from New York, and staying with the Grazers for, as Mary put it, as long as they wanted. Todd sat on the bed listening to the jumble of voices and was just as delighted to hear the noise as much as he dreaded facing them. He was happy to have the company; his own teenagers, Cynthia and Luis, were complete now that their cousin, Rebecca was back in their lives after moving two years before, and Mary now had the companionship she needed with her sister beside her. But having to face them now, after the night before – *how much do they know?* – and having to explain why he wasn't going to the office would prove difficult.

He threw the covers off him, to the side of the bed, and the stench of liquor seeping from his pores burned his nostrils and made his already nauseous stomach turn in disgust. Sliding off the bed, he attempted to straighten his back and the muscles in his body seized at first then screamed in agony as though he had used every square inch of his body aid in his bender the night before.

He cursed into the air in a whisper, it's all his dry mouth would produce.

He flipped the switched to the master bathroom and the light stung his eyes for a moment, his headache knocking on his temples as a result. He rubbed his eyes, stumbling toward the sink's faucet and splashing his face with cold water.

It felt amazing; his skin, like the rest of his body, dehydrated by the intake of alcohol the night before, absorbed the water like arid soil. It was complete rejuvenation, though a careless scrub of the bruise on his left cheek proved displeasing. The memory of Hector's fist flying toward his face flashed somewhere beyond the headache and Todd closed his eyes again in an attempt to ignore it. Avoiding his reflection in the mirror above the sink, Todd turned the faucet off and looked to the tub.

A shower would wash away his sickening feeling, he thought, as well as the sins of the night before. The cleanse would do him well he thought, but the moment his bare feet stepped onto the cold tile, the image of Mercedes Rodic's skinned body resting on her shower floor possessed his mind and took the rest of his thoughts hostage.

She was still alive he thought to himself. He could only imagine what was going through the poor woman's mind as she desperately hung on to life. Did she think she could actually survive? Was she frantic with the thought that she was going to die? Were her thoughts on her family just before she took her last breath?

Todd closed his eyes, allowing the warm water to roll down his body and soothe his aching muscles. His head hung below his shoulders, his hands, resting on the wall before him, turned to fists. After a few moments, his mind cycling through the list of victims that had been numbered over the course of six months, he slid his right hand toward the shower's chrome faucet. Slowly, he turned the handle up and to the left, the water falling over him becoming even warmer. Steam began to rise around him like spirits rising from the earthly graves. The shower doors began to fog, and Todd watched the curtain of mist spread over the glass until almost all of it was covered.

He lifted his finger to the glass and slowly cut the fog, first with a straight line, then with a series of curves and strokes until the word *RUOF* was before him. Reminiscent of the way Rodic was numbered, Todd stared at the word, then just underneath, he wrote *EVIF*. Underneath that, *XIS*. He wanted to write the number *NEVES*, if for nothing else, just to see what it would look like, the way condensation would drip from the curve of each letter like droplets of clear blood, but in doing so, he thought he was somehow completing Mason Bayer's work for him. It was bad luck to finish the numbers. He swept the glass door with the palm of his hand, wiping away the backward writing.

He turned the shower's handle to the left some more, the water becoming hotter still. The heat hurt upon his skin, but it wasn't exactly a burn, so he turned the faucet to the left until he could turn it no more. It didn't take long for him to feel the temperature rise – the skin on his face, shoulders and chest turning red from the hot water that was falling onto him. It soon became intense, making it hard for him to breath, the pain becoming too much to bear, and he turned the nozzle to the right, making the water lukewarm once again. His mind was on Mercedes Rodic – her skin melted off and lying beside her in a slimy clump on the shower floor. *How hot does the water have to be?* Beyond boiling, he answered himself. The second question he asked himself struck him as worse; *How much did she feel?* She was still alive when they arrived, albeit unconscious until she reached out to Billy for help. Without flesh, her muscles, tendons, veins, even some bones were exposed, yet she managed to stay alive long enough for them to witness her demise – and for the number *RUOF* to almost magically appear before them. *How much pain was she in?* Surely, the brain would shut down its own sensors in order to defend the body against the onslaught of pain, but how long did it take to get to that point? And again, how much could the poor woman *feel?*

He shook his head and turned the shower off. It wasn't his job, as a member of law enforcement, to concern himself with such trivial matters as how did the victim feel during death. To become attached to a victim is to hinder his ability to do his job as a detective and in that, Todd realized he and Mason Bayer had more in common than he realized. To Bayer, Mercedes Rodic was victim number *RUOF*, and to Grazer, she was also just a number; the fourth in a string. That's it. Thinking of her as a defenseless victim made her human.

Grazer stood before the mirror above the sink, a towel around his waist and dark circles under his eyes. Perhaps Roth was right to suspend him. Maybe he was becoming too obsessed with the case. *But that's what makes me a great detective*, he thought to himself, rubbing the three day beard on his face. What should he be if not fixated on finding the most elusive killer he'd seen in his twenty year career? Perhaps Roth was right to suspend him, but he also knew that from the get go, Roth was doing everything he could to interrupt the investigation, even instructing them to ignore the prime suspect for a while. If he was no longer on the Mason Bayer case, he would do a little of his own investigative work and find out exactly what Roth's motives were.

He knew just the person he would start with.

*

Dressed in his usual attire, slacks and a button down shirt, Todd made his way into the dining room where his wife and her sister were already seated, sipping coffee and gossiping about whatever reality show they both watched – *Housewives of Somewhere-or-Other*. But their conversation came to a halt the moment he entered, both of them immediately looking to him. The smile on his face was not met by either one of them, and while Mayra's look went back to her coffee, it was Todd's wife who kept her eyes locked on his.

"Good morning, ladies," he said.

"Good morning," Mayra said without looking up.

Mary said nothing.

Mayra stood from the table, her mug in hand. "I'm going to shower and get the kids up," she said to Mary. As she passed Todd, she gave him a slight smile. "Have a good day," she said.

Todd thanked her and watched as she left the room. "Well that was a little less awkward than I was expecting," he said to his wife, still smiling.

"What happened last night?" Mary asked.

The question rang in his head as the vague images of the night before flashed before him. Arguing with Hector, Hector's fist, the wet gravel. He gathered Hector had taken him home, but with Mary's question, he wondered how much Hector had told her, if anything.

"Had a little too much to drink is all," Todd said, figuring it wasn't a lie, but hoping to coax more details out of her if she knew anything more.

Mary nodded. "I know that," she said. "What happened, though? You got off of work and went drinking by yourself instead of coming home to me? To your kids? We hardly see you as it is."

Todd hung his head and nodded. "I had a rough day, is all. I needed to clear my head, and I over did it. It's nothing personal."

Mary shook her head and curled her lip at him. She stood from the table and walked to the kitchen to refill her mug and Todd followed. "Hey, I'm sorry, okay? This case is just…"

"This case is doing the same thing to you that the other one did. You're not sleeping, you're not eating, you're drinking too much, and you're never here. I mean, even when you are, you're locked in your office looking at these horrid pictures."

Todd didn't respond. He couldn't think of what to say.

"After the shit you went through last time, you promised me that if you ever got too wrapped up in a case, you'd stop. Well here we are, Todd."

"I can't stop, Mary. I have a job to do, and I promise you this is nothing like the last time. For crissakes, I was responsible for the death of an innocent man! Of course that messed with my head. This is different."

"It may be different, but you've become the same person you were right after it happened. And you stumbling in drunk last night the way you did, it's disgusting. Who the hell brought you home? Was it Hector? And do you even know where your car is?"

Hector hadn't told her anything. He probably pushed Todd out of his car and drove off without a word, thankfully. Mary didn't know about their confrontation, or the fact that he had been suspended.

"I'll take care of it," he told her. "I have to go."

Mary shook her head slowly.

"I love you," he said.

After a moment, she looked to him. "Every day when you leave this house, I pray you come back safely. It's no secret that I hate what you do, and I'm so worried that you're going to get shot or something. Even after twenty years. I even have your badge number memorized in case I need it. But Todd, I don't know how much longer I can keep worrying about you and seeing you do this to yourself."

Todd frowned, his eyes narrowed. "What are you saying?"

"I love you, Todd," she said. "But not like this. Take that for what it is." Without another word, Mary left the kitchen, passed him and disappeared up the stairs.

Todd took a deep breath, and allowed his shoulders to slump.

He hated Mason Bayer for turning him into the man he had become, what he had done to his family, his relationship with Hector. And the hate that brewed inside of him was just what he needed to fuel his need to find the son of a bitch.

Leads

Leddy met Michael O'Neill months before when he and Corona interviewed him after Cabello's and DeCocq's murders. He was a well-manicured man, tall and lanky with a head full of silver hair with just a touch of brown left at the temples. He was in his mid-fifties, and despite the silver hair, the only indication of his age were the slight laugh lines that outlined his cheeks, and though it was something Leddy would have never taken notice of, their distinction was affable.

Those same laugh lines were still visible, but Michael O'Neill was nowhere near smiling. His head hung off the couch's cushion, the features of his face falling victim to gravity and pulled toward his creased forehead. His eyes hung open wide as though he were in a state of shock, and it took a while before Leddy could snap his gaze away from them. The rest of his body was spread out on the couch, his arms and legs spread out in awkward angles as though his last act was a desperate attempt at escape. Most of his intestines had fallen to the floor beside the couch, but the trace of their journey was marked on the brown sofa. Like the other victims, O'Neill's stomach was sliced open and his insides fell outward onto the couch before sliding off and landing beside him with in a wet slop. The word *EVIF* was written, in blood, on the wall in which the couch rested against. Despite that much resembling those of victims *ENO – RUOF*, something was very different.

"His skin," Kux said. "He still has it."

"Very good," Corona followed.

Though Corona was notified of the victim at nearly four in the morning, he decided to hold off calling in Leddy and Kux until he had the chance to analyze the crime scene himself. In the past six months, their team had grown from two, just he and Grazer, to five including Hood, and though he was never opposed to the additional brain power (especially in a case as numinous as the one they were on), it had been a long time since Corona had visited a case with nothing more than his thoughts to guide him through.

He arrived at the small house before sun up, and he wasn't alone after all. The first officer on the scene was a young man Corona had met before, but couldn't remember his name. The officer filled him in on his findings, describing the victim and his surroundings in detail, no sign of forced entry, no one else in the house all sign pointing to the fact the victim lived on his own. Assuring the detective that nothing was touched since he'd arrived, Corona nodded, thanked the officer, and began to approach the house's entry when the young officer stopped him.

"Detective Corona," he said, his voice cracking.

Corona turned to face him.

"It's like nothing you've seen in there, sir. It's horrible."

Corona gave the officer a slight smile and a tight nod. *Nothing you've ever seen in there?* Doubtful. The fact was, it was the least grotesque of the murder scenes in the case so far and that was primarily because the victim still had his skin. The rest of the small house seemed untouched, just as Corona expected. No one had broken in, no one had even appeared to leave after disemboweling their victim, almost as though O'Neill had done it to himself. It was just like the other murders, but something seemed different – *off* even.

This is when Corona not only missed his partner, but needed him. Having someone to bounce ideas and thoughts off of was just an important part of the investigation as observing the crime scene. There were benefits to investigating alone, to think things through in quiet, but a second pair of eyes might pick up on something that one couldn't.

Though he agreed with Roth, that Grazer needed to step away from the case, Corona had no intention of it going as far as it did. Suspending Grazer may have been a bit too extreme, but he was able to talk Roth into letting Grazer come back to the investigation, if only behind the desk. Of course, Hector was never able to tell Todd the news because of the encounter they had the night before, the one that still caused a throbbing pain across his right knuckles. Words were spoken, threats were handed out, and a single punch to the face was thrown. When Hector looked at his watch, he wondered if it was too early to call Todd, if his partner was still sleeping off the bender he had sent himself on. And if he did call, would an apology be in order?

Hector shook his head in an attempt to rid his mind of the thoughts lingering from the night before. *Concentrate on the scene* he told himself, looking at the dead body, the word written on the wall above him, his intestines on the floor, his skin still intact.

Why leave the skin on this time? Was it that fact alone that pecked at Corona's brain telling him something about this murder was off? It was the only thing he could see that was completely different from the others – the house even smelled the same as in the other cases; a lingering smell of rot and sulfur, no doubt caused by the gasses that were released by the exposed guts.

Corona closed his eyes, his mind going through the other murders in a slide show of gruesome pictures; *ENO*: Cabello on her bed, disemboweled. *OWT*: DeCocq sitting on the floor of his living room, his hand holding onto a phone, his insides resting beside him. *EERHT*: Shaw on the bed he shared with his wife. *RUOF*: Rodic on the floor of her bath, her skinless body and innards soaked by the running shower. And now, Michael O'Neill was before him, and the moment Corona opened his eyes, he knew exactly what was so different about the fifth victim.

It was then that he called Kux and Leddy to the scene.

Kux bounced out of his bed as though he had slept for hours. He showered, dressed in his brown and khaki uniform, and was in his car in less than fifteen minutes, during which Leddy had called and asked to be picked up. With both of them rushing to the scene of the newest murder, and with Leddy in the car, Kux's mind began to, once again, confuse itself with the prophecies of a teenage psychic and the possibility of a possessed officer.

"Have you heard from Tina?" Kux asked Leddy, against his own will.

Leddy smiled, and before he even said a word, Kux felt relief. A smile meant good news.

"She's gone," Leddy said. He went on to tell Kux what he found in her clean apartment – the note she left behind claiming she was leaving to get help.

"Where do you think she went?" Kux asked.

Leddy shook his head. "Knowing Tina? Probably checked herself into a clinic or something, but she's too proud to say. I'm pretty sure that's not the last we'll hear of Tina Hood, though. She's stubborn that way."

Kux nodded. "So, do you still think she's possessed?"

Leddy smiled sheepishly as he slowly shook his head. "I think something was different about her. But she's better now, and that's what's important."

"You're willing to forego everything you told me just because she cleaned her apartment and left you a note? Seems unlike you, Leddy. Especially since you were convinced there was some outside force at work here."

"What do you want me to say, Kux?" Leddy asked defensively. "All I can go by is what I see, and what I saw is that she was better."

"Without actually seeing her."

Leddy frowned. "When the hell did you start to believe all this, anyway. I thought you didn't believe in possession."

Kux shook his head. "I never said I didn't. It just seems to me that if she was under the influence of a spirit or whatever, then it wouldn't just vanish like that."

Leddy took a deep breath and looked out the passenger side window. The night's streets were desolate, many of Miami's residents still slumbering before alarm clocks started buzzing around the city and the drones set out for their work day. The sun would begin its ascension in a couple hours, and the darkest part of the day was illuminated by street lamps. "When I said that her apartment was clean, I meant that literally. I also meant that the air itself was clean. These past six months, there was a weight in the air around her – as if something was smothering her entire apartment. When I walked in before I found the note, I could feel the difference." He shook his head again. "I don't know if you understand what I'm saying."

"I do," Billy said.

"I think she's clear of whatever it was holding on to her. I truly think so."

Billy nodded. "Until she shows up at your doorstep with that toy gun you always wanted."

He meant it as a joke, but Leddy did not laugh. They made the rest of the trip in silence, both of them relieved it was only five more minutes before arriving at the crime scene.

Corona was already there as expected, but when they walked past the crowd of officers and forensics geeks, both men stopped and looked around.

"Where's Grazer?" Leddy asked.

Corona ignored the question and instructed the men to observe the body and point out any differences they saw. That was when Kux pointed out the victim still having his skin.

"What else?" Corona asked.

Both Kux and Leddy inched closer to the couch, closer to the victim, searching for any details that were different from the other crime scenes.

"His pose," Leddy said. "It's not as staged as the others."

"You've come a long way, Leddy," Corona said.

Kux walked toward the victim, snapping on latex gloves. He pinched O'Neill's left wrist and carefully began lifting his arm. The resistance from the victim's shoulder and the lack of bend of the elbow told him more. "He's been dead for quite a while," he said. "He's starting to stiffen, over twelve hours, I'd say."

Name Not One Man

Before anyone could respond, a blade fell from the crevice in O'Neill's shoulder, from just underneath his arm pit. Covered in blood, it fell to the floor with a sloppy *clang*.

Kux jumped away from it, unsure what it was it first, but after it settled from the quick bounce, the three men stared it at as though their eyes had been fooled.

Could this be the break they were waiting for?

"You've got to be kidding me," Leddy said, his eyes locked on the large knife.

The handle was made of wood, but not something fashioned by knife manufacturers. It was rigid, no finger grips and no smooth finish. This was something someone made themselves. The blade was large, nearly twelve inches long, and though it was covered in blood, the sharp edge could clearly be seen.

Kux rushed to the supplies case set out on the coffee table and retrieved a plastic evidence bag.

"Get it analyzed ASAP," Corona told him, unable to contain the excitement in his voice. "I want to know what kind of wood that's made of, where he got it from, and for fuck's sake, if we get some kind of DNA or prints on this son of a bitch."

Kux was nodding, the knife already in the bag. "This doesn't make any sense," he said. "Four murders and he leaves no trace. Now, all of a sudden he does this? Something's not right."

"He must have been interrupted," Leddy said. "Why else would he leave that behind? Someone must have seen him or something."

"We're still trying to determine who called it in," Corona said. "It was an anonymous call, a female, from a payphone a few miles from here. We're pulling any surveillance from the area already. If someone saw him, we don't know it yet."

"Either that or he's playing with us," Kux said.

"How do you mean?"

"Think about it. This guy's elusive. He wouldn't make this careless mistake. He wanted us to find this."

"Why?"

Kux and Leddy exchanged glances, and as though through osmosis, Leddy suddenly realized what his partner was getting at. "To keep us occupied," he said, almost in a whisper.

Kux nodded. "We just said that this man wasn't posed like the others, but he was indeed posed for us. He made it look like he was rushed or caught because he knew it would keep us here longer."

Corona missed Grazer even more now. Surely the two of them would have come to the conclusion together. "Which means he could be watching us right now, or going after his last two victims as we speak."

Without another word, the three men ran out of the house, Kux instructing the few officers around to scout the area for anyone who looked suspicious. There were no spectators at the moment, so if Bayer was around watching them, he was hiding somewhere, and he was close.

Corona was on his phone barking orders for available patrol cars to go to each Patricia Greer's and Tomas Brewer's residences.

The three of them were running on adrenaline. This was the closest they had been to finally catching Mason Bayer, and neither of them was about to let the opportunity pass.

A New Union

Todd Grazer did not have an appointment, so Jennifer Leppe was surprised to see him standing outside her office. He was pacing in the small hallway just in front of her door. Immediately, she could see he was pensive and preoccupied with his own thoughts so much that he hadn't realized she stepped off the elevator. And why wouldn't he be? Just the day before, Roth told her that he had suspended Grazer and took him off the Bayer case indefinitely.

The poor guy is probably having a breakdown, she thought.

Still, she was somewhat happy to see him. Roth was breathing down her neck about the Bayer evidence box, and now that Grazer was standing before her, she needed to find out where it was and somehow get it back.

"Good morning, Todd," she said, retrieving a set of keys from her brown leather briefcase.

Todd snapped out of his daze and seemed relieved when he saw the doctor. There was even a slight smile. "Good morning," he said. "I know I don't have an appointment, but I really need to talk to you."

"It's okay," she said, unlocking her office door. "Please, come in."

He did as he was told and followed her into the office. After flipping the light switch on, she stopped in her tracks. What was placed on her desk was not there the day before when she left, and as she heard Todd close the door behind her, her heart skipped a beat.

She slowly turned to face the detective, the smile gone from both their faces.

"I thought maybe you'd like that back," he said, nodding to the evidence box he placed on her desk. He had arrived nearly half an hour before she did, picked the simple lock on her office door, placed the box on her desk and simply waited for her to discover it.

"I did nothing wrong by giving that to you," she said.

Todd nodded. "I know. And I appreciate you doing that. But I think you and I need to talk about a few things; like why did you give it to us in the first place? And more importantly, why is Roth so desperate to see us fail and why are you protecting him?"

Leppe's shoulders slumped and she shook her head. After tossing her briefcase on the chair opposite the desk, she pulled her hair back with both hands and took a deep breath. "Would you like some coffee?" she asked.

"I'm good, thanks."

She nodded, her hands now on her hips. "I'm going to get a cup for myself, so I'll get one for you, too. I'll clear my schedule. You and I will be here a while."

*

It was a Saturday, that much she remembered. What the date was specifically, she didn't know. But it was a while ago; six maybe seven months. She received a call from Lieutenant Jack Roth, but she let it go to voicemail because it was after all the weekend. His voice sounded urgent on the voicemail he left, something about needing to talk to her, that it was important, and very private.

She was free that day, and though she made it a point to not work on the weekend, she did have to visit one patient at the county jail for a report that was due on Monday, so she didn't intend to call Roth until after the weekend. This, apparently, angered the lieutenant who was waiting for her at her home once night had fallen and her day had finally come to an end – or so she thought.

He was sitting on the step to her porch, the smell of bourbon on his breath and a box beside him. She remembered the night was cold because after parking in her driveway, she could see the smoke of his breath leaving his mouth, and the slight shiver his torso carried. Concerned, she rushed beside him and asked if he was okay.

"Can we go inside?" he asked her. "I need to ask you a favor." His words were somewhat slurred, but he stood and walked like someone who was completely sober.

After serving him a mug of tea, she sat on one side of the coffee table, he on the other, the evidence box before them.

She knew what the box was because of her years of profiling criminals, but she didn't know any details – didn't even recognize the name labeled on the box; Bayer.

"What is this?" she finally asked.

Roth took a sip of his tea. "I know you don't profile anymore," he said. "But I need you to look into this for me, if you will."

"What exactly am I looking for?"

Roth took another sip of his tea, but Jennifer knew it was a stalling tactic. "Jack, I have a full schedule the next few months. Surely, you can find someone within your department to go over whatever it is that you need."

"It can't be within the department," he said, almost in a yell. "I need you." He cleared his throat, regaining his composure. "You're the best profiler I know," he said.

She decided to play along, humor him. But she also knew something was not right with the whole thing, and that's when she began to use her skills as a psychiatrist. "Tell me what I need to know," she said.

Roth took a deep breath. "Eighteen years ago," he began, "there was a boy who watched his parents die; his father killed his mother then hanged himself." He told her everything there was to know about the Bayer farm and the case that ensued; dead pigs everywhere, search for the boy, and the closing of the case with the boy never to be found again.

"And why is it you want me to look through the evidence box of a case that was closed almost twenty years ago?" Jennifer asked.

"Because, odds are, he's back."

He told her of Samantha Cabello, of the way she died; the same way a pig is slaughtered. And he told her of the word *ENO* written in blood. There was no doubt, according to Roth, that this was the work of Mason Bayer.

*

"Wait a minute," Grazer said, holding up a finger, interrupting Jennifer's story. "You say this happened on a Saturday?"

"I'm almost positive."

"January 7th?"

Jennifer thought back for a second then nodded. "It could have been."

Grazer shook his head. "Un-fucking-real. That's the day we found Cabello. Roth knew it was Mason Bayer before we did, and he told us nothing."

Leppe sat back on her chair. "There's more," she said then continued with her story.

*

He asked her to profile Mason Bayer based on the information that was in the box, and ultimately she agreed. She went through the box, looked through the pictures, read as many of the case files as she could, and she came up with absolutely nothing. It didn't take long to realize that Roth had done some doctoring of the files, and she had no doubt that he was hiding the more important pieces of evidence.

She tried to make sense of it, tried to find out as much as she could without going to him or the rest of the police force; public records, newspaper articles, she even drove out to the farm on a Sunday, but ultimately, she found nothing more than she had already been told. Still, there was no doubt that Roth was hiding something.

By the time Roth asked for her findings on Mason, how she had profiled him, she came up with the most generic of profiles to keep Roth at bay and to keep him from getting suspicious of her own suspicions. It was also at that point that she knew he wanted to the box back to ensure it wouldn't land in the wrong hands, primarily the hands of the two detectives on the case.

*

"That's when I handed the box over to you two," she said.

Todd, sitting on the opposite side of her desk, shook his head. "It doesn't make sense. Why not just tell us? Why use his phone to get Hector to the box? That's rather risky."

"Because I didn't want it to lead back to me. I don't want to be involved any more than I already am."

Todd smiled, laughed almost. "Did you forget we're detectives?" he asked.

Leppe shook her head.

"So, you're not protecting him?"

"Absolutely not," Leppe said. "I've been investigating Roth longer than you have. I just don't have the resources you do. But here's what I do know that you may not; he thinks Mason Bayer will come after him."

Todd frowned. "Why?"

She shrugged. "Maybe he knows his whereabouts. Maybe he is somehow connected to what happened before."

Todd was suddenly on his feet, pacing again. "Holy shit," he said. "The files in the box, all of the names of the officers and investigators were blacked out. Do you think he was there? He was a part of the case?"

"It's crossed my mind."

"Son of a bitch."

"Don't you have the property to confirm that?" Leppe asked.

Todd slapped his thighs. "If he's gone this far to protect himself, I'm sure I won't find anything else."

"He's doing all this to protect himself? He's afraid Mason Bayer is going to come after him?"

Todd shook his head. "He's been setting us up to fail. At every turn, he dissuaded my suggestions of going after Bayer, investigating the farm. He took me off the case for crissakes. No, Roth is hiding something, something we're not supposed to find out."

Jennifer nodded, knowing that was the case exactly. She stood from her chair and walked to the other side of the desk so that she and Todd were face to face. "I can help you," she said softly as though someone might over hear. "He's said some things to me that I cannot divulge because it's never been a confession."

"Like what?" Todd asked.

She shook her head. "I can't. But he's on the brink. He's waiting for me to take that box back to him, and I will. I'll get him to tell me."

"Dr. Leppe, if you know something that you're not telling us…"

"I don't. Not yet. But I'm close."

Todd shook his head. "I don't like this."

"I know. But if what I believe is right, then Roth will go down. I just need to get him to tell me the truth."

"I'm going with you."

"Absolutely not. If he sees you, he'll never talk. He's confided in me. Let me handle it. I will call him to set something up for today. I'll return the box and get him to talk."

Grazer crossed his arms over his chest. "How are you so sure you can get him to tell you what he knows?"

Leppe smiled. "It's what I do."

"Fucking Pig"

Corona received word that the Brewer residence was secure, Tomas Brewer was home with his family and everyone was safe and accounted for. However, Patricia Greer was nowhere to be found. She was not home, and according to one of her neighbors, she had left for work the afternoon before, and her driveway remained empty all night.

Remembering when he and Grazer interviewed her, Kux said told Corona she volunteered at the library at the university. Despite the thought that it would be a bold move to kill someone at the university, Corona, Kux and Leddy left the O'Neill crime scene and rushed to the library, Corona instructing any free units to meet him there.

The sun was out in full force by the time they arrived, bringing with it the thick blanket of humidity of a Miami morning. Kux wiped his brow as they jogged through the desolate parking lot and toward the massive building.

Leddy reached the sliding glass doors first, and when they didn't automatically open, he slapped his thighs. "They're not open," he said, first trying to force the doors open, and when they didn't move, cupping his hands on the glass for a look inside. "I can't see shit!"

"Break the glass!" Kux said.

"Wait," Corona said. "No need."

A golf cart with the word *SECURITY* stamped onto it strolled up, a middle aged man pulling it to a halt directly in front of the building. "Library's not open until 7:30, gentlemen," he said, oblivious to the uniforms both Kux and Leddy were wearing.

Corona flashed his badge. "We need it open now," he said. "We have reason to believe there might be a dead body in there."

The security guard laughed. "A dead body? That's highly unlikely. We have security cameras all over the place, and if someone died in there, we would know it."

Corona curled his upper lip. "Open the doors, sir. The longer you wait, the more you're interfering with our investigation."

The security guard shook his head. "I couldn't even if I wanted to. I don't have the keys."

The explosion of glass shattering stunned both Corona and the security guard. They looked to the sliding doors, one of them in a million pieces on the floor. A fire extinguisher in his hand, Leddy nodded at both of them, and said, "I found the key."

"You can't do that!" the security guard yelled, but they were already on their way inside, Corona first, followed closely by Leddy, then Kux.

Their guns drawn but aimed to the floor, the three of them entered the darkened, vast space slowly and quietly. It was a lobby of sorts; a reception desk placed on the center of the tiled floor, large columns rising beside it reaching toward the second level of the library. Small rooms lined the lobby on either side, each containing a work station and computer, and none of them occupied. In fact, the entire library seemed unoccupied. The building was silent save for the sounds of the officers' footsteps.

Once past the reception area, Corona looked to the men behind him, signaled Leddy to take the right of the room, Kux to the left. He would remain in the center, thereby initiating the strip method of searching a crime scene; they would sweep the room from one end to the other then proceed in the opposite direction provided nothing was found on the first trip. With the immense space around them, plus the second floor, they were bound to miss something if they weren't precise and consistent. That is if there was something to find.

The sun guided their view into the building, but the further they walked, the more the darkness of the building enveloped them. Uniformed, both Kux and Leddy were equipped with flashlights that they both turned on almost in unison.

After a few paces, the men came upon a clearing of sorts; the second floor above them breaking off allowing view of the spectacular ceiling, some twenty feet above. A banner hung from a balcony beside the stair case showing the school's color and mascot; a panther ready to pounce. Corona glanced at the animal and shook his head at the irony.

A coffee shop on the left and a drug store to the right of the center room, Kux thought the library looked more like a mall. Aside from the study rooms, there was no indication that they were in a university's library. Not a single book had been seen.

A noise snapped him out of his daze. It was barely audible, the sound of a beast grunting or snorting somewhere around them, but far enough away that he couldn't exactly pin point where it was coming from – or if he actually heard it. He stopped for a closer listen.

"What is it?" Corona asked in a whisper.

"I thought I heard something," Kux said.

The three of them remained silent, looking to the air as though the remnants sound was hovering around them.

"I don't hear anything," Leddy whispered at the same exact moment the Kux heard the grunt again; a short burst of a gurgling snort, wet and smacking.

Corona nodded at him. He heard it too.

Still, it was low enough to miss if they weren't listening *for* it. Muffled and distant, it was as though it was coming from within the walls surrounding them.

"Look," Leddy said, surprise in his voice that almost broke his whisper.

The others did as they were told and looked to Leddy, the beam of his flashlight a pace forward on the floor directly before him.

There was no doubt it was blood, set upon the beige tile floor, the crimson mark would probably have been missed completely until the halogen lights above were switched on. Corona looked at it, his brain processing the mark, and despite how many of the murders he had seen recently, this particular mark was enough to make the hair on the nape of his neck stand. It was not just a random splatter or drop – the smear was made to form the letter *X*.

Kux moved the beam of his light a few paces away from the letter, sweeping the room forward and stopped when he found another mark; *I*.

The beastly noise erupted again. It was then that they realized it was coming from the direction the letters were leading.

They moved slowly following the letters, Leddy holding his beam to the floor, Kux's flashlight revealing every concealed corner of the room, Corona's grip on his gun tightening.

"This way," Leddy said, finding a third letter slanted toward the left; *S*.

They followed its direction and came upon the last of the study rooms on the first floor. Unlike the others, the door to this one was closed.

"Look," Kux said, his beam on at the bottom of the door where a pool of blood was seeping through from the inside of the room.

The revolting sound of wet gurgling came from within the room.

Corona nodded at both men then pointed his gun at the door. Leddy holstered his flashlight and quickly moved toward the door, his back against the wall directly beside it. Kux reached for the door's knob, looked to Leddy, then to Corona. The three of them nodded.

Kux gripped the door knob with a sweaty palm, the grunting noise sickening his stomach with the possibility of what he would find once the door was opened. Mason eating his victim? Victim number *XIS* trying desperately to stay alive after being disemboweled? He wouldn't be able to take another victim dying in his hands. So many more possibilities flew through his mind in the one second he stood at the door, but duty called, so he smothered his thoughts, gnawed his jaw and in one swift motion, Kux twisted the door knob and pulled the door open.

He dropped to one knee, aiming his gun into the now open room as Leddy half turned into the doorway, Corona behind both of them.

The pig startled the three of them as it burst out of the doorway, squealing and grunting. Covered in blood, it pushed passed Kux, nearly knocking him to the floor and ran circles around the room until it found the path of sunlight and headed toward the building's exit.

"What the fuck!" Leddy yelled – his flashlight on the pig.

"Grab him!" Kux followed, finding his balance and standing.

"Forget it!" Corona yelled at both of them, as though unfazed by the swine. His cold stare was transfixed on the open room.

When Kux and Leddy returned their attention to the room, they saw why Corona cared less about the pig and more so on what was inside.

Victim number *XIS* was Patricia Greer, Kux remembered her soft voice and librarian looks from when he and Grazer interviewed her. Now, seated on the office chair of the work station and facing them, her pale skin displayed death, her mouth hanging open and her arms draped lifelessly beside her. Her stomach was a bloody mess, gaping open and exposing the empty cavity that once held her intestines.

"Where are they?" Kux asked, swallowing hard.

There was blood all over the floor; a massive puddle had formed underneath the body and there was no doubt Greer was disemboweled like the previous victims. Unlike the other crime scenes though, the pile of intestines were not beside the victim in a slimy mess.

"Where are her entrails?" Kux asked, looking at the blood marked hoof prints left behind by the pig, his stomach turning as he recalled the wet, smacking, gurgling sound it made.

Corona closed his eyes in disgust, barely able to physically say what he was thinking; that her intestines were now in the digestive system of the animal that was locked in the room with her.

Leddy covered his mouth, forcing back the bile and vomit that was creeping up his throat. He turned away from the room, feeling short of breath as his body went cold.

Corona looked into the room again and shook his head. Mason Bayer was not only elusive, but clever. His murders were becoming more creative, more vicious with each passing one. Corona's face burned with heat at the thought that they still had not captured him;

xis murders in as many months, and they were no closer to capturing him since the first. *Fucking pig* he thought to himself.

He frowned. The pig. "Why the pig?" he asked himself out loud.

"What?" Leddy asked, his face still filled with disgust.

"The pig. Why the pig? What's he telling us?"

"That he's a sick and twisted son of a fuck," Kux said, catching his breath.

Corona nodded. "Beside that. Where did Mason grow up? Where would he get a pig?"

"A pig farm," Leddy said.

"Right."

"You think he's at the farm?" Kux asked. "It's already been cleared."

"Find all the pig farms in the county," he told Kux. "We need to get every single one searched."

Kux nodded.

"Leddy, get a team together and go to the Bayer farm. Make sure that son of a bitch didn't go back home."

"What about you, sir?" Leddy asked.

"Six victims are now crossed off our list," he said, extracting the mobile phone from his pocket. "We know of one more. I'm going to get the Special Response unit to set up at the Brewer house. We're going to catch this son of a bitch today, mark my words."

He turned away from the men and headed out toward the exit, looking at the display on his cell phone.

The Special Response Team was a tactical unit made up of the toughest men and women in the county's law enforcement. He would have them set up snipers and surveillance all around the Brewer home and the moment Mason showed up, they would take him down without a doubt.

As Corona walked back into the sunlight, he squinted and looked up to the sky, the thought of finally catching Mason Bayer making his stomach hurt with excitement. Before he called for the deployment of the SRT, there was one call he needed to make. Corona looked at his phone and dialed his partner, Grazer.

*

Kux sped away in his car while Leddy was instructed to take Corona's. He jogged out to the empty parking lot, the sounds of police sirens in the distance. Leddy felt uneasy about leaving Corona alone at the scene, but his backup was arriving shortly.

The keys to Corona's car in his hand, Leddy walked to the driver's door and was about to open it when he felt the tap on his shoulder.

He turned, and the last thing he saw before the darkness took him was the face of Mason Bayer.

The Bayer Farm

When Todd arrived, he recalled his last visit to the farm. The place was empty as it was dilapidated when he arrived, but that was not the case for long. Just as he found the staircase that lead to the basement, he heard the unmistakable sound of the front door opening and someone else entering the structure. He made his escape by hiding in darkened corners, peering over wall breaks to ensure a clear path to the front door, and in less than a minute, Todd was back in his car and heading back to Krome Avenue and civilization, leaving the basement unexplored.

The basement was not the reason for his return that afternoon. In fact, his return had nothing to do with finding Mason Bayer at all – though finding the killer would prove Roth a fool for taking Grazer's badge. Todd's visit was strictly for the investigation of a different man.

Hours earlier, he and Dr. Leppe came to the conclusion that Roth was hiding something, something big, and something that had to do with the Mason Bayer case eighteen years before. Grazer had gone over the details of the case in his head over and over again, and the only piece he was missing were the names of the officers involved in the case as the reports had them blacked out. Neither Grazer nor Corona had reason to believe it before, but after his conversation with Leppe, Todd was convinced the name of Jack Roth was amongst those that had been blacked out – and that Jack Roth himself hid those names.

But for what possible reason? Todd asked himself several times on the forty-five minute drive to the farm. *What are you hiding?*

He thought of calling Corona, tell him of his meeting with Leppe, but decided against it. Corona was dealing with Bayer, and Todd knew distracting him would only delay the case. Investigating Roth was something that he and Leppe were doing together – and while she had made arrangements to return the evidence box to Roth that evening in the hopes coaxing some information out of him, Todd was left with two options; sit idly by and wait to hear back from her, or go to the place where it all began.

The Bayer Farm.

His last visit was during the dark of night. Now, the sun blared in the warm summer afternoon, allowing Todd clear view of the vast property. He had seen the pictures of pig carcasses scattered all about, the earth saturated in their blood. Dozens of dead pigs rotting in their pens and the surrounding property, all at the hands of a young boy – Mason Bayer – who witnessed his own father kill his mother then hang himself. Todd looked around the area and wondered what it would have been like to actually see it, the dead swine, the rot in the air, the state of the farm inside, the secret that Roth was harboring.

He wasn't sure if it was, indeed, in the farm, but Todd figured it was a good starting point. He reached to the back of his waist where his personal gun was holstered between his back and his belt. It was an M11 pistol, small enough to conceal, powerful enough to get the job done. He kept it in a lock box under his bed and rarely had the need to use it, but since Roth took his issued weapon, he had no choice. As he double checked the magazine, he prayed he didn't have to use it once inside the farm. He reached into the pocket of his jeans and extracted a small pen light. He turned it on, the small, thin instrument providing a surprisingly powerful light visible even in the bright afternoon.

Equipment in hand, Todd took a deep breath and made his way into the farm.

*

He stood at the stairway to the basement, the beam of his flashlight illuminating the stairs descending into darkness. His gun aiming forward, Todd thought of calling out a warning indicating his presence, but ignored his inclination and took a step down.

The wood beneath him cried out with a squeak, and continued to do so until Todd reached the basement floor, made of dirt and grime.

He stood at the bottom of the stairs and studied the room, rusted farming tools; hack-saws, picks, a hatchet and various others were hanging from chains lining the ceiling and by the look of them, they had not been touched for the twenty years that the farm had been abandoned. A work table was set in the middle of the room, covered in dirt and mud. Or was it blood? Todd couldn't tell.

There was nothing else. The rest of the basement was empty, and he took a deep breath, his mouth drying with the lingering dust and dirt in the air. He spat it out, and did not allow himself to be disappointed in the lack of new evidence since he still had the second floor of the farm, not to mention the barn behind it, to investigate.

Halfway up the stairs to the main floor, Todd heard the whisper. He stopped dead, his heart jumping at the sound.

"Grazer," it said, followed closely by, "help me…"

Todd frowned, the beam of the flashlight bouncing around the basement and the rest of the stairs before him as he tried to pinpoint the source of the whisper.

"Who's here?" Todd demanded, his gun poised.

"Grazer," the whisper responded after a moment.

It was coming from the main floor.

Todd fled up the rest of the staircase, taking two steps at a time, until he reached the main floor. Pushing the movable wall aside, Todd entered the center room in a hurry then came to a sudden stop when his eyes fell upon the scene before him.

They were standing just inside the house, the front door behind them. One of them was a young officer, the other, a tall lanky man dressed in black, a ski mask covering his face and holding the officer at gunpoint. Their killer had been hiding, and now, he had a hostage.

Todd went still as the entire room around him shrunk immediately. He looked to the hostage, his mouth going dry, and whispered, "Leddy…"

*

Todd's heart pounded against his temples and sweat was stinging his eyes. He locked eyes with the rookie, trying to convince him that it was going to be okay with a simple glare, but the fear in the young man's eyes made it clear that he did not get the message.

"Take your shot!" the perp yelled. "Shoot me and this pig gets it before I hit the ground!"

Todd's sweaty palm gripped the gun tighter. "There's no way out of this," he told the killer, trying his best to remain composed.

How the fuck is this happening? Todd thought to himself all the while keeping his eyes on Leddy.

"Come on!" the perp yelled. "Do it! You fucking pig!"

There was no back up coming, that much Todd knew. No one knew he was there, and he instantly regretted his decision to not call Corona. The realization that they were completely alone made Todd more nervous than the perp holding the gun at the rookie.

The killer laughed and said something Todd didn't hear. He was busy looking into the eyes of the sacred rookie; his eyes begging to be saved, and Todd was his only chance.

Please the rookie said, but without making a sound. Todd read his lips followed directly by, *Help me.*

Todd pursed his lips, clenched his teeth and wrapped his index finger around the trigger.

"Do it!" the killer yelled.

He took a deep breath and made a conscious effort to control his adrenaline. His heart was pounding relentlessly making his hand slightly quiver.

"Come on, asshole! Shoot!"

Ignoring the perp's taunt, he closed his right eye, aiming the pistol at the killer's forehead. "Last chance," he said. "Let the officer go."

The killer laughed. "You're all dead," he said. "You, your friends, your family. I'll kill you all."

The explosion that followed was deafening. Todd wanted to yell out, but his throat would not produce a sound as the explosion echoed in his head like a jackhammer – as though God himself was knocking on his brain with all his might. He watched as Leddy fell to the floor once the killer released him.

Todd's pistol, still smoking, fell to his side. He had aim of the killer and fired the shot, but the masked man pushed Leddy aside just before and ran out of the open doorway, dodging the bullet.

Leddy collapsed to the floor, gasping for air and within seconds, Todd was kneeling by his side. "Are you okay?" he asked, helping Leddy sit up.

Leddy nodded. "That was him," he said between breaths. "That was Mason fucking Bayer."

"Call Corona. Tell him to get here right away."

Leddy nodded. "I'm fine," he said. "Go find that son of a bitch."

Without another word, Todd ran out of the house, and as Leddy composed himself enough to make the call to Corona, Todd made his way to the barn – the only place left for Mason Bayer to hide.

Hiding

Kux explained the situation to the Brewers as gently as he could. Tomas Brewer and his wife sat side by side on the living room couch and listened to the officer seated in front of them as he spoke, both of them nodding and digesting the information.

"So this Mason Bayer will come after us now?" Ruth Brewer asked.

Kux took a breath. "We do have strong evidence to show he will come after you," he said, looking at Tomas then looked to his wife. "We can't say for sure whether you or your daughter will be safe. We have a team that is going to set up around your house to protect your property in the hopes that we find him as he attempts to make his way inside, but to be safe, we ask that you leave until this is done. Do you have somewhere you can go? Family? Friends?"

Ruth nodded. "We can go to my sister's."

"You should. As quickly as you can."

"No," Brewer said suddenly.

Ruth quickly turned her attention to him as Kux frowned.

"I am not going anywhere," he said.

"Mr. Brewer," Kux said, "I don't think you under…"

"I understand exactly," he interrupted, waving his finger in the air. "But I am not leaving my house."

"Tomas," Ruth said to him. "I think we should listen to what he is saying."

He was already shaking his head. "I have been away from my house and my family for a long time, and we've worked hard at building this up again." He turned his attention to Kux. "My wife and my daughter will leave, but if Mason Bayer wants to come for me, then I am not going. I've read the papers. I know what he's done. Sounds to me if Mason Bayer wants to kill me, he'll find me wherever I hide, so I ask you; why would I go with my wife and daughter and put them in danger when he just wants me?"

Kux pressed his lips together. Months before, Tomas Brewer was on the brink of lunacy, wandering the streets of Miami while uttering nonsense then slipping into a coma only to awake a week later with no recollection of anything. But what he said to Kux made perfect sense, and Kux found himself without argument.

"I will stay here," Brewer continued. "I will protect myself and my home."

Kux looked to Ruth expecting a rejection. She had none.

"Mr. Brewer," he said, "that is a very noble position you are taking. I cannot force you to leave, so if you do decide to stay…"

"I have."

"Then you have my assurance that my team and I will do everything we can to ensure your safety."

Ruth was looking at her hands folded on her lap and just as Kux asked if she had any questions for him, he saw a tear fall onto her hands. He reached across the coffee table and placed his hand on top of hers. "Mrs. Brewer," he said. "You have my word that we will be watching from this moment until Mason Bayer is caught."

She looked at his face, green eyes heightened by the moisture surrounding them. "What if you don't catch him?" she asked. "Are we supposed to hide forever?"

Kux looked to Tomas, then back to Ruth. He took a deep breath, knowing full well that he could not promise anything. "Your husband is very brave for staying here," he said, almost in a whisper. "And with his help, we will be closer to catching him. But you need to collect your things and your daughter, and you have to leave here. The sooner the better."

She nodded, looked to her husband once more, then stood from the couch and made her way toward the stair case. Before ascending, she turned to them once more. "If my husband is to bait to capture this maniac," she said to Kux, "I want your word that he will be okay. I want you to promise me that you will catch him, and that my husband will not be a victim."

Kux cleared his throat and stood to face her. "Mrs. Brewer, as an officer, it is impossible for me to promise you that we will in fact catch Mason Bayer. What I can promise is that we will do everything we can..."

"What about as a human?" she asked, her voice trembling.

Kux frowned. "I beg your pardon?"

"You said as an officer, it is impossible for you to promise anything. But what about as a human being? You're asking me to leave my husband here to be used as bait, so I need your word that you will capture him before anything happens."

Kux looked to his feet. To offer such a promise would be allowing upset. It would be the same to offer a promise to desperate parents that their missing child would be found alive and well. Such promises were impossible to make, especially by officers of the law. Kux shook his head and closed his eyes tightly for a moment. He took a deep breath and looked upon the visibly shaken Ruth Brewer, tears streaming down her cheeks and desperation upon her face.

Kux pursed his lips, arched his eyebrows, and his stomach sank, he looked Ruth Brewer in the eyes. "I promise," he told her.

And he believed it.

*

After Corona received Leddy's call, he quickly rushed out of the university's library, obtained a squad car, flipped the siren on and rushed toward Krome Avenue. Whipping through the city streets at over 80 miles an hour, Corona could not believe what Leddy had told him transpired.

More so than being held hostage by Mason Bayer, Corona wondered what was going through Todd's mind.

Det. Grazer was here, Leddy told him. *Mason had me at gunpoint and Grazer had him in his sights.*

The way Leddy described it, it was the same scenario as what caused Grazer to have the reoccurring nightmares, and he was desperate to get to his friend and ensure he was okay.

After Corona used the radio to order all available officers to head for the Bayer farm, his phone rang. Considering the circumstances, he would have ignored the call, but after checking the phone's display, he decided to take it. Moments later, he wished he hadn't.

The prints on the make-shift knife found at the O'Neill's crime scene had come back. The murder weapon did indeed have prints on them, but they weren't of Mason Bayer's. They were of the victim's.

"How is that possible?" Corona barked into the phone, knowing full well that the only way it was possible was if O'Neill had sliced open his own stomach and killed himself.

*

The structure was twice as large as the house. The door to the barn was missing, and unlike the house, there were plenty of windows; more than a dozen throughout the building, and most were completely broken through to allow the sunlight in. Todd was thankful it wasn't as dark as the house, darkened corners and hiding spots were scarce.

The large opening entered into a narrow hall that ran the entire length of the barn. At the end of the hall, a wooden door was halfway open leading to a room that was unseen from his viewpoint. Todd slowly approached it, his gun steady, his ears peaked, and sweat staining his shirt.

The entire facility was made of lumber, and the smell of wet, rotting wood filled the surrounding air. Its walls were dark and murky, rainwater dropping from cracks in the high ceiling and landing in echoing puddles that formed on the ground. Every inch of that ground was moist and soaking in some areas. He watched his own footing while trying to find wet footprints indicating which direction he went.

There were none.

He reached the door and peered into the room careful not to push it open. If Mason was hiding in the next room, Todd wanted to surprise him.

It was a kitchen, and it was larger than the farmhouse itself. An industrial sized stove lined the furthest wall from corner to corner, and countless cabinets and cupboards hung loosely on the wall to its left. There was a door on the east wall, and it was left half way open.

It led to another hall, running parallel with the one from which he entered, and much wider. Wooden gates standing nearly four feet tall lined both sides of the hall, four on either side, were all open and all leading to small rooms parted by broken walls. They looked like small jail cells, but they weren't intended for human use.

The holding pens... It was the area in which the swine were kept, probably from birth until they were transferred to the outside pens.

But it was all empty. There was no Mason Bayer hiding inside the barn.

Todd retraced his steps to make sure he didn't miss anything, even pushed against some walls in the event the led to hidden rooms like the one he found inside the house. But there was nothing.

It was like Mason Bayer completely vanished.

A New Manhunt

Once the ambulance arrived, the paramedics forced Leddy to sit upon the gurney to be checked on even though he insisted he was fine.

The farm lands were swarming with officers, and as though it were a recreation from the case eighteen years before, they were on the search for Mason Bayer.

Leddy watched as another squad car sped onto the grounds, and after the car came to a sliding halt, Corona stepped out and made eye contact with the officer immediately. One of the paramedics had just cupped Leddy's arm to monitor his blood pressure, but was on the move to approach Corona.

The paramedic forced him back.

"What's happened?" Corona asked, half jogging toward Leddy. "Are you okay?"

"I'm fine," Leddy said. "I have a splitting headache, but I'm fine."

"What's the situation here?"

Leddy shook his head. "Nothing so far. That son of a bitch has to be around here somewhere, but no one's found anything."

Corona shook his head. He filled Leddy in on the results of the finger prints – that only Michael O'Neill's prints were found on the weapon. Leddy frowned at the information, his mind reeling.

"Grazer?" Corona asked. "Do you know where he is?"

Leddy nodded in the direction of a cluster of officers several yards away, near the barn. Grazer was speaking to several of them, and from Corona's view, it was unclear if they were interrogating him or if he was willingly giving them information.

"You sure you okay?" Corona asked Leddy.

"I'm fine," he said again.

Corona gave him a tight nod then walked toward the officers, toward Grazer.

Leddy watched him as the information he received of O'Neill's prints lingered in his head. Was it possible that O'Neill killed himself? He sliced his own stomach open then and wrote the word *EVIF* on the wall before succumbing to his death? And if that was the case, was the same true for the rest of the victims?

It surely explained why no finger prints outside of the victim's were found in either of their homes. It would explain why there was no sign of forced entry. It would also explain why no one – neighbors or the spouse sleeping directly beside them – ever heard or saw anything out of the usual.

But could someone pour boiling water over themselves enough to skin them then slice their stomach open to spill their intestines and write their own number before dying? Was it possible? And even if it was, how would a group of people know who had nothing but a twenty year old case file in common simply decide to do it, one by one?

Leddy sat back on the gurney, his head pounding even more with the thought. There was no doubt Mason Bayer was involved in their deaths, but perhaps his involvement wasn't exactly what they thought.

*

Todd saw Hector arrive at the scene but tried not to watch him. The moment he saw his partner's face, the events of the night before came screaming back, the accusations, the snide comments and the punch to the face that still burned his cheek. When he saw Hector begin to approach the several officers that were questioning, Todd looked to his feet as his mind flipped through the many different ways their conversation would go.

"Officers, I'll take it from here," Corona said to the group. "There's a man out here somewhere we need to find, so get to it."

The officers nodded and dispersed and Corona watched them all until they were out of ear's shot.

"How did you know to come here?" Hector asked.

Todd shook his head. "I didn't. I came here on other business."

"Other business? Like what?"

Todd gnawed his jaw.

"I could charge you with trespassing," Hector said, a crooked smile on his lips.

Todd nodded. "I think you can over look that considering the events that just transpired here."

"Speaking of which, are you okay?"

"If you mean whether or not I'm going to slip into another catatonic depression, don't worry. I'm fine."

"I don't mean that. I mean, considering the situation. It sounds to me like it was a lot like the previous situation you were in."

Todd looked to the floor, shaking his head. He took a breath as he replayed the events of the year before in his mind, young Officer Lanza held at gunpoint by a lunatic. He then replayed the events that happened with Leddy. "It was exactly like the previous situation," he said finally.

"It must have been hard for you," Hector said with a nod. "I understand that."

"No, you don't understand," Todd said slightly shaking his head. "I mean, it was *exactly* like before."

Hector frowned.

"It's almost like Bayer knew what happened before. He said the same exact things to me the other son of a bitch did. Word for word. It's like he lived in my head and showed me my worst nightmare." He looked to his feet again. "I thought for sure Leddy was a dead man."

"But he's not," Hector said. "You saved him. That much is worth concentrating on."

Todd nodded slowly. "About what happened last night," he said. "I'm…"

"Don't worry about it," Hector said. "We both did things we're sorry for. Call it even."

There was a beat of silence between the two of them, and though Todd was relieved for Hector's response, he felt an apology was necessary. He promised himself he would deliver that apology the moment they could celebrate Mason Bayer's capture.

"So," Hector said after taking a deep breath. "Do you want to fill me in on this 'other business' that brought you here?"

Todd allowed a short laugh escape. "You have a killer to find, Detective Corona. Don't allow me to get in your way."

"Yeah, I have the feeling that I may need to know what you know, Detective Grazer, and what kind of partner are you if you're not willing to share?"

Todd nodded. "Roth will have your badge too, you know."

"Leave that to me. We have lots to catch up on and a killer to catch," Corona said. "Roth is the least of my worries."

*

The plan was to meet at Roth's apartment at 8 PM. Jennifer Leppe pulled into the parking garage at 7:50, the evidence box in her trunk and a small tape recorder ready to go in her purse.

She took the elevator to the seventh floor, carrying the box with all its contents exactly the way he had handed it to her. Throughout the short ride up, she played the conversation out in her head, what questions she would ask, what she might say depending on his answers, all in the hopes of making him reveal whatever it was he was hiding. She wasn't leaving his place until she had something. Hopefully, he'd had a few glasses of wine or some other liquor that would loosen the morals and let the truth come spilling out.

She rang the doorbell to the door marked 77 and waited patiently. She could hear soft music playing inside, jazz of some kind. It wasn't loud enough to smother the sound of the door bell, so when it took longer than a minute for Roth to answer, she rang the doorbell again.

"This box is kind of heavy," she said to the door, and in attempt to knock on the door with her foot, she realized it was never shut to begin with as it opened with the tap of her foot.

Jennifer frowned and peered into the apartment – the small hallway leading to the living area empty. The only sound was that of the music, clearer now, seeping through the apartment and into the hall.

"Jack," she called into the apartment.

No response.

She was hesitant to simply enter. What if he was in the shower or somehow indisposed in an awkward way? She was early, after all.

"Jack, I'm coming in," she said, and did so.

She entered the apartment, leaving the door open before her and stepped into the living room. He was not seated on the couch, nor was he in the kitchen on the other side of the room.

Calling for him again, Jennifer placed the box on top of the coffee table. Hands on her hips, she looked around the apartment until her eyes fell upon the door to the east of the living room – the door to Roth's home office. It was slightly open, and it was the source of the jazz music.

Immediately, she was unsure why Roth decided it should be her to find him.

It appeared as though he slit his wrists. A pool of blood covered most of the desk and whatever case files he was working on. Drops had begun to fall off the desk recently as the small amount of blood on the floor had not begun to puddle just yet. He was faced down on his desk, his body propped up by the chair he was sitting on, his head lying on the blood seeping from both wrists at his side.

"Shit," Jennifer said to the air, taking in the scene while rushing toward the lieutenant's side. "What the fuck, Roth!"

Wishing she had a pair of latex gloves on her, Leppe checked for a pulse on the base of his neck, careful not to touch any of the fluid from Roth's veins. There was no pulse in his carotid artery. Roth was indeed dead, taking with him the information Leppe was there to discover.

She quickly picked up the phone on his desk and dialed 911, but before the call was answered, she put the receiver back down, her eyes transfixed on something on the wall before her.

Sorry.

It was written on the wall opposite the desk where Roth now sat. Surrounded by pictures of his career in law enforcement, the word was written out by hand, and in blood.

She stepped closer to the wall, noticing that all the pictures had been tampered with; his face had been removed from each, cut or torn out.

Looking back to the man on the desk, Leppe frowned. Now more than ever, she wanted to know what it was that he had done. What secret he harbored that caused him to hate himself so much, he defaced his own pictures. What was he so *sorry* for?

She was disappointed at his death, and with the realization that she will never know was the reason behind it, she called the police.

CHAPTER XIS

"Now come on, come with me," Jack Roth called out to Mason.

The boy shook his head, still peering out toward him from behind the wall.

"Mason, come on. There are a lot of people upstairs who are going to be very happy to see you."

Mason looked down at his feet, considering it. "Are my mommy and daddy there?"

Jack took a deep breath. He didn't know if the boy meant whether his parents were waiting for him along with the others, or if their bodies had been removed because the child did not want to see them again. Either way, he had to choose his next words carefully to not lose the boy. "They're not there now, Mason. But if you want to see them again, we can make that happen."

The boy neither nodded nor shook his head. He took a step out from behind the wall.

"Is this where you've been hiding all this time?" Jack asked.

Mason nodded.

"You don't have to hide anymore," Jack said. "You're safe now. We're going to take care of you."

"Like my parents took care of me?"

Jack smiled at him, deciding not to answer.

"I need to take something," Mason said. "Will you help me?"

"Sure," Jack said.

Mason turned back to the room he was in, and Jack approached the opening.

The child's attack came quick. He jumped out of the room and lunged at Jack with a sharp blade, his lip snarling and a growl ripping his throat.

Jack stepped back quickly, nearly dropping the flashlight as he tripped over the slaughter table's leg.

The boy swiped at Roth's stomach, coming within an inch of him.

Jack tried to regain his balance, but there wasn't enough time before Mason made another attempt.

"Die, pig!" Mason screamed. "I want to see you bleed!"

"Stop!" Roth said, trying to reach for his gun.

"You sound like my mom," Mason said, his lip curling.

Mason's charge was fast – faster than Jack expected. On reflex alone, Jack lifted his arm, gripped his flashlight tightly, and brought it down on Mason's head with all his might.

The boy stopped, looked up at Jack, his black eyes dazed. Blood trickled from his scalp down both sides of the boy's face.

Jack forced one more blow to boy's head, feeling his skull give way to the flashlight. He fell to the floor quickly, his body convulsing for a few seconds before it finally remained absolutely still.

Bait

Turns out, Leddy was not okay. His splitting headache was a result of the hit he took that knocked him out and caused a mild concussion. He was forced back to the hospital for further evaluation, leaving the task force at the Brewer residence with one man less.

After Ruth and Katherine Brewer left the property, Kux and a team of officers inspected the entire house, searching in closets, bedrooms, even cupboards and pantries to ensure that Tomas Brewer was indeed safe inside the house. A would-be-victim determined to protect his home was the perfect bait, and though Kux never voiced it to anyone, he was excited at the idea that Mason Bayer would be captured that night.

At an hour before midnight, Corona, Grazer and Kux were seated in an SRT van filled with surveillance equipment; monitors displaying the views of the tactical team's members, six in total, and all of them fixed on the two story house from different angles. The three men inside were all wearing ear pieces and microphones so that each of them can give the team direct orders and hear responses. They also had access to contact the seven unmarked cars cruising the surrounding streets looking for anything or anyone suspicious or out of the ordinary.

"If you see a dog eating cat food," Kux had told them, "we want to hear about it."

The waiting game was under way.

Kux was relieved to see Corona and Grazer when they arrived an hour before. Though he had been given the privilege of being put in charge of the surveillance and the SRT, it was an immense amount of pressure to handle it on his own. Aside from that, they came with coffee and burgers.

After a quick update of the events, or lack thereof, Kux shook Grazer's hand and followed immediately with, "Where have you been all day?"

Corona and Grazer exchanged glances.

"I'm not actually here as a detective, Billy," Grazer said. "I'm just an advisor."

Kux frowned, looking at Corona. "Roth," he assumed.

Corona gave him a tight nod.

"Unreal."

"How is Mr. Brewer doing?" Grazer asked.

"He seems okay," Kux said. "That's one brave son of a bitch, I'll tell you."

"If I had the Special Response Team surrounding my house watching me, I'd be pretty brave, too," Corona said as his mobile phone erupted to life. "Check on them, make sure there's nothing going on." He popped the earpiece out before answering his phone.

Kux nodded and pressed on the microphone attached the Kevlar vest opening the lines of communication.

Grazer leaned in toward the monitors and looked at all the angles of the Brewer home. All seemed quiet.

Too quiet.

*

Tomas Brewer knew his house was being watched, but kept the small revolver at his side.

He was instructed by the officers to go about his normal business; eat dinner when he normally does, shower if he needed to, prepare himself for bed when he normally would. But he wasn't hungry, he had showered earlier, and though he dressed himself in his light blue pajamas and climbed into bed, sleep was the furthest thing from his mind.

He and his wife had a troubled bout and divorced. During the six months prior though, they had reconciled and became family once again, she even stopped correcting people when they called her Mrs. Brewer. His thoughts were on her and their daughter while he lied in bed – wondering how they were doing, wanting so much to call them even though he was instructed not to. As much as he was worried about them, he knew they were even more so worried about him. His only solace was that Kux had promised an officer watch over her sister's house and would update them the moment anything happened.

Aside from his family, there was the killer, Mason Bayer. He was a target on the maniac's list, and according to the officers, the *last* target. He knew the names of the people who had died before him, even worked with them, and though the details of their deaths were not elaborated on, he felt he needed more protection than just the Special Response Team outside.

The small revolver actually belonged to Mrs. Brewer. She purchased it after Tomas left, leaving the woman and her daughter living in the house alone. Though she hated the gun, she felt safer with it inside the house. It was now in Brewer's hand, and as he stared at it, he let out a small smile.

Everything happens for a reason, he thought to himself.

He took a deep breath, placed the gun on the night stand beside the bed – still at arm's reach, and checked the time: 11:07PM. A prayer for his safety and the safety of his family in his head, Tomas Brewer reached for the lamp and switched it off.

He waited until his eyes adjusted to the darkness before closing them, and within minutes, he began to fall asleep.

It was then that the window in his bedroom began to open slowly and without a sound.

*

Corona hung up the phone, his eyes glazed over and his mouth partially open.

"What happened?" Grazer asked. "You okay?"

Corona looked at Grazer, then to Kux. He swallowed then shook his head. "It's Roth," he said. "He's dead."

"What?" both men exclaimed.

"How?" Kux asked.

"Was it Bayer?" Grazer followed.

"Suicide," Corona answered. "Leppe found him with his wrists slit."

"Holy shit," Kux whispered, sitting back in his chair.

"No note, nothing."

The conversation came to a quick end as a loud pop echoed through the air outside, a flash of light exploding from the inside of the house for only a moment.

"What the fuck was that!" Grazer said.

Their earpieces came to life with a crackle. "Shots fired! A shot was fired from inside the house!" the filtered voice said.

"Move in now!" Kux responded.

Corona threw the van's door open and the three men jumped out, running toward the Brewer residence just across the street.

Kux was too preoccupied with the idea of catching Bayer to realize the adrenaline rushing through his system. His heart was racing though his breath was controlled, and while he was the first to reach the front door of the house, he waited for Corona and Grazer before slamming it open.

The three of them swept the entrance.

"All clear!" Corona yelled.

"In here!" they could hear Brewer yell from the upstairs. "In the bedroom!"

"Brewer, are you okay?" Kux called back as they began ascending the stairs single file.

"I shot him!" he called back. "I shot Mason Bayer!"

Manipulation

Kux ordered the SRT to stand down as they entered Brewer's bedroom followed closely by Grazer and Corona.

Brewer stood at the end of his bed, a small gun in one hand, the other pointing at the man on the floor beside the window.

Just as he was when Grazer saw him, the man was dressed in black and wore a ski mask that covered his face.

Kux ordered Brewer to put the gun on the bed, asking him to take a seat and asked if he was okay all in one breath as Grazer and Corona rushed to Bayer. The last six months of aggravation came to a boil as Corona grabbed him by the shoulders and threw him to his side, then rolled him onto his stomach. Grazer pulled his arms back and held them in place as Corona reached for his handcuffs then slapped them onto the killer's wrists.

Grazer forced him back into a seated position, slamming Bayer's head against the wall before gripping the top of the ski mask and slipping it off his head.

Grazer, Corona and Kux all looked upon the killer as blood began pooling beneath him from the bullet wound on his upper thigh.

His face matched his thin frame; sunken temples around his head, eyes large enough to bulge out of their sockets, his narrow nose prominent amidst his caved in cheeks. His wiry hair was jet black and just as unkempt as the dirty beard that was long enough to cover his neck.

"John Doe," Grazer said between breaths. "Son of a bitch."

The smell that came from him was that of sulfur and rotting meat – the smell of a corpse or of a man who had never once met a shower. Grazer and Corona both held back their refluxing throats as they covered both their mouths and noses with their hands.

"I fucking touched this disgusting piece of shit!" Corona said into his hands. "He's probably wretched with disease and germs."

Bayer looked at the two men with black eyes, looking at one, then the other, his thin lips forming a crooked smile.

"We have a special place for you," Grazer said to him. "You're going to wish you'd never been born."

Bayer laughed – a noise that emanated from his chest and filled the room with a beastly noise. "Fucking pig," he said. "I've just begun. Lock me up and I will come after you next."

Grazer turned to Kux. "Get Brewer out of here, and call this in. We're going to need to escort Mr. Bayer here with maximum security."

Kux nodded, and he held Brewer's arm as they left the room.

"Can you walk?" Corona asked, looking at Bayer's leg.

Bayer tilted his head to the side. "Probably better than your daughter can after I'm done fucking her sweet, juicy cunt."

Corona did not hesitate. Bayer hadn't even finished his sentence before Hector charged and pulled his arm back, fist in place, then slamming it onto the side of Bayer's head.

Bayer fell to his side, laughing.

Grazer pulled his partner off just as he was ready to throw another one. "Stop it!" Todd ordered. "Let him be. He's all talk. Go call your daughter and make sure she's fine."

"She's fine, she's with her friends," Corona said through grit teeth, still eyeing Mason. "I would have heard if she wasn't."

"She's fine for now," Bayer said, sitting up. "Until I bash her head through glass and make her my pig..."

"Shut the fuck up!" Grazer yelled, pulling his gun and pointing it at the dirty man.

Hector's back stiffened at the man's words.

"You're not going to do shit from the inside of a padded cell, so sit quietly until you're asked a fucking question!"

Sirens filled the air outside. Grazer and Corona looked at each other before Grazer turned his attention back to Bayer. "You hear that?" he asked. "That is the sound of your demise. You're done, Bayer."

Bayer licked his thin lips with a white tongue then showed his yellow, rotting teeth with a smile. "Aren't those the same words you told the man who killed young Officer Daniel, detective?" Mason asked. "The boy that died because you were too much of a pussy to shoot?"

Grazer felt the drop of adrenaline soar throughout his stomach. His heart beat in his temples, Grazer looked to Hector.

"Tell me detective," Bayer continued. "Is the reason you no longer share a bed with your wife because of that blood on your hands or because you no longer like the rotting scent between her legs?"

"Enough!" Grazer yelled, pointing his gun at the man again. "God help me I will put you down right now you piece of shit."

"Todd…" Hector said softly.

"Do it," Bayer said through clenched teeth. "Put me down."

Grazer's hand trembled as he wrapped his finger around the trigger. A simple squeeze and Mason Bayer was out of their lives for good. At that moment, Grazer had no interest in learning how the killer did what he did, he didn't care whether or not he ever had any of the answers to the questions the case set forth. He just wanted Bayer gone – for good.

"Todd, look at me," Hector called out.

But Todd didn't. His eyes were locked on the killer.

"Your kids," Mason said. "What are their names? Cynthia and Luis? If you don't put me done now, I will have my day with them. I promise you."

"Don't listen to him," Hector said. "He can't touch them. He just wants you to pull the trigger."

Grazer's finger caressed the trigger and he snarled at the monster before him. The sirens outside were growing closer, and though the words the killer said had penetrated his mind, he also knew Hector was right.

He lowered his arm and slowly approached the killer. Kneeling before him, gun still in his hand, Grazer leaned toward the killer, ingesting is scent without affect.

"I'm going to enjoy watching you waste away in that cell, you son of a bitch."

"Your shackles can't contain me," he said. "I will see you soon."

"Yeah, you will," Grazer said. "I will be there front row to watch your execution."

Mason's smile widened and his eyes narrowed as he looked directly into the detectives. "I hope so," he said. "I really, really hope so."

Grazer's rose his arm quickly and brought the butt of the gun down on Mason's head with such force, Grazer thought he felt Bayer's skull crack under his hand.

Bayer fell to the side once more – unconscious.

*

Leddy was in the hospital's parking lot when he received the call from Billy Kux with the news. He cheered out loud when he heard Mason had been caught, but the moment he hung the phone up, a feeling of despair fell upon him. He missed the climax. Six months of chasing the son of a bitch, and he missed the end because of a stupid mild concussion. If he had been released just moments before, he might have had the opportunity to be a part of it all.

Still, he was delighted to hear the news, and could only imagine how happy the rest of the team was. No doubt there would be a celebration, and he would certainly be a part of it.

Suddenly, his thoughts were on Tina. He wanted to share the news with her as well and wondered if he should call her. Since finding her note, he's stayed clear of her number figuring that if she wanted to check in, she would call. Despite wanting to hear her voice, he once again decided against it and instead got into his car when the phone rang.

He looked at the display; *Tina Hood*.

Letting out a small laugh, he answered the call with, "Holy shit! I was *just* thinking about you! How are you?"

There was a moment of silence, and Leddy's smile was gone the moment he heard her voice.

"Scott," she said, her voice trembling as though she had been crying.

"Tina? What's the matter? Are you okay?"

"Scott, I need your help," she said.

"Where are you? What's wrong?"

Another moment of silence.

"Tina, are you there?"

"I was trying to help," she said. "Get back into the swing of things on my own."

"Help with what?"

"The Bayer case."

Leddy frowned. "What do you mean?"

"I came to the farm to see what I could find," she said. "And I'm lost. Please help me. I'm scared."

Leddy shook his head. "What the f... Why are you... Okay. Stay right where you are. I'm going to get you. Don't move." He ended the call, tossed the phone onto the passenger side of the car and fled the hospital's parking lot.

For the second time that day, he would go the Bayer farm, and after going through such a traumatic experience, one would be hesitant to return to the farm so quickly, if ever. But his concerns were tamed. After all, Mason Bayer himself had been caught so what danger could possibly come from going to the farm now?

Transfer

It was just past midnight by the time Mason was locked into a high security transporter; a black and white van with bars on the windshield and the only other windows on the back doors. The bullet wound on Bayer's leg was clean; entering the front of his thin thigh and exiting on the opposite side, no bone fractures. A simple bandage was applied by a paramedic once Mason was strapped into the metal bench in the van. Comments of the man's stench were tossed around by all those new to the scene.

Roth and Leppe had made the agreement that when Mason was caught, she was to be notified immediately. He was to be taken to be given a psyche evaluation at the Palm Water Psychiatric Hospital for the Criminally Insane and more than likely, he would spend the rest of his time then until the courts took over to determine the monster's fate. With Roth dead however, Leppe told Corona that the hospital would handle him for the evening and she would report to him in the morning. She'd had a long night, finding Roth dead, and all.

Corona and Grazer followed the van to the hospital located in Fort Lauderdale. The trip would be shorter than usual since most of Miami and surrounding areas were off the streets. Sirens blaring, their speed reached over eighty miles an hour at points making the forty plus mile trek in just about twenty minutes.

The first few minutes were spent in silence, both of them reveling in the fact that Mason Bayer was finally apprehended – but neither of them as excited as they should be.

"How did he know so much?" Hector finally asked. "He knew about my daughter, your kids. How?"

Todd shook his head at first, but his mind was questioning the same. The only reasonable answer he could come up with was; "We've been after this guy for six months. He's probably been watching us, too."

"Be that as it may, but he knew details about you that he wouldn't know just by watching you. I mean, the way he talked about what happened to you and Lanza. That's not something he would know unless someone told him."

Todd shrugged. "He's done his homework. He's researched us, maybe."

Hector grunted, keeping his eyes on the road. "That piece of shit looks like a homeless vagabond who has never once felt water and soap on his skin. You think he walked up to a computer and used the internet to find out about us? I doubt he'll even know what a computer looks like let alone use one. No, something's up with him – something different."

"Different?" Todd asked. "Like what?" He could see Hector was hesitant to continue, his lips pursed together and his jaw flaring. "What is it?"

"What he said about Jo," Hector said. "Bashing her head through glass."

"Hector, that's all talk. Don't listen to him."

"I know it is. But I had a dream not too long ago that I walked into Jo's room, and she was sitting up on her bed, staring back at me, and her face was all fucked up. Her forehead? It was full of shards of glass. When I called out to her, do you know what she told me?"

Hector took his eyes off the road to glance at his partner who was looking at him with a deep frown.

"What?" Todd asked.

"She said 'I killed this fucking pig'. And it was the same voice as this son of a bitch."

Todd's mouth fell open a bit, but he didn't notice. For a moment, he thought of telling Hector about the vision he had of his son Luis, bashing Jo's head against a car's dashboard before slamming the car against a pole. Before he could, Hector continued.

"And I got a call from forensics recently regarding the murder weapon we found at the O'Neill murder. Only O'Neill's finger prints were on it. What if…" he hesitated. "What if Mason has some kind of mind control power?"

Todd didn't respond. He looked out of the passenger side window at the dark streets whizzing passed them in thought.

"What if he forced the victims to do that to themselves? That's why we never found one single shred of evidence it was him outside of their connection."

Todd shook his head. "Then why break into Brewer's home?"

"So that we can catch him? I don't know. What I do know is that we had several cameras on the house, and no one was able to see him scale the house to the second story?"

"You think he has the power to trick our eyes? Nothing is what it seems?"

"I know it sounds ridiculous, but this guy's been missing eighteen years," Corona said. "Who knows what he's learned to do in that time."

"Well, super powers or not, he's in the hands of the state now. Not our responsibility." Todd ended the conversation not because he thought it sounded ridiculous as Hector said, but because it made perfect sense.

They arrived at the hospital where they were greeted by armed personnel who were to take Mason in. He was transferred to a gurney where his legs, arms and head were tied down with leather straps and metal buckles. To the surprise of both Todd and Hector, Bayer did not say a word, nor did he struggle while he was rolled into the building, passed one security door, through another, and out of their sight.

They watched from a glass partition where administration forms were awaiting them. Hector filled out the paperwork, signed his name, and before long, they left the hospital, leaving Mason Bayer behind for good.

As they approached Hector's sedan, Hector put a hand on Todd's shoulder. "Hey," he said. "Thank you. For everything. We wouldn't have been able to close this without you."

Todd shook his head. "I did nothing." He looked at his watch. "Now the real fun begins. You have a shit ton of paperwork to do, and I have to fight for my job back."

Hector laughed. "I'll drop you off at home and head back to the station."

"You're not going home now?"

He shook his head. "Like you said, shit load of paper work. I'm working on that now then taking the next month off. I think we've deserved it."

"I'll help." Todd nodded. "Besides, there's much to go over, what with Roth's death and all."

Though Bayer was gone, their work was far from finished. When they arrived at the station, despite the late hour, they were greeted by their peers, including their Captain and Chief of Police who gladly handed Todd his badge and weapon back. A wave of applause filled the station, led by Officer Billy Kux.

Both men thanked everyone for the kind gesture, both of them hiding their newer concerns behind forced smiles and fake handshakes and hugs.

"It's been an honor to work beside both of you on this case," Kux told them as he shook Grazer's hand, then Corona's.

"You did good," Corona said.

"It's just a shame Leddy couldn't be here to enjoy this," Kux continued.

"Something tells me you'll be a valuable force in this department," Grazer continued, then looked around the room. "Leddy still in the hospital?"

Kux shrugged. "Tried to call him, but he doesn't answer," he said. "Who knows what he's up to."

Skeletons in the Closet

"Tina? Are you here?" Leddy called out into the darkened house.

Though he knew Mason Bayer was locked up in a high security mental facility, his confidence in going to the farm was stripped away the moment he entered the house. He could still feel Mason Bayer standing behind him, his arm around his throat and his own pistol pressed against his temple. He could see Grazer standing just beyond the opened wall, gun pointed at them and matching looks of despair on their faces.

His flashlight was on the gaping opening as he stood at the entrance. He didn't want to go in any further if he didn't have to.

"Tina!" he yelled. "Where are you?"

There was no response. He looked to the stairs and followed it upward. He looked to his left, then right. The house was silent, and it appeared empty, until he heard the soft whimper calling out his name.

It was Tina's voice, of that much he was certain, and it was coming from the wall's opening.

"Shit," he said, stepping toward the makeshift doorway. He half entered; one leg in, the other out facing the house's entrance. He pointed the beam of his flashlight down toward the basement, and though he could hear Tina's cry a bit clearer, he still could not see her.

"Tina, come on up, honey," he said softly. "I'll take you home."

"Scott, I need you," she responded. "Please come down here and get me."

He hesitated, unable to shake the feeling that he was walking into a trap of some kind. But how? Mason was locked away. Tina was his friend and she had come here to help, to prove she was still a good officer and prove that she didn't need to be on a medical leave. Something must have happened to her, he thought. Twisted an ankle or broke her leg as she made her way down the stairs and rendered herself immobile in a dark, scary basement of a killer's home. No wonder she was in tears.

Scott stepped onto the landing and began the descent slowly. "I'm coming," he said. "Are you hurt? Do you need me to call an ambulance?"

When she didn't respond, his rational thinking was replaced by the images of Tina spewing blood and obscenities. Her dark black eyes, her clenched jaw – her possessed form.

She was seated on the dirty floor of the basement, her back turned to Leddy as he stepped off the stairs. His light on her back, her golden hair was tied in a bun and her black shirt stained with brown dirt. He could see her back trembling with her soft cry, still he kept his free hand on his holstered revolver.

"Tina," he said, approaching her slowly. "Are you okay?"

She was seated with her legs crossed over each other and her dirty hands covered her face. As Leddy made his way around her to face her, he found himself frightened to actually approach her.

"Hey," he said. "Look at me." He gripped his weapon in the event he came face to face with the demon he saw inside her before.

Her hands fell to her knees and she hung her head low.

Leddy took a step back.

Slowly, she raised her head to look at Scott, and her light green eyes seemed even brighter in the beam of his flashlight. He sighed in relief and finally kneeled before her.

Her face was flushed red and her eyes were bloodshot. Her bottom lip was quivering as she tried to talk to him, but her emotions keeping her from doing so.

"Hey, hey," he said softly, holding her trembling shoulders. "What's the matter?"

"I came here to help," she said through her tears. "But I feel sadness here. Something happened here."

Leddy shook his head. "You shouldn't have come here, Tina. Let's go."

"No!" she said, almost yelling. "It's like… I feel a connection to this place. It's familiar somehow. I came down here and I was overcome with this… depression. This horrible feeling."

Scott took a deep breath, wondering how long it's been since she took her medication. Despite having been relieved by the note she left him in her apartment, he was never more convinced that she needed professional help. "Tina," he said.

"It's not the medication, Scott," she told him with a frown. "I know you're thinking that."

Leddy's eyes widened.

"It's this place. I feel like I belong here."

"You don't, Tina. None of us do. It's over. Mason's been caught and it's over. So we can leave now."

She shook her head. "I found something," she said. "This place told me where to look, and I found something you should see."

Scott's flesh erupted with goose bumps. "This place told you?"

She nodded, wiping her eyes and leaving smears of dirt across her eyes.

"What did you find?"

Tina pointed toward the east of the room, toward a darkened corner. "I found his room," she said.

Scott stood quickly, facing the area she was pointing to. He aimed his flashlight toward the area, and his back stiffened. Just like the wall that opened leading to the basement, there was a wall that was partially opened in the east end of the basement itself. From where he stood, he could see the room was empty, still Scott approached it slowly, his hand on his gun, and his flashlight holding steady at the area.

He studied the wall, found a small hole at eye length and quickly surmised that Bayer must have used this room to hide in and keep watch over the basement.

He looked back at Tina with a frown who was crying into her hands again.

Scott slid the door open completely and studied the room inside. It was no larger than a closet and it was obvious the room was built by someone without experience. The walls were not finished with plaster or sheet rock. They were just dirt as though it was dug out by hand, as was the ground beneath.

He reached in and felt the uneven surface of the wall to his right, even took a piece off to smell it. The soil smelled moist – impacted with water to keep the walls up.

A pile of dirty, torn clothes were on the floor, and with his foot, Scott moved them about. A pair of torn jeans, a shirt marked with sweat stains, something someone had warn for a very long time. A homeless man, perhaps. Leddy knew they weren't Bayer's clothes as Bayer was draped in black when he was held hostage by him. Moving the clothes suddenly filled his nostrils with a horrid scent – sulfur. Mixed with rotting meat. Leddy thought of calling in to put out notice of a possible missing homeless person, but what good would that do?

He froze. There was something underneath the clothes that he could feel even through the sole of his boot – something hard. Leddy pushed the clothes aside completely and nearly jumped back at the revelation.

The small pile of bones shifted when Leddy rubbed his foot against them. They were stacked together, the clothes on top of them covering them before, but now that they were exposed, they rolled over each other and the small pile collapsed. It was a skeleton, there was no doubt. The skull that rolled forward had a gaping hole at the very top, the suture. A blow to the top of the skull is what killed this victim, there was no doubt, but the reason why Leddy was taken aback by it even more so was that the skull and bones were all small. The skeleton belonged to a child, his training kicking in gear suddenly and realizing that the width of the rib cage and shoulders, that this child was a boy, and no more than eight to ten years old when he was killed.

A doll made of leathery skin was resting beside the bones; a doll stitched together at the seams and housing a crooked smile was more suited for a girl than for the boy whose bones Leddy was looking at.

Leddy's mouth went dry suddenly. His hand trembled as he took a step backward, out of the closet.

"Tina," he said, almost unable to do so. "Who is this?"

He turned. The black eyes that were facing him startled him. Tina was inches away from him and they were face to face. "It's me," It said, its voice heavy and rumbling through its clenched teeth.

I was right.

That was the last thought Officer Scott Leddy had before the thing in front of him grabbed his face and snapped his neck with one swift move.

Saturday, June 6th

Mary slammed the phone down onto the receiver. She crossed her arms, her foot bouncing on the kitchen floor, then began chewing on her thumbnail.

The sun had just begun to rise over the eastern skies, and when she woke without Todd in the house, she immediately checked her voicemail for any missed calls. There were none. Todd had not come home from work and without word from him, it was not good news – not in his line of work.

"I'm sure he's fine," her sister told her, seated in the dining room, smoking a cigarette. "He's a good detective." Smoking was not normally allowed inside the house, but more pressing matters were at hand.

Mary shook her head. "He always calls if he's going to pull an all-nighter," she said, then picked up the phone again, dialed his number. It went straight to voicemail. She slammed the phone down again.

"Try Hector," Mary's daughter said, suddenly standing at the entrance of the dining room.

Mary quickly realized her worried voice must have woken Cynthia. "We already have," she said, tears welling in her eyes. "We can't reach him, either."

Luis appeared behind his sister. "What's going on? What's wrong with dad?"

"Nothing's wrong," Cynthia sneered over her shoulder. "Go back to bed."

"Shut up!"

"This is *not* the time, you two!" Mary said, almost in a yell. "Both of you go back to your rooms!"

Her children exchanged glances.

"Now!"

They quickly moved toward the staircase, each of them rumbling toward each other as they did as they were told.

Mary took an exhausted seat at the end of the dining table. "I don't know what I would do if something's happened to him," she told her sister. "The last words I spoke to him were horrible."

"I'm sure he's fine," Mayra said, lighting another cigarette. "If something happened, you would have heard by now."

"I don't know. It's not like they just ring your doorbell and tell you as soon as it happens," she said.

The chime of the doorbell suddenly echoed throughout the house, and Mary shot a wide-eyed stare at her sister. Her blood pressure rose, her heart pounding in her chest and pulsing in her temples. Against her will, Mary rose from the table and slowly made her way through the dining room and into the living room, her eyes on the doorway that would possibly provide the worst news he had received. Never before has a single door been so menacing.

She gripped the doorknob with a sweaty hand, took a deep breath and said a silent prayer before finally opening the door.

The first thing she saw was a handful of red, beautiful roses. The hand holding them belonged to her husband, standing at the doorway with a large smile on his face.

Relief waved over her, weakening her knees, and comforting her. Still, the only words she could muster were, "Where the *hell* have you been?"

"We put the son of a bitch away!" he said, almost in a laugh, then tossed the flowers aside, picked Mary up in a massive hug, kissing her cheek several times.

Mary laughed as he put her back down and took hold of her face. Their kiss was a long one, and Mary knew that, though her worries were for not, her husband was home. Really home.

*

When Hector walked into his home, he found his daughter sleeping on the couch in the living room.

She was dressed in jeans and a t-shirt, and a quick study of the room told him that she had fallen asleep in front of the television, probably waiting for him.

He stared at her for a moment, her porcelain skin and dark hair, and reveled at her maturity, her willingness to be a major part of the household despite being just a teenager. It wasn't fair, he thought. Forced into adulthood because her mother was selfish, and him leaving her for hours at a time as he worked the force.

He and Todd both had many conversations about their job, that they do what they do to keep scum off the street to protect their families. Mason's threats were deafened by the fact that he was put away, and Hector suddenly felt that Mason, specifically, was the reason he went into law enforcement – his swan song. He decided he would retire from the police department and find a job that allowed him more time with his daughter.

He walked into the living room and switched off the television, approached the couch and gave her a soft kiss on her forehead.

She flinched, but remained asleep.

Thoughts of retirement in his mind, he walked into the kitchen and began making breakfast, the kind she would make for him; eggs, pancakes, the whole nine. He would announce his decision to retire soon, perhaps that evening when they would all unite at Grazer's house for a celebration of their victory amidst family and friends, or perhaps on a day when it would just be he and his daughter.

Hector Corona never felt the happiness he did that morning, a new start in his mind and his daughter in his heart.

*

By sundown, Billy Kux was on his third beer, and on his couch watching a comedy movie marathon – nothing to do with murders, cops, or anything of the sort.

Grazer had called him earlier and invited him to his house for a small party he was having in celebrating the capture of Mason Bayer, but Kux respectfully declined. He was tired. He wanted to do nothing more than sit in his darkened apartment and relax his mind.

He thought about turning his phone off so that he wouldn't be bothered, but knew he couldn't. If an emergency happened and he was needed, he would be called out. But he prayed it wouldn't.

He thought of Leddy and Tina and wondered if they were okay. A few times, he thought of calling Scott to see how his headache was, if it had gotten any worse, but he knew the conversation would lead to Mason Bayer, and that was a name Kux did not want to hear or say for at least a month.

His phone rang suddenly, and when he looked at his display, he rolled his eyes. So much for a relaxing evening.

He answered the call, and the beer that was in his other hand slipped out, crashing to the floor and shattering once he heard the news. He didn't have time to stop and clean it up. Moments later, Office William Kux was in uniform, and fled his home.

Not calling Grazer or Corona was his decision. They deserved the time off. He would handle the emergency on his own. On his way back toward the Brewer home, he called the SRT back out, then called the Brewer family to warn them that Mason Bayer had escaped and was more than likely returning to finish what he started.

Escape

"How the fuck does he escape a maximum security hospital?" Kux asked, almost in a yell.

Leppe held her hands up in surrender. "It's not my fault so don't take it out of me," she said.

It was almost midnight when she entered the surveillance van, a badge hanging from her neck on a leather necklace and a briefcase in her hand.

They were seated at the same spot observing the Brewer residence. Members of the SRT were set in the same positions, plus a few more covering each entrance of the house with specific instructions that they weren't to even blink to avoid the same mistake made the night before.

Leppe set the briefcase on her lap once she sat next to Kux and opened it. "I had a conversation with Bayer earlier this afternoon," she said. "I tried to get him to tell me about the eighteen years he was missing, where he was hiding, how he managed to kill six people without being caught, etcetera."

"And?"

"He didn't say a damn thing, of course. Once I heard he escaped, I demanded video from the hospital's surveillance system." She extracted a DVD enclosed in a clear jewel case. "I think you'd be very surprised to see how he managed to do it."

She inserted the disk into TV / DVD combo resting beside the monitors displaying the Brewer house. The TV came to life and a grainy picture split into four quadrants came filled the small screen.

"This is video from a few hours ago," she said. "This is the ward he was being held in." She pointed to the feed on the upper right hand corner of the screen.

It was of a hallway, several closed metal doors lining each of the walls. "That's his room there," she said, pointing to the middle door on the left. The door opens slowly and large man dressed in white exits the room, followed closely by Mason, dressed in black. He held a cloth of sorts in his right hand. His ski mask.

"Whoa, wait a minute," Kux said. "Did that guy give him his clothes and let him free?"

"Keep watching," Leppe said. "I'll get to that."

The feed on the upper left hand side of the screen showed a security door, guards lining it with heavy artillery. "That's the door to the ward itself," Leppe said.

Bayer approached the door and looked at the two guards. They each nodded at him, and one turns to a red button beside the heavy doors. He pushes the button, the doors slide open and Mason walks through. As they close, the guards retake their stance as though nothing happened.

"What the fuck!" Kux yelled at the screen.

The bottom right feed was a hallway filled with doctors, nurses and officers in what seemed to be a very busy section of the hospital. Leppe didn't bother pointing out which area of the hospital it was because it wasn't necessary. Mason Bayer walked amongst the crowd as though he belonged, none of the officers, doctors or nurses paying him any mind.

The final feed was of the last security door, the one that lead to the hospital's exit. It was manned by officers behind a glass partition. Mason stood before the door, looked to the officers, then back to the door. It slid open, revealing the outside world. Before he left however, Mason looked up to the security camera and smiled, revealing his crooked teeth.

Kux sat back, a chill running up his spine as though Mason was looking directly at him.

The feed suddenly turned to static, and Mason was gone.

Leppe ejected the disc and took a deep breath. "He just walked out."

Kux shook his head slowly, frowning, his mind processing what he just saw. "I don't believe this," he said.

"We spoke to every single person on that video, the nurse who left his room, the guards who let him through the security doors. Not one of them remembers what happened. Even when we showed them the video, they were shocked. One of them even began trembling once he saw the video, he was so shocked. Hasn't spoken since."

"It's like he had everyone hypnotized or something."

"Exactly," Leppe said. "We're not dealing with someone normal here," she said. "He was completely catatonic all night. Almost like he wasn't in his own head, and then today, he pulls this off. How? Who is this guy?"

Kux shook his head. "I think we should call Grazer and Corona," he said softly.

"I'm surprised you haven't already."

"They were celebrating. Last time I spoke to Grazer he was already pretty drunk and I can hear the party in the background. Figured they'd be useless by now, but they should at least know what's happening."

"I'm going back to the hospital in the morning. In the meantime, I'm going home to rest."

Kux nodded. "I'll have one of the officers around here follow you. Just in case."

Leppe nodded, and left the van.

Kux grabbed his mobile and dialed Grazer first.

It rang, but went to voicemail.

He called Corona next.

No ring, just voicemail.

Kux shook his head; they were either drunk and passed out, or the party was so loud they didn't hear their phones.

He hit a couple more buttons and found Grazer's home number. He dialed it and received a repetitive tone – busy.

Kux frowned.

He tried again.

Busy.

He tried both of the detective's numbers, then the house number once again, all of them with the same results.

Fucking pig, I've just begun. Lock me up and I will come after you next.

The words suddenly hit Kux like a truck – the words Mason Bayer told Grazer in Brewer's room after having been caught.

Kux stood, his body going cold, his breath short. He looked at his phone, his head spinning with the fact that he could not get in touch with either detectives. He swallowed hard and reached for the microphone attached to his vest.

"Kux here," he said, his voice trembling. "Pack it up and move out." Every word he spoke rose in volume. "We have the wrong house!" he said. "I repeat, we have the wrong house!"

Fallen

By eleven, Grazer, Corona and friends had eaten too much and drank even more. The Grazer household was filled with six adults and just as many teenagers.

Todd and Hector were both celebrated for their achievements, and to top it all off, they received a call from the Mayor himself congratulating them on their victory. It was a happy day, Todd had told everyone, and happy days were to be celebrated.

With the teenagers tucked away in the pool house in the back yard, and the adults too inebriated to drive, it was decided everyone would spend the night and deal with the hang over together as a group come sun up.

Hector insisted on sleeping on the couch in the living room, leaving the others to spread about the random bedrooms on the second floor. His head filled with visions of the day, he smiled. He didn't announce his plans on retiring. Everyone was having a great time, and though his retirement would no doubt make his daughter happy, it would upset his partner, and the last thing he wanted to do was upset Todd Grazer. *It was a happy day, and happy days are to be celebrated.*

Hector took a deep breath, the room around him spinning a bit.

He closed his eyes, his thoughts on the bright future ahead of him, but was jarred out of his sleep when he heard the sound of a tap against glass. He opened his eyes and immediately thought of his gun. Where had he left it? *It's at home*, he thought to himself. He left it thinking he wouldn't need it at a party.

The noise had come from the dining room somewhere, and he had a direct view from the couch. He remained still, listening for another noise, and when it came, his body stiffened. The sound of the sliding glass door slowly rolling on its track filled the kitchen. Someone was coming in from the backyard.

His back relaxed – the kids. They were coming into the house. He saw the silhouettes of two teenage boys – the Sheyer boys; Nick and Logan, he thought – enter the dining room and disappear into the kitchen. Moments later, they reappeared, one of them holding a six pack of beer that was dripping wet. He couldn't tell which of the brothers it was, and though he wanted to bust them using his cop status, he simply smiled.

He was a teenager once.

Besides they were all in safe in the pool house and if drinking beer was the worst they were doing, so be it.

He closed his eyes again, and he fell asleep within minutes; a drunken induced slumber that completely sealed out the world and left him with no awareness of his surroundings.

That is why he never heard Mason Bayer opening the living room window and making his way into the Grazer home to fulfill a promise he had made.

*

Kux jumped out of the car, the siren still blaring, and tried the door. It was locked. He knocked hard, his hand burning with pain with every punch, and there was no answer.

Without much thought, Kux withdrew his gone, fired two rounds into the lock and kicked the door open. He rushed inside the darkened house, gun aimed, and saw the bloody mess that was once Hector Corona on the couch.

"Help us!" a girl's voice cried from the kitchen.

Kux peered into the dining area and the sight made him lose support of his arms and back. His knees almost gave way when he saw Mason Bayer's unmasked face, his body on the floor, a bullet hole in his head.

Standing above him was a young man whose eyes were transfixed on the killer. He looked like a young version of Grazer, and Kux's heart sank with the realization that Luis Grazer had killed Mason Bayer. The gun he used was at his feet, and the stress of the event was in his eyes.

Several teenagers were strewn about, a girl on the floor passed out in a pool of her own vomit, a teenage boy bleeding profusely from his thigh, and three others all crying and desperate for answers.

"They're all dead," Kux heard Luis say. He locked eyes with the boy whose eyes were solid black. "All of them."

Kux swallowed hard, looking to the living room and Hector's mutilated stomach. *They're all dead*. He closed his eyes for a moment knowing that meant Grazer and his wife, too. And anyone else in the house, more than likely.

When he opened his eyes again, a tear rolled down his cheek and his eyes settled upon the word *NEVES* written in blood on the wall just above the couch.

He looked back to Mason Bayer dead on the floor. Shot in the head. Something he should have done back at the Brewer home when he had the chance.

He then looked to the crying kids, now orphaned, and the words Angela Ortega told him before echoed in his head, finally having meaning. Finally making sense.

Don't let the kids get involved, she said.

CHAPTER NEVES

Roth hyperventilated. He stared at the dead boy before him.

"What the fuck did I just do?" he asked the air.

He heard muffled footsteps coming from the second floor, then the muffled voice of Chiovitti calling out for him.

In a panic, Roth dropped his flashlight and grabbed the boy's wrists, careful not to get any blood on himself, and dragged him back into the small closet he came out of.

He almost didn't hear the soft whimper coming from the makeshift room in all the commotion, but as he dragged the boy's body toward it, he heard the soft voice loud and clear.

His heart sank when the little girl, no more than two years old, looked up at him. Her dirty hair was blond once, and her light green eyes were filled with fear. Holding a doll close, one made of leathery skin, she looked to Roth as tears began to roll down her cheeks.

They have a daughter, Roth thought.

"Roth!" he could hear Chiovitti calling for him.

He looked up to the ceiling of the basement, then back to the little girl. "Stay here," he told her. "I will come back for you and help you. I promise."

When he reached for his flashlight, he saw blood on the end that killed the boy. He left it behind, ran up the stairs in darkness, and pushed open the wall enough to squeeze out of it.

"Roth!" Chiovitti called from the second floor.

Relieved, Jack pushed the door closed, dusted himself off and adjusted his clothes. "Down here," he called.

Chiovitti came down the stairs. "Where the hell were you?"

"Out back," Roth lied.

The detective frowned. "You okay? You look like you seen a ghost."

"I'm fine."

"No sign of the boy, huh?"

Roth shook his head.

"Okay, let's get out of here, then," Chiovitti said. "The longer he's out there the less likely we are to find him alive."

"Agreed," Roth said.

Both men left the house, and Jack Roth decided he would return come nightfall and rescue the girl on his own. He would take her to a shelter where she would be tended to and lead a new life; a shelter he would later volunteer at, and look over her – until she came to know him as Uncle Jack and work with him law enforcement.

Excerpt of NEVES
The continuation of "Name Not One Man"

CHAPTER ENO

T HE DEATHS THAT STAINED HER memory and infected her mind were still with her though the war was over. They would be with her until she exorcised them. There were those who would not believe her stories of the war, but that was of no concern to her. First, she needed to find refuge; a place where her mind would settle and her body would rest.

What if Death followed me? she wondered as she entered the hotel's lobby.

The automatic doors slid to a close, sealing out the night's storm. The stale air of the building hit her at once, her breath falling short at the sudden claustrophobia, and she gripped the handles of the plastic bags in her hand tighter on reflex alone. A hotel, she thought, would be the safest place to hide; once she was in her room, alone, away from anyone and everyone who posed a threat. But the moment she stepped foot in the lobby, she second guessed herself. Could it be she just walked into another trap?

She glanced over her shoulder to make sure her car was visible before taking count of the people in the lobby. There was a young couple waiting for the elevator, a mother and child near the souvenir boutique, and an elderly woman at the check-in desk attended by a young man. None of them noticed her enter, but Cynthia knew that each of them were a threat. Her death could be *inside* one of them.

Stepping onto the cheap carpeting, she hissed when a jolt of pain ricocheted from her right calf and settled around her waist. The wound was bandaged with a piece of torn cloth wearing heavy with the mixture of rain and blood. It served its purpose and stopped the bleeding, but the pain was a different story. She prepared herself for another jolt, taking a slow step forward, keeping a steady eye on the check-in desk.

The elderly woman turned toward the lobby's doors giving Cynthia nothing more than a passing glance, and for that, she was thankful.

She moved slowly toward the check-in clerk, a young man dressed in a burgundy uniform that seemed out-dated. Avoiding eye contact with him, her eyes went to the nametag on his lapel.

Danny.

"One room, please," she said, making sure no one else could hear her.

He smiled then began pecking away at the computer's keyboard.

She could feel his eyes studying her as he checked the vacancy, and the voice in her head began with yet another prayer.

Please don't recognize me, please…

"Aren't you Cynthia Grazer?" he asked. "The writer?"

Defeated, Cynthia took quick glances around the lobby. It was empty.

Vocally, she didn't answer, but the look on her face was more than a whisper of confirmation. She looked at his face for a second and found his young eyes focused on her. Cynthia saw his face had yet to meet a wrinkle or seemingly feel the steel of a razorblade. She quickly estimated his age to be, at most, twenty.

"I've read all your books," he said. "I'm a big fan."

They were the same words she heard from her fans many times before, but their delivery was different. Most fans smiled, even laughed when meeting her, but Danny seemed concerned.

And why wouldn't he be? Beside the fact that she was limping the entire way to the check-in desk, Cynthia knew she didn't look like the publicity photos on the backs of her novels. He had every right to be concerned after seeing her limp and discovering the bruises on her face's delicate skin.

Cynthia kicked herself for not thinking of being less conspicuous, but she couldn't think right about anything at all. Still, she forced a smile as she readjusted her hair in the messy bun above her head, inadvertently revealing the bruised tear on the center of her forehead. She combed her hair back over it, praying Danny didn't notice.

But he stared directly at it then frowned at her. "Are you okay?" he asked.

"I'm fine," she said. "One room please."

He didn't continue to pry.

"The length of your stay?" he asked, trying hard not to stare.

"One night," she answered immediately.

Danny pecked some more and the printer beside his computer erupted to life. He took a key card and swiped it in a reader much like a credit card machine and a wave of relief fell over Cynthia. He found a room for her – hopefully on a floor that was otherwise empty.

"Danny," she said softly. "Can I ask you a favor?"

His eyes widened, obviously surprised by her voice. He nodded, meeting the writer's green eyes for the first time that night.

"No one is to know I am here," she told him. "Please don't tell *anyone* that you've seen me, and if anyone calls for me, tell them that you've never heard of me, you've never read one of my books, you don't know me. Can you do that?"

Danny nodded still in obvious surprise.

"Thank you."

She paid for the room in cash, and when he handed her the key card, his eyes widened again. She knew at once that he noticed her hands. Both sets of knuckles were bruised, the skin healing from numerous wounds as though they were forced through a cheese grater. His grip on the key tightened.

When she was unable to pry it from his hand, she looked back at him in surprise.

"Are you okay?" he repeated, demanding it the way she demanded her orders.

Cynthia sighed and looked away. "Send up a first-aid kit, please," she told him, his finger gently touching hers across the key card. The touch of the stranger felt somewhat comfortable to her, unexpectedly relaxing her. She met his eyes again and forced a thankful smile. "I'll be okay."

Danny released the key. "Seventh floor," he said. "Room 77." He watched as she limped towards the elevators weaving the plastic bag's handles between her thin, damaged hands.

*

The elevator doors opened on the seventh floor revealing a long, lonely corridor. It was dimly lit; small light fixtures were set between each wooden door on both sides of the hall. She studied the beige walls and matching carpeting until the hall turned left and out of her sight. The rattling of a distant ice machine filled the air, but beyond that, there was complete silence.

She stepped off the elevator cautiously, the doors sliding closed behind her, trapping her in the hall. The first door to her right was marked with a golden *70*, the door to her left was tagged *71*.

Room 77, Danny's voice echoed in her head.

She could see her number on the fourth door to the left.

Fifteen paces…I can do this.

She began her descent, limping toward the door without looking away from it. Seek your goal and aim to achieve it, her therapist told her a hundred times before, and as Cynthia passed the door marked *73*, the motivation began to set in. Though she only took a few steps, she was that much closer to her room and that much closer to her salvation.

The bell that echoed suddenly throughout the hall was not loud, but it was enough to bring Cynthia to near panic. It came from behind her, and she immediately realized she heard the same bell moments before.

The elevator...

She stopped, her heart pounding relentlessly in her chest as the doors slid open behind her. She felt the burn of a stare, sending her body into tremors. Death followed her after all.

It was in Danny...

She wasn't ready to face her enemy. Not again. Still, she strained her neck to turn just her head, keeping her body facing forward in case she would have to sprint away. She could barely walk, let alone run, yet recent experience taught her that when the body soared with adrenaline, amazing things happened. A mere flesh wound would not keep her from saving her own life.

The light fixtures began to flicker on and off before she had a full view of the elevator, but they remained burning at full power. Cynthia wanted to believe that it was due to the storm, but she knew that if Death *had* arrived, they might have flickered from Its presence. She saw stranger things in the past week.

But the elevator was empty. The bell was still ringing in her ears as she scanned the small lift. There was no room for anyone to hide in its corners, nor had there been enough time for someone to have stepped off and into one of the rooms behind her. It was as if the elevator opened on its own.

She rushed to the door marked 77 and quickly unlocked it, not daring to look over her shoulder. The door opened inward into an abyss of darkness and Cynthia cursed her luck. Her hands felt for the light switch on the walls before she entered, and when she found it, she quickly flipped it upward. Just as the soft light filled the room, she entered swiftly and slammed the door behind her.

Turning the bolt above the knob, she locked herself into the room before inspecting it.

One lock, she reluctantly thought. She would have felt better if there were a second.

The room was as small and simple as the hallway. The carpet and walls were matching beige, and there were several landscape paintings hung in no particular fashion. A television set atop a small dresser was a short distance from the foot of the queen-sized bed, and as Cynthia looked to the opposite wall, she froze.

She caught her own reflection on the sliding glass door amidst the night's sky. It led to a small balcony where the beach's shores could be seen just beyond the parking lot below. Tossing the plastic bags onto the bed, Cynthia crossed the room and pulled the verticals closed in a hurry. The blinds would remain closed that night.

The door tucked in the east corner of the room led to the bathroom. A single bulb hanging from a fixture in the ceiling nearly blinded Cynthia when she flipped it on, revealing the room's contents. A stand-up shower stall, a toilet bowl set beside it, and a small sink next to a rack stocked with clean, fresh towels. Without a second's thought on how small the room was, she turned on the sink's faucet, and splashed her face with cold water.

It felt amazing; her skin, dried by the recent sweat and tears, absorbed the water like arid soil. It was complete rejuvenation, though a careless scrub of the abrasion on her forehead proved quite displeasing. Avoiding her reflection in the mirror above the sink, she reached for a towel and walked out of the bathroom, promising herself a full shower when she was done with what she planned to do, even if it meant waiting until sunrise.

After adjusting the pillows by propping them onto the headboard, Cynthia slowly brought her tired body down, becoming weak the moment she felt the softness beneath her. Her head pounded with exhaustion and her blood shot eyes grew dry and heavy as the thought of undisturbed slumber entered her mind. She wanted to give in, but she couldn't because sleeping was out of the question.

Slowly, she brought her legs upward onto the bed then unlaced her sneakers. After reaching for one of the plastic bags at her feet, she sat back on the fluffed headboard and allowed a moment to recoup.

She emptied the bag, spilling its contents onto the bed; three spiral bound notebooks and a five pack of pens with foam grips. She stacked the items neatly, deciding to make immediate use of the contents that were the last to fall out; a pack of menthol cigarettes and a brand new disposable lighter.

She didn't ask Danny for a smoker's room and, frankly, she didn't care whether she was in one or not. A quick glance at the night table beside the bed told her that her luck was improving; between the lamp and the telephone, and beside the alarm clock was an ashtray. Without another second passing, Cynthia placed a cigarette between her dry, pale lips and lit it.

She listened to the sound of its burn as she puffed it slowly taking a deep breath to inhale the sweet poisons. Cynthia's head fell backwards onto the board, and she closed her eyes. It was her first cigarette in nearly twenty years. She admitted missing it, and remembered how much she loved it. She puckered her lips and exhaled, watching the gray smoke dance around her until it vanished. Her shoulders relaxed, *slumped* in fact, as though the tension was lifted.

The pack would probably be emptied before sun-up.

She glanced at the alarm clock; the red digital numbers reading 9:07 P.M. After taking another puff, Cynthia placed the cigarette onto the ashtray and one of the notebooks on her lap.

Each notebook contained 150 college ruled pages, and she wondered if it would be enough to tell her story. She had not written an entire novel on notebook paper since her first, but it was not a novel she intended on writing.

It would be her first deviation from fiction, and she would be criticized for it. Not because it was nonfiction, but because of its contents. She wasn't discouraged, though. In fact, it was quite the opposite.

She opened the notebook to the first blank page then opened the pack of pens.

Cynthia Grazer was the first thing she wrote. She stared at her handwriting at the top of the page, and as though she were dissatisfied with it, she wrote her name again…

Cynthia Grazer

…and once again…

Cynthia Grazer

Satisfied, she closed her eyes and took a breath delving into the memories so fresh in her brain. Her mind ran through the events of her life that she wanted to put on paper, but Cynthia was uncertain as to whether or not she was ready to relive it. It was a story that she deemed necessary to tell, not only for herself, but also for those who would believe. It was the story of the events that led her to the hotel on that very night.

She thought of beginning with a formal introduction; expressive words explaining her deviation from fiction to a story of her life. She wondered if she should elaborate on the fact that she was risking her career and reputation by swearing to a story that many people wouldn't believe. Knowing that some of her peers would call her story nothing more than a publicity stunt, she considered insisting that her story was true. But just as those thoughts entered her head, she shook them away. An introduction was not necessary to begin her story.

She puffed her cigarette once more, deciding that the best place, the only place, to start her story was obvious; at the beginning.

NEVES is available now